The story of Josephine Cox is as extraordinary as anything in her novels. Born in a cotton-mill house in Blackburn, she was one of ten children. Her parents, she says, brought out the worst in each other, and life was full of tragedy and hardship – but not without love and laughter. At the age of sixteen, Josephine met and married 'a caring and wonderful man', and had two sons. When the boys started school, she decided to go to college and eventually gained a place at Cambridge University, though was unable to take this up as it would have meant living away from home. However, she did go into teaching, while at the same time helping to renovate the derelict council house that was their home, coping with the problems caused by her mother's unhappy home life – and writing her first full-length novel. Not surprisingly, she then won the 'Superwoman of Great Britain' Award, for which her family had secretly entered her, and this coincided with the acceptance of her novel for publication.

Josephine gave up teaching in order to write full time. She says, 'I love writing, both recreating scenes and characters from my past, together with new storylines which mingle naturally with the old. I could never imagine a single day without writing, and it's been that way since as far back as I can remember.' Her previous novels of North Country life are all available from Headline and are immensely popular.

'Josephine Cox brings so much freshness to the plot, and the characters . . . Her fans will love this coming-of-age novel. So will many of the devotees of Catherine Cookson, desperate for a replacement' *Birmingham Post*

'Guaranteed to tug at the heartstrings of all hopeless romantics' *Sunday Post*

'Hailed quite rightly as a gifted writer in the tradition of Catherine Cookson

JOSEPHINE COX

Nobody's Darling

HEADLINE

First published in hardback in 1993 by
HEADLINE BOOK PUBLISHING PLC

First published in paperback in 1994 by
HEADLINE BOOK PUBLISHING PLC

This edition published in paperback in 2017 by
HEADLINE PUBLISHING GROUP

1

Cataloguing in Publication Data is available from the British Library

ISBN 978 1 4722 4573 1

Typeset in Times by Avon DataSet Ltd, Bidford-on-Avon, Warwickshire

Printed and bound in the UK by Clays Ltd, St Ives plc

Headline's policy is to use papers that are natural, renewable and recyclable
products and made from wood grown in well-managed forests and other
controlled sources. The logging and manufacturing processes are expected to
conform to the environmental regulations of the country of origin.

HEADLINE PUBLISHING GROUP
An Hachette UK Company
Carmelite House
50 Victoria Embankment
London EC4Y 0DZ

www.headline.co.uk
www.hachette.co.uk

For Chloe Louise, our first grandchild.
A sweet darling, long awaited

Also, a loving thought for little Alexander,
who will never be forgotten

Contents

Contents

Part One

1890

THE PROMISE

'His lordship may compel us to be equal upstairs,
But there will never be equality in the servants' hall'

J.M. Barrie 1860–1937

Chapter One

'Don't go putting on airs and graces, my girl. Fame and riches ain't fer the likes of us, and you'd do well to remember that.' Lizzie Miller shook her head and blew out a sigh. 'God help us, but I can't help wondering what's gonna become of yer,' she muttered impatiently.

Seated in the old horse-hair armchair, with the contented bairn sucking at her flat drooping breast, Lizzie had been secretly watching her eldest daughter for these past ten minutes or so. Not for the first time she wondered how someone as plain and unbecoming as herself could ever have given birth to such a perfect and lovely child as Ruby. The girl didn't take after *her*, and was unlike any of the other childer. All the same, Lizzie thanked the good Lord for sending her such a precious little parcel. But, oh, wasn't it shocking how quickly the young 'uns grew up? she asked herself now.

Going on fifteen years old, Ruby was already showing the signs of womanhood. On a Friday night when all the childer were washed in the old tin tub, Lizzie had been astonished at the changes in her daughter's body; the small budding nipples and the fine dark hairs just poking through above her private parts; the way she seemed suddenly to be losing the awkwardness of a child, and gaining that special grace with which some young

3

women are blessed. With her small shapely figure, the abundant spill of rich brown hair and those magnificent blue-black eyes, it was plain to see that Ruby Miller was set to be a beauty. And, for some reason she couldn't rightly fathom, Lizzie was fearful for the girl. It was true what they said about there always being at least one child who would cause a mother the greatest worry, because of all her brood – and there were six of them – it was Ruby who gave her the worst sleepless nights.

Surprised and embarrassed, Ruby swung round. 'Oh, Mam!' she cried, blushing bright pink as though she'd been caught in the act of thieving. 'You've been peeking at me again.' Lately it seemed that her mam was always peeking at her.

'It ain't surprising that I'm fascinated with yer comical antics, is it, eh?' Lizzie asked with a chuckle, thinking Ruby looked the grandest little lady in the cast off clothes which she herself had worn as a young woman; the long flouncing skirt with its deep frilly hem, the cream-coloured shawl with pretty lace workings all round the edge, and a big-brimmed hat decorated with long black feathers above large silk flowers. In that moment, Lizzie realised with a little shock that she hadn't always been ugly and clumsy. When Ruby's dad came courting her some eighteen years ago, she had been thin enough for him to encircle her waist with one arm. She was twenty-one then, foolish and full of dreams. Now she was going on forty, with six young 'uns round her arse, and a waist as far round as the gas works at the end of Albert Street. Life hadn't been easy, what with three childer taken young by the whooping cough, and always a struggle to make ends meet. Yet, for all that, the thought of her husband Ted brought a warm glow to Lizzie's tired heart. 'Yer a pretty little thing, our Ruby,' she said now, 'an' yer deserve pretty things.'

Ruby looked thoughtful as she chewed her bottom lip and thought on her mam's words. Presently she said softly, 'Dad says *you* looked lovely when you were young.'

4

'Aye, well, yer dad's a silly ol' bugger,' Lizzie laughed. 'Anyway, he were in love, an' it's a known fact that fellas are daft as brushes when they're in love.'

'But you *did* look lovely, didn't you, Mam?' Ruby insisted. She couldn't imagine her dad being 'daft as a brush'. And anyway, sometimes, when her mam smiled at the babby, Ruby thought how pretty she really was; and when she raised her face for a kiss from Ruby's dad, Lizzie's soft hazel-coloured eyes sparkled like jewels. Anybody could see that she had been a good-looking woman, and Ruby wouldn't have it any other way. 'I expect you think I'm fancying myself, don't you?' she asked, shame washing through her; if her mam had taught her anything, it was that she must never get carried away with grand ideas. Ruby found that very hard because she had so many 'grand' ideas, and the greatest of all was that one day, she might somehow be able to give her mam and dad a better life. Day and night, she never lost sight of that dream, although she was careful not to say it out loud to anyone, not even to Johnny Ackroyd.

'Aw, bless yer heart, it don't matter if yer fancy yerself in yer mam's old togs,' Lizzie told her, carefully shifting the babby from one shrivelled titty to the other. 'So long as yer don't forget yer station in life, it don't hurt to pretend, just a little bit. Only don't forget what yer mam's allus told yer.' She shook her grey head and stared hard at the girl. 'It don't do no good to spend yer life dreamin' for what yer can never have, lass. Wishing for the stars can only end in heartbreak. The plain truth is that when yer born poor, yer meant to end yer days the same way, an' that's a fact.'

'Who says so?' Try as she might, Ruby had never seen the reason for that.

'*I* say so, my girl!' In the early days, Lizzie had dreamed her own dreams, and had been bitterly disappointed when they came to nothing. She had never revealed her own secret longings, and she never would. But she didn't want any child of hers to suffer the feeling of being 'second-best', in the same way she had. In time Lizzie had come to accept her lot, and now she wanted her young 'uns to do the same. 'Wanting what you can't have is a sure way to hating what the good Lord has already seen fit to give you,' she retorted sharply. She didn't like putting Ruby down in that way, but she believed it was for the best. There was something about the girl, that strong, deep-down yearning. Such ambitions were dangerous.

'But, I *like* to dream, Mam,' Ruby said wistfully. She dropped the hat on to a chair, then slipping out of the garments, sat opposite her mam by the empty firegrate. 'I don't think the good Lord would mind me wishing, 'cause I don't want him to give me anything for nothing. I'll work hard, Mam, I promise, and I won't be bad. All I want is for you and our dad to have lots of nice things, like you deserve.' She smiled widely. 'Oh, our mam, wouldn't it be lovely if the childer could have grand presents of a Christmas, and if our Lottie could have a pretty white shawl like the grocer's babby?' She lowered her gaze until it rested on her mam's face, and the magnificent blue-black eyes were dark and serious. 'I don't think it can be wrong, wanting special things for people you love. And I don't think it's wrong wanting to live in a house where the rats don't come in from the brook and run round the young uns' legs when they're playing in the yard.'

'Well, it *is* wrong!' Lizzie yelled. 'And I don't want to hear you talking like that, d'yer understand? Get rid o' them fancy bloody ideas, my girl . . . else I'll have to ask yer dad to knock 'em out of yer.' Ruby put Lizzie in mind of herself when she was younger, and it frightened her. 'D'yer hear what I'm saying?' she insisted. 'Yer ain't rich and famous, and yer never will be.'

It took a moment for the girl to answer. In her young heart she was convinced that she was right, but she wouldn't upset her darling mam, not for all the world, she wouldn't. 'I'm sorry, Mam,' she said, wounded, her gaze falling away to the threadbare mat. There was bitterness in her then, and it tasted nasty. She was angry and hurt. Part of her wanted to promise that she would never again think above her station, but she couldn't bring herself to say it. Her dreams were too precious, and the thought that one day she might make them come true was too fierce inside her. Sometimes in the middle of the night, when it was dark and she lay in her chilly bedroom listening to the fidgeting and snoring of the other childer, it was only her dreams that kept hope alive. She couldn't give them up. They were too much a part of her.

Getting up from the chair, Ruby came to kneel at her mam's feet, and there was such love in her eyes that it made the woman ashamed. 'I'm sorry, our mam. I didn't mean to make you mad at me,' she said, stretching out her hand to stroke the infant's sleeping face. There was so much more she could have said, but not now, because the words wouldn't come easy. She could have said how she hated to see her dad come home from work worn and weary; she could have explained how sad it made her when little Lottie was laid to bed in an old orange box instead of a proper cot. She might have reminded her mam about the ragged clothes that the childer went to school in and how the other kids from better families made fun of them. And what of Mam herself? When was the last time she had had something new to wear? When did she last go out and enjoy herself? Why was there never enough money to buy that dear woman a new frock or a pair of boots? Ruby had thought and thought about all of these things, and it only made her all the more determined. She wanted to speak of it, but she knew it would only hurt her mam all the more so said nothing except: 'I do love you, Mam.' She saw Lizzie's gaze soften, and her young heart was full.

One glance at Ruby's downcast face had warned Lizzie that she might have been too harsh. No mother should have a favourite, but if she was to tell the truth and shame the devil, Lizzie would have had to admit to herself that her first-born was closer to her than the five that came after – although hell and high water could never drag that admission from her. Lowering the sleeping child to her ample lap, she fastened her blouse and smiled at the girl. 'Aw, lass,' she said in a gentler voice, 'I'm sorry an' all, 'cause I should never 'ave shouted at yer like that. Yer know I wouldn't ask yer dad to do any such thing as knock yer about . . . not that he ever would,' she added with a wry little chuckle. The laughter died away and she was serious again. 'But I want yer to listen hard to what I'm saying, sweetheart. Dreamin' and wishing can make yer bitter if yer let them get out of hand. Oh, I expect it don't do no harm to pretend now and then. But, yer have to know which is pretending and which is real.' She hoped she was making herself understood.

'I know what you mean, Mam,' Ruby assured her. 'And I *do* know the difference.'

Lizzie was visibly relieved. 'That's all right then,' she said, 'just so long as yer know.' She struggled forward in the chair and waited for Ruby to stand up before placing the child in her outstretched arms. 'Mek her comfortable, lass,' she instructed. 'Then yer can help yer mam get summat on the table afore yer dad comes home from his work.'

Lizzie watched with pride as Ruby pressed the infant close to her, making for the makeshift cot in the corner. Here she laid the child down and fussed about it for a while, tucking its legs beneath the patched eiderdown and stroking its face with tender fingers. There was no doubt that Ruby was very special . . . 'An old head on young shoulders' was how her dad described her, and he wasn't far wrong. Lizzie deeply regretted the harsh scene that had just taken place between her and the lass, and was eager to make amends.

'Set the table, sweetheart,' she instructed, 'then see if yer can round the others up for their teas. Afterwards, yer can fancy yersel' all yer like.' She strutted across the floor, mimicking the manner of a fine lady. 'Oh, la de da!' she said in a grand voice, clasping the girl to her when they both collapsed with laughter. 'Only don't break that there mirror with all yer rouge and finery,' she warned, ''cause it were a present from yer old Irish granmer. I don't want the ol' bugger turning in her grave when that mirror cracks from top to bottom at the sight of you in yer old mam's long begones. We don't want the divil to come down on us with a sack full o' bad luck, do we, eh?' she teased.

'No. It's all right, thanks, Mam,' came the reply. Ruby looked into her mam's hazel eyes, putting the fear of God in her when she said firmly, 'Your clothes are lovely, Mam, but they're not *mine*. And you needn't worry about Granmer's mirror because I'll put it back in the cupboard where it'll be safe. The next time I look in it, I'll be wearing my own finery.' Realising she had said more than she intended, she promised, 'I'll put the clothes back upstairs when Lottie settles.'

'Aye, you do that, lass,' Lizzie told her softly. When Ted came home, happen she would persuade him to have a quiet word with his daughter.

'Isn't she lovely, our mam?' Ruby was fascinated with the infant. When her mam had gone into labour with this latest addition to the Miller family, Ruby had been the only one there and so she had seen the whole birth from beginning to end. It was an experience she would not easily forget.

'Yer *all* lovely,' Lizzie retorted. And you most of all, she thought, gazing at the dark brown tumbling hair and the sparkling blue-black eyes that looked on the tiny infant with such wonder. In that moment Lizzie knew instinctively that never again would Ruby dress up in her mam's old clothes. Never again would she allow others to see her 'pretending'. It was a sad thing but suddenly she knew that her little girl was gone for ever. It was

9

another stage in Ruby's development, another step towards being a woman.

'Take the things back upstairs then, and put them in the box where you found 'em,' Lizzie said. She watched the girl a moment longer; loving her all the more when the child began crying and Ruby's soft lilting voice sang her back to sleep. It made a very special picture for Lizzie, one that she would cherish 'til the end of her days.

Still singing, Ruby gathered the clothes together and went up the stairs two at a time. In a minute she was running back down, and in another could be heard at the front door, calling out to the childer, 'Come on, you lot. Mam says you've to get washed for your teas.'

Lizzie smiled to herself and shook her head. 'Kids!' she moaned. 'Nowt but trouble.' Taking a small oval tin from her pocket, she opened the lid and with finger and thumb pinched out a generous helping of the brown snuff, afterwards pushing it up into her nostrils and coughing from the shock. Taking snuff was a weakness of Lizzie's and she rarely did it in public, although the tell-tale brown signs beneath her nose were an obvious giveaway. 'By! That's some strong stuff,' she spluttered, quickly putting away the tin before the childer should come rushing in through the door.

Glancing at the mantelpiece clock, she was astonished to see that already it was nearly five o'clock. In less than an hour her husband would be home, wanting his tea after a hard day's work. She hurried into the scullery where she filled the big old black kettle to the brim with water. As usual when she placed it on the gas ring, Lizzie stood well back. The rusty ring had an unnerving habit of spitting and popping the minute a lighted match was put to it. All the same, this was the time of day she loved best; when Ted was on his way home, and soon all the family would sit round the table, cosy in each other's company. Lizzie smiled at the thought. The sight of her man seated at the head of the table always gave her a rush of pleasure. It was strange how she and Ted could still be so much in love after all these years of ups and downs and so many childer between. A feeling of warmth and contentment spread over her as she went about her work.

But suddenly a strange premonition rippled through her, and somehow she couldn't seem to settle inside herself. It was a peculiar feeling, an instinct that something awful was waiting to happen; and yet there was no rhyme or reason as to why she should think it, unless it was because of those few hasty words with Ruby just now. 'Aw, stop worrying about the lass,' she muttered. 'Yer daft ol' bugger, Lizzie Miller! She'll sort herself out, you see if she don't.' Then she launched herself into the business of peeling the onions, and in spite of the burning tears streaming down her face, was soon in a happier mood.

The foundry buzzer rudely interrupted the men. It was six o'clock; another back-breaking shift was over and already the night workers were beginning to filter in. One by one the men put down their tools and stretched their weary limbs. With grim expressions and tired eyes, they began the slow, hazardous journey along the narrow terraces, a long snaking line of dark-blue overalls and dirty faces, all heading for the fresh air and daylight beyond that awful place. Hell itself could hold no greater horror than the foundry. Immediately below the terraces, monstrous cauldrons roared hungrily, deep bubbling furnaces of unimaginable heat with wide-open mouths and licking tongues of flame; the slightest mistake, one foot wrong, and the cost was too horrifying to contemplate. Only a few years before, two men standing on a platform lost their footing and fell into the glowing mass beneath. There was no saving them. There was nothing anyone could do.

From the higher reaches, the manager oversaw the change of shift, his sharp eyes surveying each man as he passed beneath.

When the small balding fellow came within hearing, the manager called out to him, 'Ted! Ted Miller.' When the little fellow stopped and looked up, he would have called again, but the roar of the fires below was almost deafening. Instead he made a sign, jerking his thumb backwards to indicate that he wanted Ted to come up to the office. He waited for a nod of acknowledgement before returning to the relative safety of his tiny office. Here he sat down behind the desk and waited.

It wasn't too long before the polite knock came on the door and Ted Miller poked his face inside. He didn't say anything, but his thoughts were troubled. It wasn't a good sign when the manager summoned you to his office; and the fellow was smiling. That alone was disturbing.

'Come in, Ted,' the manager urged, sitting on the edge of his seat and trying not to seem too serious. When Ted came in and closed the door behind him, he pointed to the chair opposite. 'Make yourself comfortable,' he said in a kindly voice.

'No, thanks all the same.' Ted sensed the other man's nervousness and it conveyed itself to him. 'I'll be more comfortable when I know what's on your mind. If it's summat bad, then the sooner you spit it out, the better.' This last week there had been rumours of a cutback in manpower. Ted prayed he wasn't here for that particular reason.

The manager looked at Ted. He took up a pen from the desk and began chewing on it, then he got out of the chair and walked round the desk. His face was grim, 'I'm sorry, Ted.' He shook his head slowly and dropped his gaze to his feet.

Ted's heart sank but he found himself smiling, because if he didn't smile he might show his deeper emotions. 'So, the rumours were true?' he asked, and his voice shook. The other man looked up. His expression was answer enough. 'Why me?'

'Not just you, Ted. You're only the first.'

'I've not been singled out then?' He needed to know that. He wanted reassurance that he wasn't being finished because he was too old, or too clumsy, or not pulling his weight.

'You're a good worker, Ted. Like I say . . . there'll be others soon enough. It's a higher decision to cut the workforce.' He wasn't lying, but neither was he telling the whole truth. He had long been envious of Ted Miller's standing with the men, and an incident when Ted had undoubtedly saved a man's life had been more than he could stomach. There wasn't a man here who didn't believe Ted should have been promoted long ago, and there was a deal of bitterness when it failed to happen although Ted himself was content enough. The truth was, Ted Miller was one of the best men in the foundry; a reliable, conscientious man who knew this work better than any of them. The manager was a jealous insecure soul who saw Ted as his enemy, so, when the moment came, he availed himself of the opportunity to be rid of him once and for all. It wasn't hard to convince them who mattered that Ted spelt trouble. It was easy. Too easy. But then there were other things at stake here.

Even as the truth of the matter was running through the devious manager's mind, Ted was voicing his own suspicions. 'I hope you're being square with me, matey,' he said. 'Me being finished here – it wouldn't have anything to do with that business a while back, would it?' Anger rose in him. 'If I thought the bastards were putting me out for that, I swear to God I'd fight 'em tooth and nail.' He breathed in hard and held his head high. Presently he said in a gruff voice, 'They were in the wrong and the buggers know it. *You* know that upper platform wants shoring up. All the men know it! Jacob Darnley could have gone the same way as them two poor sods a while back if I hadn't been there to grab his shirt-tail.'

'I know what you're saying, Ted.' The manager felt they were skating on dangerous ground here. Ted was right. When that platform swayed, his colleague could so easily have gone to a fiery grave. From his vantage point, the manager had seen the whole thing. Afterwards, he saw how Ted Miller was held in respect by the men, saw how they looked up to him, how they hung on his every word, and his jealousy was like a canker eating away at him. When Ted made a formal complaint with regard to the condition of the platforms, the foreman duly relayed it to a higher authority. He also pointed out in graphic terms how such a man as Ted was a potential troublemaker who should be watched very carefully. All this was reported to Oliver Arnold and the inevitable order was given; that Ted Miller must be discreetly removed at the first opportunity. The same applied to other men, real mischief-makers, and so the rumours were deliberately started soon after, implying that lower demand and higher competition might soon force a cut in manpower.

'Look, Ted. As far as I know, the owner took kindly to your suggestions regarding the rickety platform. I'm assured they've got all safety matters under review. This business of cutting the workforce – well, that's a different matter altogether. Like I say, you won't be the only one to go.' He sighed and looked suitably sorry for himself. 'Who knows . . . I might be next in line!'

'It's a lousy business all the same,' Ted replied in a serious voice. 'What's to be done about it?'

'Nothing. I only wish to God there was. Confidentially, Ted, orders have been dropping off for some time,' the manager lied. 'There's still plenty of work in the mills though. You shouldn't have any trouble getting fixed up there.'

When Ted gave no answer but stared stonily ahead, he went to his desk and took out a long brown envelope from the top drawer. 'I really am sorry,' he said lamely, handing the envelope over. 'Best take this and be on your way, eh?' For one brief moment he hated himself, but then he remembered how it would only have been a matter of time before Ted was noticed as supervisor material by the management, happen even by Arnold himself. He had his own position to think of, and if Ted was put up for promotion, it wouldn't be too long then before he was looking to the foreman's job. And then who knows what he might find out? No, he couldn't take no chances. Besides, he told himself, Ted would find work. He wasn't a man to be out of work for long. All the same, he felt a burning shame at what he'd done. Ted Miller was no troublemaker. He was a decent man, justifiably concerned about the well-being of his fellow-workers. 'I'm sorry, mate,' he said again. The hair stood up on the back of his neck when he recalled what Ted had said just now. 'I swear to God I'd fight the buggers tooth and nail!' Aye, and happen he'd break the manager's jaw an' all, if he was to learn that the cowardly fellow was lying about the reason for Ted being finished here at the foundry.

'Away home to your missus, Ted,' the manager urged now. 'You'll need to break the news to her, won't you, eh?' Lizzie Miller was a stout woman in more ways than one, and both men knew that she would be a source of strength in any crisis.

Without another word, Ted walked away, the envelope clutched tightly in his closed fist. The manager watched him go along the gangway and down the steps that would lead him to the outer doors. In all the years he'd known Ted Miller, he had never seen his narrow shoulders so bowed, nor his step so heavy. 'I pray to God you'll never find out what I've done this day,' he murmured fearfully, shaking his head and returning to his duties. Even now, he wondered at his own despicable action in bringing Ted to the notice of Oliver Arnold, a strong character who had built an empire from the smaller legacy left by his father. It was never wise to cross such a man, and with this in mind the manager bent his head to the communication he had received some days ago. With a heavy heart, he took up his pen and carefully ringed round the names of four other men. Unlike Ted Miller, each of these men was known to have made trouble in one way or another.

* * *

Normally, Ted would have made straight for home after alighting from the tram at Whalley Old Road. In spite of being bone weary, he would have quickly covered the few hundred yards to the little house on Fisher Street, with thoughts of Lizzie and the young 'uns filling his heart and lending wings to his feet. Tonight, though, there were other, more pressing things on his mind. He was a sorry soul, a man lost, one without work or sense of direction. He had never been an ambitious man, never greedy or proud. His two interests had been his family and his work. Now the work was gone and with it his ability to support Lizzie and the young 'uns. The foreman had said there was plenty of work to be had, but he was lying, Ted knew. He was no fool. For every vacancy that came up, there were always any number of men waiting to fill it.

'How do, Ted?' Len Taylor's familiar voice sailed across the road, bringing Ted out of his deep reverie. 'A bit off the beaten track, ain't yer, matey?' He laughed, a loud raucous sound that grated on the ear. 'Fisher Street's that way, yer silly ol' bugger,' he said jovially, pointing in the opposite direction. 'Your Lizzie thrown yer out, has she?' he laughed again, and Ted turned away with a wry little smile. The cabbie shrugged his shoulders and climbed up into his carriage. As a rule, Ted Miller would have stopped and chatted. Not today though. Today, he seemed a million miles away.

Coming out of Lodge Street, Ted stopped to lean against the lamp on the corner. 'What do we do now, eh?' he asked, looking up to Heaven as though for guidance. When none was forthcoming, he took his pipe from the pocket of his jacket and a wad of baccy from his waistcoat. The very act of packing the baccy into the wooden bowl was soothing to him, but he didn't reach for the matches to light it. Instead, his attention was caught by the huge sprawling building before him. Like a man entranced, he gazed at it.

Brookhouse Mills made a daunting and magnificent sight. Like a monstrous stone cake, its grime-covered tiles were the chocolate icing and the long cylindrical chimneys were gigantic candles. The out-pouring smoke snaked through the sky, making weird dark patterns against the bright sunlight which in their very ugliness appeared uniquely beautiful. Through the many long narrow windows he could see the upward-reaching iron struts and heavy machinery, could hear the awesome noise from within where the men, women and children scurried about like insignificant ants flitting in and out of the looms, all intent on one thing: survival. They might have their dreams, in their heart of hearts they might aspire to greater things, but they knew their limitations and so for now, it was enough for them to survive. 'That's all any of us want,' Ted murmured, 'just to survive.'

The image of his eldest child came into his mind and his face broke into a grin. Ruby was unlike any of his other children, a little woman who wanted to take on the world. Merely 'surviving' would never be enough for her, he thought proudly. And he couldn't understand why that bothered Lizzie so much. 'Wanting more is always a road to heartache,' she claimed, but to tell the truth, he'd wanted more all his life. It hadn't broken his heart, yet it hadn't brought him a fortune either, he admitted wistfully.

He looked again at the building across the road, then stared up at the calm evening sky. June was always a lovely month. In that moment Ted felt oddly at peace with himself; beneath that blue uncluttered sky, the fumes and hellfire of the foundry seemed a million miles away. Happen his sacking was a blessing in disguise, he told himself. And there was hope. There was always hope. 'The Lord helps them as helps themselves, ain't that right?' he whispered, his eyes upturned to the sky as though they might suddenly see something else there, *someone* else, gazing back at him. Suddenly he felt ashamed. What was he doing, standing on a street corner, feeling sorry for himself? Shaking his head, he muttered, 'Get yourself off home to your family, Ted Miller. Arnold's Foundry ain't the only place of work round these parts. You mustn't let the buggers beat you. You ain't finished while you've got two arms and a strong back, and never forget that!'

He thought of Lizzie and his face lit up. He could see her now, cursing him up hill and down dale for not being home on time. But then another thought suddenly occurred to him and his back stiffened against the lamp post. 'Bugger it!' Lizzie was bound to think the worst when he didn't come home as usual. In his dilemma, he hadn't given that a thought, but now he was frantic. Thrusting his pipe and baccy into the pocket of his jacket, he went on his way home with renewed vigour, half walking, half running, his mind assailed by all manner of things: his work at the foundry, Brookhouse Mills and all the other mills around here that were going full strength. The foreman was right. There *was* other work to be had. He couldn't do anything about it at this time of night, but first thing in the morning he'd be out there looking for work, and today would be just a bad memory.

Ted Miller's heart was a good deal lighter as he hurried down Lodge Street, along Whalley New Road and into Fisher Street, wending his way between roaming dogs, boisterous children rolling hoops along the cobbles, and grown-ups standing in little groups, where they busily swapped tittle-tattle and set the world to rights. He had been so steeped in his own troubles, he hadn't noticed them before. Now, though, they exchanged greetings as he hurried on his way.

It was gone seven o'clock. Lizzie was beside herself with worry. 'Where in God's name is he?' she asked, looking at Ruby with frantic eyes. 'He ain't never been late in all the years we've been wed.' She wrung her fat little hands and sighed noisily. 'Oh, our Ruby, summat's happened to yer dad, I just know it has.'

'No, it hasn't,' Ruby told her firmly. 'Happen they've asked him to do some overtime and he couldn't let you know,' she suggested. 'Or the tram was late. It'll be something like that, you'll see, so don't go getting yourself worked up all over nothing, our mam.' She didn't tell Lizzie how she too was worried to the pit of her stomach. Every night since as long as she could remember, her dad always walked through the door on the stroke of six. He should have been home a good hour since, and still there was no sign of him. 'I'll take another look down the street,' she said, going quickly out of the parlour and down the passage. Her heart was in her mouth as she opened the front door and peered out.

In the parlour, Lizzie paced anxiously up and down in front of the fire. 'I just know there's trouble,' she mumbled. 'I can feel it in me bones.'

'Our dad's not run away, has he?' The small tearful voice caused her to stop and stare at the group of children seated round the table, everyone washed and scrubbed and waiting for their dinner. It was Dolly who had spoken, and she looked at Lizzie now with frightened hazel eyes, her chubby little face pale and worried and her hands clenched tight together on the table.

'Aw, bless yer heart, darlin'.' Realising how she was frightening the young 'uns, Lizzie painted a smile on her face and went across the room to the table where she stood behind Dolly's chair. Reaching down, she lovingly wrapped her two arms about the girl's neck, saying in a voice that belied her fears, 'Course yer dad ain't run away.'

'Where is he then?' This time it was Lenny who asked the question; a tall skinny lad not yet eleven, with sandy hair and eyes the same colour, he appeared sulky. 'I'm starving hungry,' he moaned. 'Why can't we have our dinner *now*?'

When Ruby had called the children in for dinner, she'd found Lenny rolling about the cobbles with a lad from Viaduct Street. The two of them had been itching for a fight for some days now.

Although the lad was four years older and nearly twice his size, Lenny was getting the better of him until Ruby angrily pulled the two of them apart. Now, he would have to do it all over again, he thought angrily. What was worse, Ruby had called them in for nothing, because they couldn't have their dinner on account of their dad being late home. Lenny wasn't concerned about his dad being late, because he believed his dad had gone off for a jar of ale or a game of dominoes with a mate. Or, at least, that was what he would do if he was a man, especially on Friday night, and especially if he'd just been let out of Arnold's foundry. The thought of working in a foundry, in all the heat and the fumes, horrified Lenny.

'What! Start without yer dad at the head of the table?' Lizzie was mortified at the suggestion. 'Whatever are yer thinking of, Lenny? Since when has this family sat down to a meal without yer dad here to say grace?' The look she gave him was withering. 'I don't want to hear yer talk like that agin, d'yer hear?' Her hazel eyes were hard and angry as she waited for an answer.

'Yes, Mam.' Biting his bottom lip, Lenny turned bright pink. He felt embarrassed in front of the other children, and was greatly agitated. Beneath the table he crunched his fists together and imagined he was strangling that lad from Viaduct Street.

A strange silence settled over them all. Lizzie sat hunched in the rocking chair beside the empty fire, frantically pitching the chair back and forth on its runners, her eyes downcast and her heart troubled. The children quietly fidgeted in the hard stand-chairs set round the big square table. The boys entertained themselves by pulling faces at each other; Dolly busied herself by discreetly playing with the tassels on Lizzie's best green cord tablecloth, and above the ominous silence the ticking of the mantelpiece clock echoed the beat of every heart.

Once or twice Lizzie raised her eyes, to peep into the makeshift cradle where the youngest of the Miller family was peacefully sleeping after its fill of milk. She surreptitiously ran her gaze over the children; all out of her and all but one, by the same father, and she never ceased to be amazed how each one of them could be so different in character. The starkest contrast was between the twins. Eight years old, Frank and Ralph were of the same colouring and build, freckly, fair and sturdy. Yet where Frank was a happy amiable lad, Ralph was surly in nature, greedy and spiteful; only recently Lizzie had confined him to the house for a week after he deliberately squashed Frank's pet frog between two bricks. The only other lad in the family was Lenny, and he was different again; a handsome young man in the making with his tall lean figure and shock of sandy-coloured hair, he seemed to be always angry and quick to lash out with his fists. 'He has the temperament of a boxer,' Ted would say with a twinkle in his eye, but, like any mother might, Lizzie feared his temper could well land him in trouble one day.

She and her man had been blessed with three lads and three lasses. Ruby was the first-born, and although all the children were dearly loved, Ruby had a special place in her mam and dad's heart; fiery, strong in character, and fiercely protective. Lenny was the next, then came the twins. A year after that, Lizzie and Ted lost a newly-born girl-child to the whooping cough, before they were blessed with another healthy lass. Dolly was never a beauty like Ruby, because where Ruby was perfectly proportioned, her sister was round as a dumpling, with small hazel eyes much like Lizzie's, and the same unruly light brown hair. She was a delightful child, though, loving and warm, and right from the start there had been something very precious between her and Ruby. Last of all came Lottie, a pretty infant with carrot-coloured hair and vivid green eyes. She was unlike any of Lizzie's brood in that she was unusually quiet, sad even. After being fed and washed, she would lie in her cradle for hours, watching what was going on; she hardly ever smiled, and in spite of Ruby's constant efforts, had never been heard to laugh out loud. 'There's nothing wrong in being of a serious nature,' Ted was quick to point out. 'She's got two arms and two legs and they all move, she's got a loud enough voice when she wants her titty, and them pretty green eyes don't miss a single thing.' He had a way of stating the obvious. Lottie was different, that was all, and she was no less loved because she didn't laugh and gurgle every time one of the children played the clown for her.

Ruby's heart lifted when she rounded the corner of Fisher Street and there, not too far away, was a familiar figure striding towards her. 'Dad!' she yelled excitedly, running over the distance between them. 'Where've you been? Our mam's worried out of her mind.'

Breathless, she slipped her hand in his and together the two of them continued with quickening steps, Ruby's shorter legs doing two strides to Ted's one. For a while there was silence between them. But then Ruby became impatient for an answer to her question. Looking up, she studied her father's face; it was grim and tense. 'What's wrong?' she asked, sensing that he had something to tell. 'Something's happened, hasn't it?' She could tell from his downcast face.

Ted reassuringly squeezed her hand, saying firmly, 'You're a sharp little thing and no mistake.' He could never fool this one no matter how hard he might try, and so he admitted as much as he was prepared to. 'Happen there is summat, sweetheart, but it's nowt for you to worry about.' It was a frightening thing to be suddenly out of work, and it was best if he waited until the children were all abed before he talked to Lizzie about it. 'I expect your mam's waiting for me with a rolling pin, eh?' he asked, forcing himself to laugh out loud when, with a rueful expression on her face, Ruby slowly nodded. Lizzie was right, the lass really did seem to be an old head on young shoulders. 'We'd best get a move on,' he suggested, going at a gentle run and taking her with him. When they reached number twelve, breathless and laughing, the door was flung open and there stood Lizzie.

'What time d'yer call this, Ted Miller?' she demanded, but the relief in her eyes was unmistakable. 'And what's so funny, eh?' She glared at Ted, and then at Ruby. All the way down the passage to the back parlour, Lizzie ranted on at them. 'Shame on the pair of yer . . . there's neither of yer deserves any dinner.' As for *you*, you've got some explaining to do,' she told her husband. 'I've been out of my mind . . . imagining all manner of terrible things happening to yer.' Anxiety had given way to relief, and now relief had given way to anger. Ted went straight through the parlour, greeting the children as he headed for the scullery where he quickly stripped off and washed himself. He paid little mind to Lizzie's chastising. After all these years, he knew her well enough to realise that she was only letting off steam.

Ruby took her place at the table. Like her mam, she too had been anxious, then relieved, but now she was glowing inside because her dad was safely home, and because they had laughed together; although her instincts told her there was trouble brewing. But Ruby didn't want to think about that now. She looked forward to the times when they were all seated round the table and tonight felt special somehow, though she didn't know why. She loved the familiar sounds and smells in this house; the sound of splashing water when her dad was having a strip-wash, the smell of her mam's hot-pot, and that strong aroma of lavender polish and snuff that permeated every room. She even enjoyed her parents' good-natured bantering, because that was the way they had always been, and she couldn't imagine them any other way. Outside the factory-sirens called the mill-workers to shift, the high-pitched wails invading the room like uninvited guests at their table. There was nothing of any value in their humble home; thick ageing furniture, a profusion of ornaments on every surface, tatty rag-rugs made by her mam's own hands, cheery floral curtains, second-hand beds with patch-quilts, a rusty old gas cooker and a crockery cupboard bought from old Joe for a shilling. Nothing grand but it was home.

Lizzie fetched the large enamel bowl from the oven and placed it on the board in the centre of the table. 'We'll wait for yer dad,' she warned Lenny when the lad reached out with his plate. He didn't have to wait long because even as Lizzie spoke Ted came in from the scullery. His clean-shaven face was scrubbed rosy and he looked decidedly handsome in his clean white shirt. Smiling at one and all, he went to the head of the table where he seated himself in the carver chair. Bending his head, he folded his hands together and closed his eyes. It was a moment before he spoke, and this was so unusual that the children became restless, opening their eyes and peeking at him from between their fingers. They weren't to know what was on his mind, how he was wondering whether or not he should thank the Lord at all. After all, his work had just been taken from him, and that wasn't much to be thankful for, was it? He thought about Lizzie then, and about the children, and his faith was restored. 'Our deepest thanks, Lord,' he murmured softly. That was all, but it was spoken with such feeling that Lizzie was made to look up and wonder. Later, when the children were in bed, he would tell her the reason for his being late, she knew. It was Ted's way. But somehow, as she dished out the steaming helpings of hot-pot, she was suddenly afraid.

After the meal there were the usual protests about having to go to bed. 'It's only nine o'clock,' wailed Lenny. 'Other lads of my age can stay out 'til dark.'

'I don't give a fig for what "other lads" do,' Lizzie retorted with a determined toss of her head, 'I'll not have you wandering the streets 'til all hours, and that's an end to it.' Another time she might have relented, but not tonight. Not with Ted looking at her in that certain way which told her there were matters to be settled.

Soon all the children were washed and abed. The younger ones quickly fell asleep but Lenny stubbornly forced himself to stay awake and stare out of the window at the children playing on the cobblestones beneath. Convinced that they had deliberately chosen to play right below his window in order to annoy him, he vowed to dish out a few black eyes at the first opportunity.

'You can leave that,' Lizzie told her eldest. Every night, after the evening meal, Ruby would clear away and begin the washing up. Tonight, though, Lizzie suspected that her man was itching to tell her something, and from the way he was discreetly glancing at Ruby, it was obvious he didn't want any of the children to hear.

'It's all right, Mam, I don't mind,' Ruby replied. She piled up the plates and carried them into the scullery.

Ted followed her, saying in a serious voice, 'Do as your mam says, luv. You get off and spend a while with yer friend next door but one, but mind you're back afore dark.' He tried not to show his anxiety, but it was there, in his voice, and in his eyes which softened to kindness when he smiled on her as the two of them came back into the parlour. 'I expect young Maureen will be glad to see you. Her dad tells me she's been asking after you, and it's all right for her to have visitors now.' When Ruby seemed hesitant he added with an apologetic little smile, 'Me and your mam need to talk, d'you see?'

Ruby did see, and sensed that there was real trouble. She met his gaze with dark steady eyes. 'All right, Dad,' she said, lovingly returning his smile. Without another word she departed the room, deliberately leaving the door slightly ajar. Outside in the passageway she lingered a moment, listening for the soft hum of voices. When none came, she hurried along the passage to the front door, where she opened and shut the door with enough noise for them to realise that she was gone from the house. If there was trouble, she would hear about it soon enough, she reckoned. And anyway, the thought of seeing Maureen Ackroyd cheered her up. Three times over the past two weeks Ruby had gone next door but one, and each time she'd been turned away because 'The lass ain't fit to see nobody,' her mam had said. It would be grand to sit and chatter. Maureen always made her laugh.

Outside, the street was still alive with the sight and sound of busy folk. The cobblestones echoed beneath the wheels of passing wagons, children squealed with delight as they chased each other up and down, and numerous yapping dogs took up pursuit, diving in and out between thin little legs and occasionally pausing to fight playfully and roll about the pavement.

One shawled woman sat on an upturned box outside her front door, counting her pennies and shouting abuse at her husband, who had the good sense to stay inside where she couldn't fetch him a right-hander. The immediate neighbour of the Miller family, Ma Collins was well known all over Blackburn, a large formidable figure in a brown trilby and woollen chequered shawl which folks swore she'd worn every single day for the past ten years. 'Never been washed yet mended,' they claimed; which could account for the many holes and stains that made a pattern of their own in the long fringed garment. She sported a handsome dark moustache which made her look more masculine even than the coalman – and he was six foot tall with hands the size of shovels and a back as wide as a tram-car. She was loud and vulgar, and she smelled to high heaven, but if ever there was a birthing, a laying-out, or a pair of strong hands needed to stop a man from strangling his wife, Ma Collins was available. Down the pub of a Saturday night, she was a music hall turn all of her own. She could outsing, outwrestle and outshout anybody, and she was always good for the lend of a shilling or two – at an exorbitant rate of interest, of course. She was a woman of many talents, a good friend and a bad enemy.

Ma Collins' unfortunate husband was a tiny nervous fellow

whose physical attributes seemed to have withered beneath her insatiable demands. Not a day passed when he wasn't reminded of his shortcomings. 'What bloody use are you, eh?' she yelled out now, as Ruby passed, and for one dreadful minute Ruby thought she was alluding to *her*. 'You're neither use nor sodding ornament!' she screeched. Suddenly she sprang up from her stool and charged into the house. 'I'm no fool, you bugger. There's a woman somewhere, ain't there? It's *her* that's getting the best from you, ain't it, eh? By! I swear to God, if ever I find out who she is, I'll have her bloody eyes on the end of me fingernails!' Her voice echoed the length of Fisher Street. 'Look sharp, Bill Collins. Upstairs this minute!' she ordered. 'Get your arse up them bloody stairs and let's see what you're made of.' She laughed out loud, and every man in the street thanked the Lord it wasn't *him* who'd run up the stairs.

Ruby was still chuckling when she knocked on her friend's door. Almost immediately she could hear the sound of footsteps coming along the passage, and when the door opened it was Maureen's brother who smiled down on her. 'Ruby! Come to see our Maureen, have you?' he asked, wishing it was him she'd come to see.

Johnny Ackroyd was some four years older than Ruby, with coal-black hair and brooding eyes. A well-built lad with handsome gaunt features and long lean limbs, he was the only son and the breadwinner, since his father was always too drunk or too lazy to provide for his own. 'My mam's up there with her now, making sure Sis eats something. But I expect it'll be all right for you to go up,' he said, opening the door and stepping aside as she came up the steps and into the passage. Ruby would have brushed past him but he closed the door in such a way that she was trapped against the wall.

'Is she better?' Ruby asked. 'My dad heard that she could have visitors.'

27

'Aye, thank God. She's sitting up and taking notice now. The doctor says she's to take things easy, but she's better. You'll see that for yourself.' His easy manner was comforting, and when he looked down on her with those smiling dark eyes, Ruby's heart turned over.

'I'll go up then, if you're sure your mam won't mind?' She was deeply conscious of his closeness. Things were happening to her lately, things that went on inside her, strange thrilling things that she couldn't really understand.

'Stay a minute,' he said, leaning over her, his fingers reaching out to secure a stray lock of her dark brown hair. He knew every inch of her lovely face: the dark blue eyes that were marbled with streaks of black, the wide arched eyebrows and those thick dark lashes, the full mouth that turned gently up at the corners, and the shock of rich brown hair that framed her small heart-shaped face. He loved her. He had always loved her. But he wasn't yet man enough to know how to deal with this all-consuming emotion. He wanted to reveal all of this to Ruby. He longed to tell her how he dreamed of her at night, and how he made himself imagine what she was doing every minute of the day. He even imagined her without her clothes on, and he was not ashamed. The kind of feelings he had for Ruby were not the kind that brought shame.

'I'd best go up,' she said. She was confused by those dark brooding eyes and the way he was touching her. She could feel his finger, gentle and loving, shaping the outline of her breast, sending frissons of delight down her spine. She didn't move away, even though he was no longer blocking her path. Her heart was fluttering, and her insides were churning like her mam's mangle. Even before he bent his head to kiss her, she knew what he had in mind. His face had coloured up in anticipation and his manner was clumsy, but when his lips came down, warm and soft, melting into hers, her senses reeled, and all manner of longings coursed through her.

Reluctantly, she pushed him away. Their eyes met and she saw the passion still smouldering in his gaze. She was ashamed then. Ashamed and deeply afraid. That was her first kiss, and she liked it too much. It was never her intention that Johnny Ackroyd should be the very first boy to kiss her; she had always meant to save herself until *she* thought it was time. Anger spiralled up in her and she opened her mouth to speak, but the words which she might later have regretted were suppressed when another voice intervened. 'What are you doing there, you two?' Meg Ackroyd made her way down the stairs, peering into the gloomy passage with inquisitive eyes. 'Oh, it's you, Ruby!' she exclaimed with relief.

She had known for some time how her son felt about this pretty lass. A mother always knew. Somehow, though, she had an idea that he was setting his cap too high. Young Ruby Miller was a godsend to her mam, and she was a lovely bonny creature, but she would never be satisfied with a tiny back-to-back house and a dozen bairns to keep her down.

'I'm sorry, luv, but you can't see our Maureen. She's sleeping just now, and I don't want her wakened.' She turned to go into the parlour. 'Come back tomorrow. She'll be glad to see you then, I know.'

She sensed the atmosphere and suspected they'd been kissing. A curious little smile flitted across her mouth. 'A boy yesterday, a man tomorrow,' she murmured. She only hoped her son wasn't heading for a broken heart.

Johnny opened the door to let Ruby out. His voice was low and intimate as he asked shyly, 'You didn't mind me kissing you, did you, Ruby?' It was his first kiss too, and he loved her all the more because of it.

'It's all right, I expect,' she said, and in spite of a small twinge of regret, her face was still flushed with the pleasure of that wonderful kiss. Unable to bear his dark, searching gaze, she quickly turned away and ran down the road. The knowledge that he watched her all the way gave her an odd feeling of pleasure.

Ruby was in a lazy, dreamy mood as she came softly into the house and closed the door. She could still feel Johnny's strong hands on her, and her skin tingled deliciously. Suddenly she couldn't face her parents, so she went down the passage on soft footsteps. Her curiosity was aroused when she heard what sounded like crying. She paused to listen, but all she could hear were muted tones emanating from the parlour; her mam and dad were still deep in discussion. Something about the timbre of her mam's voice made her afraid. On tiptoe and holding her breath, Ruby made her way as far as the parlour then pressed herself against the back wall and climbed up the stairs to the third step. Here she sat down, wedged her elbows on her knees, bent her head to her hands and listened hard. She felt no shame at her actions, because this was her family and, for some reason known only to herself, Ruby had taken on responsibility for their welfare.

'Don't worry, sweetheart,' her dad was pleading, 'I'll get a job the morrow, I swear to God I'll not be out of work for long.'

'Aye, I know you won't,' came Lizzie's reply. 'And it ain't your fault, I know that too.' She said something then, something that made Ruby sit up and take notice. 'I can't make it out though. *Why* would they finish a good worker like you, eh?' Before he could answer, her tone hardened. 'Are you sure it weren't Oliver Arnold himself who instructed it, to punish yer for complaining about them dangerous platforms?' She made a noise like a sob. 'If I thought a fella like that could deliberately fetch a heap o' trouble on us heads . . . well, I reckon I'd swing for the bugger!'

'Aw, to hell with Oliver Arnold! It don't really matter why he finished me, and harping on it can only create bitterness.' His tone softened. 'Come on, Lizzie. We've bounced back from worse things than this, ain't we now, eh?'

There was a quiet, poignant moment then, a moment when

Ruby imagined her dad with his arm round her mam. When Lizzie spoke again, it was in a small trembling voice that belied her words. 'Yer right, Ted. It ain't like me to worry over nowt. But we've six childer to feed and clothe now.' Pride surged through her voice. 'Still . . . I know we'll be all right, 'cause I've got the grandest fella in the world to take care on us.' It was the best thing Lizzie could have said to restore Ted's flagging confidence, because it wasn't long before the two of them were chuckling and canoodling and he was light-heartedly blaming her for the number of bairns they'd accrued. 'Yer too pretty, that's the trouble,' he complained. 'A man don't know how to keep his hands off yer!' And she laughed like a young bride on her first night.

Creeping back to the front door, Ruby made a great fuss about coming in. 'Goodnight, God bless!' she said, poking her head round the parlour door.

'Goodnight, God bless, lass,' they called in unison; Lizzie's face was a picture as she hastily straightened her hair and fastened the top button on her blouse. Ted just smiled knowingly. But it was a nervous smile.

Upstairs, Ruby stripped down to her pants and climbed into bed beside Dolly. As usual, the bed struck cold; the damp had a way of creeping out of the walls and seeping into everything. The child was fast and hard asleep. Ruby couldn't sleep though. She was in too much of a turmoil. She thought about her dad being out of work, and couldn't forget how her mam blamed Oliver Arnold. She remembered that sobbing sound she'd heard on coming in at the front door, and the way her mam had tried not to show how worried she really was. It was this which touched Ruby most. There was something wonderful about the way her mam and dad loved each other.

Suddenly, she found herself thinking about Johnny's kiss: warm soft lips brushing her mouth, dark handsome eyes that

31

looked into hers and stirred her deeply. She was dreaming again, and lay back in the bed, her eyes turned to the ceiling, her imagination taking her right out of the room, out of the house, out of Fisher Street, and into a grand place filled with grand things – and *him*. Suddenly it was Luke Arnold who was filling her thoughts, and she was both thrilled and ashamed; thrilled because he had smiled at her when she was waiting for her dad outside the foundry last week, and ashamed because of what she'd just heard. She knew he was the boss's son, because she'd heard two men talking nearby.

Long after her mam and dad had gone to bed, Ruby lay in the darkness, thinking about the events of the evening. The thing that stood out in her mind was that her dad was out of work and her mam was worried – and all through no fault of their own. Her dark eyes shone with tears and her young heart hardened with bitterness. Tonight she had learned three important lessons. The first was that love was a foolhardy luxury that cost a body too dearly. The second that it was dangerous to trust your future to others. And the third was the most important of all. If you were rich, you were powerful, and if you were powerful, you couldn't be frightened the way her mam and dad were frightened.

Those were the things she had learned that night, and the far-reaching consequences of these revelations would shape Ruby Miller's destiny for many years to come.

Chapter Two

Oliver Arnold peered out of the carriage window at the familiar landmarks. After a long hard day he was glad to be home. Lately the challenges of big business didn't seem quite as exciting as they once had. But then, he reminded himself, he was no longer a young man. This year he would be fifty years of age, and he was lonely. Even after four years without her, he still deeply missed his late wife. All the same, he could not afford to wallow in self-pity for she had left him with three children and he must keep going for their sake. He thought of his son, Luke, and a frown creased his forehead; he had not done such a good job on raising that one, he thought. Teresa, his eldest daughter, had been a source of strength to him, yet still he couldn't love her in the way he loved his youngest child. Ida was only eight when her mother died, but she was everything that lovely woman had been – warm and caring, a joy to be with, and as Oliver thought of her now, he couldn't help but smile. She would be watching for him to come home, and he was waiting for the moment when she would run out to greet him.

The carriage came up the top of Buncer Lane, the big grey horses going at a trot through the huge wrought-iron gates that led to Arnold Lodge, a grand old house with timbered gables and tall bay windows. On this glorious July day, the entire front of the house was hung with clematis and honeysuckle that spilled out a profusion of blossom and filled the air with heady fragrance. The long winding driveway meandered past lawns of velvet green interspersed with crescent-shaped flower beds where humming bees and many-coloured butterflies buzzed and fluttered in and out of the open blossoms. Great oaks and silver birch trees lined the way. Here was paradise, a haven of peace and quiet away from the noise and smog of a busy industrial town.

Less than two miles out of Blackburn, Arnold Lodge had been built by Lucas Arnold some thirty-nine years before. His son Oliver was a boy when he watched the house grow out of the naked earth, from the laying of the first brick to the hanging of the last lampshade. The house was his pride and joy, a sanctuary in an acre of valuable land which developers would have given their eye-teeth for. Yet there wasn't one of them who would ever have dared approach the mighty Oliver Arnold.

In time, though, his son Luke might prove to be of a different mind altogether. Now twenty-two years of age, immature and selfish, Luke Arnold was motivated only by greed and an insatiable need for excitement and danger. He spurned responsibility in any shape or form, and had no regard for either his family home or his father's discipline. Expelled from every school he had ever attended he strongly protested his innocence of the many crimes of which he was accused; crimes that had involved fraudulently making money out of his peers, blackmail and corruption of a kind that quickly earned him the reputation of being a bad lot. It was only because of his father's wealth and influence that scandal had been avoided time and again. But even so, he was not grateful. Instead he resented his father's intervention, and grew increasingly more sullen and defiant. Lately, though, he seemed to have mellowed, apparently wanting to make amends. Always hoping that his son would one day make a man he could be proud of, his father was ready to give him the benefit of the doubt. There were those who claimed that his mother's death some years ago had sent him off the rails, but there were others who insisted that he was rotten through and through. And this was all the more surprising because his father, although hard and ambitious in business, was not a ruthless man nor ever knowingly unjust.

Since his wife's death, Oliver Arnold had done his best for Luke and all he had received in return was heartache. Yet he loved his wayward son and against his better instincts was convinced that all would come right in the end. Indeed, after being given some authority over safety measures at the largest foundry, Luke seemed at last to be settling down and accepting his role as heir to the Arnold fortunes and all the responsibility that went with it.

At long last Oliver had hopes that his son would come to realise the prominent role he was expected to play as a leading figure in a vast and thriving business concern. However, being the astute fellow he was, he had limited his son's responsibilities until such time as Luke proved himself to be worthy. In fact, having spent a year under his father's strict tuition, and a further six months assigned to the manager at Arnold's largest foundry, Luke had shown himself to be surprisingly capable and this was encouraging. Oliver was pleased at his son's progress, and soon he would pass over much more responsibility. These days he was feeling his age and felt his decisions were not as sharp as they once had been. It would be good to have a son's broad shoulder to lean on.

But Oliver was fooling himself. Instead of teaching him to be a better man, the experience of being monitored by his father and then by his father's 'trusted' manager, who was required to report on his every move, had succeeded only in making Luke Arnold dangerously bitter and more deceitful. Already he was secretly colluding in a very underhand and dangerous activity which was bound to end in shame and scandal.

The carriage drew to a halt at the entrance to the house. Oliver Arnold climbed out, his weariness showing in the stoop of his shoulders and the slowness of his steps as he went to speak to the driver. 'I won't be needing you any more this evening, Thomas.' He looked up at the little man in the driver's seat. 'You're free to get about your other duties.'

The driver's homely face broke into a smile. Respectfully tipping the neb of his flat cap, he nodded gratefully, replying in a gruff voice, 'Right you are, sir.' As the other man walked away, he regarded him closely and muttered under his breath, 'By! There ain't even a smile for us tonight, is there, eh?' In fact, he had never seen his master look so worn. These past years had been a terrible strain on him, but Thomas believed that if his master was looking for the son to share his heavy load, he was heading for another disappointment. The father was good, the son was bad, and nothing would ever change that.

Thomas continued to watch as the older man approached the door. There were only two years between himself and the master but there might well have been ten, because while Thomas himself was carefree and jolly, the other man was white-haired and bowed down by the weight of office. Nearing fifty years of age, Oliver Arnold could never be described as a handsome man. He was tall and as thin as a pike-staff, with wispy iron-grey hair and a matching moustache; his best features were his strong blue eyes and his straight white teeth. Like many tall men, he stooped slightly at the shoulders, and had a noticeable habit when angry of stretching his thin neck upwards, until the sinews in his throat stood out like tram-lines.

Many years ago Oliver Arnold had inherited a small fortune from his father; this consisted of a working foundry and a number of tenanted houses throughout Blackburn. Lucas Arnold had been an exemplary businessman, with a modest instinct for making money. He had also been a fair-minded, honest man who always had the welfare of his workers at heart. His son Oliver was made in the same mould; although neither man ever gave an opportunity to troublemakers or those who would disrupt the orderly running of the business concerns. Like his father before him, Oliver Arnold chose his managers with the utmost care, trusting these same men to uphold Arnold traditions and values, one of their duties being to keep a sharp eye out for mischievous trouble-makers who were then dismissed without a second thought. Conversely, if a man showed promise, he was always rewarded with more responsibility.

Oliver Arnold never engaged in underhand deals or shady speculation. He was a shrewd, ambitious man with an instinct for making money. It wasn't long before the legacy left him by his father had become an immense empire.

'Arnold Holdings' now amounted to three foundries, a cotton-mill and two warehouses. Always seeking to expand his fortune, Oliver was presently in negotiation with the owners of a small merchant fleet operating between Liverpool and America. The company was reputed to be in deep financial trouble and so had attracted his attention. No one doubted his ability to acquire a troubled company and turn it into a thriving concern. He hoped that soon he would be able to unload some of the responsibility onto his only son's shoulders.

As he walked up the steps to the front entrance, Oliver Arnold had sensed the driver watching him. Puzzled, he glanced round, asking, 'Is there something else, Thomas?'

'No, no. There's nothing, sir. I'm on me way,' Thomas Miller was quick to assure him, at the same time slapping the reins against the horses' rumps and causing the animals to start forward. The way round to the stables was narrow and winding, which meant that he must keep the horses at a steady gait. Thomas

Miller loved his job and he had a deal of respect for the man of the house, but he saw things here that nobody else saw. His master was one man to the outside world and another here in his own domain. Thomas had seen the deep abiding love that drew him to his family; and he had seen the pain and disappointment when his only son returned a failure time and again. He recalled how weary his master was just now, and it made him think.

'Aye, it makes yer count yer blessings,' he murmured to himself. 'I ain't got no family, except my brother Ted and his brood. I ain't rich nor handsome, and I don't know much except horses, but I do know this . . . I wouldn't want the master's life for a gold clock. He may have a fine big house and an army of servants at his beck and call, and happen he's the wealthiest man in Blackburn, but it don't mean to say he's a *happy* man, do it, eh?'

As the carriage approached the stable-block, he gently pulled on the reins. 'Whoah, me beauties,' he coaxed. In a moment the carriage was still and the horses impatient to be free of their harness. Climbing down from his lofty seat, the little man called out, 'Johnny! Give old Thomas a hand, will yer?' He continued muttering to himself as he began undoing the cumbersome harness. 'Johnny!' he called again, looking about impatiently, 'Where are yer, lad?'

The 'lad' appeared then, a broad-shouldered young man with smiling dark eyes and a quick strong stride. Johnny Ackroyd was stripped to the waist and carrying a pitchfork. 'The stables are cleaned out,' he said, 'and I've got the feed waiting.' He hung the pitchfork from the timber beam above the straw-bales. 'Miss Teresa's just gone. She wanted to see the big greys before we settled them down for the night.'

He came to the horses and began lovingly stroking their noses. The big greys knew him and nuzzled into his work-worn hands. 'It's all right, Thomas,' he said, 'I'll see to them. You look tired.'

He freed the horses from the shafts, then he set about loosening the brass buckles that secured the harness. 'I'll clean up these brasses while the horses are feeding,' he said. 'Oh, and there's a fresh brew simmering on the stove for you.'

'Bless yer heart, lad, what would I do without yer, eh?' Thomas asked. He watched Johnny skilfully remove the harness before leading the greys into the stable. Following behind, he thought how capable the lad was and how he had taken to this work like he was born to it. He often wondered how he'd managed before Johnny was hired as his assistant. 'You say Miss Teresa came to see the horses?' he asked mischievously.

'Aye. She's only been gone a few minutes. I wish she wouldn't hang about when I'm trying to work, though.'

'Hang about, did she?' Thomas chuckled. 'That's 'cause it ain't the horses she came to see.'

'What do you mean?'

Thomas was surprised that Johnny hadn't already seen through Teresa's dangerous little game. 'The lass came to see *you*,' he remarked. But then his voice changed and he warned, 'Don't be tempted though, lad. Women is trouble. And rich men's daughters is the worst trouble of all.'

Johnny didn't answer straightaway. He was thinking of Thomas's niece. There was only one girl for him and that was Ruby Miller. 'You're imagining things,' he replied somewhat sharply. 'Miss Teresa came to see the horses, like she said.'

'Aye, well, have it your own way. But I'm warning you, Johnny lad, be on your guard. Temptation comes in many shapes and forms.' Having delivered his warning, he slapped the lad on his bare back and chuckled mischievously. 'I forgot, though. It's our Ruby as takes your fancy, ain't it?' He shook his head. 'She's a quality creature is that. Oh, but she's proud! All the same, one o' these days, she'll make some fella a grand wife.' When he saw the deep red flush that crept from Johnny's muscular neck right up to the roots of his hair, he thought he had teased him enough. 'Aye, well, just think on what I said about that one in the big house.' He rubbed his hands together and chuckled again. 'There's a brew o' tea, you say?' he asked, going to the stove and licking his lips in anticipation.

He set about the serious business of pouring out the tea, and it wasn't long before he was seated in the old torn armchair that he'd rescued from the gardener's bonfire. With his hands wrapped round the enamel mug of steaming liquid, and thankful that the day's work was almost over, he took a moment to contemplate. 'I can't stand this July heat,' he complained, 'it saps a body's strength. It's all right for you, lad,' he muttered, 'you're finished for the weekend. But my work ain't never finished.' A sudden smile lit his face. 'Still, I won't complain, 'cause I've a great deal to be thankful for after all's said and done.'

Appearing not to have heard the other man's ramblings, Johnny placed the bucket of water where both horses could reach it. Stretching up, he told Thomas in a serious voice, 'One of these days, I'll have to punch that Luke Arnold on the nose.'

'Hey! We'll have none o' that, young fella,' Thomas rebuked him. 'I've told you before . . . don't let the bugger rile you.' He supped his tea and sighed, all the while aware of Johnny's anger. 'What's he done this time?' he asked impatiently. Running through his mind was the incident when Luke 'accidentally' dropped one of the best saddles in the horses' trough after Johnny had spent a full hour polishing it. Luckily Johnny was busy fetching the hunters in from the top field and didn't see the damage until later or there might have been a punch-up then. As it was, Thomas had his work cut out to stop Johnny going after the master's son. There was deep bitterness between those two, and it was a great source of worry to Thomas.

'He's a bad 'un,' he said in a whisper. 'And he'd like nothing more than for you to lunge at him, so he can have you chucked out of your job. Is that what you want, eh? How do you think your mam would feel if you went home and told her you've no wages coming in, 'cause you let yourself be drawn into a fight with that good-for-nothing?' He shook his head. 'What was it he done, anyroad?'

'Nothing you could put your finger on. He just stood by the stable door, kicking at the ground and watching me. Whenever I turned round, he was there . . . watching and sniggering. Going out of his way to aggravate me.' Johnny's fists clenched and unclenched at his sides. 'If he does it again, I swear I'll black his eye and face the consequences. At least I'll get the satisfaction out of knocking him flat on his back!' The prospect made him smile.

'You'll do no such thing. Luke Arnold can be a bad enemy. You'll *ignore* him, that's what you'll do, young fella-me-lad. If he comes round again, just get on with your work and pretend he ain't there.'

'He's a bastard, and he deserves a thrashing! If it weren't for what you said, about me going home without any wages for my mam, I'd knock all sorts out of him, I would.' His eyes darkened with rage.

'By!' Thomas had never heard the lad use such strong language before. 'He really has got under your skin, ain't he? Well now, you can forget about giving him a thrashing, because that's for his father to do. You and me, we do as we're told, and we keep ourselves to ourselves. That way we don't get in trouble, do we, eh?' He waited for Johnny to answer, but it was plain to see that the lad was still in a black mood. 'Did you hear what I said?' he insisted sharply. 'We don't want no trouble, so we get on with our work and we mind our own business, ain't that right?'

'I suppose so.'

'There ain't no suppose about it.' He pointed to the straw-bale beside him. 'Sit down here, lad,' he said kindly. When Johnny was seated beside him, he went on, 'I ain't saying as the bugger don't deserve a thrashing, because he does. What I'm saying is, it won't be *you* as gives it him, 'cause then he'll have you right where he wants you. Don't give him the satisfaction, lad. You know he ain't worth it, don't you, eh?' He nodded with approval when Johnny grunted his agreement. He lit up his clay pipe and began sucking contentedly on it, and the two of them were quiet for a while, each thinking his own thoughts; the old one wondering whether he should have taken a wife to comfort him in his old age, and the young one dreaming of walking down the aisle with the lovely Ruby on his arm.

He thought about the way she had looked up at him when he took her in his arms the other day, how her eyes told him all he wanted to know. He remembered how she ran from him, and how she had always given him the impression that she didn't really care for him in that way. But in his heart Johnny truly believed that Ruby loved him as much as he loved her. He had to hope that there would come a day when she would be his wife – and, oh what a proud man he would be then. Thomas was right though, Ruby was proud, and if anything dimmed Johnny's hopes in that moment it was the knowledge that she was different from any other girl he'd known. Loving and delightful as she was, there was something frightening about the way she talked of 'fine clothes and a big house, and an army of servants for our mam, so she can put her feet up when they ache'.

Anger rose in him then. God Almighty! Where did she get such grand ideas? For himself, he never hankered after things like that. All he ever wanted was Ruby. But if he could provide her with the things she craved, he'd work his fingers to the bone. Sometimes, in the early hours when he was taking the horses out to the top field and the air was heavy with dew, he would marvel at God's wonderful world, and he'd think of Ruby, of how she ached for other things, things that didn't really matter, and his heart would turn over with fear. He feared her ambitions would separate the two of them for ever.

Then he'd see Luke Arnold galloping across the fields, a man only a few years older than himself, a layabout who'd never done a proper day's work in his entire life, rich and spoilt and with all the things that Ruby put such great value on. Johnny was consumed with bitterness then. Luke Arnold didn't deserve such an easy life. If there was any justice in this world, a man would reap only what he sows. That way, all men would get their just rewards.

Thomas spoke again to issue a warning, 'Stay well clear o' that one next time the bugger tries to rile you, remember you're worth ten of him!' He shook his head and sighed, 'It'll be a sorry day when Luke Arnold is master of this house. Twenty year I've worked for Oliver Arnold, and I can't remember a time when he's ever caused me pain. I've seen his eldest son grow from an infant, and I've seen him become a father twice more. I watched him break his heart when his wife was taken, and I've been proud o' the man he is. Oh, but I tell you, Johnny lad . . . the greatest sorrow he's endured has a name, and that name is Luke – a bad 'un if ever there was one!'

'Where did he get his bad ways?' Like Thomas, Johnny had immense respect for the master, and often wondered whether Luke was more like his late mother. 'You can see he didn't get 'em from his father.'

'No, and he didn't get his bad ways from his mam neither,' Thomas informed him. 'Some folks are just bad, and there ain't no telling why. But like I say, lad, it'll be a sorry day for all on us when he's the master of Arnold Lodge. But most especially for young Ida. Miss Teresa can take care of herself, 'cause she's cut out of the same mould as her brother. But the young 'un's a different kettle o' fish altogether.' He shook his head forlornly and his spirits plummeted until he told himself that none of it was his concern. He didn't have no worries, and wasn't about to take on anybody else's. All the same, thoughts of the gentle Miss Ida being left at the mercy of Luke and Teresa made his blood run cold.

'That's enough of other folk!' He rose from his seat and carefully put out his pipe. 'Come on, lad. We've a deal o' work to do afore you can make your way home. The sooner we're done, the sooner I can retire to my own quarters.'

Thomas had lived over the stables these past twenty years, and now he was content to end his days here, with a hearth he could call his own and a good master to serve. His only fear was that he might outlive the master, because then he, like young Miss Ida, would be at the mercy of a hard and spiteful young man.

By six o'clock the horses were fed and stabled, the harness hung in the tack-room, polished and gleaming, the carriage cleaned inside and out, and everything ship-shape, as Thomas put it. At ten past six, he straightened his back from his labours and told Johnny, 'Right, lad. There ain't nothing else to do for the minute, so I'm away upstairs to my quarters. I reckon it won't be too long before I go to my bed, 'cause more often than not, that young bugger Luke will have me out at midnight to run him here or there. If his father knew he was dragging me from my bed at all hours, I reckon he'd skin the hide off him.'

'Why don't you tell him, then?'

Thomas groaned. 'Don't think I haven't been tempted. But no, it ain't worth causing trouble for. You should remember that, lad. You don't go making trouble for yourself with the gentry, unless you want to come off worse.' He saw Johnny was about to protest, and so quickly instructed, 'When you've had your swill, get off home. Mind you check the horses just before you leave. Oh, and don't forget to secure the stable doors behind you.' He patted

Johnny on the back, adding an apology, 'Sorry, lad. I know I can trust you to do what's needed, eh?'

'Don't worry, I'll see to it,' Johnny promised, and the older man knew he was leaving everything in safe hands.

'I'm tired, I'll not deny it,' he said as he made his way towards the far end of the stables to climb the narrow stairs there. 'I ain't so young as I was, and that's a fact.'

'You'll be fine when you've washed and eaten. It's been a long day, that's all,' Johnny assured him. 'But if you want me to come over the weekend, you've only to ask.'

'No need for that.' Thomas would never admit that he couldn't manage on his own for two days. 'I'll see you five o'clock Monday morning, and don't be late.' Johnny was never late, but Thomas felt the need to assert his authority just then. Without a backward glance he went on, up the stairs and into the haven of his tiny quarters.

'You're a proud old fella,' Johnny whispered. 'Proud and stubborn, just like your niece Ruby.' Even the mention of her name warmed him all over, and he began whistling a merry tune. Taking the bucket to the pump, he filled it to the brim with water then carried it back to the stables; Thomas had warned him never to strip-wash in full view of the house. 'The master don't want you offending the young ladies.'

Inside the stables, Johnny poured half the water into a smaller bucket before making his last check of the evening. The hunters were bedded and content, and the big greys nuzzled him in turn as he went from one stable to the other, forking over the straw beds and checking the water level in the trough. 'You'll do, my beauties,' he said softly, caressing each nose in turn. He loved these animals, and they sensed it. 'I'll be away soon as ever I've had my wash, but Thomas'll see to you first thing.'

Johnny was always reluctant to leave. For a long while he leaned against the rail watching the horses and taking pleasure in their every move. It was warm in the stables and the smells invaded the air like a physical presence; the sweet warm aroma of horses' sweat, the pleasant dry smell of newly polished leather – familiar things that gave him a feeling of great contentment. The big old barn with its great oak beams and high wide roof, the tack-room hung with saddles, working-harness and riding gear; he knew every inch of it, his hands had touched every surface, and his fingers had ached from polishing the harness until it shone like a mirror. This place was like his second home and he understood why Thomas had bided here these many years, content to live out his life in the rooms above. There was something very special about this way of life. Not like the mills and the foundries where so many men earned their living. Huge monstrosities that belched black acrid smoke over the land, places that were more like jails, where a man could choke from the noise and chaos. Here there was peace, and beauty, and a wonderful sense of freedom.

Glancing out of the doors to the church steeple that towered above a nearby village, Johnny read the time on the clock face. It was already twenty minutes past six. If he didn't get to the main road by quarter to seven, he'd miss his tram. 'All the same, I can't get aboard with the muck and sweat still on me,' he muttered. After collecting a towel and soap from a small cupboard, he tied the towel securely around his waist and tucked it into the top of his trousers. Placing the larger bucket on a stool, he plunged his two arms in and gasped aloud. The water was ice-cold, sending a ripple of goose-pimples over his skin. Yet it was gloriously stimulating in the close heat of the evening. Now he dipped the soap into the water, vigorously working up a green frothy lather which he rubbed all over his bare chest, then his neck and arms and as far round his back as he could reach. That done, he scooped handfuls of water from the bucket and followed the same pattern, until the soap was washed away and his skin glistened beneath the incoming shaft of sunshine. Taking up the smaller bucket from the floor, he leaned forward, straddled his legs wide, and poured the entire contents over his head, at the same time running his free hand through his thick black hair and allowing the water to run over his shoulders and down his back.

Blinded by the water, Johnny couldn't see the girl standing in the doorway, her avaricious brown eyes following his every move and with a look on her face that would have given old Thomas a heart attack.

Moving forward with soft footsteps, she was careful not to betray her presence there, and all the while she kept her gaze on that magnificent body, the strong shoulders broadened by work, the thick muscular chest, that rich dark hair and those distinct handsome features that had first drawn her to him. Johnny was nothing to her. She felt no compassion, no tenderness, no conscience as to the possible consequences of her desire to take him to herself. She thought only for the moment, and of her own needs. Soon she would be seventeen, and Teresa Arnold felt the stirrings of womanhood within her. She ached for a man, *any* man; but the forbidden fruit was always the best. Johnny was 'forbidden fruit', and she resented that.

She was almost on him when she changed direction, her silent fleeting footsteps taking her into the tack-room where she saw Johnny's jacket flung over the back of the chair. For a long delicious moment she stroked her delicate white fingers over the rough cord material, her imagination running riot and her senses tingling. She knew he would come in here before he left for the weekend, and the thought spurred the wanting in her. When he came in, she would be waiting. Bending low, she put her face against the cloth. In her mind's eye she saw the two of them writhing on the ground, their naked bodies merging. Trembling now, she straightened up, smiling knowingly as she began undoing the tiny pearl buttons on her blouse. At the same time she looked out of the door and glanced over to where he stood. He was combing his hair now, almost ready. His back was to her, a broad wet expanse, taut and tanned by his hours in the fields. For some long time she had planned this evening, the way she would greet him when he came in through the door, how his senses would be so overcome by her beauty that he would not be able to resist.

The last button slid open and she slithered the blouse over her arms. It fell to the ground. Her small white breasts were bared now, excitement flooding through her. Soon. Very soon. She could hear him now. Her trembling fingers undid the belt around her waist. In her mind's eye she could see him naked, wanting her.

Upstairs, Thomas was puzzled. From his tiny window he had seen the girl hurrying towards the stables, but as yet, he hadn't seen her come out again. 'She means trouble,' he muttered, frantically pulling on his boots. 'Bloody women! – they can be wily as foxes when they've a mind.' His thoughts flew to Johnny and he was afraid. At the door he paused, his instincts telling him to peer carefully out before he went barging down the stairs. Happen he were wrong and she weren't making for the stables after all.

He winced when the door made a small squeak as he came out onto the wooden platform. In the same moment a movement caught his attention, causing him to glance down into the tack-room. She was there, hiding in the shadows. For one shocking minute he couldn't believe what he'd seen; he didn't want to believe it. What in God's name was she thinking of? The master's daughter, half-naked and waiting in the tack-room. Looking beyond, he saw that Johnny was making his way there. What to do? God above, what to do? He couldn't rightly betray her, even though she deserved it, the little hussy! But then he couldn't let Johnny walk in on her like that. By! Before this night was through, both he and the lad could be out on the streets looking for another job. The thought spurred him into action.

'JOHNNY.' His voice carried the length of the barn. 'Hold on a minute, lad.' He came down the stairs in a hurry, rushing towards the younger man and keeping him from entering the tack-room. 'I meant to ask you if you'd take a look at the master's hunter. I've an idea she might be going lame, but for the life of me, I can't find a cause.'

'Why didn't you tell me before?' Johnny recalled fetching the horse in from the fields. 'He seemed all right when I brought him in earlier.'

'Aye, well. Happen you'd best take a look at him. We can't be too careful.'

'If you're that worried, Thomas, all right, I'll take a look.' He didn't want to miss his tram because he had ideas of calling on Ruby tonight. All the same, he wouldn't leave a horse in distress. Like Thomas said, you couldn't be too careful where animals were concerned. Without hesitation, he swung round and made haste to the hunter's stable. As he went inside, he glanced round, visibly surprised to see Thomas going in the opposite direction. 'Did you check all four hooves?' he called out. 'If he's picked up a stone, I can't think where it came from because that top field's clean as a whistle.'

'Just give him the once-over, lad. See what you think.' Thomas paused outside the tack-room. 'Soon as you've done, you'd best get straight off. You don't want to miss that tram do you, eh? I'll fetch your jacket . . . save you a few minutes.'

Deliberately keeping his eyes averted from the shadows where he knew she was lurking, and pretending not to notice the silken garment lying crumpled nearby, Thomas went straight to the chair, snatched up Johnny's jacket and made haste out of there, closing the door behind him.

'Well, there's nothing in his feet and his limbs seem sound

enough.' Johnny came forward, a puzzled look on his face. 'Are you sure he was limping?'

'Aye, well, happen I were wrong,' Thomas chuckled. 'Happen it's me as is crippled.' His relief at having defused a very dangerous situation showed in his ready smile. 'If you go at a run, you'll just make that tram.' He gave the jacket to Johnny.

'If you're still concerned on the morrow, it might be best to call the veterinary.'

'Naw. The natural way you have with the animals, lad, I reckon your opinion is as good as any "veterinary".'

'But you *will* call him if you're worried on the morrow?'

'Aye. Now get off home.' He walked Johnny to the door, remaining there until the tall familiar figure was out of sight. Only then did he climb the stairs to his own quarters. As he went inside and closed the door, he was aware of furtive movements down in the tack-room. 'You've been outfoxed, you bugger,' he chuckled softly. But he knew he must be ever vigilant, because she wouldn't give up. Folks like her set their sights on a particular possession, and neither hell nor high water would stop them from owning it. The smile slid from his face. If it came to it, he might be better to let Johnny go. He was young and strong, he had a good head on his shoulders, and he was unusually quick to learn. He went to the window and stared out. A great anger welled up in him when he saw the girl going at a run towards the house.

'Why did you have to set your sights on this particular lad?' he asked bitterly. 'There must be any number of young men who would give their right arm to break in a bad filly like you.' Sighing, he turned away. 'I hope you'll not be the cause of me losing him. Johnny Ackroyd is the best I'm ever likely to find. He's a good lad, hard-working and with a natural knowledge of horses that comes straight from the bone. You can't teach that kind of instinct.' He was angry now, 'He's my right arm, you bugger. It would be a sin and a shame if I have to let him go because of a flighty wicked thing that don't know right from wrong.'

Luke was preening himself in front of the hallway mirror, pressing the palms of his hands over his temples in a bid to flatten his wayward fair hair, and at the same time discreetly admiring the handsome, thick-set man who stared back at him. He certainly looked splendid in his brown cords and burgundy jacket. After dinner, he had a very important date to keep; although his father would never approve of the long-legged brunette who blatantly chased him for his money and not his looks.

He saw Teresa in the mirror, so was not unduly surprised when she came rushing in through the door. However, on closer inspection he saw that she was in a foul mood, her face aflame and her mouth set in a thin grim line. 'Where's Father?' she asked rudely, her brown eyes glittering with anger. Deeply frustrated by what had just taken place, she felt cheated and bitter, bent on inventing some dreadful story about the stablehand making approaches to her. At this moment in time, she didn't care if she never saw him again. She wanted him dismissed, shamed, sent from Arnold Lodge with a slur against his name that would prevent his ever again gaining employment in a house of gentry. It didn't matter that it was Thomas who had ruined her devious little plan. All that mattered was that it had been ruined. She felt humiliated and scorned. There was a deal of loathing in her, and this was unjustly directed at the young man she had meant to seduce.

'My, my!' Her brother turned slowly round to regard her with some curiosity, softly laughing when his dark blue eyes alighted on the wisps of straw caught in the hem of her skirt. 'What have you been up to?' he asked cunningly, noting how her shoulder-length light brown hair was unusually dishevelled and the upper buttons of her blouse done up in the wrong order, 'You certainly like playing with fire, don't you?'

'What do you mean?' At once she was on her guard.

'You know very well what I mean,' he whispered, glancing furtively towards the drawing room from which emanated the sounds of Oliver Arnold and his youngest daughter laughing, delighting in each other's company. 'If I were you, sister dear, I'd tidy myself up before Father sets eyes on you.' He grinned. 'You little bitch,' he teased. 'Was he to your liking . . . our brawny stable-lad?'

Incensed by his taunting, she lunged forward and kissed him full on the mouth. 'Don't be jealous now!' she retorted. Then, before he could recover his composure, she laughed in his face, turned quickly and went in great haste up the wide stairway to her room. She was still smiling when she closed the door. Somehow her fury had subsided. No, she didn't want the young man dismissed. But she *did* want him. Oh, yes. And next time she would plan it all much more carefully.

It was ten minutes past seven when Johnny stepped off the tram at Blackburn Boulevard. The sun was still high in the heavens and the evening air was clammy. He felt tired and hungry, but as always was glad to be making his way home to the bosom of his family. Even in his work-clothes and with his hair tousled from crawling about beneath the horses' bellies, he was handsome enough to turn a few heads. Two young factory-girls giggled as he strode past them, his broad shoulders set square and his eyes fixed on the road ahead. He was amused but not affected by their girlish antics. They were pretty enough, and no doubt they would make good companions, but they were not Ruby. It was she who filled his mind at the moment. She who had filled his mind all day. Ruby held his heart and his future in the palm of her tiny hand.

From the corner of his eye he saw a familiar figure approaching. He recognised the terrier-like features and the way the man's flat cap was perched on his greying hair at a jaunty angle. He saw how the man swayed from side to side and his heart sank. The man was his father, and even before the pubs were properly open, he was already drunk.

Reluctantly, Johnny stopped and waited. 'Aw, Dad, have you no decency?' he asked, neither ashamed nor proud of this once charming man now hopelessly afflicted with a craving for drink. 'Just look at yourself! You can't put one foot before the other.' He stretched out his arm. 'Come home with me, eh? Mam'll be wondering where you are.' It was a strange thing, but he loved and hated his dad all at the same time.

'Away with you. Your mam knows where her ol' fella is, and she knows he'll come home when he's ready.' He chuckled and said with a cheeky wink, 'I saw them two lassies, giggling an' giving you the eye. You're a chip off the ol' block, sure you are, Johnny Ackroyd.' He stretched his little figure to its full height. 'There was a time when I could turn a few heads. Oh, aye! You ask your mam, she'll tell you . . . had to fight the little buggers off, she did.' He cocked his head and thrust his two hands into his pockets, almost falling over when he unbalanced himself. 'Gerrof!' he yelled when Johnny thrust out an arm to grasp him. 'I ain't drunk.' He was indignant though. 'I ain't coming home for a while yet, tell your mam. There's this bloke, y'see, and he's got a bloody good idea for making money. I've a chance to get in on it. Your mam'll understand.' He glanced at Johnny's pocket. 'Got your wages, have you, lad?'

'Yes, Dad, I've got my wages, but you'd better not say what's on your mind because these wages are going home with me. I'm not interested in your get-rich-quick ideas, and I'm certainly not going to give you my hard-earned wages, just so you can squander them on some fella who spins you a likely tale.' When the other man cast his forlorn gaze down, Johnny was struck with remorse. 'Aw, come home with me, Dad. You know our mam'll be worried about you.' His father's weaknesses for gambling and booze were widely known, and there were plenty of crooks who would take advantage of a soft-hearted individual like Leum Ackroyd.

'I've told you, I *can't* come home, not yet. I've a fella to see. Do as you're told and tell her I'll be home shortly.' He gave a loud hiccup and grinned broadly. 'Did you hear that, eh? I swear I'll never touch a hot chestnut as long as I live. Tuppence a bag from the barrow on King Street. By! They turn my stomach upside down an' that's a fact.'

'It couldn't be the drink then?' Johnny had to smile.

'The drink? Never!' He saw the glint of humour in Johnny's face and was not a man to lose an opportunity. 'I need a shilling or two, son. As God's my judge, I'll pay it back.'

'You know I can't give you Mam's money.'

'Oh, I know that. But your mam don't take all your wages.'

'I keep enough back to see me through the week, that's all.'

'Aye. And a bit to save.' He leaned closer and Johnny could smell the booze on his breath. 'Saving, ain't you? Saving for the day when you're ready to ask that bonny Ruby Miller to be your wife.' He saw the surprise on his son's face and was encouraged to add boldly, 'You didn't think your ol' dad knew that, did you, eh?' He rolled his eyes upwards and sighed. 'By! I remember when your mam was a slight young thing. She were bonny too.' He made a choking noise in the back of his throat and his eyes welled up with tears. 'I've not been much of a husband to her, have I, eh? I wouldn't blame her if she were to pack her things and leave me for good.'

'Come home, Dad.'

'No. Not yet. I'm sorry for what I am, son, but I can't be no different than the good Lord made me. I shouldn't be asking for your wages, and I'm ashamed. You keep them. Take them home to your mam. Tell her I'll be along, I've some business to see to first.' He turned away, his shoulders bowed as though the weight of the world was pressing him down.

To the young man watching, it was a heart-rending sight. This was his father, and like he said, he was only what the Lord had made him. 'Wait on, Dad.' Johnny went after him. Digging his hand into his trouser pocket, he brought out two silver shillings. 'I'll expect it back when you're able. Don't waste them on booze, will you, eh?' he said, pressing them into his father's outstretched palm.

Leum was never a man for making promises he couldn't keep, so he didn't answer. Instead he muttered, 'You're a good lad.' Then he patted Johnny's shoulder, winked in that endearing way he had, and soon was going down the road, whistling to his heart's content and leaving Johnny to reflect on his impetuous action. He thought it best not to tell his mam that he'd given away his own share of the week's wages; though he would tell her that he'd seen his dad and that he would 'be home shortly'. All the same, if past experience was anything to go by, it would be gone midnight before Leum Ackroyd came rolling down the street, his voice uplifted in song and his pockets empty.

'Got any sweeties for us, Johnny?' The little boy ran towards his hero, and all the other children close on his heels; snotty-nosed, raggy-arsed kids who had been playing in the street, rolling their hoops along the cobbles and chasing the dogs in circles. When the smallest one saw Johnny, though, the play was abandoned. They all loved Johnny Ackroyd. He always brought them sweets of a Friday night.

'I'm sorry, fella,' Johnny apologised, 'I didn't have time to stop at the shop.' In fact, he'd been so dismayed at seeing his father in such a state, he'd forgotten all about the children's sweets.

'Ain't you got none in your pockets?' The little lad cuffed a running dewdrop from his nose onto the back of his shirt-sleeve. 'Have a look, go on,' he pleaded. And just to please him, Johnny dug into his trouser pockets. It was hard to tell who was more surprised, him or the little fella, when he produced a handful of liquorice lumps. 'Thanks, Johnny!' the lad cried, grabbing the sweets and running full pelt up the street with the others on his tail. 'Come back!' they yelled. 'You'd better share 'em or else!' Johnny chuckled. He was glad he'd found the sweets. The children expected it.

As always, Johnny looked for Ruby when he strode down Fisher Street. Sometimes she would be home and sitting on the doorstep, and he would sit down beside her and they would chat and laugh and enjoy each other's company. Not tonight though. There was no sign of her. He might have called down the passage if the front door had been open, but it was not and so he passed by. Later, when he was washed and changed, he meant to call on her. It suddenly occurred to him that she might be up in the bedroom with his sister Maureen, and with this thought in mind he quickened his footsteps towards his own front door.

'Do you think he'll find work, our mam?' Ruby was bouncing Lottie on her lap, while Lizzie put the finishing touches to the dinner table. 'I asked Miss Cicely if there was any work in her dad's foundry, and she said there might be, 'cause it seems they're working full stretch.'

'Oh, Ruby!' Lizzie swung round to stare disapprovingly at her daughter. 'What have I told you about discussing our business with your employers?'

'It's only Cicely, and she's all right.'

'Cicely Banks might be "all right", lass, but you're paid to do a day's work at her father's house, not to stand about idly gossiping. By! Will you never learn that we're different from these folks? They're *monied* folk. Gentry, that's what they are.

Jeffrey Banks and his daughter ain't no different than the Arnolds even if they do seem nicer folk. They live in a big house where they're waited on by servants such as yourself, they feed off fine china and their tables are laid with the very best that money can buy, they own dandy clothes and grand carriages that ordinary folk have no need of, and they talk a different language.' She heaved a deep sigh. 'Will you do as yer mammy tells yer and keep your distance. Do your work and keep yourself to yourself, lass. Else, God help us, it'll be *you* looking for work next!'

Ruby wrapped her two arms round the infant on her lap, kissing and cuddling her, 'Oh, our mam!' she replied fondly. 'Mr Banks would never get rid of me, not while I'm working hard and doing a good job. Besides Cook, there's only me and a live-in maid, and we do the whole house between us. When I've finished my housework, I run about for Cook, and she always says she's never had such a good worker. She's even told Mr Banks what a "treasure" I am.' In truth, Ruby enjoyed her work at the Banks household. She delighted in all the fine things about her – the expensive walnut furniture and the handsome drapes that swept the great casement windows, and, oh, that beautiful grand piano that she often secretly tinkered with when no one could hear. 'Anyway, it isn't me who talks to Cicely. It's her that talks to me.'

'Well, she shouldn't!' Lizzie could see the makings of trouble here. 'And you've no right calling her "Cicely".'

'Why not? That's her name.'

'She's *Miss* Cicely to you, and her father isn't "Mr Banks" neither.'

'Who is he then?'

'He's the *master*, that's who he is, my girl. These folks have titles and they like to be addressed correctly. Start showing disrespect and they'll have you out the door faster than your feet can touch the ground.'

'Oh, don't worry, our mam.' Ruby put the child in its makeshift cot and came to where Lizzie stood. Putting her arms round her broad squashy waist, she cuddled herself into her mam's ample bosom. 'I always address them correctly when I'm there, and I always treat them with respect. They're nice people though, Mam. Cicely is awful lonely, and I think her dad likes it because she's found a friend in me.' She was startled when Lizzie swung round and caught her fiercely by the arms.

'Don't you ever look on these folk as *friends*, Ruby Miller!' Lizzie's pretty hazel eyes opened wide in horror. 'These are the folks who pay you to wait on 'em, and that's all you are . . . a servant to fetch and carry and pander to their needs, nothing more than that. Don't you ever forget it, my girl!'

'But I'm the only friend Cicely's got.'

Lizzie shook her then, and Ruby was visibly shocked. 'NO! I'll not have it. And when your dad gets work, happen it might be best if you left the Bankses and found something more suitable.' She pushed Ruby away. It was the first time Ruby had ever seen her mam in such a state.

'You know I can't do that, Mam. Mr Banks is the best employer I could find, and he pays me good money that we couldn't do without.' Her dark eyes were confused as she looked up at her mam, but there was a certain defiance in her voice. 'I'm sorry if I've angered you,' she said. 'I promise I'll try to be more careful.'

Lizzie was angry with herself too. She shouldn't have gone on at the lass like that. In spite of having ideas above her station, Ruby was a good girl. But there were things that Ruby didn't know. Things that she would *never* know if Lizzie had her way. 'Aw, I'm sorry I lost me temper, luv,' she said, cuddling the girl to her. 'But you mustn't get too familiar with folk who employ you. It never pays. Don't forget, when I was a young lass I did the very same kind o' work that you're doing now, and

I've seen a lot o' heartache come from humble folk mixing too close with the gentry. It's wrong, child. Believe your mammy when she tells you, it's allus best to keep a distance between yer.' She held Ruby at arm's length. 'Promise me you'll think on what I've said?'

'I promise.' Ruby was glad she hadn't been asked to promise that she would never talk to Cicely as a friend again, because that poor girl had nobody else to confide in. Cicely Banks had told her things that she'd never told anybody else; she was never one for making friends and really looked forward to seeing Ruby. Like all young girls, she couldn't talk to her dad about certain things, and so confided in Ruby who always appeared much more mature than her fourteen years. She told Ruby how her mam had walked out soon after she was born and was later killed in a train accident somewhere in London. Being a shy and delicate creature, Cicely hardly ever left the house, and Ruby was like a ray of sunshine to her. The idea that she should 'keep her distance' from this lonely soul was unthinkable to Ruby. And yet, she didn't want to cause her mam any distress. 'Don't worry,' she said now, 'I will think on what you've said, and I'll try harder to remember my place in future.'

Ruby was never sure what her 'place' was, though. Sometimes, she frightened herself by the very scale of her ambitions.

'That's all I'm asking of yer, lass.' Lizzie was in better spirits already, and anyway Ruby was right. This family could never do without the wages Jeffrey Banks paid her. 'You keep your eye on Lottie while I fetch the brood in from the street,' she said kindly. 'And let's hear no more about it, eh?' Her answer was a bright and lovely smile that lifted her heart as she went from the room and on up the passage to the front door.

Ted opened it just as Lizzie reached it. He shook his head. 'No luck, sweetheart,' he groaned. 'I've fair worn me feet out, but there ain't no work to be had this side o' Liverpool.'

Lizzie recalled what Ruby had told her. 'Did you try Jeffrey Banks's foundry?'

'I had it in mind, but then some fella on the docks told me as how Oliver Arnold was after buying Jeffrey Banks out. If there really is a tug-o'-war going on, Banks won't be looking to take on more labour. Still, happen I'll go and see for myself on Monday, eh? Sometimes you listen to gossip, and get the wrong end of the stick.' He leaned forward and planted a kiss on her mouth. 'I'm home now, and I'm tired. I'll start again first thing Monday morning. You're not to worry, d'yer hear? Trust your old man and he'll see you right, you know that.' He deliberately brightened his face and rubbed his hands together. 'I can smell hot-pot. By! I'm a hungry man an' no mistake.'

'You've done your best, luv. You can't do more than that,' Lizzie said in a voice that belied her fears. 'The meal's ready. We were just waiting on you, but you've time to have your wash, 'cause I'm just about to fetch the young 'uns in.'

Her sorry eyes watched him go down the passage. She saw his stooped shoulders and the weariness in his footsteps, and her heart ached for him.

At nine o'clock, Lizzie sat in the rocking chair, her mind fleeting from one thought to the next. Another week gone and still Ted was out of work. Lizzie wondered whether she would ever have peace of mind. The childer were fast and hard asleep in their beds; all but Ruby, who was sitting outside on the front doorstep with Johnny Ackroyd. Ted was snoozing in the chair opposite, and only the ticking of the clock disturbed her troubled thoughts. Through the parlour window she could see the sun going down. It would be a while yet before the sky was darkened and the night set in. She felt uneasy, strangely unsettled. Uppermost on her mind was Ruby, and then the question of how they would manage if Ted didn't soon get work. Suddenly she felt the need to get out of the house.

'Where are you off to, Mam?' Ruby was surprised to see Lizzie come out wearing her best Sunday shawl and her navy straw hat pulled over her hair.

'I'm off to stretch my legs.'

'Do you want me to come with you?'

'No, lass. I'll not be gone long,' came the reply, and with that Lizzie went at a smart pace down the street.

'I'm glad she didn't want you to go with her.' Johnny loved to be close to Ruby, and the thought that she'd been willing to leave him there cut through him like a knife. 'There's things I want to talk about,' he explained.

Ruby looked at him with inquisitive dark eyes and his heart turned over. 'What things?' she asked.

'Oh, just "things",' he said lamely. How could he tell her that he intended to wed her one day, and that he wanted her promise right now? She was so unpredictable. If he said the wrong thing she would be up and off. He didn't want that. No. Happen it would be best if he just sat here and enjoyed her company for a while. 'You look real pretty tonight,' he said softly, hesitantly touching her hair and cursing himself when she inched away from him. 'Our Maureen's been asking after you,' he added swiftly, changing the subject.

'Will it be all right if I come and sit with her awhile tomorrow?' Ruby's eyes lit up at the thought. But her heart had leaped at the touch of his fingers. Johnny was so handsome, so gentle with her, and when he touched her like that, she could almost forget the other things she wanted out of life – and it was this which frightened her. Being poor was bad. She must *never* forget that.

St Peter's church was where Lizzie's mam and dad were buried. Whenever there was something deeply troubling her, she always came here. Now, a forlorn figure kneeling at the altar, she let the quietness and solitude wash over her and then asked in a whisper, 'Please help him to find work, Lord, for all our sakes. And I think you know what's on my mind where our Ruby's concerned. It were a cruel stroke o' fate as took her to Jeffrey Banks's house. Oh, dear God . . . if she were ever to find out that he were her father, there'd be no rest for any of us! Oh, I know it's hardly likely, 'cause there's only you and me knows the truth, ain't there, Lord? Neither Ted nor Jeffrey Banks has any inkling of it but our Ruby's a restless, wanting little soul, and I'm afeared she's got the taste for finery in her blood.'

The tears spilled down Lizzie's face at the thought of how she herself was once a maid at the Banks household and how, in one unforgiveable weak moment, she and the man of the house were drawn to each other. 'Forgive me, Lord,' she asked. 'It ain't her fault. She's the dearest little soul on this 'ere earth, and I'm asking you please to keep the lass safe from harm.'

As Lizzie walked home, she felt lighter of spirit. In all these years she had never confided the truth in anyone, and she never would. But then, the good Lord had always known, and she felt in her heart that he had forgiven her long since.

Chapter Three

It was the last Friday in July and still Ted hadn't found work. At five o'clock that morning, even before the knocker-upper made his rounds, he stood on the doorstep of the little house on Fisher Street, leaving Lizzie with the same hope he'd given her every morning since losing his job at Arnold's foundry, 'Today, lass. I'll get work today, you see if I don't.'

Lizzie smiled and encouraged him "Course yer will,' she murmured warmly, then pouted her lips for a kiss, put the snap-tin in his hand, and waved him away down the street until he was out of sight. Then she visibly sagged and the smile fell from her face. 'God go with yer,' she sighed, before going back inside to her little parlour where she would make herself busy so as not to brood about the future. Money was desperately short now, and she didn't know for how much longer she could keep things going.

Upstairs, Ruby remained at the window a while longer. She too had watched her father go down Fisher Street. She too had waved him out of sight. But she didn't make her presence known. Something told her that these few minutes when her mam and dad hugged on the doorstep were precious and meant only for the two of them. 'You'll get work, Dad, I know you will,' she whispered, staring at the place at the bottom of the street where she'd last seen his familiar figure. But she had said the same thing every day for the past few weeks, and still he was searching from morning to night. To make matters worse, twenty men had been laid off from Waterfall Mill and there were rumours of others to follow. 'You're a good worker, Dad, and everybody knows it,' Ruby added forlornly. 'All the same, it's a miserable day to be trudging the streets.'

She stared out at the grey skies. All week it had rained with a vengeance, and even now there was no sign of it letting up. Any minute now the skies would darken and the clouds would burst asunder to drench everything below. 'There's no use moaning though,' Ruby said aloud, her dark eyes following the drips that fell past her window from the guttering above. 'They do say as how every cloud has a silver lining.' With that thought in mind, she drew the curtains back together again, until only a narrow chink was left to admit the half-light of the morning, then she collected her work-clothes from the far wall where they were hanging on the picture-rail and tiptoed her way to the door. She didn't want to wake Dolly at this early hour. Besides, she needed a quiet word with her mam before the whole house was awake.

'I'm cold,' Dolly's voice whimpered into the gloom, causing Ruby to redirect her steps to the bed where she pulled the blankets over the shivering child.

'Keep still then, and you'll soon get warm again,' she whispered.

'I won't!' The child didn't open her eyes. Instead, she put out her arm and felt for Ruby's hand. 'I need you to cuddle,' she said, grabbing Ruby's thumb tight. 'Come back to bed, Ruby.'

Her answer was to wrap the blanket more firmly round the child. 'Go back to sleep,' she told her softly. This old house was damp at the best of times, but when it rained the air was especially dank and it seemed to strike right to the bone. Then there was the smell, a damp sweet smell that clogged the throat and clung to everything. It was that which Ruby hated most because even when she had put a distance between her and Fisher Street and was standing in Cicely's beautiful bedroom, that awful pungent smell seemed to follow her, until she could almost taste it.

'You won't be long, will you?'

'No, I won't be long.'

'All right then.' Dolly smiled as she wormed down under the blanket. In no time at all she was fast asleep and Ruby left the room, softly closing the door behind her.

'Aw, lass, there was no need for you to get up so early.' Lizzie was astonished to see Ruby come into the room, still wearing her night-shift and with her work-clothes draped over her arm. 'I would have called you in plenty of time for you to catch the seven o'clock tram.' She was busy setting out the breakfast things, although it was becoming harder and harder to satisfy the many mouths that gathered round the table. On seeing Ruby, she straightened her back from the task and looked at the girl with concerned eyes. 'Yer could have slept another half-hour yet, lass,' she muttered.

'Once I woke up, I couldn't get back to sleep,' Ruby said truthfully, coming to the table and laying her clothes over the nearest chair.

'What about the others?' Usually Lizzie loved to have her childer about her, but right now she felt low and couldn't be doing with their aimless chatter. 'They ain't follering yer, are they?'

'It's all right,' Ruby assured her. 'They're all hard and fast asleep. Dolly woke up because she was cold, but I tucked the blanket round her and she soon went off again.' She reached up to kiss her mammy on the cheek. 'If you want to sit down, I'll set the table for you,' she offered.

'No, lass. I'll tell yer what though, yer can keep a look out for Joe's horse and cart, 'cause there's only just enough milk to make the childer's pobs. I've washed the small churn ready. But there's time enough for yer to get your wash afore the others come down and fill the place up. They all need a lick over afore they come to the table.' She laughed then. 'I sometimes wonder whether it wouldn't be easier to put the buggers in the dolly tub one after the other.'

The laughter was a strange choking chuckle, and then, as though it had opened a dam somewhere inside, another sound followed – a low sobbing that startled Ruby. She was sitting in the chair about to put on her boots. She looked up, staring at Lizzie curiously, not certain whether her mam was laughing or crying. When she saw the tears running down that darling face, she prepared to spring up and throw her arms round her, but Lizzie was having none of it. Whatever troubles she and Ted shared were not to worry the childer. 'By! I reckon I've got a chill on me,' she lied, taking out the hankie from her pinnie pocket and dabbing feverishly at her sore little eyes. At the same time she turned away from Ruby and continued with the setting of the table. 'There's hot water in the kettle,' she said. 'Use it for your wash then fill it up again, will yer? Be sharp though, lass, 'cause they'll all be down the stairs soon enough, then it'll be like all hell's let loose on us!'

Ruby made no reply but bent her head and fastened the laces on her boots. She knew her mam had been crying, and she knew why. Yet no amount of reassurance from her would help her mam just now. The only thing that would bring the smile back to Lizzie's face was the sight of her fella going to a regular place of work again. Ruby could do nothing about that. She felt helpless, and hated herself for not being able to do more. Suddenly she recalled something her dad had said last night, and a thought had crossed her mind. It cheered her, yet she daren't think too hard on it. Not yet. And she daren't mention it to her mam or there would be hell to pay.

Twenty minutes later, Ruby was washed and dressed, her face scrubbed and her dark blue eyes shining. In her light grey, long-sleeved blouse and the dark over-smock, she looked smart as a new pin. She had worn the same outfit all week but each day, on arriving home, would heat up the flat-iron and press out all the creases; afterwards she would hang the two garments very carefully on the picture-rail in her bedroom, where they would stay until morning. On Friday evening she washed them and hung them out to dry in the back yard, before putting them away in the big cupboard in her mam's room, where they would stay until Monday morning. 'Shall I go and wake the young 'uns?' she asked, seeing that the table was laid and the bread-pobs were boiling in the pan on the gas-ring. When her dad was in work, there were boiled eggs and soldiers too, but not now, not any more.

'By! Look at you.' Lizzie was astonished at how quickly Ruby had got herself ready. 'What's the hurry, eh?' She winked cheekily and into her mind came the image of that nice young man, Johnny Ackroyd. The whole street knew about the love-hate relationship between these two. Lizzie had long hoped that in the fullness of time Fate might smile favourably on them, because she knew that if Ruby were to search far and wide, she would be hard put to find a more suitable and hard-working young fellow. 'You ain't looking to walk the length of Fisher Street on the arm of young Mr Ackroyd, are yer?' she asked mischievously, adding in a more serious voice, 'You're too young yet for serious thoughts, my girl!'

'Don't be daft, our mam,' Ruby chided, and a hot blush suffused her face until she wished the earth would open and swallow her whole. 'It's just that I want to catch the first tram this morning.'

Lizzie's eyes popped open in surprise. 'Oh? Why's that?'

'No particular reason, except I might get paid extra if I show up early.' She wasn't about to reveal the real reason for wanting to get to the big house before Mr Banks left for his office. Not when she suspected her mam's strong views would swiftly put paid to her little idea.

'I shouldn't count on it, my girl,' Lizzie remarked with a cautious smile. 'In my experience the gentry are more fond of taking than giving. I wouldn't want you to go working extra hours with the wrong idea that you might get paid for it.' She cast a suspicious glance on her daughter. 'Mr Banks hasn't asked you, has he? To work extra time, I mean?' Always at the back of her mind was the fact that every minute Ruby spent in Jeffrey Banks's house was a minute too long. However, there was no chance the lass could find out that he were her father, and it was nigh on impossible that the fellow himself should suspect anything; even though Ruby had a certain look that put Lizzie in mind of Jeffrey Banks . . . the dark blue eyes that were speckled black, and that particular proud way she held herself. 'Afore yer go, lass, take a look out in the street and see if Joe's there.'

Joe was already halfway down the street and his cart was surrounded by women, each carrying a churn, and each waiting to be served. By the time Ruby got there, most of them were already making their way back to their parlours with a gill of milk securely poured from Joe's ladle into their cans. The only people still waiting were a young lad and Mrs Donaldson from number ten, a big friendly woman who owned a wardrobe of nice clothes and a parlour that was reputed to be the 'grandest' in Fisher Street thanks to her five sons who were all earning. But nobody begrudged her that, because she was a widow, and had never found a man to take her late husband's place.

'Serve the lass first,' she told Joe when he'd filled the boy's can and been paid for it. She smiled at Ruby, noting her smart smock and knowing the girl was employed in one of the big houses off Preston New Road. 'Off to work, are you?'

'Thank you, Mrs Donaldson. Yes, I mean to catch the first tram if I'm not too late.'

'Best hurry then, eh?' Mrs Donaldson turned to smile at a neighbour who had joined them. 'The lass is in a hurry,' she explained, and while Joe set about filling Ruby's can, the two women got talking about lace and shawls and feather trimmings, and how the drapers in Ainsworth Street was selling a new range of 'the cheekiest little hats'. Mrs Donaldson vowed to get herself one that very day, while Mrs Armstrong tutted at the idea. 'I've got much more important things to spend me money on than "cheeky bloody hats"!' she retorted, swinging round and rolling her eyes at Lizzie who had just come out to send Ruby on her way before the tram went off without her.

'That'll be tuppence.' Seeming reluctant to give the full milk-can to Ruby, Joe held out his hand for payment.

'Oh, that's all right,' she said cheerfully, stretching out her two arms to take the can from him. 'Put it on Mam's bill.' She hadn't seen Lizzie come up behind her.

Joe shook his head and frowned, though his voice was kindly. 'Sorry, luv. No money, no milk.'

'But you *always* put it on Mam's bill!' Ruby was shocked, and when she realised that everyone standing behind had gone quiet, she blushed red with humiliation. 'We're not likely to run away without paying,' she said, summoning her dignity.

'Can't do it. There's too many folk owing me money, and by all accounts your dad ain't got no work.'

As far as Ruby was concerned, he had said the wrong thing. Now, when she stared up at him, her dark eyes glittered with tears. 'That's only a matter of time,' she said proudly. 'But when he does find work, you can be sure of one thing . . . we won't be getting our milk from you any more!' She swung away and was surprised when Lizzie stepped forward to tell the milkman, 'Joe Leyland, I'm surprised at yer. Haven't I allus paid me way?' He nodded and she went on, 'How do yer expect me to manage with six young 'uns and not a drop of milk in the pantry, eh?'

'Sorry, Mrs Miller, but I'm having to be careful. I'm owed money everywhere, d'you see?' He seemed relieved when Lizzie nodded her head and dropped her gaze.

'Well, I'm more fortunate than most, so you can put it on my bill.' Mrs Donaldson snatched the can from his hand and pushed it into Ruby's. 'Take yer mam home, lass,' she said softly.

'Thank you, Mrs Donaldson,' Ruby said, holding the can out, 'but we can manage all right.' Her mam had never accepted charity, and as far as Ruby was concerned, she was not about to start now. If needs be, she would buy milk from Cook and pay out of her wages next week.

'No, child,' Lizzie's sad voice intervened as she closed her fingers over Ruby's small hand and pressed it down until the can was almost touching the floor. 'We mustn't be ungrateful.' Turning to Mrs Donaldson, she said, 'It's very kind of yer, but we can't accept.'

'Would you do the same for me?'

Lizzie smiled. 'Aye,' she admitted, 'yer know I would.'

'Then let me help. Treat it as a loan.'

Lizzie nodded her head. 'Thank you,' she murmured. 'You know I'll pay yer back soon as ever my husband fetches a wage home. And, God willing, that won't be too long.'

'Thank you, Lizzie. I'm only doing what any one of us would do for the other. What are good neighbours for, eh?' Mrs Donaldson's comment brought a murmur of encouragement from others who had appeared and, as Lizzie began her way home with Ruby at her side, they thanked the good Lord that their own husbands were still in work, and that he shouldn't overlook Lizzie Miller in these hard times because she was one of the best.

'You'd best get off or you'll miss your tram,' Lizzie said. 'Leave the childer to me, and remember what I said . . . if they don't pay you for the extra time, then you're never to do it again. I'll not stand for it.' Like Ruby, Lizzie had been deeply humiliated by what had just taken place, but she wouldn't let Ruby know it for the world. She was close to tears, and on top of that was the fact that Ruby was becoming more and more attached to Jeffrey Banks's daughter who, unbeknown to Ruby, was her half-sister. By! If there was a way she could get Ruby away from that house without arousing suspicion, Lizzie would have done it long ago. But there was no easy way. And, like Ruby said, they badly needed the wages she earned, because now with Ted out of work and Lizzie's crafty savings almost gone, the money the lass brought home was all that kept them from the workhouse. 'And put yer coat on, 'cause it's bound to rain,' she instructed impatiently, muttering under her breath, 'Pissy weather for July!' When there came a bumping sound from the back bedroom, she rolled her eyes to the ceiling. 'The buggers are awake,' she groaned.

'Are you sure you'll be all right, Mam?' Ruby asked. She had hated the scene out in the street just now, and sensed that her mam was hiding her real feelings. Going to the parlour door she took her long-coat down and shrugged herself into it. Usually her mam was a bundle of good nature in the mornings, but today she was troubled and irritable. 'I can stay behind and help you with the young 'uns if you want?' Ruby suggested. She sighed within herself when Lizzie shook her head. 'Be off with yer,' was all she said. And Ruby didn't need telling twice, because hadn't she got a very important thing to do this morning? Something that would hopefully make that awful scene the last of its kind.

When Ruby came to kiss her goodbye, Lizzie clung on to her, saying grimly, 'Aw, lass, I pray your dad'll find work.'

'He will,' Ruby promised. At the front door, she paused and listened, thinking she could hear her mam softly crying. All the way down Fisher Street then on to the tram stop, Ruby prayed that she wasn't promising the impossible.

The tram was only half full. The recent laying off of labour made itself felt in the empty seats that once had been filled, and there was a strange quietness where once there had been a busy murmur of conversation. There was something soul-destroying about being put out of work, and something equally soul-destroying about being left in work when a neighbour was made idle; though it was the lesser of two evils. All the same, on this particular morning there were still a number of mill-workers and foundry folk all making their way to work, neighbours from Ruby's own street who knew and exchanged greetings with her, and those who were strangers yet nodded and wished her 'good morning'. But there was no sign of Johnny. In her secret heart, Ruby had hoped he might be travelling on the same tram.

It was just coming up to seven when she came in sight of Billenge House, a sprawling homely place situated at the top of Billenge End which led from Preston New Road. All the way along the lanes she'd expected at any minute to see Johnny making his way to Arnold Lodge, which was en route, but he was nowhere in sight and she supposed he must have caught an earlier tram. In one way she regretted not having met him, then in another she was glad. Lately, he was taking up too much of her thoughts, and there was no good could come of it.

Turning in through the stone pillars, she went at a run down the wide carriageway that led to the stables and the back of the house; there were no horses kept here because no one rode. Neither Mr Banks nor his daughter had any yearning to hunt, and as they each preferred to stroll the few hundred yards to hail a carriage on Preston New Road, there was also no need for a carriage, although there was one gathering dust in the far stable, a magnificent black ensemble with plush red leather and handsome wooden wheels. There had been a time years back when the carriage was in constant use and in the rooms above the stables had lived a groom whose job it was to keep ready the two bay geldings; now, though, the groom was employed elsewhere and the geldings pulled one of Thwaites' beer wagons. The carriage, however, had remained, to rot and rust, growing old alongside its owner. Its usefulness was long gone, its wheels never turning against the cobbles, nor the crack of a whip urging it ever onward. Once it was a part of daily life; once it had swiftly and efficiently carried out its duties, employed in the routine transportation of Mr Banks to his foundry. It was dressed in black silk and ribbons when they laid old Mr Banks to rest, and it had rushed the doctor to Cicely's birthing some eighteen years before. There had been only one more duty. Soon after the child came into the world and brought her father joy, the mother went out of their lives and brought him sadness.

It was said that she had been deeply disturbed by the trauma of Cicely's birth, but whatever the reasons for Anne Banks's untimely disappearance, she died in a train-crash before she could explain them, leaving Mr Banks a widower and his daughter without a mother. The carriage which took her to Blackburn Railway Station had stood isolated and unused from that day to this. Only Cicely ever went near it, and that was when her father was out of the house. On these occasions she would sit in the leather seat and imagine how her mother must have felt on the night she ran away. All manner of questions would race through her mind, and she would wonder how any woman could leave a child so newly born, and desert a man who professed to idolise her.

Billenge House was not a grand place. Instead, it was homely and welcoming, a low-roofed dwelling with several dormer windows, and lovely gardens all around. Inside the furniture was serviceable and much used: delightful bureaus and light-coloured walnut dressers with fine curved legs, comfortable floral-covered settees that cocooned you when you sat down, and all over the house the windows were dressed in pretty curtains depicting garden scenes and fine ladies beneath parasols.

Cook gaped open-mouthed when Ruby came rushing in through the back door. 'Good Lord above!' she exclaimed. 'You gave me a fright. Whatever are you doing here so early?' She glanced at the big old clock on the wall whose face was round as her own, and saw that it was not yet seven. 'You haven't wet the bed, have you?' she asked in a chuckle.

''Course not!' Ruby declared, and her sharp answer brought her a severe look from Cook, a large and formidable lady who liked to exercise order in her own kitchen. 'It's just that – well, I wanted to see Miss Cicely,' Ruby explained in a more subdued voice. She didn't want to upset Cook, not when as a rule they got on so well. 'And I thought you might have need of me, what with the tea party this afternoon and everything,' she quickly added. Occasionally Cicely was obliged to please her father by receiving a number of 'guests' for tea; wives of prominent citizens and, as Cicely herself put it, 'intrusive and nosy individuals'.

'Hmmh.' Cook regarded Ruby through curious eyes. 'Can't say I've ever heard of a servant coming in early to help out without being paid.' A thought suddenly occurred to her, and she squinted her bright merry eyes into a scowl. 'You're not being paid, are you? I mean, you've not been asked behind my back, have you?' She prided herself on knowing everything that went on in this house. If there was extra money being paid out, then *she* should be first in line.

'No, I've not been asked to come in early, and I've not been offered more money neither.' Ruby was well aware of what was going through Cook's mind. 'Like I said, I thought you might be glad of me, and I really do need to have a word with Miss Cicely.'

'I've never known such goings on,' Cook tutted loudly,

mimicking Ruby in an unkindly fashion. '"Need to have a word with Miss Cicely" indeed! She shouldn't encourage you in the way she does, and you shouldn't take advantage of her lonely disposition.' She continued to glare at Ruby, but when she saw that her words were not having the desired effect, she tutted again, adding sourly, 'She'll not be properly dressed yet, and anyway I dare say there'll be time enough during the day when you can have a quick word with the mistress. Goodness knows she seems to have taken a very unhealthy liking towards you.' She was a little bit jealous.

Wisely ignoring Cook's attempt to antagonise her, Ruby went into the pantry. A moment later she reappeared, wearing a dark ankle-length dress and a little white pinafore. Her thick dark brown hair was pressed down beneath a frilly white mop-cap, and while she busily fastened the upper corners of the apron to the bib of her dress, she noticed the suspicious manner in which Cook was observing her. 'Is it all right then, if I go and see Miss Cicely now?' she asked respectfully.

'Huh! If I say no, you'll probably sneak away from your duties to see her, and if I say yes, you'll happen not be back down here within the hour.' It was obvious to Ruby that Cook had got out of the wrong side of the bed, especially when she added with a grunt, 'Pardon me if I seem difficult, Ruby Miller, but I was given to understand that you were employed here as *general* help, not as M'lady's maid.'

'I'll only be a minute.'

'And that's all you'd *better* be! I can't stop you, I suppose, being as it's your own time.' Her voice changed. 'All the same, I could do with an extra pair of hands this morning, what with jellies to make and cakes to mix.' She had been rolling the pastry on the pine table, but now she threw out her two hands and the flour shot into the air in a fine white spray. 'Go on, and be quick!' she ordered. 'And while you're at it, knock on that lazy girl's attic door.' She glanced up at the clock again. 'See that? It's gone seven and there's still no sign of the wretched creature. In another hour the master and mistress will be coming down them stairs wanting their breakfasts. The table's not yet laid, nor the dresser set out. On top of that, there's a chill in the air, so happen the fire should be lit.' With a noisy sigh, she plunged her hands into the flour bowl and sent up a mushroom of flour which tickled her nose and made her sneeze. She was still complaining when Ruby sneaked out of the room to make her way upstairs.

On the way she crossed paths with the parlour-maid, a grim-faced soul with a thin piping voice. Above the sound of the grandfather clock which was presently striking seven, she wailed at Ruby, 'I expect the ol' bugger's moaning, taking notice of that kitchen clock, which she deliberately sets fast. Well, I ain't late, so I'm not hurrying.' And she didn't. Ruby suspected the rebellious girl might come to regret it.

As Ruby had thought, Cicely was already awake and dressed. When the tap came on the door, she recognised it at once, quickly flinging open the door and showing great surprise when she saw it actually was Ruby there. 'You're early,' she exclaimed, her narrow face alight with pleasure. Suddenly the smile fell away as she asked with concern, 'There's nothing wrong, is there, Ruby? Your family are well, are they not?' While she spoke, she ushered Ruby inside.

The room was bright and spacious, simply furnished according to the young lady's taste; there was a large bed which was covered with a pretty floral eiderdown, a small oak dresser whose surface was filled with dainty little artefacts including a large china powder bowl, the most beautiful silver brush and comb set, hairpins and other such things as might suit the purposes of a gentlewoman; two tall oak wardrobes stood against one wall and a large cream patterned carpet covered most of the polished floorboards. The deep windowsills were filled with all manner of toys;

brown teddy bears, brightly painted wooden carousels, and a porcelain doll with a look of childish innocence that always put Ruby in mind of Miss Cicely herself; with its long fair hair and clear blue eyes, it was tall and elegant, softly rounded in all the right places, and except for the occasions when it was duly dusted, the doll was rarely moved from the sill, where it had lain these many years. In comparison, Miss Cicely could often be found in her room, and would only leave the house when circumstances obliged her to.

'I hope you don't mind me bothering you, Miss Cicely, but I need to have a quiet word before the master sets off for the foundry.' Ruby knew Mr Banks's routine well. Mondays and Tuesdays he worked from his office at Billenge House, Wednesday was given over to receiving certain men of authority in his employ, Thursday was the day when he either rested in his room, strolled the surrounding countryside, or travelled into town to see his accountant or financial adviser. Friday was always the same; every Friday since Ruby had come to work at the house, and probably every Friday before then, Jeffrey Banks attended personally to his foundry in the heart of Blackburn.

Today was Friday, and the reason for Ruby coming in early. Before her courage failed her, or before she might forget everything she had silently rehearsed on the way here, she quickly spilled out the story, feeling so nervous that the words tumbled one over the other and made her breathless. 'Miss Cicely, I expect you remember me asking a while back whether there were any vacancies at your dad's foundry?'

Cicely looked puzzled, but then she smiled and nodded and Ruby went on, 'Well, I weren't just being nosy. There was a reason. You see, my dad was finished at Arnold's foundry some weeks back, and every day since he's trudged morning and night from one end of Blackburn to the other, and still he ain't found work. It's bad, Miss Cicely, 'cause there's only my wages coming in and it's hard for Mam to keep us fed and pay the rent and Dad don't know what to do next, and Lottie has to have new boots, and the coalman won't leave coal no more because Mam still owes him, and . . .'

Her voice broke, and feeling deeply ashamed that she was made to confide such private things to this quiet lovely creature, she cast her gaze to the floor, adding lamely, 'I was wondering whether you could please ask your dad if he could find work for one more man?' She looked up then. 'He's a good worker, Miss Cicely . . . the best!' Having humiliated herself, there were tears in her deep blue eyes, but the pride shone through. 'You only have to ask anybody and they'll tell you that Ted Miller would break his back to do a good day's work.'

In characteristic manner, Cicely reached out and placed her hand on Ruby's shoulder. 'If your father is anything like you, Ruby, he must be a real asset to any employer.'

'Thank you, Miss Cicely.' Ruby's embarrassment quickly melted beneath the gaze from those soft pale blue eyes. 'Will you ask your dad then?'

'I will ask him, you know that,' came the reply. 'But you must also know that there are the beginnings of a depression, and my father has said that employers are more cautious about taking men on.'

'But you will ask?' Ruby boldly insisted.

'I'll do it this very minute.' She paused before asking the next question, because she knew how fiercely proud Ruby was and how it must have cost her dearly to bare her heart just now. Yet she also knew that Ruby saw herself as being responsible for her family, so was encouraged to speak what was on her own mind. 'Ruby?'

'Yes, Miss Cicely?'

'Your family is going through a hard time, I think. Won't you let me help?' She felt Ruby's shoulder stiffen beneath her touch

78

and instantly regretted her offer. 'I'm sorry,' she said simply, drawing her hand away. 'I meant well.'

'I know. And you mustn't think I'm not grateful.'

'But you won't let me help?'

Ruby shook her head. 'Us Millers have never taken charity. We've always worked for what we've got. That's all my dad wants now . . . a chance to work.'

'I understand, Ruby, and I'll do what I can.'

'I know. Thank you, Miss Cicely.' She stepped away then. 'I'd better get back down to the kitchen. There's a deal of work to be done, and Cook needs me to help her get ready for your tea party this afternoon.'

Cicely groaned. 'Think yourself fortunate you don't have to endure such trials,' she said, and Ruby agreed.

'Will you let me know what the master says?' Ruby wouldn't rest until she knew.

Cicely nodded her head, half-smiling as she quietly regarded this young girl whom circumstances had matured before her time. Cicely thought it wouldn't be long before Ruby was snatched up by some handsome young man who would cherish her for ever. With dark blue eyes and strong proud features, she would stand out in a crowd. There was something else too, something that set Ruby above other girls of her own age; it shone out of her, like a light from within, a kind of strength and determination which told the world that here was a force to be reckoned with. Yet she was good and loyal, and it was that which had first drawn Cicely Banks to befriend her. She had never regretted it, because now, in spite of the differences between them and the fortunes bestowed on them by accident of birth, she had come to love Ruby almost like a sister. 'Don't worry,' she told her now. 'As soon as I've spoken to my father, I'll come and find you. But please, Ruby . . . don't let yourself be too disappointed if my errand isn't successful.'

She daren't think on it. Nor could she speak just then. Biting her lip, she merely inclined her head to let the young woman know she understood. Then, with her heart in her mouth, she retraced her steps to the kitchen where Cook received her with an anguished cry, 'About time too!' She was in the act of grabbing a cloth to wrap round the great pan on the stove, and with the deftness born of practice, lifted it from the heat effortlessly. 'I've only got one pair of hands,' she complained bitterly. 'And just when I need you most, both you and that useless article of a girl go missing. Must I do everything myself?'

'I was as quick as ever,' Ruby protested.

'Well, you weren't quick enough then, were you?' Cook glanced at the table. 'See that?' she asked sullenly. 'I'm not paid to work myself into the ground, you know. You can be sure I'll have something to say to the pair of you when this little lot's been seen to.' Cook had been desperately busy in Ruby's absence, because the tureens which were standing on the table when Ruby first arrived, were now set out in a more orderly fashion, with their lids tipped to one side. Soon they would need to be filled and sent up by dumb waiter to the dining room, the many aromas of freshly cooked kippers, muffins browning in the oven, bacon sizzling on the hob and newly-baked bread all mingled together as Cook darted about, lifting lids and opening doors and getting herself in a dire state.

'Goodness knows where that wretched girl's gone,' she snapped at Ruby. 'Get up to the dining-room and see what the divil she's playing at.' As Ruby hurried out into the hall, she glanced back when the Cook began cursing, having just set a large pan on to the table and burned her thumb against its handle. 'Go on!' she told Ruby in a shrill voice. 'Or I'll flay the pair of you!' With Ruby going swiftly on her way, the big woman reached down to the shelf below the table and drew out a brown earthenware jug from which she took a great swig. 'I deserved that,' she chuckled, then replaced the jug and set about her work with renewed vigour.

The routine was always the same. Once the table was laid and the food set out on the dresser, Ruby would inform the master and he would accompany his daughter to the dining-room without delay. Usually he greeted her with a warm smile and a cheery 'Good girl', but not this morning; because this morning he seemed a million miles away, and his face was set into a grim thoughtful expression.

'Thank you, Ruby,' Cicely murmured as she followed her father into the dining-room.

Ruby stood by the dresser as always, waiting to clear the plates soon as ever they were dirty, and hoping against hope that Miss Cicely would pass her the wink that she had spoken to her father and that he had agreed to employ Ted Miller in his foundry. All she got was a downcast expression and a shrug of the young lady's slim shoulders. Ruby's heart fell to her boots.

Coming to the dresser to serve himself from the various tureens, Jeffrey Banks didn't even glance at the two young women standing either side of the dresser; Ruby to his right and the wretched girl to his left. Instead, he seemed greatly preoccupied and somewhat troubled. As a rule he piled his plate with a healthy helping of bacon, sausages and eggs, with a slice of liver besides, but this morning he returned to the table with only one egg and a crispy piece of bacon; although he filled his cup with tea several times throughout the hour-long ritual.

'Surely you need a more substantial breakfast?' Cicely remarked with concern, helping herself to scrambled eggs and toast. 'You're not ill, are you, Father?' She had gone straight to the library after speaking with Ruby, but had been unable to approach her father about the matter she and Ruby had discussed, simply because he was not in a listening mood. There was something on his mind, she knew. Yet he was a man who kept things to himself; a trait in his character which often frustrated her.

'Don't fuss, child,' he replied impatiently, looking up with a frown on his brow. 'The breakfast I have is quite enough. And, no, I am not ill.'

'Oh.' She was hurt by the sharpness of his voice and the dark scowl in his eyes. Her father was a kindly man, and rarely showed ill temper. 'I haven't angered you, have I?'

He looked up and dabbed the corners of his mouth with a napkin. 'Of course you haven't,' he said warmly, the scowl being quickly replaced with a loving smile. In his autumn years, Jeffrey Banks was still a handsome man although the dark brown hair that had once had much the same rich vibrant quality as Ruby's was now streaked with silver. His features were fine and strong, with only the suggestion of age creeping over the skin, and he walked tall, with a proud bearing that could still draw a flicker of admiration from the ladies. 'How could you anger me?' he asked charmingly, and his face became serious once more as he thought long and hard as to whether she should be told of recent developments. Cicely was his only child, and he loved her dearly. Suddenly it did not seem right that he should keep her in the dark, for if he didn't tell her the state of things, then someone else would.

He glanced across to where Ruby and the wretched girl were keeping duty, and it crossed his mind that perhaps he should wait until he and his daughter were alone. But then he realised that these two young people knew of Oliver Arnold's determination to acquire the one remaining foundry he did not yet own; no doubt they had relatives who worked either at his own or at one of Arnold's foundries, and probably knew more than he himself did. So he decided to speak out.

'Oliver Arnold has made me an excellent offer for the foundry.'

'I see.' Cicely was not surprised, although she sat up at the news, a look of disappointment on her face. 'And will you accept it?' she asked, placing her fork against the plate and playing her long fine fingers against the tablecloth.

His answer was slow in coming, and when he spoke it was with great dignity. 'I think not.' He exchanged smiles with her then, and she thought with amusement that Oliver Arnold could never be the man her father was. The conversation took a different turn when he glanced through the morning paper, making comment on this or that, and in particular remarking on: 'The City and South London Railway . . . the first deep "tube" some forty feet below the surface. Doesn't bear thinking about, my dear,' he said with alarm, and Cicely thought she would never have the courage to go so deep underground.

In a moment the two of them were leaving the room, arm in arm and quietly talking, although Ruby was rewarded with a covert smile from Cicely which told her all was not yet lost. With the tiniest flicker of hope rekindled, she helped the wretched girl to lay the tureens in the dumb waiter and send them back down to the kitchen, where Cook threw out her arms in horror on seeing that the food which she had so meticulously prepared, was hardly touched. 'Why in Heaven's name do I bother?' she asked the ceiling. 'When I could just as well serve them dry bread and shoe-soles!'

Ruby was in the scullery washing the breakfast dishes when Miss Cicely came in search of her. 'I asked him, Ruby,' she said, 'but Father says it's difficult times, and while he'll keep it in mind, he can't promise anything.'

'That's all right, Miss Cicely, I understand,' Ruby said. But it *wasn't* all right and she *didn't* understand. The master had a foundry, and a good man wanted work. She couldn't really see what the problem was. All the same, it wasn't Cicely's fault, and Ruby put on a brave face. 'My dad is sure to find work somewhere,' she said brightly. When Cicely had gone to prepare for her visitors, Ruby went about her duties with a fervour that prompted Cook to tell her, 'Slow down, before I faint with exhaustion just watching you!'

That night there was cause for celebration. Because of Miss Cicely's tea party, it was eight when Ruby got off the tram and made her way towards Fisher Street. Johnny came to meet her. He looked especially handsome, his long legs clad in his best brown cords and wearing a blue cotton jumper over his white-collared shirt; his smile was dashing as he looked down on her. 'You must be dead on your feet,' he said, taking up step beside her and longing to put his arm round her waist. 'Your mam tells me you went to work on the first tram this morning?'

'Cook needed extra help on account of Cicely having a tea party.' Ruby almost confided about her talk with Cicely, but then thought better of it. If it ever got back to her dad that she'd been going behind his back to get him work, there'd be Hell to pay. 'How's Maureen?'

'Getting better by the day.'

'I'll be along to see her later, if that's all right?'

'She'll like that.' They went along in silence for a while, until he spoke again. 'Ruby?'

'Yes?'

'I was thinking, why don't we go for a picnic on Sunday?'

She came to a halt, her dark blue eyes looking up at him in surprise. 'Is she able to go out? Did the doctor say she could?' The thought of Maureen up and about again – oh, that would be wonderful!

It was his turn to be surprised now. 'Oh, I don't think Maureen could stand up to that.' How could he explain that he was thinking of just the two of them? He gazed down on her, his eyes drinking in her lovely face and his arms aching to fold her to him. He had never been so impatient – impatient to be the man she wanted, impatient to make love to her – and always she seemed so unattainable.

Ruby saw the look in his eyes and her heart turned somersaults. 'You mean just the two of us, don't you?'

'Is that so wrong?'

'No. It isn't wrong. It's just . . .' She paused, thinking of the right way to put it. How could she say it without hurting him? How could she tell him that she was saving herself for a man who could give her all the things she wanted out of life? How could she explain that she would never put her own happiness before the well-being of her family? Johnny would never understand.

Things were straightforward for him; you fell in love, you got wed, and then you had babies. There was nothing wrong with that, it was what most girls wanted. In fact there were times when Ruby herself would have liked nothing better than to spend her whole life with Johnny. He was quite the most handsome young man she had ever seen, and he could have the pick of the girls from one end of Blackburn to the other. He was kind and good and he loved her. Although she could never confess to him, Ruby had come to realise that she loved him too, loved him with all her heart. It was a wonderful and painful thing. But love wasn't everything. She had learned that life wasn't quite so simple. There were other things to be taken into account, and her instincts told her that it would be fatal to let the heart dictate.

Whenever she felt herself weakening, Ruby would remind herself of the difference between being poor and being rich. Being poor could mean being hungry. It was being cold on a winter's night, huddled together in bed beneath two thin blankets while the wind howled through the chinks in the window frames and the rain trickled in to rot the sill; it was seeing her baby sister lying in a cradle made out of an old orange-box found on the cobbles in the market-place. Being poor was never seeing her mam dressed up, and it was being helpless while her dad was out of work. It was seeing the wrinkles deepen in her mam's face, and her dad going grey before his time. Being poor was working like a dog, and being afraid when the work was taken away. Being poor was being humiliated on the street when a kindly neighbour was moved to pay your bills. The scene out in the street with the milkman haunted her still. Ruby didn't mind for herself. But she wanted her family to have the very best in life.

Maybe if she had never been employed at Jeffrey Banks's lovely old house, she might never have seen the better things. But she *had* seen them. And now she wanted all of these things for her mam and dad and the young 'uns. And if that meant she had to sacrifice love and marriage, then it was a sacrifice she was prepared to make.

Johnny was angry. He knew Ruby had ideas that didn't include him. Yet he sensed her deeper feeling for him, and he warned himself to be patient. 'It was just a thought,' he said, beginning to walk on.

Ruby followed him. 'All the same, it was a lovely thought.'

'But you won't come?'

'Not this Sunday.'

'*Next* Sunday?' He wasn't about to give up that easily.

'Maybe.'

Her answer made Johnny smile. 'Be careful. I might hold you to that.'

'I only said "maybe".' She was smiling now. He always did that. He always warmed her heart in spite of her trying to harden it against him. They were at Ruby's house now. 'Don't forget to tell Maureen I'll be in to see her later.' She walked up the white-stoned step to the front door.

He made no answer but gave her a long lingering look that bound them together for one exquisite moment. 'I'll tell her,' he promised. Then he strode away.

86

Ruby watched him go. 'Don't wait for me, Johnny,' she murmured lovingly. 'Or you'll wait for ever.'

As it was bath-night, Lizzie had decided against waiting for her husband before they had their evening meal: a few meaty tit-bits got from the butcher for a few coppers, thrown into a pot of vegetables to make a wholesome stew. Ted's helping could stay warm in the oven. It wouldn't spoil. 'He said we weren't to wait, 'cause there was no telling what time he'd be home,' Lizzie told Ruby.

'But it's nearly nine o'clock, Mam.' Ruby was worried. 'Where can he be until this hour?'

'Happen he's gone to see the shift-foreman at one o' the mills.' Lizzie was worried too, but she wasn't about to show it in front of the childer. There'd been enough upset in this house, what with Lenny fighting again and Lottie screaming with her first teeth coming through. 'He'll be home soon, you'll see,' she said, dropping to her knees before the tin bath which was placed in front of a small cheery fire. 'Meanwhile, you an' me have to get the young 'uns washed and abed.' She rolled up her sleeves and dipped one elbow into the water. 'That'll do. Fetch the babby, will yer, lass?'

When she looked up at Ruby, her small hazel eyes betrayed none of her own apprehension. 'Aw, an' stop fretting. Yer dad'll be home soon enough, I tell yer.' She collected the babby from Ruby's arms and lowered her gently into the water.

Little Lottie screamed all the while she was being bathed, and screamed after she was dried and handed back to Ruby. 'Little sod. Anybody'd think I were trying to drown her,' Lizzie said indignantly. Then, feeling sorry, she added, 'Poor little thing. It's still cutting its teeth and there ain't much anybody can do about that.' She gave orders that Dolly was next, and the girl came obediently to her side. In a minute, she was stripped and sitting in the bath. 'Don't get the soap in me eyes, Mam,' she pleaded, and Lizzie was quick to assure her, 'If yer sit still an' stop fussing, I'll be finished afore yer know it.'

When her head was bent into the water and the soap was rubbed hard into her scalp, with Lizzie promising to 'drown any lice that might be hiding there', Dolly screwed up her eyes and feared the worse.

'Can I play out 'til it's my turn?' Lenny had been sulking in the scullery, but now, when it seemed his mammy would be too busy to worry about him, he came out to try his luck. He was bitterly disappointed because Lizzie told him to get back in the scullery and have a strip-wash at the sink. 'Then get to yer bed, young man. Happen you'll think twice next time yer tempted to go punching some lad in the nose!'

She shook her head and tutted as he strolled sullenly back into the scullery. 'Think yourself lucky yer dad ain't back yet, or yer might have felt the weight of his boot on yer arse, yer little bugger!' In fact, both Lizzie and Lenny knew full well that Ted Miller was not the kind of man to lift his boot to anybody, let alone his own son; although that son might have felt the weight of Lizzie's hand round his ear if she'd seen how he gave the scullery wall a good kick that split the plaster and sent it fluttering to the floor like a snowfall.

The next half-hour was like bedlam. Lenny whistled defiantly in the scullery, splashing and banging about in the sink, the twins rolling about on the mat laughing and playing and waiting their turn in the tub, Dolly yelling and crying when her hair was being washed, and despite Ruby walking her up and down, little Lottie screaming blue murder throughout. 'Gawd love and save us, I think I'll go mad!' Lizzie yelled above the din. Then came the sound of somebody singing at the front door, and the twins bolted up and out into the passage.

When they came rushing back again, they were laughing and shouting. All eyes turned to the parlour door, and Ruby couldn't

believe what she saw there. Her dad was drunk! Never in her life
had she seen her dad drunk. Clutching a small earthenware jar,
he clung to the door-jamb, swaying and chuckling, with the twins
clinging to his legs and holding him upright. 'He's tipsy like
Johnny's dad!' laughed Ralph, and Frank hugged himself with
glee.

In a minute Lizzie had scrambled to her feet, leaving Dolly
splashing in the tub. 'Ted Miller!' she cried, putting her hands on
her hips and glaring at him through narrowed eyes, 'Shame
on yer!' She was so astonished at the sight of her husband that
she couldn't think of anything else to say. 'Shame on yer!'

He fell on her then, almost knocking her to the floor. 'He set
me on!' He was laughing through the tears. 'The bugger set me
on!' He flung his arms round her and squeezed her until she
laughed and shouted, 'Who? *Who* set yer on?'

Breathless with excitement and unable to stand up straight
because of the booze, he held her at a distance, swaying and
winking, until, having teased her long enough, he told her, '*Jeffrey
Banks*, that's who.' He gave Lizzie the earthenware jar. 'I've
brought you a drop o' the good stuff so's you can drink to us
good fortune.'

He looked sheepish under Lizzie's disapproving glare. 'I'm
sorry, lass – but, oh, I were that excited. And, well, I had a
shilling left and I felt I should drink to the occasion. I bumped
into an old mate from Arnold's, and what with one thing and
another . . . well, I am sorry, lass, honest to God I am.' He
laughed out loud and fell into the chair. 'Oh Lizzie . . . Lizzie!
Yer old fella's got work at last. But it were a close thing. Oh aye,
it were a close thing. The foreman had just finished telling me
how they weren't setting on yet, and that he'd take me name and
let me know if owt turned up, and when I were giving me name,
who d'yer think stepped out of the inner office, eh?'

He winked and grinned until Lizzie felt like pushing him out of the chair. 'Go on,' she encouraged, and he set himself back into the chair, saying in a grand voice, 'Jeffrey Banks himself, that's who. He asked me if it were our Ruby who worked at his house, and I said it were, and, well . . . he said he'd heard that I were a good worker, and that he had need of a responsible boiler-man.'

Suddenly, a thought occurred to him and he peered at Ruby, who was smiling broadly at the news. 'I hope it weren't *you* that told him I were a good worker?' When she looked suitably indignant, he appeared satisfied, telling Lizzie, 'I'm to report for work on Monday morning. There! What d'yer think to that, eh? Ain't yer proud o' yer old man?' His chest seemed to swell to twice its size.

Lizzie was torn two ways. She was thankful that he was in work again. But now there were *two* members of her family working for Jeffrey Banks, and so she was twice indebted to him. 'I'm very proud o' yer, sweetheart,' she said softly, hugging him close. That said, she straightened her back and looked about at the childer who had been both amused at their father's unusual appearance but delighted at his news. Now they grinned at their mam and she shook her head. 'This is the first time a Miller's ever been the worse for drink, and so long as I'm alive, it'll be the last.' She looked from Dolly, who was bent in the bath with her hair dripping all over her face, to the twins who were cuddling each other, then at Ruby, who was beside herself with delight, and finally Lenny, who had come to the scullery doorway and was still scowling. 'Is that understood?' she demanded. 'There'll be no drinkers in this house. Not while I'm alive, there won't.'

Heads nodded all round; all except for Lenny, who dropped his gaze to the floor and shuffled his feet back and forth. Lizzie didn't notice. 'Good!' she remarked, turning to her husband. When she saw that he was sound asleep, she tutted loudly and shook her head. 'Shame on yer, Ted Miller,' she muttered. All the same, there was a smile on her face as she tucked his legs in and made him more comfortable.

It was growing dark when Ruby made her way along Fisher Street to number ten. 'I'm sorry, lass, but if it's our Johnny you've come to see, you'll be disappointed, because he's just this minute gone out.'

Mrs Ackroyd didn't reveal the reason for her son having 'gone out', which was to search for his dad who was probably keeping company with drunks and the like. Although she still had a fondness for her feckless husband, there were times when she wished he could have been different. He was more like a child than a man. Yet there was no bad feeling between them. She had grown used to his coming home at all hours of the day and night, wildly excited about this scheme or that, and none of them ever coming to anything. 'You can come in and see Maureen though,' she invited, opening the door wider. 'She's a deal better, and I know she'd be that pleased if you went up and had a chat with her. Although you mustn't tire her out,' she warned, adding with faint amusement, 'Happen Johnny will be back before you leave.'

Stepping inside the passage, Ruby told her firmly, 'It was Maureen I came to see.'

'Oh, I'm sorry, dear.' She felt foolish, especially when her daughter and Ruby Miller had long been best friends, and Ruby had asked every day for these past weeks when she might be able to come and visit her. Then there were the little notes that had passed between the two girls by way of Johnny or the Miller children. But Mrs Ackroyd reminded herself of the little intimate scene that had taken place in this very passage between her son and Ruby, and she thought it was no wonder that she'd made a simple mistake in thinking the lass had come to pay him a visit – although from what she could see, Ruby gave him very little encouragement.

91

Nevertheless, it was painfully obvious to Mrs Ackroyd that her son had set his sights on this particular young lady. Under the circumstances, *anyone* would have thought Ruby had come here tonight with Johnny on her mind. 'You go straight up,' she said brightly, closing the door behind Ruby and pointing along the passage towards the stairs at the other end. 'You'll not be disturbed. The lass has finished her supper and she's had her wash. I left her sitting in the chair staring out of the window. After being so long confined to her bed, it's a real treat for the darling girl to look out on the world. I would have moved her bed to the window long before, but the doctor left strict instructions that she was to be kept out of any likely draught.'

She chatted on and on. 'As it is, I'm not sure I've done the right thing in allowing her to sit in the chair there. Mark you, it's a warm evening, and she's on the mend now, thank God.' She led the way down the passage, occasionally looking back to make certain that Ruby wasn't far behind. 'I shouldn't be at all surprised if she didn't see you coming up the street,' she said, nodding her head up and down and smiling to herself as though she had said something very wise.

Maureen was delighted to see her old friend. Ruby tapped twice on the door and when there was no reply, edged it open. And there was Maureen – her thin waif-like figure seated in a dome-backed wicker chair, a brown checked blanket over her knees, and her face turned towards the window. Her brown eyes were round and intense, staring up at the darkened sky with such wonder that anybody might think she had never seen the sun go down before. The window was closed, the sparsely furnished room was stiflingly hot, and even then the girl's face was grey as parchment.

Ruby was shocked. Maureen was much thinner than when she had last seen her some weeks since; her cheeks seemed to protrude at a sharper angle and her eyes had sunk deep within their sockets;

her mousy-coloured brown hair hung fine and lifeless over her narrow shoulders, and her whole countenance had a look of starvation that frightened Ruby so much that she gasped softly, causing Maureen to turn around. Her eyes lit up then filled with tears as she stretched out her arms in welcome, 'Ruby!' she said in a laugh. 'Oh, Ruby, I've missed you so.'

'And I've missed you.' Rushing forward, she threw her two arms round that tiny figure, astonished when it felt like she was holding fresh air. They clung to each other and laughed, and Maureen cried until the tears spilled down her face on to Ruby's shoulder. 'Thank you for your notes,' she said, 'I read them over and over. Oh, Ruby! I knew you'd come as soon as ever you were allowed.'

Ruby pushed herself away, sniffling and giggling and trying to see her friend's face through a veil of tears. 'Look at you!' she cried, lifting a stray lock of hair from the other girl's forehead. 'You're as thin as a pikestaff. You'll need to put some fat on your bones before I take you out. I'm not having folk staring at me and thinking I've brought a scarecrow out for a walk.'

She drew the girl against her and they held each other quietly for a minute. Presently Ruby told her in a soft sober voice, 'I won't let you be ill any more, and I won't let anybody keep us apart again.' She had been shocked to her roots by Maureen's gaunt appearance. 'Did the doctor say when you could go out?'

Maureen pulled away, smiling now, her face lit from within. 'Soon, he said . . . next week maybe, if I'm feeling stronger and the sun's shining.' Her smile widened. 'I *am* feeling stronger, Ruby. Every day I'm feeling stronger.'

'Then we'll have to make the sun shine for you,' Ruby promised. Falling to her knees and lovingly gripping her friend's frail white hands, she murmured, 'I'll get my mam to have a little word with him up there.' She turned her deep blue eyes to the sky outside. 'She knows him better than I do.' Ruby believed in God, and had felt his presence inside her, but she rarely talked to him because, in spite of going inside his house to gaze at the beautiful things there, she didn't know how to hold a 'conversation' with someone she couldn't see; not like her mam who reckoned she could 'see the good Lord at every turn'.

There was so much to talk about, and as Maureen said, 'Reading notes isn't the same as talking proper to each other, is it?'

''Course it's not,' Ruby agreed. She had sent the notes via Johnny, or sometimes just slipped them under the front door; mostly at night when thoughts of her friend weighed heavy. Being too weak at times to hold a pen, Maureen had written back only once, and that was when she dictated a reply to Johnny, saying, 'I want to talk about so many things, Ruby. But I'd rather wait until we see each other like we used to.' She'd understood, and had returned a message telling Maureen that she too was looking forward to the day when: 'We can walk side by side down Fisher Street, just like we used to'.

'But I'm here now,' she said warmly. 'Your mam promised we won't be disturbed for a while yet, so we can talk to our hearts' content.'

And that was exactly what they did. Maureen talked about how she hated being shut up in this small room, although she was never lonely because her mam and Johnny wouldn't let her be. 'And he's promised soon as ever he can afford it, he'll do the front parlour up and move me downstairs.'

Wisely, Ruby didn't dwell on Maureen's illness. Instead, she related all her own news to the inquisitive girl, vividly describing the two new gowns that Cicely had bought in Manchester only last week. 'A pale blue one with pretty ribbons round the hem, and a grey walking-out one with a bonnet to match.' She didn't tell how Cicely had promised to find her a bundle of gowns that she didn't have need of any more; somehow it didn't seem right to Ruby that she should be bragging about a thing like that, when poor Maureen was still confined to wearing her nightshift.

She went on instead to reveal how her dad had been thrown out of work and how the whole house seemed to have grown darker these past few weeks, with her mam worried about paying the rent and feeding her little army. 'But now everything's all right again, because our dad came home this very night with the news that he is to start at Banks's foundry on Monday morning.' Ruby's dark eyes shone with merriment and her voice dropped to a whisper. 'He was drunk too! Our mam gave him the length of her tongue, but he didn't pay no attention, because he went right off to sleep. I don't think our mam really minded though, because now she can pay Mrs Donaldson back, and we won't have to hide from the rentman next week.' She actually clapped her hands and laughed. But then the laughter died away as she said in a gruff voice, 'I hate being poor.'

'We're *all* poor,' Maureen said thoughtfully. But it didn't seem to worry her; not like it worried Ruby. She merely shrugged her shoulders and said Johnny had told her how his boss, Oliver Arnold, had set his mind on getting hold of Banks's foundry at any cost, and Ruby explained how she heard Jeffrey Banks tell his daughter the very same. 'But he won't sell,' she remarked knowingly.

'Bet he will if the money's right,' Maureen argued.

Ruby thought different. But there were other matters she would rather discuss, and soon the pair of them were deeply engrossed in talk of what they would do when Maureen was better; of how things used to be before she was taken badly; of friends who had left the street, and of boys she used to 'fancy', like the ginger-haired young man who had moved to Leyland Street a year ago and who, according to Ruby, was now working for the undertaker. 'He's tall and thin as a lamp post, and grown awful coarse in the face,' she said. Maureen sighed and said wasn't it a shame how people changed when they got older? Then Ruby was shocked when Maureen asked if she loved Johnny.

'No, I don't,' she lied, and her face went a deep shade of pink.

'Well, he loves *you*.'

'I know.'

'Has he told you?'

'Sort of.'

'What does that mean?'

'Well, all right then . . . yes, he *has*.'

'And did you say that you don't love him back?'

'No.'

'Why not? You just told *me* you don't love him?'

Ruby hated being asked all these questions, and she hated herself because she had lied to her best friend. 'I'd forgotten how nosy you can be,' she said, but she had to smile.

'You do love our Johnny, don't you?' Maureen was insistent.

'All right then. Yes, I do.' Ruby dropped her gaze to the floor and shifted uncomfortably against the rug.

Maureen was quiet then, sensing that she had probed too deep. Stroking Ruby's hair, she said softly, 'I'm sorry.' Then, in a lighter tone, 'Like you said, Ruby, I'm too nosy.'

'No. It's all right. I don't mind you knowing, so long as you don't tell Johnny.' She paused then, not certain how to explain her innermost thoughts to her friend, not even knowing whether Maureen would understand her. And how could she expect her to, when her own mam didn't understand her? 'Johnny frightens me,' she murmured.

'*Frightens you!*' Maureen gaped at her in disbelief. 'How can our Johnny frighten you?'

'Because I like it when he walks down the street with me. I feel proud and warm inside. And when he kissed me the other day, I didn't want him to stop.' Strange, she thought, how she could reveal all her deepest secrets to Maureen when she couldn't talk to anyone else about them, not even her own mam.

'I don't understand.' Maureen's thin white face was creased with confusion. 'How can that frighten you?'

'Because he makes me forget all the things I've promised myself.' Ruby leaned back her head and gazed out of the window. The sky was fringed with darkness, a safe and beautiful mantle enfolding the world like a mother's arms. Darkened clouds like puffs of gossamer drifted slowly over the chimney tops, making Ruby feel especially dreamy. 'I don't want to live in Fisher Street for ever,' she whispered, as though some higher being might hear her and put a stop to her dreams. 'One day, me and our mam and all the young 'uns will live in a big house, and Mam can have whatever she wants for the rest of her life. We'll have servants to light the fire, and a carriage to take her into Manchester where she can shop to her heart's delight. It won't matter how much money she spends because we'll have plenty more where that came from. She can buy as many fine gowns as she wants, we'll build extra wardrobes to fit them in, and shoes too . . . black patent ones for best, and stout dark boots for walking; she can have hats with feathers that touch the ceiling, and a pretty little maid to help her dress.'

She brought her gaze back to Maureen and her expression was deadly serious as she went on in a quiet voice, 'One day, when I'm old enough, I intend to have all these things. In all my life, I never, never want to be poor again.'

She saw the horror in her friend's eyes and was sad. 'Try and understand, Maureen,' she pleaded softly. 'Being poor frightens me more than anything in the world. Money could buy so much happiness. I know that now. All the time our dad's been out of work, our mam's been hard put to feed the family. I've seen her push her own food on to the young 'uns' plates when she thought no one was looking, and at night when she's sent us all to bed while she waits downstairs for our dad, I've heard her crying. For years, she's worn the same two skirts and the same tattered old shawl. There's never enough food in the cupboard, and we don't have enough blankets to keep us warm, even on a summer's night. In the winter we have to count the number of cobs we put on the fire, and even when our dad was in work, there were times when he had to walk because he couldn't afford the tramfare. Our mam always puts on a brave face, but I know how she's feeling inside, and I can't stand it.'

She sighed, and when she spoke again it was from the heart. 'Sometimes I don't understand why I feel the way I do, and sometimes I feel ashamed because I'm never content. But I can't help it, Maureen, and I want you of all people to try and understand how I feel.'

'Money won't buy happiness, Ruby. Life isn't like that.'

'How can you tell? All we know is what we have. Every working day I see the difference money can make, and it makes me sad to see how folks such as we have to scrape for every penny.' She stiffened, a hard determined look coming into her eyes as she said firmly, 'I've seen what it's like to be rich, and I know what it's like to be poor. My mind's made up, Maureen. I want to be rich. I *will* be rich one day.'

'And what about love?' Maureen wanted to know. She could never remember Ruby being this way, and suddenly felt the need to protect her. 'What if you don't love this rich man you intend to wed?'

Ruby thought hard, her face turned downwards and her brow creased in a deep frown. She had asked herself the same question so many times, and each time it hurt to think about it. It hurt now. Presently she looked up, her dark eyes filled with a kind of wonder yet strangely saddened. 'It won't matter,' she lied, 'I don't know if I can even say that I love Johnny, because I'm not really sure what it is to love in that way. I only know that I love my family with all my heart, but that's a different kind of feeling than the one I have for Johnny. If it's "love" to feel happy with someone . . . if it's "love" to think about someone day and night, and to glow inside whenever they look at you, then, yes, I do love Johnny in that special way.' Her voice fell to a whisper and Maureen had to lean forward to hear. 'Anyway, happen I'm too young to know about that kind of love.'

'My mam wasn't much older than you when she got wed,' Maureen said brightly. 'So you're wrong to think that way.' Ruby was right about one thing though: Maureen didn't understand her. She didn't understand the intensity of these strange feelings that lived inside Ruby and made her so restless. She didn't understand the point of someone longing for what she couldn't have. But she adored Ruby, and hated seeing her so unhappy. Johnny could make her happy though. If only she would let him take care of her, things would be all right. 'You and Johnny would be good together,' she suggested hopefully. 'Then, later on when you got wed, he'd work his fingers to the bone for you.'

'NO!' There was a look of determination in Ruby's dark eyes as she shook her head. 'We're neither of us old enough to be thinking like that. And even if I was, I couldn't let myself love him. If I'm to get out of Fisher Street, then I mustn't think about marrying. Love can spoil things too, you know.' Suddenly she was angry. Her dreams were too important to be threatened.

'What do you mean? How can love "spoil things"?' Life was wonderfully simple to Maureen. A man and a woman fell in love and then they got wed. Every day she dreamed about it happening to her.

'It can spoil things because it can force you to make decisions that you might spend the rest of your life regretting. I've thought long and hard about what I want to do with my life, Maureen, and my mind's made up. I'd rather wed a rich man and not love him, than wed someone I love and be poor for ever. I owe it to my family, to find them a better way of life, and I promise you . . . the very first chance I get, I'm going to take it.'

'Oh, Ruby! Ruby!' Maureen grabbed her hands and shook them hard, but her eyes were soft as she said, 'I can understand now why our Johnny "frightens" you. It's because you do love him, and because you're afraid he might make you forget these other things.' She bent her head to Ruby's and the two of them were lost in deep thought. After a while, Maureen whispered, 'I really will try and understand all the things you've said, Ruby. But if our Johnny "frightens" you . . . then you frighten me even more.'

'I know.' Ruby felt what was in her friend's heart. She knew what Maureen was trying to say, and the truth was that sometimes she even frightened herself.

That night, Ruby lay awake in her bed, unable to sleep. Maureen's words dripped into her thoughts like raindrops wearing away a stone. 'Oh, Ruby, it's because you love him, and you're afraid he might make you forget these other things.' For the very first time she began to wonder whether she was wrong in preferring riches to someone special like Johnny. But then she thought about this tiny house with its cold damp rooms and windows where the rain poured in; she pictured her three brothers in the room across the landing, all sleeping in the same narrow bed and huddling together to keep warm. She thought about the empty food cupboard downstairs, and remembered how her mam had cried herself to sleep so many times. And her resolve was strengthened. Just now there had been a moment, one fleeting moment when she had questioned the wisdom of her ambitions. That was what 'love' did. That was why Johnny 'frightened' her. And that was why she vowed never again to lose sight of her goal.

The sound from her parents' room attracted Ruby's attention; a low murmuring at first, then the familiar rhythmic squeak as the bed went up and down beneath her dad's weight. Ruby was embarrassed. She knew about these things, because Meg Brown at school had told how she caught her mam and dad in the act when she went bursting into their room one Sunday morning.

The sounds from next door intensified and Ruby's face grew a dark shade of pink. Burying her head in the pillow, she cuddled up to Dolly. Strange pictures rushed through her mind, of her mam and dad, frantic shapes locked together. The sounds grew louder, there was an agonised moan, and then silence.

Ruby wondered what it was like, to have someone make love to you. *Someone like Johnny*. The thought had popped into her mind without her realising it. Quickly she thrust it out, wrapped the blanket over her ears and forced herself to think about the clothes that Cicely had promised her. She wondered whether any of them could be made to fit her mam.

Chapter Four

Cicely announced her intention to invite Oliver Arnold and his son Luke to the Christmas Eve party.

Her father's voice betrayed astonishment but not total disapproval; in fact he seemed a little amused by the idea. 'Are you saying you really mean to invite Oliver Arnold inside this house? Have you forgotten how he intended to add your inheritance to his own endless list of properties?'

Cicely smiled and kissed him lightly on the face, 'No, Father, I haven't forgotten. But that little war is over now and we have to build bridges. It won't do to make enemies of our rivals . . . and there's nothing wrong with having rivals, you've told me that often enough.'

He laughed. 'Very true. And, of course, I have it on the best authority that Mr Arnold has abandoned the idea of acquiring the foundry. Any good businessman knows when to give up the ghost, and he must realise by now there was never any chance of him becoming the owner of my foundry.' Sinking into deep thought, he pursed his lips and played his finger and thumb over his chin, his eyes downcast for the while as he said in a soft voice, 'Yes, indeed. I feel the man is a little wiser than I gave him credit for. Perhaps, after all, it would be a sensible move . . . to invite him here and bury old bones, eh?'

'I think so.' Although she hated being hostess at any time, Cicely was obliged by tradition to arrange this end of year celebration, and had long toyed with the notion of using it as a means by which Mr Arnold and her father might meet on social terms, rather than communicating through solicitors. Indeed, she saw it as a charitable gesture that was long overdue. 'You have said yourself that, although he has a reputation for being shrewd and tenacious, Mr Arnold has also earned the reputation of being a gentleman, with much the same principles as yourself?'

'So I'm given to understand.'

'And he has abandoned the prospect of buying you out?'

'By all accounts.' He chuckled, putting his arm round her and walking her to the half-dressed tree. 'No doubt he saw the measure of my own determination.'

'Then there are no objections to my sending him an invitation?'

'My dear, *you* are the woman of the house. The guest list has always been your responsibility. And no, I have no objections to speak of.' At first he had been surprised and reluctant, but now the idea was growing on him by the minute. 'Do what you think best, my dear.'

'But do *you* think it's for the best?' Cicely sensed that her father was not wholeheartedly convinced.

He looked at her then, a long hard look that betrayed his deep love for her. 'What I think is this . . . you and me are two of a kind, Cicely Banks, too forgiving and soft-hearted by half.' He put his hands on her shoulders and held her at arms' length. 'You don't like us having enemies, do you, child?' he asked lovingly.

'I think it's a great pity that we can't see the best in each other.'

He gazed at her with a father's pride. 'You make me feel ashamed,' he told her, his eyes darkening when he warned in a serious voice, 'It's a sad truth but sometimes we do come across people who are all bad. You're such a gentle, trusting soul, child. I pray no one will ever take advantage of that.'

When she seemed troubled by his words, he shook her gently, his wide smile beaming down on her. 'But of course you're right. Yes! Yes, indeed! I think it's a very good idea to invite Arnold Oliver. Oh, and his son of course. By all means add them to the guest list.' He chuckled, and she could almost see him thinking. 'Besides, I do believe it could be fun,' he said mischievously, and when she began outlining her plans, bent his head to hers and concentrated on her every word. He was well aware that she was apprehensive about the occasion, although he was immensely proud of the fact that she grew more capable and accomplished with every such event.

Suddenly, Ruby came rushing into the hall, breathless and excited and carrying a large wicker basket which hid her from sight. 'I found it!' she cried, surging forward and almost going headlong when she caught her toe in the carpet-edge. 'I found the old decorations. Oh, but what a business! I tell you, Miss Cicely, I hope you never send me up the attic again. A draught from above blew the lamp out and it was pitch black, except for the chink of moonlight coming in through the hole in the roof-tiles.'

She was obviously unnerved by the experience, 'And, do you know, I swear I could hear rats scurrying about. I didn't waste much time, I can tell you. I found what I was looking for and then I took myself out of there like the devil was after me . . .' She peeped round the side of the basket and was even more flustered when she saw the master looking at her with curious eyes.

'Oh, I'm sorry, sir,' she remarked, 'I didn't know you were here.'

She realised she might have interrupted a deep discussion between father and daughter. 'I've been helping Miss Cicely to decorate the tree,' she explained, pushing the basket from her with the intention of carefully setting it down before she departed.

Instead, it fell from her arms and clattered to the floor, spilling its contents across her feet.

'I am sorry, sir.' She apologised, her aching arms falling to her sides. She stared from one to the other, feeling a fit of giggles coming on when she saw that Cicely was trying not to laugh. Ruby wasn't to know what a sight she looked, with her dishevelled hair covered in cobwebs and her apron belt dangling lopsidedly to her boot; there were dusty marks all over her uniform, and a smut of dirt reaching from one side of her face to the other.

'No, leave it, child.' Jeffrey Banks stepped forward when Ruby stooped to retrieve the paper and glitter that was strewn across her feet. On seeing him come towards her, she straightened up and feared the worst. Fancy barging in like that, when these two were talking privately. He was standing before her now, surveying her from top to toe, and when he spoke, she was relieved to hear it was in tones of amusement. 'Good heavens, child. You look as if you've been twice up the chimney and back down again.'

'Yes, sir.' Out of the corner of her eye, Ruby could see Cicely smiling, and prayed that the tickling feeling in her own stomach would not erupt into laughter, because while the master was kindly, he would never tolerate such rude behaviour.

'I'll have the roof-tile fixed, of course.'

'Yes, sir.'

'We can't have the wind and rain coming in and rotting the timbers, can we now, eh?'

'No, sir.'

'Still, you found what you wanted, and you're to be commended.'

'Yes, sir.'

He looked at her more closely, scrutinising her lovely face, and seeming to search for something there. Suddenly time fled away and he was looking at her mother; Ruby had the same trim figure that Lizzie had had at her age, and the same proud presence. He remembered how she had felt in his arms on the night when they had made illicit love, when each was married to another and he the father of that little girl who was now Cicely, woman of the house. So many years, so much had happened between, and still he suffered a deal of affection for the young maid who had worked in this house and whom he had taken shameful advantage of, although he believed with all his heart that Lizzie had loved him too. There were days and nights when he had fought hard against his instincts to persuade her away from her husband. Even now, deep down inside, he still regretted the day when she turned her back on him; even though she had since become a plump and motherly soul. He and she had come face to face some two years back when he was walking through the town. He knew her at once, and there was still a great warmth between them. Her eyes were still bright and pretty, and she had that certain feminine way that attracted a man and made him feel comfortable inside. He had wanted so much to talk with her, but Lizzie appeared greatly flustered, hurrying away before he could stop her.

'Shall I clear the mess away now, sir?' Both Cicely and Ruby were puzzled by his long silence.

He felt his face colour, and was smitten with a cruel pang of conscience as he brought his attention back to her. What would Lizzie's daughter say, he wondered, if she knew how he had seduced her mother? He liked the name by which Lizzie had called her. Ruby was a handsome name, with a particular strength. The girl had the most marvellous eyes, deepest blue and marbled with black . . . they were fathomless. He thought how they were nothing like her mother's eyes; oddly enough, he clearly recalled Lizzie's eyes which were not particularly unique but the warmest, prettiest shade of brown.

Suddenly a great feeling of loneliness came over him and he

longed to see her again. It didn't matter that she was not slim or young any more. All that mattered was that they had shared wonderful moments together; perhaps even more wonderful because they were forbidden. It wasn't just a master taking advantage of his maidservant. Lizzie Miller had made him feel like a real man, and he truly loved her. He wondered if he did still. He wondered also whether he would ever shake off the memory of Lizzie. 'Your mother was maidservant here, did you know that?' he asked in a strained voice. 'You bring the same delight into this house as she did.'

Such was the strangeness of his voice that Ruby was made to stare at him and Cicely actually stepped forward. At once he sensed their curiosity and smiled brightly, saying, 'But of course you know. If I remember rightly, you gave your mother as a reference when you applied?'

'I did, sir.'

'And is she well?' He was greatly relieved that the moment had passed, and warned himself never to lower his guard like that again.

'She's very well, sir, thank you.'

'Like yourself, she was a very valued member of this household. You do her proud. Tell her that, won't you?'

'Thank you, sir. I will.'

'Good!' He began to turn away. 'Very well then. I'll leave you two young people to your task.'

'Excuse me, sir.' When he stopped and turned to face her, Ruby came forward.

'What is it, child?'

'I want to thank you . . . for helping my dad to get a job in your foundry.'

Seeming embarrassed, he waved his hand in a dismissive gesture. 'No need to thank me,' he said abruptly. He glanced at Ruby and thought again of Lizzie, then he smiled at his daughter and thought of her mother, the woman who had deserted them both. The comparison was painful to him, and he went quickly from the room.

When the tree was dressed, Cicely took Ruby up to her room. 'These are for you,' she said. One by one she brought out a number of dresses and laid them gently over the brass bedhead.

Ruby could hardly believe her eyes. The dresses were the loveliest she had ever seen. There was a sea green one with black lace at the hem and throat, a slimmer cream-coloured one with a little evening bag to match, a blue one with a huge flouncy skirt, and a most beautiful dress in richest burgundy, with layer upon layer of fine ribbon encircling the skirt from hem to waist. 'Oh!' That was all she could say, because the breath caught in her throat and choked her. She felt the tears well up in her eyes as she collected the burgundy gown and pressed it to her face; it felt like smooth running water against her skin.

'Try it on.' Cicely was excited, taking Ruby by the hand and ushering her to the long mirror where she told her, 'Look! Oh, Ruby, it's just the right colour for you. Try it on. Do try it on!'

'I can't. I've still got a deal of work to do before I'm finished, and Cook will be chasing after me any minute now.'

'Then we'll just have to chase her away, won't we?' Cicely laughed. She was thoroughly enjoying herself. 'Oh, Ruby. You must try it on. Please?' Seeing how Ruby was just itching to try the dress on, she began undoing the buttons on the back of her work-dress. 'With your dark eyes and rich brown hair, the colour is perfect for you.' She chatted on, working quickly to undress the slim small figure. 'Of course, it will need to be shortened and altered here and there, but you're not to worry about that. I'll arrange for the dressmaker to come in and we'll get you a fitting.' She looked in the mirror and saw her own excitement reflected in Ruby's face. Somehow it made her sad.

'You're so lovely, Ruby . . . far more beautiful than I could ever be. You should always be dressed in the finest gowns that money can buy.'

Ruby shivered exquisitely as the gown touched her bare shoulders. 'Don't say that,' she chastised gently. 'I think you *are* beautiful.' Just like the china doll in the window, she thought.

Cicely made no reply. She knew her own limitations, and knew too that Ruby was very special. It had often crossed her mind how cruel Fate was, to give one girl such beauty yet place her where she might never know the better things in life, and to make another girl merely plain and pleasant, with all the money and material things that she could ever want. But then she reminded herself of how she had only her father, while Ruby had her family, a family she doted on. Life was a strange and unpredictable carousel of ups and downs, and it was a great pity when some people had more than their fair share of downs. 'Let me look at you,' she said, dashing with her handkerchief at the smut on Ruby's face.

Taking up the silver-backed hairbrush from the dresser, she swept it through Ruby's thick dark-brown hair. Then she fastened the last button at the tiny waist and fluffed out the sleeves of the gown before drawing Ruby into the centre of the room. 'Where I can see you better,' she explained, stepping back to take a look. And she looked so wonderful that Cicely was moved to cry out, 'Oh, Ruby! You look like a princess.' Even though the hem of the dress trailed on the carpet, and the sleeves were too long, the gown might have been made for her. It was as though wearing it had touched something deep inside her, making her especially vibrant and grand; she appeared much taller and wonderfully elegant. Her hair shone in the light from the window, and her eyes glowed like burning embers. She was proud and defiant and exquisite, and Cicely was suddenly afraid that she had unlocked some dark and wonderful demon. 'You look . . . different,' she said, her voice quiet and strangely reverent. In all her life she had never seen such loveliness.

'I *feel* wonderful!' Ruby cried, spinning round and round until she was dizzy. 'Oh, Miss Cicely. I never dreamed I would own anything so fine.' When she came to a stop, Ruby was laughing so much she was crying. 'How can I ever thank you?' she asked sincerely.

Cicely's answer was to grab Ruby in her arms and dance her round the room. 'By coming to the Christmas Eve celebrations, that's how!' she replied, breathless with excitement. The idea had occurred to her in the moment when she first saw Ruby in the gown, and already she was having fun thinking about how the other guests would react to Ruby's flawless beauty. 'Everyone will think you're the most exquisite creature they've ever seen.' She brought Ruby to a halt and stared at her with wide childlike eyes. 'Oh, Ruby, you know how I hate these parties. Please say you'll come? It will be such a treat for both of us.'

Ruby was thrilled and horrified all at the same time. 'I can't do that,' she protested. 'Whatever would your father say? And my mam too?' she added with a shock.

'They won't say anything, because we won't tell them.'

'But they'll find out, and then there'll be hell to pay,' Ruby said. Her stomach was turning somersaults and she wanted to fling her arms round Cicely's neck and shout: 'I DON'T CARE WHAT THEY SAY.' But she was afraid. And she was angry because she was afraid.

Cicely was laughing. 'Oh, what fun! Can you imagine their faces when I bring you in? All the young men will be panting to meet you, and every woman in the room will hate you at first sight.'

'You devil. You'll get us both locked up,' Ruby chided, but in her mind's eye she could see it all: the music playing from the stand, the guests all dressed in their finery, then she would sweep in beside the hostess and all eyes would turn in their direction. It wouldn't frighten her. She wouldn't want to hide behind Cicely. Instead she would be proud and defiant, and she would look them in the eyes and say in her mind, 'This is me, and I'm as good as any of you.' Oh, how wonderful it would be! The thought excited her beyond reason. 'Oh, Cicely, you're right. It would be fun,' she had to agree.

'Then you'll come to the party?'

'Oh, yes. YES!' No sooner were the words out of Ruby's mouth than she and Cicely fell into each other's arms and hugged and laughed until the wretched girl came with the news that Cook had sent her to fetch Ruby. 'On account of she wasn't born with four pair of hands,' she said in parrot fashion, whereupon Cicely sent her away with instructions that Ruby was presently employed and would be down shortly.

After the wretched girl scurried away, Cicely returned to the room to find that Ruby had already slipped out of the gown and was in her work-dress. 'I'd better go,' she said anxiously. 'Or Cook will have me scrubbing 'taters for a week.' She would much rather have stayed here with Cicely, but she must never forget her place in this house. Better folk than her had overstepped their mark and lost their job. As to this idea of Cicely's, well, it was probably spur of the moment high-spirits that she was regretting already. 'Can I really have the dresses?' she asked hesitantly.

Cicely was shocked. 'Of course you can, Ruby. Haven't I already said so? And I meant what I said, about having them altered to fit you.'

'I'm very grateful, Miss Cicely. But I had a mind to alter all but the burgundy one, to fit my mam.' Thoughts of Lizzie had a sobering effect on her and her heart sank to her boots. How could she have imagined that she could actually go to a gentry party? A maidservant, dressed like a lady and mingling with the wealth of Blackburn? The like had never been known. What foolish notions would she be thinking next? she asked herself crossly. By! If her mam could have been in this room not five minutes since, seeing her and Cicely swinging each other round and making such outrageous plans, she would have given her daughter what for and no mistake! 'If you'll excuse me, miss, I must get back to my work.' For some reason she couldn't quite fathom, Ruby was deeply angry.

'Ruby.' Cicely stepped forward, bending her head a little so as to see Ruby's face the better. She knew there was something going on in that quick mind, and feared it would put an end to their wonderful arrangement.

'Yes, miss?' Like the atmosphere in the room, Ruby was subdued, and it showed in her voice.

'You haven't forgotten what we planned?' Her voice was soft, persuasive.

Ruby looked up. There was surprise in her face, astonishment in her voice. 'So you did really mean it? The party and everything?' She daren't think about it now. It was too wonderfully frightening.

'I meant every word. You will be there, won't you, Ruby?' The corners of Cicely's mouth were lifting in a smile, and her bright blue eyes were twinkling. 'You did promise,' she reminded Ruby.

Ruby's face was a picture of delight. 'If we can do it without arousing my mam's suspicions, I'm all for it,' she said. Before anything could happen to change things, she clutched the handle and flung open the door. 'You'll stay with me, though? I mean, you won't leave me at the mercy of everyone?' Suddenly it was too real. After waiting hand and foot on the privileged, it would be a strange thing to be on the other side of the fence. Somehow, though, Ruby had a feeling that was where she belonged.

'I'll be at your shoulder all night if you want me to,' Cicely said. 'And we'll think of a way to allay both your mother's and my father's suspicions. Trust me.' She slipped her long fingers into Ruby's small hand, saying softly, 'It will be fun, but most of all I want you there because you're my one and only friend.'

'I'm glad.' Ruby could only imagine how lonely Cicely must be, and the thought of being an only child was abhorrent to her. 'I'll try not to let you down.' As she went out of the door, Ruby could hear Cicely's voice reminding her, 'I'll arrange for the burgundy dress to be altered, and I'll have the others packed and waiting for you when you go home.' Ruby refused Cicely's suggestion that Ruby should take a cab at her expense. What! Her mam would have a fit when she arrived home with a pile of 'fancy' clothes, never mind about turning up in a cab paid for by the gentry.

The rest of the day was spent in a frantic rush. Ruby believed that Cook had it in for her, because she piled so much work on her that there was hardly time to breathe. By the time she put on her coat at the end of the day, Ruby had cleaned all the silver in every cupboard throughout the house, each and every mat had been taken out and slung over the line, where it was beaten until it hung like a limp rag, the legs of every table and chair had been first dusted and then polished: 'Until I can see my face in it,' threatened Cook peevishly. Following that, Ruby was made to take the long feather-duster and sweep the many curtain valances throughout the house.

'You old bugger, Cook,' she muttered when the older woman's voice called out a merry 'goodnight' as she left for the evening, with the carefully wrapped bundle of gowns tucked under her arm. 'Thanks to you, I feel bow-legged and worn to a frazzle!'

All the same, Cook had not been able to dim her excitement about the coming event. All the while Ruby had been going about her work, she had counted the days to Christmas Eve. It was now the twenty-fourth of September. In just over twelve weeks' time, on the very day before her fifteenth birthday, Ruby believed she would be attending the most important occasion of her entire life.

As she boarded the tram and sat in the farthest corner where she could be alone with her daydreams, the thought of herself in that gown, at that party, made her shiver with delight. The thought of her mam finding out made her shiver with horror.

Lizzie was adamant. 'You'll take them rags straight back where you got 'em. You'll never see the day when I take charity from the rich.'

'But it's *not* charity!' Ruby was devastated. She had come into the house quietly and hidden the bundle in the front parlour. All evening she had been bursting to tell her mam about her wonderful surprise. Now, when her father was snoozing in the chair and the young 'uns were abed, she had taken her mam into the parlour and proudly unfurled the gowns at her feet. There were tears in her eyes as she and Lizzie faced each other now.

'If it ain't charity, what the divil is it then?'

'It's a present.'

'I don't want no "presents" from gentry.' Even as she spoke, Lizzie was thinking about another 'present'. That present was her own precious Ruby. And wasn't she got from the gentry? she asked herself. Got in a tide of love? Got between two people who had a passion for each other? And wasn't it *more* than passion? Wasn't it something very wonderful? A longing for each other that Lizzie felt even to this day, in spite of the fact that she had enough love for her husband to keep him content? In her deepest heart, Lizzie was made to acknowledge the truth and it was this . . . in the whole of her life, two things had happened to bring her a deal of joy that would carry her to the end of her days. The genuine love of Jeffrey Banks, and the birth of her darling daughter.

Lizzie knew she had many reasons to be grateful to the good Lord. After all, he had seen them through some very bad times, he had forgiven her for the shocking thing she did, and had brought her happiness many times over with the birth of her beloved children. But, to Lizzie's mind, every woman deserved to keep a secret, and that secret should bring them the greatest happiness of all. Through the years, because of what she had done outside her marriage, Lizzie had suffered in all manner of ways; she had been first ashamed, then guilty, fearful, then lonely; she had been torn in so many ways, and there were times when she believed that the good Lord would turn away from her for ever.

Now, though, she had come through all of that, and every time she looked at Ruby, her heart would soar at the memory of how that delightful girl came to be. She looked at her now, and her heart swelled with love and gratitude. In that fearful moment, Lizzie was closer to confessing the truth than she had ever been.

'Please, Mam?' Ruby had seen how her mam had gone into a quiet mood. She had seen the hardness melt from her eyes, and sensed that it would take only a little persuasion for Lizzie to accept Cicely's wonderful gift. 'Won't you at least try one on . . . for me?' She deliberately chose the cream-coloured one to hold against the candlelight; it was slimmer in style than the others, and she believed the soft colouring would flatter her mam's light brown hair and pretty hazel eyes. 'Cicely is a wonderful, kind lady, and she did so want us to have them.'

Lizzie shook her head. 'No, lass.' Her face creased into a smile, and Ruby knew her mood was changed. 'Whatever would the neighbours think? And wherever would I go in such a fancy thing? That's provided I could get into it in the first place!'

'The neighbours would think you were very lucky,' Ruby said hopefully. 'You could wear it every Sunday to church. And I can alter it to fit you. Thanks to you, I'm an excellent seamstress, so I can put your teaching to good use.' While her mam was still considering, Ruby held the dress against her. 'It won't take a lot of work,' she fibbed.

Lizzie threw back her head and laughed loudly. 'Oh, yer little liar, Ruby Miller!' she cried. 'May the good Lord forgive yer. It would take a wagon and four to get me into that there dress, and well you know it.' She pushed it away. 'No, sweetheart. Once upon a time it might have fitted yer mam . . . when she were slim and the fellers cocked an eye at her, but after nine bairns, a body goes to seed. No. You tell your lady I'm grateful, but such things is wasted on the likes of me.' Suddenly there was a movement at the door, and Lizzie swung round to see her husband standing there.

'You're too hard on yourself, Lizzie Miller,' he murmured lovingly. 'You may not be the dainty little thing you once was, but any man with half an eye could see that even in the sad clothes I can afford you, you're still a fine handsome woman. You always will be. What's more, I think you should let Ruby alter that pretty gown to fit you, because nobody could look more fetching in it than my lovely wife. Ruby asked you to wear it for her,' he said softly. 'If you won't do it for her, then will you wear it for me?' He had said what was in his heart, and now he gazed at her with smiling eyes and a proud look in his face.

'Oh, Ted.' Lizzie was overwhelmed. The tears trembled in her bright eyes as she looked at him, this humble, hard-working man whom she had wronged so long ago, the man who had been at her side through thick and thin. And, yes, although she would always keep a special place in her heart for Ruby's real father, she loved this man in a different and wonderful way. She went to him then, and he opened his arms to embrace her. 'I don't tell you often enough how much you mean to me,' he murmured, pressing her close to him.

Thrilled and silenced by the depth of emotion between these two people whom she adored, Ruby gently laid the dress down and prepared to tiptoe past them. But Lizzie turned round to tell her softly, 'See what you can do then, lass.' She might have said more, but Ted took her by the hand and led her down the candlelit passage, then on up the stairs, leaving Ruby alone with thoughts of a young man only a few steps away from where she was.

Earlier, when she had gone in to see Maureen, Johnny had sat in with them for a while. Afterwards he had walked her home. When it seemed he would kiss her at the door, Ruby had pulled away. She regretted it now. After all, what was in a kiss?

Oliver Arnold came into the dining-room where his three children awaited his arrival. The table was laid to perfection, the chandeliers were lit, and he bestowed a smile on each of his children in turn, before bowing his head to: 'Thank the Almighty for the food we are about to eat, and for the well-being of all those who are gathered at this table.' He was not unaware of the impatience of his son, who fidgeted throughout and whose attention was caught by every little movement. Somewhat irritated, he curtailed Grace and gave the customary signal, a discreet nod of the head, for the meal to begin.

At once the maids stepped forward: neat little figures in black garments and starched white aprons with their hair scraped back beneath frilly caps, and their faces impassive as they served the first course. The evening meal was a traditional ceremony, beginning with Grace, eaten in silence, and ending only when the man at the head of the table placed his neatly folded napkin on the china plate beside him.

The room was splendid with mellowed oak panels all around the walls; against the far wall stood a magnificent huge dresser displaying silver tureens surrounded by all manner of glassware and pretty condiment sets. The grand table was covered with a stark white cloth and dressed with the very best that money could buy: beautifully embroidered napkins, hallmarked cutlery, best china, and food enough to feed a small army.

The meal always began at seven and ended precisely one and a half hours later. For Oliver it was a time of complete relaxation, when he could be with his family – yet remain quiet with his own thoughts. For Luke it was precious time wasted, when he would rather have been elsewhere; preferably with a woman of the town who would show him a good time without shame or conscience. The eldest daughter saw it as an occasion when she could play at being mistress of the house; while the youngest member of the family saw only that her beloved father was home. During the meal she would glance at him with soft green eyes and he would discreetly reward her with a smile. On Oliver Arnold's instructions, there was no discussion at the table. They were gentry, and it was not the done thing to speak while eating.

Later though, when the meal was over and the family retired to the drawing room, the talk spilled over. Young Ida sat by her father's knee and excitedly outlined every minute of her day, of how the tutor was pleased with her Latin, and how she had played the piano to excellence. 'And I finished my whole sample of embroidery.' She sprang up and ran to the dresser, bringing him the very sample. 'There!' she said proudly, her pleasant round face beaming from ear to ear as she held up the beautiful piece to show him.

'Well now, let's see.' Oliver Arnold took the embroidery from her chubby fingers and turning it this way and that, he made a great fuss of examining it. 'And what's this?' he asked, pointing to a strange shape sewn in bright orange thread.

'That's *you*!' Disappointment clouding her eyes, she pressed herself between him and the sample. 'Look . . .' She pointed to the odd shape, painstakingly tracing her finger over it. 'There's your nose, and that's your mouth, and these little bits are your eyes.' She lifted her gaze from the sample and smiled brightly. 'See?' she asked hopefully. Ida was twelve years old, but delightfully immature for her age.

He nodded his head. 'Of course! I see it all now,' he lied. 'It's a wonderful likeness.'

'And you love it, don't you?'

'I love it.'

'Here you are then. It's a present.' She placed the piece into his hands. 'You can hang it on the wall over your bed if you like.'

'And I will,' he promised. 'Where else would I keep such a splendid portrait of myself?'

He was teasing her and she knew it. 'Oh, you . . .' She laughed, throwing herself into his arms. 'I do love you,' she whispered into his ear.

'And I love you,' he whispered back. Kissing her on the forehead, he held her at arm's length. 'Leave me now, Ida. Your brother and I need to talk.' He glanced up at Luke who was standing with his back to the fireplace, his hands thrust deep into his trouser pockets and a sullen look on his face At his father's words, he groaned and jerked his head to one side, staring down at the casement doors and out to the star-lit night beyond. He wanted to be away, laughing and frolicking in some whore-house with better company than he would find here. Damn his father. Damn the bloody business, he thought vehemently. But then he reminded himself that he must be careful not to let his father suspect his deep resentment. As it was, it had taken far too long already to fool him into believing his son was coming to accept the weighty responsibilities of his inheritance.

'What about me?' Teresa stood up then, her face set hard as she stared from her father to Luke, and finally at her sister, who was still lovingly enfolded in her father's arms. Teresa Arnold was as different from her sister Ida as it was possible to be. Where Ida was small and round, with curly fair hair, bright green eyes and a wide open face that was quick to smile, Teresa was tall and elegant, with a certain cold beauty; her auburn hair was long and straight, sometimes drawn up in a coil into the nape of her neck,

119

and sometimes hanging down her back to her waist, always brushed into a high sheen, and jealously treasured as her best feature. Her large oval-shaped eyes were almost the same shade as her hair, reddish brown, but wonderfully brilliant and often frightening to look upon. Through her eyes, Teresa could be all things. She could be bold or coy, loving or hateful, she could draw a body to her or cause them to cringe away. As she spoke again, her eyes almost snapped and her whole countenance was hostile. 'I *asked* to speak to you after dinner, Father. Surely you remember?' The words were spat out. Continuing to stare at him, she came forward and awaited his answer.

'Of course. I'm sorry, my dear. Speak out then?'

'Not in front of these two,' she said bitterly, nodding her head first at Ida and then at her brother. 'It has nothing to do with either of them.'

Her father frowned. 'Can it wait then? I do have a business matter to discuss with your brother.'

'No, it cannot wait.' She flared her nostrils angrily.

Sensing another of her tiresome complaints, he sighed wearily. 'Oh, very well.' Leaning forward in his chair, he put the younger girl on her feet. 'Sorry,' he said simply.

Ida's buoyant mood was spoiled, and she suspected, quite wrongly this time, that her sister had done it on purpose to separate her from her father. 'You will come up and say goodnight, won't you?' she asked. When he answered that he would, her bright smile returned and, after hugging him fondly, she went away satisfied.

'Now then, Teresa. What is it that's troubling you?'

'Huh! Need you ask?' She tossed her head indignantly.

'Well, yes, my dear,' he replied with immense patience, 'I do need to ask, otherwise I won't know what I'm supposed to be dealing with.'

She seemed suddenly to realise that her brother was still in the room. 'I would like him to leave,' she said sulkily, stiffening when Luke merely smiled at her in that infuriating manner.

Her father's impatience deepened. 'There is no time for that, Teresa. As I have just explained, your brother and I have an important business matter to discuss. Either say what's on your mind now, or leave and we can talk about it tomorrow.'

Seeing that he was irritable, she reluctantly told him, 'It's that old fool in the stables.'

'Thomas, you mean?' He knew exactly who she meant, because hadn't she derided that harmless old man time and again? In fact, as she went on, he found to his dismay that he knew every word even before she spoke it, he had heard them so many times before. And so he listened while she predictably complained about how Thomas was growing senile and unreliable, how he took a particular delight in antagonising her. 'He's neglecting his duties, sleeping most of the time while his assistant does twice the work. It's shameful, I tell you. Do we pay him to sleep? What's more, he smells to high heaven. I shouldn't think he ever uses soap and water. In fact, I don't believe he's washed at the pump in these many months.'

Luke infuriated her by laughing and accusing in a meaningful voice, 'And *you* should know.' He stopped short of saying he had seen her watching from her bedroom window while Johnny Ackroyd strip-washed at that very pump. If their father ever suspected, he wouldn't hesitate to send the young man packing and Luke would lose his hold over Teresa. That would never do. Not when there was still much sport to be had from this whole amusing business, before the arrogant Ackroyd was made to meet his downfall.

'That's a very unkind thing to say, my dear.' This was a new one on her father, and he disliked hearing such a thing. 'Thomas's personal hygiene is really a matter for him only. I must admit, I haven't noticed anything untoward.'

'That apart, what do you intend doing about his neglect of his duties?'

'What would you *have* me do?'

'Get rid of him, of course!'

'I see.' He hadn't realised how callous she could be. 'You know Thomas has been in my employ for many years, and that he has no other home than what we provide?'

'Then he must find another.'

'Oh? And who would we put in his place?'

'Why, his young assistant of course. That young man works long and hard, and his behaviour is highly commendable.' She almost bit her tongue when those particular words came out, because she was still smarting from the way Johnny had let it be known that he was not interested in her. All the same, she believed that, once she got the old one out of the way, Johnny would be hers for the taking. 'Give his work to young Mr Ackroyd and take on a new assistant,' she suggested, and the belief that she was finally persuading her father brought a ready smile to her face.

The smile, however, was quickly wiped off her face with her father's grim reply. 'You shame me, Teresa. But you have put your case, and now I must put mine. You are of course the eldest daughter, and as such are entitled to some say in this house. But *I* say Thomas stays. I have never found him lacking in his duties, and I have never seen him sleeping when he should be working. I spend the most time in his company, when he saddles my horse or takes me about in the carriage, or when he leans across my desk to collect his well-earned wages. And not once have I ever had occasion to wrinkle my nose at this smell you mention.'

'Then you think I'm a liar?' Her voice trembled and her hands shook with temper as she glared at him.

'No, I do not say that.' He too was angry, and was giving her no quarter. These constant complaints about a good man had gone on long enough, and it was time they were put a stop to.

'What I'm saying is that you are sorely mistaken in your findings. Apart from which, I think you should bear in mind that Thomas has been a good and loyal servant to this household for many years . . . long before you were even born, my dear.'

He let the implication sink in, before he went on, 'As for young Mr Ackroyd, I *do* agree, he is a fine young man with a strong sense of duty, and it has been on my mind these past weeks to entrust him with more responsibility. Consequently he will be paid a considerably higher wage, which no doubt will be welcomed by his mother who, I'm given to understand, has a sickly daughter and a feckless husband to cope with. Also, you might be interested to learn that it was Thomas himself who put the young man's name forward.'

He drew himself to his full height and squared his shoulders. 'No, my dear,' he said determinedly, 'Thomas will stay for as long as I think fit. And as yet, I see no reason to turn him out of his home. I doubt if I shall ever be called upon to do such a thing.'

'Then in spite of my being the eldest daughter with a right to speak, my opinion counts for nothing in the end?'

'That seems a little harsh, my dear. But, yes, on this occasion, it is my opinion that matters. Now, can we let that be an end to it?'

She gave no answer. Instead, she turned stiffly on her heel and departed the room in a huff; going all the quicker when she heard Luke's soft irritating laughter behind her.

When the door was closed and the echo of her steps had died away, Oliver gestured for his son to be seated. 'That a daughter of mine could be so unfeeling is beyond me!' he sighed. Waiting until his son was seated in the brown leather chair to one side of the fireplace, he went to the dresser where he poured two brandies, a double one for himself and a smaller measure for his son. After all, bad habits were too easily formed. 'You don't believe I was too harsh on your sister, do you?' he asked, handing the glass to

Luke. 'I'm afraid she did infuriate me though.' He sank into the chair opposite. 'Sadly, Teresa has always been able to bring out the worst in me.' He sipped at the brandy, smacking his lips and sinking further down into the chair.

Luke grinned foolishly, restless to be gone from there. 'Teresa is her own worst enemy,' he stated boldly, thinking she had not yet learned the art of true conniving. There were occasions when it was most unwise to speak your mind about certain matters. Often it was far wiser to say one thing and mean another. That way you deceived your enemies and gave yourself time to review the situation.

'There are things she still has to learn,' came the reply, and it appealed to Luke's warped sense of humour because he had been thinking along those very same lines himself.

'You said you had business to discuss?' he asked. Teresa was a fool, and he had little time for fools.

Oliver straightened himself in the chair and his mood changed. 'Well, of course there are "end of week" matters we need to discuss. No doubt you have your report completed?'

Luke smothered his feeling of anxiety. When his father gave him responsibility for safety measures at the Eanam foundry, it was understood that he must submit regular reports. So far he had managed to satisfy his father that everything was being taken care of. Indeed, he had the manager's own reports to substantiate this. But he was playing a dangerous game, and was always made nervous when his father took the 'end of week' reports to read in the privacy of his own study. If it was ever made known that he and the manager were accounting for top grade materials, when in fact they used sub-standard . . . well, Luke dared not even think about the consequences. Outwardly he bristled with self-confidence, but inwardly he shrank from his father's gaze. He knew from experience that Oliver was no fool. That was why he had gone to great lengths in order to cover his tracks; even the supplier had no idea who was purchasing his goods. The entire plan had worked better than he had envisaged, and his private bank account was swelling by the minute. 'Of course my report is ready,' he said with disarming charm, 'I've taken the liberty of placing it on your desk.'

'Good!' Oliver beamed at him, delighted that his son had responded so well to the responsibilities of management, and even exceeding his father's highest expectations. 'I have to admit that I had certain reservations about placing such a heavy burden on your shoulders.'

'I know that, Father, and in view of my irresponsible behaviour in the past, I can't blame you for being cautious.' He gulped as he went on to voice the daring thought that had been burning in his mind for a long time. 'I do believe I'm ready to take on a great deal more authority.' There! It was said, and he was shockingly pleased with himself.

Oliver laughed out loud, 'Do you indeed?' He became quiet then, staring at his son through narrowed eyes, as though he was looking beneath the surface. Presently, he took a small gulp of brandy, smiled, and replied in a strong voice, 'Not yet, son.'

'But *why* not?' Bitter disappointment showed in his face as he sat on the edge of his chair, silently pleading for his father to change his mind. 'I've done as you asked. There isn't a rusty nail or a shaky platform anywhere to be seen in the Eanam foundry. Even the men are saying they feel safer than they have for years,' he lied. 'I've done a good job, you can't deny that.' He felt cheated and bitter. He had so many plans, and besides, was beginning to enjoy a feeling of power.

'Everything you say is true,' Oliver admitted. 'Your manager bears you out, and your reports are excellent. I have seen for myself how you've greatly improved the safety measures.'

'Then why can't I take on more responsibility?'

'Oh, the day will come, I promise you. But not yet.'

'But I'm your son! An Arnold. You just said yourself that I've proved myself to be capable?'

'Indeed. But you're still young, I think. Too young to be taking on an empire. As it is, you have virtually a free rein, and a workable budget, which you manage exceedingly well. The other premises are in good hands for the minute.' He smiled benevolently, urging, 'Be patient, son.' He saw the disappointment in Luke's face, but it did not change his mind. The safety of his men was too important an issue for him to let his heart rule his head. For the moment Luke had quite enough responsibility. Later of course he would be given more, but slowly, and cautiously. 'Don't be disheartened. Your time will come soon enough.'

'You don't trust me!'

'It isn't altogether a question of trust.'

'Then what is it? Are you punishing me?'

'For what?' He thought that a very strange thing for Luke to say.

'For all the years you say I shamed you.'

Oliver bent his head. Even now it hurt to think of the way his son had deliberately gone out of his way to bring this family into disrepute. But he tried so hard not to think about those times, and it hurt for Luke to mention them now. 'That's a cruel thing to say. And, no, I'm not punishing you. You forget, I have already given you the opportunity to redeem yourself, and of course you have done so. But I still can't turn over any more responsibility to you, not for a while at least.'

'But I don't see your argument.'

'There is no *argument*.' Oliver had a certain way of smiling which effectively brought a discussion to an end. He was smiling in that manner now. 'I have something to show you,' he said with a brighter face. He reached inside his waistcoat pocket and produced a small white envelope which he handed to his son. 'I think you'll find it interesting.'

Grudgingly, Luke opened the envelope and drew out a stiff white card which he read with increasing surprise. It was an invitation in the most beautiful handwriting:

Mr Jeffrey Banks and his daughter, Cicely,
would be pleased to receive you and your
son at Billenge House on Christmas Eve

The festivities will begin at 8 p.m.

Replies, please, to Miss Cicely Banks,
Billenge House,
Billenge End Road,
BLACKBURN,
Lancs.

Luke was astonished. 'I can't believe it!' he gasped. 'The man must be mad . . . inviting an enemy to his table.'

'And what makes you think I'm his enemy?'

'Huh! What else would you be, when you've been trying for years to prise his foundry away from him?'

'It's true I would dearly love to buy Banks's foundry,' Oliver freely admitted.

'There you are then.'

'But I haven't been trying to steal it. Nor have I employed underhand methods by which I might acquire it. Any offers I've made to Jeffrey Banks have been all above board. And very generous too, I might add.'

'You haven't got it though, have you?' Luke said with a cunning expression. 'For all your "above board" dealings, and "generous offers", you still haven't got it.'

127

'No, I haven't got it.'

'So you'll go on as before?' Luke found himself being drawn into the fray, and strangely enough he liked it. At the back of his devious mind, a plan was taking shape. 'You'll go on making "generous" offers and being turned down, until one or the other of you tires?'

Oliver was delighted to see his son showing such interest. 'What else would you have me do?' he teased with a wry little smile, thinking the young man still had a great deal to learn about business matters.

'Oh, I don't know.' He must be careful here. 'But you would really love to have that foundry, wouldn't you?'

'It has been an ambition of mine for too long now.' A curious thing occurred to him then, and the words tasted bitter in Oliver's mouth as he asked, 'You're surely not suggesting that I should have been less than honourable in my dealings with Jeffrey Banks?'

'Good heavens, no!' Luke sounded suitably horrified.

'I'm glad to hear that. And you might be glad to learn that at long last I have come to a decision about the Banks's foundry.'

'What kind of decision?'

'That he will never part with it. And that I will make no more offers.' By the look on his son's face, he knew this had come as a shock.

'You're letting him win?' Luke had never before seen his father the loser, and along with astonishment came a feeling of pleasure. He had been convinced that tonight his father would trust him enough to grant everything he asked – which to his mind wasn't too much, merely to be in charge of all safety measures in each of the Arnold establishments. With that kind of free hand, and the budget allocated, he saw himself becoming immensely wealthy in a very short time.

It wasn't altogether the money, though. It was the rush of

power that excited him, and even more than that, the idea that he would be out-manoeuvring his own father, the same father who was so revered in the business world, the same father who had been ashamed of his son, the same father who tired of sending him to school where he might yet again be expelled, and who had instead shamed his only son by keeping him at home and including him in instruction classes with his two younger sisters. Luke had never forgotten the humiliation, nor the way in which the tutor took malicious enjoyment in drawing him out and making an example of him. During that time a deep hatred had grown inside the boy, and it was there now in the man, a deep dark hatred that never went away. Hatred for his father. Hatred for everything that was good. A consuming hatred that dictated his every move. 'Will you go . . . to this party?' he asked, something deliciously wicked spiralling up inside him.

'First, I do not look on my decision to stop pestering Jeffrey Banks for his foundry, as "letting him win". It was never a fight, only a business proposition. As for attending the party? What do *you* think?'

Luke dropped his gaze to the carpet, pretending to give it careful consideration. He thought about the wording on the invitation. Jeffrey Banks and his daughter, Cicely . . . Replies please to Cicely Banks. Luke remembered the one occasion when he had gone to a certain business function with his father. Jeffrey Banks was there, and so was his daughter. He hadn't received a strong impression of her, because he was restless to get away. Now, though, it occurred to him that she must have considerable influence on her father or he most certainly would not have taken her to a business function. Perhaps he had even signed part of the foundry into her name? After all, she was an only child.

My! That was a thought. A *woman* owning property; perhaps even having a say in the running of a business. But no, that could never be. All the same, her father clearly doted on her, and that could bode well for a certain little plan that had blossomed even while his father was speaking. In his mind's eye he could see Cicely as she had been those twelve months ago, not a handsome young woman by any stretch of the imagination. If he remembered rightly, she was too thin, too fair, not to his taste at all. But then, she did appear to be a soft and trusting soul, and that was certainly to his taste. 'I think you should go,' he said in answer to his father's pointed question.

Oliver was amused. 'You do?'

'Well, he's asked you, hasn't he? So it follows that he bears you no grudges,' Luke said cunningly.

His father was pleased. 'My sentiments exactly,' he confirmed proudly. 'I have already accepted the invitation. It's a pleasure to be civilised about these things.'

Another small brandy and a short discussion about trade in general, before Oliver Arnold dismissed his son. 'Trust me,' he said, seeing him out of the drawing room, 'I do know best, and my judgement is usually sound.'

Luke was too disappointed to offer an answer. Instead he curtly nodded his head and went, seething, out into the hallway, where he almost collided with the wretched girl who was hurrying towards the drawing room with the master's late-night toddy. 'Ooh! I'm sorry, sir,' she stuttered, staring up at him with fearful eyes. When he bade her to, 'Take that in, you little fool, then summon Thomas to deliver himself and the carriage to the front entrance,' she began trembling and nodding her head feverishly. 'Be quick then!' he ordered, and she went on nodding her head until he sighed noisily and strode away, muttering 'Dolts and idiots everywhere!'

It was dark and cold, and as he climbed into the carriage his mood matched the night well. When Thomas clicked the horses on and the carriage moved away, Luke settled back in the soft leather seat and began to reflect on the way his father had dismissed any idea of handing over more responsibility.

Suddenly he was smiling to himself in the darkness, his mind running with mischievous thoughts. Wouldn't it be something if he succeeded in acquiring the Banks foundry where his father had failed? Wouldn't it show his father how he had wronged his only son in not trusting his ability? And wouldn't it be wonderfully satisfying to set himself up against his father? 'To ruin him once and for all,' he muttered, laughing softly at the very idea. It could be done, he calculated. 'It's time to settle this between us, Father,' he said grimly. 'Perhaps then you'll see that your "wayward" son is a better man than you are.'

As he came boldly into the club, the sound of music permeated the air, and lewd laughter, and the unmistakable smell of fancy whores. 'There's a private party in the back room,' the doorman explained with a knowing wink.

Luke was reminded of another party. And he could hardly wait. Before Christmas Eve was over, Cicely Banks would be eating out of his hand. She was the means by which he could acquire not only the Banks foundry, but in time the absolute trust of his father; especially if she was to bear him a son. The thought amused him immensely. All women were fools, and Cicely Banks would be no exception.

Chapter Five

'I can't say I like the idea of you sleeping over at the Bankses'.'
Lizzie pushed back and forth in the rocking chair, growing more
and more agitated. 'I should have put a stop to it the minute you
told me,' she grumbled. Suddenly she brought the chair to a halt,
a triumphant grin on her face as she stared at Ruby. 'It's not too
late even now. No! You're not staying over, and that's that. You
can tell 'em yer poorly, or *I* can be poorly, it don't matter what
yer tell 'em. But you're not sleeping in that house, not while I've
a say in it, my girl.'

Ruby couldn't believe her ears. A minute ago her mother was
seated at the table mending Da's socks, but now she had rounded
for a confrontation. Ruby knew her mam hadn't liked the idea
right from when she told her some weeks back, but there had
been nothing said about her not being able to stay at Billenge
House on the night of the party. 'Oh, Mam, I can't let Cicely
down now,' she pleaded, her heart sinking to her boots. 'Besides,
I've already promised.'

'Well, yer can unpromise, 'cause yer not staying, and that's
an end to it. I must have been mad even to consider allowing it.'
The thought of Ruby sleeping under the same roof as the man
who had fathered her all those years since, had haunted Lizzie
since the girl told her about the Christmas Eve party. At first, she

had tried hard not to let it cloud her judgement. After all, Ruby was a much-valued member of that household, and she would be paid good wages for her extra duties. What was more, neither Ruby nor Jeffrey Banks had any idea that they were father and daughter, so surely there was little harm in Ruby staying over?

Lizzie had fought with all those arguments over the past weeks, but now that the time was almost on them, her courage had given out and she was all of a sweat about her secret somehow being found out. 'You'd best make it clear when yer go in tomorrow . . . yer won't be staying over. You tell 'em that . . . yer *won't* be staying over.' She wagged her finger and began rocking the chair again. 'I should never have let yer think you could,' she finished, crossing her arms and fiercely tipping the rocker back and forth.

For the first time in weeks she felt more at ease with herself, although there was a murmur of regret about the way she had let the girl believe she could go, about how that nice Miss Cicely had already been promised and now would be disappointed that Ruby was going back on her word, and then there were the extra wages that she would have earned. All of these factors niggled at Lizzie, dampening her bubble of joy. But then, she reminded herself of two things: first that money could never be more important than her child, and second that her man was now in work and they were as comfortable as they were ever likely to be in this life.

'Please, Mam, I can't let Cicely down.' Ruby felt sick with disappointment.

'Hey!' Lizzie brought the chair to a halt and fixed her hazel eyes on Ruby's unhappy face. 'Have yer forgotten what I've told yer, about properly addressing yer employer?' she demanded crossly. 'Yer not to be so familiar with the lady's name.' She daren't even think about how Cicely Banks was Ruby's half-sister. 'It's *Miss* Cicely. Allus keep that in mind, my girl.'

'But I promised I'd be there,' she protested. 'Don't make me a liar, our mam.' She thought about Cicely, and the beautiful burgundy dress which had been altered to fit her like a glove. She thought about the way in which she had deceived her mam, and wondered whether she didn't deserve to be punished. All the same, what harm had she done? Was it so wrong to want to wear a lovely gown for the first time in her life? Was it so wrong to feel like a princess? And who would it hurt? No one. It would hurt no one, she thought. If it did, she wouldn't do it. She felt guilty though, guilty because she had not been able to confide the truth in her mam. Oh, how she would have loved to tell her about the things Cicely had said, about how she thought Ruby was made to wear fine things, and how every eye would be turned in her direction when she walked into the room.

Ever since that day when she had tried the dress on, Ruby had longed to tell her mam, had ached to share her secret. But her mam's fixed views about 'mixing with the gentry' had warned Ruby against it. Now it would be just another dream, a dream that would never come true. It was a cruel blow. And yet, though she was obliged to keep the whole truth from her mam, and though she was bitterly frustrated at her late change of mind, Ruby would never defy that darling woman.

So when Lizzie asked her to confirm that she understood the way of things, Ruby answered with bowed head, 'Yes, Mam. I understand.' And from the look on her mam's face, she knew from experience that the argument was lost.

During this unhappy exchange between two people he dearly loved, Ted Miller sat hunched in the chair on the other side of the fireplace, for some time steeped in his own thoughts and contentedly wriggling his bare toes in the heat from the burning coals in the grate. Since being set on at Banks's Foundry, he felt like a man again. It was good to bring home a wage and to know that you were taking care of your family. As a rule he would never interfere in Lizzie's rulings over the children.

Usually she was right, and he only exerted his own authority when there was a rebellious attitude to be dealt with; Lenny and Ralph were becoming a pair of handfuls, but then they were lads, and lads had a way of testing the measure of their parents. On the whole, they didn't get much past Lizzie. *None* of the children did.

As for Ruby, it was plain as the nose on your face that she would never do anything to hurt her mam, she idolised her too much. He turned his head to look on Ruby's face. There were tears in her dark blue eyes, and in spite of the fact that her voice was remarkably calm, he sensed that she was crushed by Lizzie's harsh words. Straightening himself in the chair, he looked at Lizzie. She was stony-faced, her neck stretched and a determined gleam in her pretty eyes. 'I'll not hear no more of it,' she said in a hard voice. 'I don't want no daughter of mine sleeping in a strange house, especially on Christmas Eve when yer should be at home with yer own family.'

'Happen you'd best go to bed, lass.' Ted's voice was little more than a whisper as he addressed Ruby, but it filled the room with a certain authority that made both women turn to look at him.

'I'm not tired, Dad,' she replied softly. 'Besides, I promised Maureen I'd see her before I go to bed.'

'You did, eh?' Ted leaned on one elbow and viewed her fondly. 'Well now, we don't want you having to break *two* promises, do we?' When Ruby glanced at Lizzie, he added, 'If it's all right with yer mam, you can get along and say goodnight to your friend.'

'Aye.' Lizzie couldn't deny her that. 'But don't be too late afore yer back.' She hated having to hurt the girl about tomorrow night, but for once in her life Lizzie was going to be selfish.

Ted didn't say anything until Ruby's footsteps had gone over the threshold and the sound of the front door being closed echoed down the passage. And then he told Lizzie, 'You were a bit harsh, don't yer think?'

'Happen,' she admitted.

'What's so bad about the lass staying over at Billenge? After all, it's her place of work. If *I* was asked to work an extra night shift you'd have no objections to that, would you now, eh?'

'That's different.'

'Oh? And how is it "different"?'

'Because you're paid to do a night-shift, and you work right through it. It ain't the same as sleeping next door to the gentry, stretched out in a fancy bed with silk sheets against yer skin.'

'Who says she'll be sleeping in a fancy bed?' He laughed good-naturedly. 'I don't reckon things have changed *that* much since you were a maid-servant at Billenge House, me beauty. Our Ruby will be put abed with the other servants at the back of the house, in a bed not too much different than the one upstairs.'

'I wouldn't put it past that Miss Cicely to treat her different. She's already got Cook's back up by taking the lass away from her duties when she sees fit.' Ruby had always kept her mam in touch with what was going on.

'Don't go reading things into that,' Ted gently warned. 'Ruby works damned hard, it's in her nature, you know that. Besides, she's fond of Miss Cicely, and you said yourself, that young woman has a good heart.' He paused when a certain memory flooded his thoughts, of how Jeffrey Banks had stood out to offer him a job when everyone else would turn him down. 'She takes after her dad, I expect,' he said warmly. 'Oh, look, lass, it's no secret that Jeffrey Banks's only daughter has taken a liking to our lass, and where's the harm in that, eh? It must be a lonely existence in that big house, with no brothers nor sisters, and if our Ruby lessens that loneliness, who are we to say it's wrong?'

'Well, it *is* wrong. No good can come of getting too close to the gentry.'

'But, where's the harm, Lizzie?' he insisted, unaware how his words struck deep when he asked, 'Are you frightened she might be stolen from you, is that it?'

'Yer can say what yer like, but tomorrer night the lass comes home where she belongs.' Lizzie's heart was fluttering fearfully, but she made an effort to keep her voice calm. He mustn't guess her fear. He must never, never guess.

Ted was not about to give up. He had seen the unhappiness in Ruby's face, and couldn't understand why Lizzie was so unreasonable over this particular issue. 'Be sensible,' he pleaded. 'You've told me yourself that these grand parties go on 'til all hours. Lord above, woman! Would you have the girl walking the streets in the dark early hours. There won't be no trams, and if she's to pay for a cab, then what's the point of her working a late shift to earn a few extra shillings?'

'She won't be waiting on at the party neither.'

'Oh, and why's that?'

'Because I say so.'

'It's her job, Lizzie. She's been asked.'

'No matter. She'll just have to make up some excuse or other, because I'll not have her sleeping in a strange bed.'

He was curious then. In all the years he'd been wed to Lizzie, he could never remember her being so stubborn. 'But, most maid-servants live in at these big houses, and when Ruby's sixteen, I've no doubt she'll be asked to do the same. Besides, didn't *you* live in at Billenge House?'

'We're not talking about me.'

He stared at her then, and suddenly he felt a shiver of something spread through his bones. 'What are you afraid of?' he asked.

Something in his quiet tone startled her. 'What d'yer mean? I ain't "afraid" of nothing.' But she was. Every day that Ruby came nearer to her sixteenth birthday, Lizzie was afraid the girl would be obliged to live in at Billenge House. Lately, Lizzie had noticed something about her daughter, and it put the fear of God in her. The older Ruby got, the more like Jeffrey Banks she looked . . . the same sapphire blue eyes, the same thick dark brown hair, and that same proud way of entering a room. 'What makes yer think I'm afraid?' she asked light-heartedly, at the same time quietly regarding Ted's kind homely features. Ruby had easily passed for his daughter these many years, and he must go to his grave believing she was his.

He shrugged his shoulders. 'I don't know,' he admitted, 'It's just that – well, to be honest, Lizzie, I can't see no harm at all in Ruby sleeping at the Bankses', not when she's duty bound to work 'til late. And I for one don't want the lass wandering the streets looking for transport home.' There was curiosity in his voice as he went on, 'Honest to God, Lizzie, there's no rhyme or reason why you should be kicking up such a God almighty fuss.'

Lizzie felt cornered. The last thing she wanted to do was to raise his suspicions. He was a good and simple man, but he had touched on something dangerous when he asked her what she was afraid of. Sighing, she fell back into the chair, 'All right,' she reluctantly conceded, 'I'll think about it. But I'm not promising anything, mind.'

'You think on it, Lizzie, and you'll see I'm right,' he encouraged with a grin. When Lizzie nodded, he too settled back in his chair. 'The lass'll be all right, you'll see. And we shall have her here for Christmas Day.' He shook his head and tutted with amazement. 'By! To think our Ruby is fifteen years old come Christmas Day.' He turned and smiled on her. 'Time flies, Lizzie, lass.'

She nodded. It was true. Time did fly. Nigh on fifteen years ago, at four o'clock on Christmas morning, she had the easiest birth ever. Ruby popped into the world like a cork from a bottle; she had always been a laughing good-natured baby, affectionate and delightful, and now here she was, almost grown up, fetching a wage to her mammy, and a handsome young man down the road looking at her for his wife. By rights it should be plain sailing from now on. Yet some deep troubled instinct told Lizzie that her daughter's trials were only just beginning. And her own too.

'You will tell me all about the party, won't you, Ruby?' Maureen's eyes shone as she looked at her friend who was standing by the window. Across the room, the tiny grate emitted a cheery glow, warming the room until the heat was almost unbearable. Beside the bed stood a narrow cupboard, littered with all manner of paraphernalia: bottles of medicine, stone jars containing body-rubs and little phials of pills. Right in the corner stood a large brass candlestick, containing a round white blob of tallow that burned brightly, the flickering flame sending weird shadows all round the walls.

The smell in this room never changed – it was the smell of illness, a damp sweet smell that told Ruby she must cherish the times she and Maureen had together. Tonight the air was cloying, but as always Maureen had spent most of the day seated by the window. The curtains were still open and the moonlight poured in. Ruby looked out at the night sky, a vast expanse of ocean above, the same deep blue as her eyes, split here and there with trailing stars and etched in its middle was a bright yellow moon. The whole beautiful creation put Ruby in mind of the surface of Maureen's little cupboard, although in truth, it could not have been more different.

Invigorated by the sight of all that splendour, and feeling less confined because of it, she drew in a long deep sigh. Then, turning to Maureen, she said, 'Of course I'll tell you all about it. The very next morning I'll come and tell you about the pretty ladies and the handsome gents, and I'll remember the things they said and the clothes they wore, and the food on the table, and – oh it will be grand, I'm sure.' She laughed then skipped to her friend's side, where she fell to her knees, rolled her eyes heavenwards and sighed, 'Oh, Maureen, whatever will I do if our mam doesn't change her mind?'

'She will. Didn't you say you thought your dad might persuade her?'

'Well, he gave me a secret little look just now, so I'm hoping it will all come right.' Taking Maureen's slender fingers into her own, she tenderly stroked them. 'I haven't told you everything though,' she admitted with a wry little smile.

'Oh?' Maureen had guessed there was more. 'Come on then, Ruby Miller . . . out with it,' she laughed. 'You're up to something, aren't you?'

'Promise you won't tell?'

'Who would I tell?'

'Johnny.' The thought of him knowing how she was going to dress up like a lady and actually attend the gentry party was somehow disturbing to Ruby. In fact, for the very first time since she and Cicely had planned it, Ruby was ashamed. And then she was angry, irritated that he should raise such deep feelings in her. 'I *especially* don't want Johnny to know,' she exclaimed stiffly.

'Don't worry. He won't know from me,' Maureen promised with her hand on her heart. 'Go on then!' she urged, prodding Ruby impatiently. 'Tell me what you've been up to, you bad 'un.'

Ruby took a deep breath, then launched into a full account of how Cicely had come up with this exciting idea of dressing Ruby like a lady and introducing her to all the guests as a friend. She described the beautiful burgundy dress, and the four sessions in Cicely's quarters where the dressmaker had fitted it to her, cutting and trimming, sewing and shaping, until now it looked like it was made for her all along. She told of how Cicely's own hairdresser was going to attend her an hour before the party got underway.

And, so that Cook and the wretched girl would not find out, Cicely had arranged for them to have the evening off.

Maureen had heard Ruby refer to the other maid-servant before, and now she voiced her curiosity. 'Why do you call her "the wretched girl"?' she asked. 'Doesn't she have a name?'

Ruby thought about that at length. Presently she replied with a frown, 'I did once ask her what her name was, but she didn't tell me. So, if she does have another name, I don't know it. I've only ever heard Cook call her "the wretched girl". "Do this, you wretched girl. Do that, you wretched girl." She doesn't seem to mind anyway,' Ruby said with a bright smile.

'Well, *I* would!' Maureen declared with astonishment. But her astonishment reverted to curiosity as she returned to the question of the party. 'Did Cook ask whether you would be waiting on at the party?'

'Yes. But Cicely just told her not to concern herself about anything, that it was all taken care of.'

'Well, I never!' Maureen's eyes grew big and round as Ruby's story began to take shape. 'Aren't you afraid of being amongst all them fancy folk, and pretending to be someone you're not?' The very idea of walking into a roomful of such people filled her with dread. 'Oh, Ruby, I don't think you should. What if the master recognises you? He's bound to wonder. You could lose your work.' She hesitated, another possibility filling her with a worse horror. 'You could even be put in prison if you're found out.'

Ruby was unmoved. She had already said all these things to Cicely, and was assured there was no danger of anyone finding out the truth. There was only one person who could put a stop to it now, and Ruby prayed that she was being talked round at this very moment. 'It's up to our dad now,' she murmured hopefully.

'Tell me about the dress again.' Seeing that Ruby would not be talked out of it, Maureen let herself be drawn in and, as Ruby told her over again, the whole exciting plan became an adventure, a wonderful secret between the two of them, something that could only happen once in a lifetime, a tale to tell their children, and the children that came after.

Johnny was on his way up the stairs when he heard Ruby saying goodnight. He met her at the top of the stairs. 'Aw, you're not going yet, are you?' he asked. 'I was hoping to sit with you and Maureen awhile. Afterwards, I was going to walk you home.' He glanced down at the cup in his hand. Thankfully, the milky liquid was still steaming. 'I'm just on my way up with Maureen's drink. I'll not be a minute. Will you wait?'

Above them the lamp burned softly, bathing them in a warm halo of light. He thought he had never seen Ruby more lovely, nor more vulnerable. 'Let me walk you home,' he asked in a whisper, his arms aching to hold her. In this moment, with her dark eyes glowing and her hair tousled, she seemed like a small child. And his fear for her was tenfold.

'I'd like that,' she answered softly, smiling when she saw that her reply had surprised him. His closeness was strangely comforting to her; little things she had never noticed before sent a thrill through her senses. The brush of his trousers against her skirt, the way his shirt-sleeves were rolled up over the thickness of his arms, with the top buttons undone to show the broad strength of his chest. He was a good deal taller than her, and when he looked down with those magnificent eyes, she felt herself trembling. He was so close, so very close. In her mind's eye she saw his arms reach out, she felt them wind around her, she remembered his kiss, and suddenly she wanted him to kiss her again. It was her eyes that told him. Those sea blue eyes that lit her whole face with emotion, raising such hopes in him that he could hardly breathe.

Slowly, he bent his head, touching his mouth against hers. When he felt her press into him, he placed the cup on the step above and slid his two arms round her waist, drawing her into him. 'Wait for me,' he murmured against her mouth, and she shuddered in his arms. A long wonderful moment when they stayed locked in each other's arms and then he was going up the stairs two at a time. At the top he glanced back to make sure she was still there. When he saw that she was, he went quickly to Maureen's room where he put the cup into her hands.

'It's nearly cold,' she remarked with surprise. Normally when Johnny brought her late-night drink it was piping hot. When he apologised, she looked at him with a curious expression. He was breathless, and his handsome face was deeply flushed. Of course! Now she understood. 'Did you meet Ruby on the way down?' she asked mischievously.

He prepared to give an answer that would allay her suspicions, but she was smiling, teasing, and he knew she'd guessed. 'You little vixen!' he laughed.

'You'd best not keep her waiting,' she warned, 'Ruby's like the shadows on the wall. One minute she's here, and then she's gone.'

Without a word, he rushed out. Even before he reached the top of the stairs he knew she was not there. The warmth had gone from the house. The magic she always brought with her had evaporated, like the shadows Maureen had described. He fled down the stairs two at a time, along the passage and out into the street, just in time to see her disappear into her own house. He called but it was too late. Behind him he could hear his mother's voice. Sadly, he returned to her.

'Whatever's the matter with you?' she demanded. 'Rushing out of the house like that, and leaving the door open when there's such a cold breeze?' A thought occurred to her. 'Ruby's gone, has she?' He looked at her without speaking. 'Have you two had words?' she wanted to know.

'I wanted to see her home safely, that's all,' he explained.

'I'm sorry for leaving the door open.' He brushed past her, but she laid her hand on his shoulder.

'Is there anything between you two that I need to worry about?' she wanted to know.

'What do you mean?'

'Oh, I think you know what I mean,' she replied impatiently. 'Ruby's what? . . . fifteen? The pair of you are far too young to be thinking serious.'

He touched her hand, and when he spoke the corners of his mouth were uplifted in a wry little smile. 'Listen to you,' he chided. 'And who was it that got wed at sixteen?'

She was cornered and she knew it. 'Oh, all right, son. But if I could turn the clock back, I would have waited longer. Besides, things were different then.' She thought about her husband, and her mood saddened. 'Don't rush into anything,' she pleaded softly. 'If you get the lass in trouble, you'll have to wed her whether you like it or not. How does the old saying go? "Marry in haste, repent at leisure".'

He looked at her anxious face, and was sorry. All the same, she couldn't know how he felt about Ruby, how he had felt these many years, ever since she was old enough to toddle down the street holding hands with him. He could never envisage a future without Ruby at the heart of it. Tonight she had given him hope, and then cruelly snatched it away. Yet she wasn't cruel, only misguided, and driven by something he could never understand. A great weight pulled his spirit down. 'Leave it be, Mam. Ruby's all right.'

'I never said she wasn't . . . only that you were both too young.'

'Do you want me to wait up for Dad?'

'No. You've to be up early in the morning.' Realising he had deliberately changed the subject, she wisely went along with it. 'Didn't you say that old Thomas has need of you this Christmas

Eve? Something about the carriage and horses being got ready to take Oliver Arnold and his family to a particular party?'

'That's right, Mam.'

'Goodnight then.'

'Goodnight, Mam.' He bent down to kiss her. 'If he's not in soon, wake me and I'll go and find him,' he told her.

'I'll do no such thing!' she retorted. 'If he isn't in soon, I'm going to my own bed and your father can bloody well stay out.' She closed the door and followed him down the passage. She watched him go upstairs, his broad shoulders stooped and a heaviness to his steps. And she knew that it was all for Ruby.

Upstairs, Johnny sat on the edge of his sister's bed, his face confirming Maureen's suspicions. 'She wasn't there when you went down, was she?' she asked kindly.

'No.'

'Did you go after her?'

'No.'

'Why not?'

'She chose not to wait. It was her decision.'

'Ruby doesn't always make the right decision. She's impulsive.'

'I know it.'

'She *is* fond of you though.'

He looked up then, his dark eyes searching her face, 'Has she told you that?'

Not wanting to betray her friend's confidence, she answered simply, 'I just know, that's all.'

His strong fingers wrapped over hers as he said in a warm voice, 'I shouldn't be confiding my troubles in you, Sis. You've got enough to contend with.'

She looked at him for a while, thinking how much she loved these two. Ruby and Johnny were made for each other, yet there was always something that kept them apart. But they were very young, time was on their side and she would not despair. 'The day you stop confiding in me, I'll shrivel up and die,' she said, patting the back of his hand.

'I'll pretend you never said that,' he remarked grimly. Then, 'I expect Ruby confides in you too, doesn't she?' he asked hopefully.

'And if she does, you wouldn't want me to break a confidence, would you?'

He shook his head and smiled. 'Only if it was to my advantage,' he replied cheekily. When she remained silent, he told her in a serious voice, 'I'm glad you have Ruby for a friend. But then she and I are both lucky to have *you*. A man couldn't have a finer sister.' He reached out and drew her head on to his shoulder, his fingers lovingly stroking her hair. 'I pray for the day when you can go out, Sis,' he murmured.

'Where will you take me?'

'Where would you like to go?'

'Corporation Park . . . a picnic!' She twisted her neck to look up at him. 'I'd love to go on a picnic, Johnny . . . you, me and Ruby.' Excitement rushed through her at the thought. Then, to his horror, her breath caught in a sob and she was taken by a coughing fit.

Cradling his two hands over her thin shoulders, he eased her away, gently pressing her head into the pillow. 'You've had a long day, sweetheart,' he said firmly. 'And I'm all kinds of a fool for keeping you awake.' He kissed her on the forehead, 'Goodnight, God bless.'

She gazed up at him with soulful eyes, 'Don't worry too much about her, Johnny.'

'I won't,' he promised. 'Now get off to sleep.' Her eyes flickered and closed. 'Goodnight, Sis,' he murmured, then took the candle from the bedside cupboard and placed it on the dresser at the far side of the room. When his mother came up to check Maureen, she would take it away with her.

In his narrow room next door, Johnny lay awake for some long time, listening for his father to come home, thinking of Maureen and praying that she would get well. But, most of all, his heart was filled with thoughts of Ruby. Maureen had asked him to 'look out for her', and it was this that was playing on his mind. Tomorrow night Ruby would be mingling with the gentry. How in God's name could he keep an eye on her there, when he was duty bound to old Thomas and Arnold House? And, even if he wasn't working, he could never get within a mile of her, what with Cicely Banks there, and the gentry all around.

Maureen dreamed awhile, stirred then woke. Ruby was still on her mind, so real it was as though she was there in the room with her. 'Look after her, Lord,' she asked. 'Sometimes she has strange notions of grandeur, and she's so determined to make life easier for her family. She can never do that, you and I know it. But you have to make *her* know it too. Deep down, she's good and well-meaning so, please, Lord, don't let her come to no harm.'

Downstairs, Mrs Ackroyd waited for her wandering husband to come home. She was tired of these vigils. Her mind turned to thoughts of her daughter. She gave thanks to God that Maureen was making progress. It would be wonderful when the girl could go outside, but now that winter was rushing in with a vengeance, it would probably be spring before she could feel the sun on her face. Still, she was never lonely. Johnny spent many an hour with her. And it was good that Ruby came so often to sit with her. She was a fine and thoughtful creature, who had always been a loyal friend to Maureen.

Suddenly, Mrs Ackroyd recalled how Johnny had rushed into the street just now, leaving the door wide open behind him. He had deliberately given her the impression that he had walked Ruby home, when in fact it was plain to see that he must have been rushing after her. There was something brewing between these two, she thought, and them so young, so inexperienced. Yet, for all that, Johnny was a man, the breadwinner in this house, and he had a mind of his own. All the same, she couldn't help but feel that there would be tears before there was laughter.

In that quiet house, the thoughts of three people found a common bond. And the house was alive with Ruby's presence.

'Get off, before I change me mind!' Lizzie grabbed the infant from Ruby's arms. 'Go on. I'll see to the young 'uns. And get a move on or you'll have to run like the wind to catch that tram.'

Ruby got her coat from the nail behind the door. 'If you're sure, our mam,' she said, going to Dolly and giving her a hug. She would have hugged the twins, but they pushed her away, 'Gerrof. We're not babies!' they protested in unison. Lenny was wolfing down his breakfast, but made time to glare at her. 'You'd better not hug *me* neither,' he warned. And looking at his miserable face, Ruby thought there were umpteen things she would rather do.

Dolly sprang from her chair and ran to be hugged a second time. 'I want you to come home tonight,' she wailed.

'Aw.' Ruby held her tight. 'Will you miss me then?'

'Yes, 'cause there won't be nobody to keep me warm.'

'You ain't sleeping with us,' the twins yelled.

'I don't want to,' Dolly replied indignantly. 'You've got stinky feet.' At that there was uproar, and after rushing into the scullery to fetch the rolling pin, Lizzie banged it on the table. 'Which one of yer wants to cause trouble then?' she asked, glaring from one to the other and daring them to speak out. The silence was deafening until the infant started screaming and thrashing in Lizzie's arms. 'Go on, our Ruby,' her mother cried impatiently, plonking herself in the chair and pulling out a withered old tit which she crammed into the child's mouth. 'And mind you keep an account of yer hours. We don't want the buggers short-changing yer.'

Shrugging herself into her coat, Ruby came over to where her mam was seated. Lizzie's words might have put the fear of God into her, but she had mentioned to Cicely that her mam would be looking for extra wages if she didn't come home on Christmas Eve. Cicely had got it all in hand, so everything was all right. 'I'll be back tomorrow, Mam,' she said, fastening her arms round Lizzie's neck, then stiffened against her. 'Sorry, Mam,' she said softly. 'I know you're angry I gave my word without asking you first.' In that moment she was riddled with guilt. She had a strong urge to spill out the truth. But she stopped herself. 'Miss Cicely said she'll see I get home all right tomorrow.' As Cicely had rightly pointed out, there was no transport on Christmas Day.

Lizzie shook her away. 'She'll do no such thing, my girl!' she said angrily. 'I'll not have you turning up in this street in some fancy carriage. Besides, you've not been asked to work on Christmas Day, have yer?'

'No. The family are going out straight after breakfast, visiting an old aunt, and they won't be back until late.'

'Right. So, I'll expect you home no later than mid-day. And not in no posh carriage neither, 'cause you'll *walk*. After all, it's no more than two or three mile from Billenge End to Fisher Street.'

'It's more like *five*!' Lenny interrupted with a snigger. 'But it'll serve her right.'

Lizzie shut him up with a withering glance. 'You'd best get off,' she told Ruby. 'You're wasting precious time.' She bent her head to the infant and kept it there, even when she sensed Ruby glancing back at her just before she went into the passage and out of the house.

'I'm sorry, lass,' she murmured beneath the ensuing bedlam. 'But I don't hold with yer sleeping at no gentry's house, an' I never will.' All the same, even when she was yelling at the young 'uns to: 'Stop yer noise or I'll tan yer arses!' she was thinking of her eldest daughter. In fact, it took only a few minutes before she deeply regretted not saying cheerio with a better heart.

Putting the infant into its bed, she rushed down the passage. 'Ruby!' she called out. 'Ruby, lass!' She flung the door open and looked anxiously down the street. There was a stream of mill-workers, and others going to the foundry, but there was no sign of her bonny child. 'Damn and bugger it, Lizzie Miller!' she moaned. 'Yer an old fool, and yer should be ashamed.'

Dejected, she returned to the parlour where Dolly told her with tearful eyes, 'You never kissed our Ruby goodbye.'

'Never mind, sweetheart,' Lizzie told her, 'I'll hug her twice over when she comes home the morrow, and we'll bake her a nice little cake for her birthday. What d'yer say to that, eh?'

Dolly laughed and clapped her hands. 'Can I put a silver threepence in it?' she cried jubilantly.

'We'll see, lass. Happen I've got one tucked away in me purse somewhere.'

'Huh!' Lenny snorted, giving the table leg a sound kick. 'I never got a silver threepence on *my* birthday.'

'That's because Dad got you a pair of boxing gloves from the tatter-man, and they cost *fourpence*,' Frank reminded him.

'Well, I'd rather have had the fourpence,' grumbled Lenny, ''cause them gloves are no good at all. They're old and stiff, and I don't want them.'

'I'll have 'em!' Ralph cried.

Lizzie was furious. 'Yer ungrateful little bugger. We've all gone without so you could have them gloves, and now yer say yer don't want 'em? You'd best not let yer dad hear yer say that, my lad.'

'Well, I *don't* want 'em. If I can't have a proper pair, I'd rather not have any at all!' He was defiant. 'I never asked for the rotten 'things in the first place.' He made a hard fist and shook it at her. 'I don't need them anyway, 'cause I could knock Roy Marner from one end of the road to the other if I wanted.'

'I'll tell yer what yer do want,' Lizzie retorted furiously, 'and that's the flat of me hand on yer arse.' She never could abide braggery. 'Get off to the scullery and wash yerself.'

'Aw, Mam, I'm only playing out. Why do I have to get washed?'

'Because I say so.'

'You're allus picking on me,' he moaned, skulking away from the table and reluctantly heading for the scullery.

'Is that so?' Lizzie was used to his pathetic little games and she was having nothing of it. 'If yer don't want picking on, yer shouldn't behave like a bone-head.' At this the twins creased up laughing. But they soon sobered up when Lizzie gave them one of her fiercest glances. She returned her attention to Lenny. 'And mind yer wash behind yer ears,' she said loudly, 'else I'll have ter take a scrubbing brush and do the job meself.'

'All right, Mam,' he answered sweetly. He knew he'd gone too far, but he wasn't a bit repentant. In fact, even while Lizzie was still talking, he hid behind the door to stretch out his tongue, at the same time waggling his fingers at either side of his head to make a demon face. 'One of these days I'll show you all,' he muttered bitterly. 'Then you'll laugh on the other side of your faces!'

Chapter Six

'I'm afraid something will go horribly wrong.' Ruby climbed into the perfumed bath-water while Cicely busied herself laying out the towels and silken underwear. 'When will you tell your father?' That was the moment she dreaded more than anything.

'Oh, there's time enough,' Cicely said with a little chuckle. 'I've a good mind *not* to tell him though,' she said mischievously.

'What do you mean?' Ruby slithered deeper into the water and sighed aloud as the smooth rich lather bathed her nakedness. 'You must tell him. But I know he won't allow it,' she murmured. 'Then all this will be for nothing.' Suddenly she was upright in the water and staring at Cicely with shocked eyes. 'Maureen said I would lose my job.' She was horrified because only yesterday Cicely had told her that, after the holiday, she was being upgraded to lady's maid. 'What if Maureen's right? Oh, Cicely, how could I ever go back and tell my mam that I'd lost my job? And worse . . . how could I tell her *why*? She'd never forgive me if she knew what I was up to right now.' When a feeling of guilt overwhelmed her, she hung her head. 'Happen we should forget the whole idea. Happen I should get dressed and help *you* get ready for this evening.' Now, at this late hour, when soon it would be too late to turn back, Ruby was beginning to have second thoughts.

'You'll do no such thing,' Cicely told her. 'I've been looking forward to this evening for weeks. Oh, don't worry, it will be all right.' She knelt down by the bath and looked into Ruby's anxious eyes. 'I wouldn't enjoy it at all if you weren't there,' she confided. 'And anyway, why shouldn't you be there? You're as good as any of us, Ruby Miller, and don't you ever forget that.'

'Aw, Cicely, I don't belong,' she protested. 'You're a lady and I'm a servant. According to my mam, the two are like oil and water. They make a bad mix, that's what she says, and I'm beginning to think she's right.'

Cicely was adamant. 'Much as I believe your mother is a wise and wonderful woman, I have to disagree . . . at least where you and I are concerned.' She clambered to her feet. 'If I had a sister, I'd want her to be exactly like you,' she said fondly. And then she said something that was astonishing to Ruby. 'What would you say if I told you my great-great-grandfather was a footman in one of the big houses along Park Street?'

Ruby was shocked. 'Honestly?' She would never have dreamed it in a million years. 'Who would have thought it? Your great-great-grandfather – a footman.' She was wide-eyed and delighted as she smoothed the soap over her arms and shoulders 'Well, I never!' she chuckled. 'Well, I never!'

Cicely was satisfied that her little ploy had made Ruby think hard. She hadn't exactly lied, nor had she told the truth. She had merely implied that one of her relations had been a footman in order to put her and Ruby on a common level. In fact, the Banks family came from a long line of wealthy aristocrats, and if her father knew what she had just told Ruby, his hair would have turned snow white on the spot. 'So you see,' Cicely said coyly, 'deep down we're the same, only somewhere along the way Fortune smiled on me. It could so easily have been you living in a big house and I could have been the maid.' She gathered Ruby's clothes from the chair and placing them over her arm, crossed to the door, reminding her with a chuckle, 'It's too late to change your mind, Ruby Miller. Miss Armitage will be here any minute to dress your hair, and soon after that the guests will be arriving.' She knew the reason for Ruby's anxiety, and if truth were told, she also was concerned about her father's reaction to this little 'arrangement' between her and Ruby. However, on occasions when it was called for, Jeffrey Banks's daughter could be just as stubborn as her father. *This* was such an occasion. There was fighting spirit in her voice as she told Ruby now, 'I'm going down to check the caterers. Then I shall see my father.' She gave a reassuring little wink. 'Don't you worry. I'll have him eating out of my hand in no time.'

'You won't be long, will you?' Ruby was convinced that within the hour she would be leaving this house bag and baggage never to set foot over its threshold again.

'Trust me.'

'I do.'

'Good girl. When you've bathed, you'll find some new undergarments on the bed.'

Ruby watched the door close. 'What have I got myself into?' she thought forlornly, looking up at the ceiling as though she might see the answer there. She thought of how the master would react when his daughter told him that she had invited a *servant* to his Christmas Eve party. The thought of father and daughter face to face because of her, sent shivers down her spine. Not for one minute did Ruby believe the master would give his approval; which was why Cicely had toyed with the idea of not telling him . . .'

'We'll let him find out on the evening,' she'd told Ruby. 'I know he won't cause a fuss in front of everybody.'

But Ruby had been adamant. 'You *must* ask his permission,' she'd insisted, 'or we'll have to forget it.'

The thought of being exposed in front of everyone was like a nightmare. Fancy the master recognising her, dressed in a fancy gown and hob-nobbing with his guests! Like as not he would send her packing there and then, in front of everybody. No, he had to be told. That way, she might escape a worse punishment.

Bearing the look of a young woman with a purpose, Cicely made straight for the dining-room where she satisfied herself that the table was laid with the very best china and that everything was as it should be. The round-faced young woman was putting the last touches to the flower arrangements. 'That looks wonderful,' Cicely said with approval. The woman glowed pink with pride. 'Thank you, ma'am,' she said gratefully, and Cicely left her to it.

Going across the main hall to the inner passage, she went swiftly down the narrow staircase that led to the kitchen. The noise of bustle and activity came to her as she approached the half-open door. Sweeping into the kitchen, Cicely glanced around. There was always a feeling of great comfort and warmth in this big old kitchen; a sprawling room with a cheery glow emanating from its huge range whose flames were reflected in the batteries of iron and copper saucepans, frying-pans, skillets, skimmers and sieves hanging from the ceiling or lining shelves.

The two confident females flitting about the range clutching steaming cooking pots turned in unison to stare at her, each one dipping ever so slightly in a curtsey. Then, when Cicely quickly moved away, nervous that her presence might cause them to drop the cooking pots, they went about their duties all the more vigorously. These two, and the young woman in the dining-room, were temporary staff, employed for the occasion. The pantry door was half-open, its many shelves groaning beneath the weight of prepared food, all ready to be put into the dumb waiter and sent up to the dining-room; there was fresh pink fish, dainty slices of beef, pork and ham, there was an enormous fowl on an oblong, flower-patterned plate and a generous selection of mouth-watering desserts, all beautifully dressed and set out in fine china dishes.

Sensing someone behind her, Cook glanced round, giving a small cry when she saw that it was the mistress of the house. Her round face was bright pink, and she looked unusually flustered. 'Good heavens!' she exclaimed with the brightest smile, although she secretly believed that Cicely was far too young and inexperienced to be in charge of such a fine house as this, 'I didn't hear you come in, miss,' she explained. Her face dropped as she went on, 'There's nothing wrong, is there?'

'Of course not,' Cicely said. 'I'm just making certain you have everything you need?'

'Oh, yes, I have. That I have.' She waved her arm to encompass the entire room. 'You can see for yourself, everything's fine,' she boasted, swelling with pleasure when Cicely told her how clever she was to have secured the same excellent help that had served them so well last Christmas. 'Well, seeing as these three came with first-class references, and seeing as, like you say, they did a good job last year, I writ their addresses down in my little book,' she replied grandly. Then a frown crossed her face. 'Sadly, there are any number of first-class servants to be had, all out of work and glad of a day's pay.'

Cicely lowered her voice so as not to be heard. 'Since I've taken Ruby as lady's maid, you'll be needing a replacement for her. I had thought to leave it until the New Year, but, if you think it advisable we can deal with the matter sooner?' She glanced around. 'Perhaps one of these three ladies here tonight might be suitable, do you think?'

'Well, yes.' Cook positively beamed. 'To my way of thinking, you wouldn't do better than the fair-haired lass over there.' She flicked her eyes towards the smaller of the two women carefully stirring the contents of a cooking pot. Somehow, she had taken a liking to that one. 'They're all hard workers,' she confessed, 'but that little miss has an instinct, if you know what I mean? She don't need telling what to do every two minutes.'

'Good. Then mark her in your little book,' Cicely told her, 'and we'll talk about it on your return the day after tomorrow.'

'Oh, dear!' Cook nervously bit her bottom lip. 'I do feel bad, leaving the house on Christmas Eve of all days.'

'Nonsense!' Cicely remarked.

'And you don't mind me taking the wretched girl with me?'

'You know I don't. In fact, I think it's a very generous idea, especially when the poor thing has no family of her own.'

'Thank you, miss,' she said gratefully. 'And to be honest, I am looking forward to it, and that's the truth.'

'Then it's settled. You can go whenever you're ready and I'll see you on your return.'

In a hurry now, Cicely went quickly from the kitchen and on up to the library. The sooner she faced her father, the better.

Jeffrey Banks sprang out of his chair like the gentleman he was. 'Cicely, my dear,' he remarked. 'Come in. Sit down.' When she was seated in the barrel-chair on one side of his desk, he rounded it and resumed his own position in the comfortable red leather arm-chair. Facing her with a gleam of pleasure in his sharp eyes, he rested his hands on the desk. 'Well, young lady,' he said, still beaming up at her with loving eyes, 'I trust everything's in order?'

'Of course, and why shouldn't it be?' Cicely leaned forward, perching on the edge of her chair and returning his smile with a confidence that belied her anxiety. She was afraid that when she imparted the real nature of her errand to him, there would likely be an explosion. Well, thank goodness he was in a buoyant and receptive mood, she thought hopefully.

'No reason, my dear,' he assured her. 'I always panic immediately before the guests arrive. You should know that by now.' Taking hold of the chain which was draped over his waistcoat, he tugged at it until the round silver watch sprang from his pocket and fell into his palm. 'It's fifteen minutes to six o'clock. They'll be here within the hour.'

'I don't think so,' she reminded him. 'The invitation was for eight o'clock, and it would be bad manners on the part of the guests to arrive before then.'

'Ah!' He tucked his thumbs into his waistcoat pocket, leaned back in his chair and laughed out loud. 'That's what you say every year, and there are still those who turn up an hour before time.'

'Only those who don't know better.'

'Ah, but they do know that I keep only the finest brandy in my cellar. The reason they arrive early is to fire their souls ahead of the others.' He smiled. 'Connoisseurs every one.' He beamed at her. 'Do you know, Cicely, I find myself looking forward to this evening.' He lifted his chin, pursed his mouth and peered at her. 'Hmh! Something tells me it will be an immensely enjoyable evening.' He waited for a like response from his daughter, then, when it wasn't forthcoming, felt a little foolish. He studied her hard for a moment, before asking with a concerned voice, 'Are you all right, young lady?'

'What makes you ask?'

'You seem . . .' He shook his head slowly, narrowed his eyes and concentrated on her face, his quick mind searching for the right word. 'I don't know – a little too *quiet*, perhaps?' He sat forward in his chair, his fists clenched on the desk as he asked in a subdued voice, 'There aren't any problems, are there?'

'No. There are no problems, Father. I've just come from downstairs now, and I can assure you, your guests will have the best of everything. I'm quite certain that Cook will outshine herself. She deserves the day off tomorrow, and I know she's bound to return in a better mood for the visit to her sister.' As was her duty, Cicely always informed her father as to every move that was made in the house. 'Did I tell you she's taking the scullery maid with her?'

He nodded. 'Cook is hard outside and toffee inside,' he said good-naturedly. 'That poor wretched girl can't be good company over the holidays. And what about *you*?'

'Me?'

'Yes. No doubt you, like Cook, will outshine yourself? Or should I say outshine Teresa Arnold?' he added with a sly little look.

Cicely smiled demurely. Teresa Arnold was very young, but her reputation went before her. Even the tradesmen had told Cook how, by all accounts, Oliver Arnold's eldest daughter cost him a fortune in fine clothes and fast horses. What was more, it was said that she was growing impatient to wear the mantle of lady of the house. On Cicely's last visit to the milliner, she herself had overheard how Teresa Arnold was not only extravagant but 'arrogant', 'bold', 'petulant', and 'quite a stranger to good manners and patience'. Cicely answered her father's remark with tact. 'I shall do my very best to please you, Father,' she said, 'Miss Armitage should be here at any moment, and no doubt she will see that I am meticulously turned out as usual.'

'So it's all running smoothly?'

She smiled demurely. 'Yes, Father. It's all running smoothly.'

'That's what I like to hear. Of course, you've never let me down yet.' He knew full well that she was a first-class hostess and nothing would be left to chance. 'All the same, what with all of your duties and everything to oversee, I do think you were wise to avail yourself of young Ruby's services this evening.'

'I meant to tell you – as from today, Ruby is employed as lady's maid.'

'Wonderful, my dear.' His head nodded up and down in fervent agreement. 'In fact, I'm delighted. You must have been the only young lady of consequence in the whole of Lancashire who was without a personal maid.'

'Ruby's duties will be more of a companionable nature, I think, Father. I shall always prefer to dress myself, thank you. If I was incapacitated, the situation might be different, but as it is I'm quite capable of brushing my own hair and choosing which shoes I wear with which outfit. Although on special occasions, such as this evening, I am more than happy to call on the admirable skills of Miss Armitage,' she told him firmly.

'You're stubborn, that's all. Just as you're stubborn about other matters which concern me.'

'And I don't think I need to ask what these other matters are?' she said wryly.

'You know well enough,' he replied in an injured tone. 'Oh, Cicely! I do wish you would think about my earlier suggestion.'

'Which was?' As if she didn't know.

'You know very well what I'm referring to,' he said wearily. 'It's all to do with your status, my dear. I still heartily believe you are wrong to take on the responsibility of housekeeper in addition to everything else.'

'Have you cause to complain?'

'Not at all, but . . .'

'No "buts", Father. I could never idle away my time while another woman kept your house. How many times must I stress that I love being responsible for the running of this house? Please don't confuse me with Teresa Arnold, who by all accounts would have half the population waiting on her if she had her way. Added to which, her father is one of the wealthiest men in the north-west.'

'We have more than enough money for our needs,' her father retaliated. 'We may not be in quite the same league as the eloquent Oliver Arnold, but we are very well-off, my dear.'

'I know that, Father. But it isn't a matter of money with me, and well you know it. I do actually enjoy running this household,' she argued. 'Besides, how else would I fill my days?' Even as she spoke, Cicely realised she had foolishly opened the way for him.

'Like any other young woman,' he replied meaningfully. 'Meeting people of your own age, and taking an interest in what goes on outside your own four walls.' He had long been concerned with her growing reluctance to leave this house.

'Do you really mean me to attend these hateful little gatherings that take place in the drawing rooms of aged dowagers and busybodies with nothing better to occupy their minds?' There was contempt in her voice. 'Really, Father! Can you see me attending these frivolous women's groups? Meetings of frustrated old women who assemble for afternoon tea and indulge in the latest gossip? Perhaps you feel it right that I should exhibit myself? Perhaps you want it known that I might be "available" if the young man is "suitable" enough?' He had touched on a delicate issue, and she resented it.

He was mortified. 'Oh, dear me! Dear, dear me!' He would have got out of his chair and pacified her, but was still held by her angry blue eyes. 'You misunderstand me, my dear,' he said lamely. 'I didn't mean to imply *anything*, and well you know it.' He hated himself for being so clumsy. Oh, he couldn't deny that he would have liked his daughter to be courted by some 'suitable' young man. And, yes, it was true that he would like to see Cicely mixing with people of her own calibre. And if, during the course of her social activities, she was introduced to members of the opposite sex – then so long as they met with his approval there wouldn't be anyone more delighted than himself. He had long felt that his daughter was in danger of becoming a hermit in this house, a spinster who would end her days all alone. The thought was a source of sorrow to him. Besides, what man didn't ache for a grandson? Especially when that man was a man of property, who craved a male heir to carry on the family name.

'I know,' she murmured, her mood suddenly subdued, 'I know you didn't mean anything. But we've gone over all this before, and you know my own views on the matter, Father. I'm happy as I am. I've never found it easy to make friends, and though I happily carry out my duties as hostess in this house, I have no love of socialising in other people's drawing rooms. You're right. Perhaps I should be thinking about young men, and becoming a wife before it's too late. But I will not deliberately go out looking for a husband, and I will not be paraded from house to house in the hope that I may meet this "suitable" young man. If I'm to be a spinster, then so be it.'

She saw the hurt in his eyes and her tongue was stilled. In her heart, she knew how desperately he wanted her to be wed and to provide him with an heir. She went to him then and murmured softly, 'Oh, look, I'm sorry if I'm a disappointment to you, Father. I've always been painfully shy amongst strangers outside my own home. It doesn't worry me though,' she lied, 'I really am content in my own company.'

'Whatever you say,' he muttered reluctantly. Although secretly he clung to his hopes of walking her down the aisle, and one day holding his own grandson in his arms.

Relieved, she kissed the top of his head. 'Anyway, I have you,' she said warmly. 'And I have this beautiful old house to live in. What else would I need?' The truth was, she was not altogether happy and realised he must sense that. There were times when she was incredibly lonely. Days when, if it wasn't for Ruby's friendship, the hours would seem like a lifetime. It hurt her to know how concerned her father was, and though she knew he was well-meaning, his words always struck home. Didn't he realise there were times when she ached with loneliness? But then, how could he know of her longing for love and motherhood? Yet, she could not change the way she was. The very idea of sitting in some archaic and dingy drawing room, sipping tea and being scrutinised by a gaggle of old and curious women who revelled in other people's business was enough to give her nightmares. Apart from her father, she had only one other real friend in all the world. That friend was Ruby. And thinking of her now brought Cicely back to her purpose. 'Father,' she began carefully, reaching out and taking the guest list from his tray, 'I said there were no problems. In fact, there is just one.'

'Oh?' He sat upright and turned his face up to her. 'Then we had better deal with it, don't you think?'

Placing the sheet of paper on the desk, she told him, 'If you cast your eyes down the guest list, you'll see that the men outnumber the ladies.'

'Really?' He was glad that the previous subject had been brought to an end. It always unnerved him when Cicely took offence at his innocent words. His daughter was everything to him and he would never knowingly hurt her. Gratefully, he brought his attention to the matter in hand. He was puzzled. 'I thought you'd rectified that particular matter? Wasn't that the reason we decided to extend the Arnold invitation to include his daughter, Teresa?' He frowned as a thought occurred to him. 'Oh dear, she's turned down our invitation?'

'No, no,' Cicely was quick to assure him. 'Along with her father and brother, Teresa Arnold has accepted the invitation.' She was cautiously leading up to an issue much more important to her, and her stomach was nervously fluttering. She had convinced Ruby that everything would be all right, but now, she wasn't sure whether her father would put paid to their well-laid plans. 'All the same, it means the numbers are uneven,' she persisted.

'Well, it's too late to do anything about it now,' he sighed. 'This only bears out what I've been saying about you having far too much responsibility. And you've always been so meticulous in the past.'

'It isn't too late, and I do have a solution. You see, Father, the numbers were not an oversight.'

'Not an oversight?' he repeated, his face wreathed in frowns. 'Then perhaps you had better explain?' He was obviously puzzled.

'I have invited a dear friend, and she'll be seated beside me if that's all right with you, Father?'

His eyes widened in surprise. 'A friend?' he exclaimed. 'Oh, my dear, that's wonderful!' He grabbed her hand and feverishly patted it. 'Who is she . . . this friend? Wherever did you meet her? Does she come from a good family? And why haven't I been introduced?' The last question was delivered with a mildly disapproving stare.

'My goodness!' Cicely exclaimed. 'All these questions. I met her here, in this very house, and yes, she does come from a good family. As for your being introduced – well now, there was no need for that. You see, she's well known to you already, Father. In fact, you see her every day.' She was beginning to enjoy her little game, especially now that she had him at a disadvantage. All the same, she was still anxious about how he would react when he realised it was Ruby who was going to be seated beside her at the dinner table, instead of waiting on it as was her normal place in this house.

He stared at her then. The smile had gone from his mouth and his eyes grew darker. 'How can I possibly see her every day, as you say?' he asked cautiously. Already he was growing suspicious. She didn't answer straight-away, and he asked again, 'Cicely, who is this young lady?'

Swallowing hard, she stood up straight and met his eye with dignity. 'It's Ruby,' she answered.

In an instant he was on his feet. 'Ruby?' His astonishment was obvious in his expression and in the low disbelieving voice in which he uttered Ruby's name. 'Are you telling me that you want

Ruby Miller . . . a servant in this house . . . to attend as a guest this evening?'

Convinced that she was just jesting with him, he forced his mouth into a nervous smile, but it fell open when she answered his question with a brave nod of the head and a bold remark that caused him to fall back in his chair. 'Ruby is very dear to me, Father. And I'm determined she will be there. If you exclude her, then you exclude me.'

There then followed a heated discussion during which Jeffrey Banks argued the order of things in society, pointing out with great deliberation how Ruby would feel ill at ease in such a situation for: 'Even you are not altogether happy surrounded by people.' He went on to talk about protocol, and he made every attempt to persuade her that she was utterly wrong to think such a thing could ever be arranged. 'What? I could never agree to it. NEVER!' he stormed. He paced the room with his hands behind his back, and ranted on, stopping every now and then to glare at her. Then he would smile and entreat her to think about the enormity of the undertaking. 'Never in my life have I heard of such a thing!' he protested. Finally, mentally and physically exhausted, he fell into his chair. Spinning himself round and staring across at the window, he said in a spent voice, 'I will not allow it.'

'Very well, Father.' She turned on her heel and began to make her way towards the door.

'Where are you going?' He swung round, lurching forward in his chair. 'What do you intend to do now?' he asked. When she turned and smiled with frustrating calm she seemed like a stranger to him, and it struck him in that moment that his daughter was made of stronger stuff than he had imagined.

'Don't worry, Father,' she assured him, 'I shall see that everything is taken care of before I leave for the evening. Of course I'll return first thing in the morning.' Her smile grew sweeter, then with a determined flourish she turned her back to him. Her hand was already turning the door knob when he spoke again. And this time he was pleading.

'It could never work, my dear. You must see how impossible it is? Ruby is a splendid young lady, and I do agree with you . . . she does come from a good home.' And who should know better than he what a proud and delightful woman her mother was. 'I have nothing detrimental to say about the girl's background. But what I *am* saying, my dear, is that Ruby is a maid and you are her mistress. What I *am* saying is that her experience of life is far different from *your* experience of life. Ruby could no more be a high-born lady than you could be a low-born servant. Oh, and what I am *not* saying is that one is any better than the other . . . just vastly different, that's all. No doubt there are those among our guests who lack Ruby's moral fibre and good manners, and there are as many "undesirables" in higher society as there are in the back streets of any town. I am not denying that for a moment.'

'Well then?'

'The whole idea is unthinkable. Besides, the poor girl would be out of her depth.'

'So you still forbid it?'

'OF COURSE I FORBID IT!' He sprang from his chair and strode across the room. 'What in God's name made you dream up such a fearful idea?'

Instead of answering his question, Cicely told him calmly, 'As I say, Father, you don't need to worry about this evening. Everything will be taken care of, you have my word.'

'Go on then,' he snapped. 'Do what you must, because I will not allow such a thing under this roof and that's an end to it.' He watched her go. He waited until the door was closed behind her. He scowled, he muttered, and he listened to her footsteps receding further and further. And he knew she had got him exactly where she wanted him, just like she always had. 'Damn and bugger it!' he groaned. The irony of the situation made him chuckle. The chuckle became louder, then became a full-bodied laugh which he abruptly stemmed for fear that she would hear.

He found himself thinking of Lizzie, Ruby's mother who had been his own salvation when he desperately needed someone to love. In all these years he had not forgotten how he had found solace and comfort in her willing arms. They had made love here in this very house, in the very bed where he still slept. How could he forget what that darling woman had meant to him?

Even now, in those private moments when he was especially lonely, he had only to close his eyes and she would be in his arms again, that delightful wide-awake face gazing up at him, filling his heart with pleasure. So many years had passed between, so much time, and they had each travelled their own predestined paths. That was the way it should be, and they both accepted that. But he couldn't deny that there had been murmuring regrets, nor could he deny the fondness he still nursed for Lizzie. Not high passion the way it had been on that first night when he had taken her to himself and she had clung to him with all the love a woman can give, but a kind of love all the same.

In a minute he had flung open the door, his frantic eyes searching the stairway for his daughter. 'Cicely!' he called, going forward into the hall.

'Yes, Father?' She was partway up the stairs when his voice caused her to turn round. She was half-smiling.

It was a moment before he answered, and when he did, it was with a great sigh. 'Have you decided to be sensible?'

'No, Father.'

'Where is she?'

'In my bath tub.'

He winced and sighed again. 'Has your dresser arrived?'

'Not yet.'

'Does she know the girl? I mean . . . has she seen Ruby Miller on her previous visits?'

'No. Miss Armitage never goes downstairs. She arrives, attends to me, and then she leaves. Usually I myself answer the door to her.'

'Then you shouldn't!' He clenched his fists in exasperation. 'You must leave that to the servants.'

'Yes, Father.'

'This woman, Miss Armitage – she must not know.'

'She will be told only that Ruby is a friend.' She sensed his weakening. '*No one* will know. Not even Cook.'

He snorted. 'No doubt this little escapade has been planned for some long time?'

'Not really.' She started forward, her eyes shining with anticipation. 'Oh, Father, Ruby will make you proud, you'll see!'

'Enough of that! What you've done has made me very angry.' He waved his hand impatiently, causing her to stop in her tracks. A thoughtful pause while they stared at each other, then reluctantly Jeffrey said, 'When she's ready, bring her before me.'

'Thank you, Father.' Her smile broadened triumphantly.

'I don't promise anything.'

'Of course not, Father.' She went on her way, quickening her steps the nearer she came to the bedroom.

Ruby's heart skipped a beat when she heard the footsteps approaching. She had bathed and dried herself though her hair was still a little damp. Now she was seated on the edge of the bed, dressed in the soft clinging undergarments that Cicely had laid out. Somehow it seemed to Ruby that she belonged here. It felt so right. And her sense of well-being only further inspired her to work her way up in the world, so that her family could savour the better things in life.

Suddenly the door was flung open and there stood Cicely. Ruby had been anxiously waiting to hear what had been said downstairs, but now she didn't have to ask because Cicely's face said it all. A tide of joy surged through her as she ran across the room to throw herself into Cicely's arms. 'YOU DID IT!' she cried. 'Oh, Cicely, how did you ever persuade him?' She could hardly believe it, and said so.

'Well, you'd *better* believe it,' Cicely told her, leading Ruby back across the room to where she swung open the wardrobe door and there, in all its glory, was the magnificent burgundy gown. 'He wants to see you when you're ready,' she said grandly.

'Oh. You mean he wants to inspect me?'

'And if he does?'

'Well, I don't know.' Doubts began to creep in. 'He has given permission, hasn't he? At least, I thought so from the look on your face when you came back just now.'

'Trust me, Ruby. Everything is going to be fine. Just fine. Miss Armitage will be here any minute, and she must see you first. Here.' She stooped to the drawer beneath the hanging robe and took out a dry towel. 'Rub at your hair. It needs to be drier before she can arrange it,' Cicely pointed out, lifting a hank of Ruby's rich brown hair and feeling it between finger and thumb. 'Meanwhile, I'd better make a start on myself. When you stand before Father, I wouldn't miss it for the world.'

In that moment the outer bell rang. Without delay Cicely rushed out of the room and down the curving stairway. Through the vestibule window she could see the outline of a woman's figure, straight and prim, with a tiny round hat atop her head and a bulky bag clutched in her hand. It was Miss Armitage, pamperer to the privileged. 'Come in, please,' Cicely said with a wide smile. 'We haven't much time. I wasn't able to let you know, because I didn't know myself until a few moments ago, but a very dear friend of mine has arrived so there'll be two of us to be got ready.'

Miss Armitage was a woman of few words, and gave none

now. She merely nodded in that marvellously confident manner for which she was renowned, and in a moment she and Cicely were on their way upstairs to where Ruby was waiting with growing excitement.

Coming out of the library, Jeffrey Banks saw the two ladies mounting the stairway. 'Heaven help us all!' he muttered. Then he dodged back into the library, closed the door and went straight to the dresser where he poured himself a small measure of brandy. 'I have a feeling I might live to regret this day,' he muttered, swilling the fiery liquid down his throat, and suffering a coughing fit.

At precisely twenty minutes to seven there came a polite tap on the door before it was pushed open to admit two young women into the library. 'What do you think, Father?' Cicely's proud glance went from her father to Ruby, and back again to her father. 'Doesn't she look every inch a lady?'

He stared and stared, and at first could not recognise the young woman before him. Dressed in a fine gown of burgundy, and with her thick shining hair rolled into a halo about her elfin face, Ruby seemed like a stranger. And, yes, as Cicely so aptly put it, she was 'every inch a lady'. More than that, she was incredibly beautiful. Her midnight blue eyes were glowing, her mouth was lightly painted and her hair was without parting, brushed and bouncing and framing her face with deep, earth-coloured waves. At her throat she wore a simple black velvet band. The gown was sheer luxury, the height of elegance, and fitted her figure with perfection. Round sleeves and a waspish waist brought out the curves of her slight figure, and where the silken folds fell gracefully to the hem, the entire effect was breathtaking. She was taller, more mature, astonishingly sophisticated. And he couldn't tear his gaze away.

'Aren't you surprised?' Cicely insisted. 'Doesn't Ruby look wonderful?' She was standing between the two of them now, looking from one to the other. 'Have you ever seen anyone so beautiful, Father?' she said in awed tones.

It was a seemingly endless time before he answered. All he could hear was the one word, 'beautiful'. And, yes, Ruby Miller was certainly that. He was shocked by the vision she made. He had always seen her as little more than a child; although in truth it was not unknown for a working girl to wed and bear a man two or three children when she was not all that much older than Ruby was now.

Beneath his scrutiny, Ruby stood tall and confident. It was almost as though, in putting on this gown, she had become someone else, someone more important. Someone worthwhile. It was a good feeling. Oh, how she would have loved for her mother to see her now. Yet, it wasn't to be. All the same, Ruby hated having to deceive her mother. She so much wanted to share this experience with the one who meant more than anything in the world to her. But Lizzie could never understand, and the knowledge that she would have ripped the gown from her daughter's back dissipated Ruby's pleasure. She stood, straight and still, her throat tight and her limbs slightly trembling, while the master continued to look at her with curious eyes. It would have been a shocking revelation to her if she had only known how Jeffrey Banks was mentally comparing her to her mother.

His gaze wandered over Ruby's lovely face. He wanted to see Lizzie there. He looked for her, but no, Ruby was infinitely different. Where Lizzie had been pretty, her daughter was strikingly handsome. Where Lizzie had charm, Ruby had something more devastating . . . a certain presence, a charisma that struck at the heart. Lizzie had stirred pleasure in him, and love, and a need for her companionship. Ruby, however, struck him dumb, as she would any man. Suddenly, Cicely's words came into his mind: 'She'll make you proud'. That was what she had promised, and now he understood. That was exactly how he felt in that moment. *He felt proud of Ruby!* Just as he had always felt proud of his own daughter. He recalled something he had said to her earlier. 'Ruby is low-born, and you are high-born.' That was what he had said. But now he continued to gaze at Ruby, and was aware of the stupidity of his words. For all her ordinary background, Ruby Miller showed a quality that many women from noble families might envy. She had a rare natural elegance. There was something about her, something uniquely special, and all of his resolve to disapprove of her melted away. 'You really are a surprising and lovely young lady,' he murmured.

At once there was a cry from Cicely as she ran to plant a kiss on his face. 'Oh, Father, I *knew* you wouldn't disappoint me,' she told him. 'So it's all right? Ruby can attend the dinner party as my friend?'

He dropped his gaze. In his mind he could still see Ruby, and Lizzie, and knew he could not refuse. 'She will need you,' he reminded her, 'but you must not neglect our guests.' He raised his eyes then and looked hard at Cicely, saying in a low strong voice, 'But this will be the *last* time. Do you understand that?' She nodded, and he turned his attention to Ruby.

'Yes, sir,' she answered, and he was satisfied.

'Very well. Leave me alone now.' He needed time to compose himself. Very soon, this library would be filled with men of consequence, and it would befall him to entertain them. After the trauma of this evening, he hoped it would not also befall him to hurt Lizzie, by ending her daughter's term of employment within this household. No doubt she had been kept as much in the dark as he had been with regard to the 'arrangement' between his daughter and Ruby.

He poured a small measure of brandy into his glass and sipped at it thoughtfully. 'Your daughter is certainly beautiful, Lizzie,' he murmured with a smile. 'And like you, she's blessed with a lovely nature or Cicely wouldn't adore her as she does. But

Ruby isn't contented like you, is she?' he asked. 'More ambitious, perhaps?' He thought a while, then chuckled. 'Still, there's nothing wrong with being ambitious.' He raised his glass to an imaginary figure. 'Here's to you, Lizzie Miller. And here's to that handsome girl of yours. I have a feeling that, one of these days, she'll bounce the world in the palm of her hand.'

Luke Arnold slouched in his chair, one leg crossed over the other and a sly grin on his face as he watched his sister preen herself in the hall mirror. 'My, my! Aren't we the little fusspot?' he said in a cruel voice. 'I'm sorry, sister dear, but Ackroyd won't be able to appreciate your finer qualities this evening. You'll be inside the carriage with me and Father, and that young skunk will be outside in the cold, where he belongs.'

She reached forward and coolly regarded him in the mirror. Her voice was equally cutting as she replied, 'Haven't you got anything better to do . . . like playing cards or bedding street women?' When he merely grinned wider, she said in a wicked voice, 'Or perhaps you might be better employed in polishing Daddy's shoes?' She knew that his greatest frustration was in not yet having been given greater authority in his father's business, and it always delighted her to play on his bitterness.

'You little bitch!' He sprang from the chair and rushed towards her, but a stern voice from the drawing room doorway made him stop and swing round.

'Just for once, try and act like civilised human beings!' Oliver Arnold had heard every word and was furious at these two, his eldest daughter and his only son. Teresa and Luke were two of a kind, with a selfish and greedy streak to their natures. Even as infants they had always brought out the worst in each other, but over recent years, without the steadying influence of a mother to temper their behaviour, their mutual antipathy had grown almost out of control. It was a source of great sorrow to him, because for all their faults they were his children and he loved them dearly.

'Sorry, Daddy.' Teresa smiled beseechingly, and as usual he forgave her.

'Always remember that you were born a lady, and there are certain ways in which a lady should behave,' he reminded her. Turning to his son, he asked, 'Have you arranged for Thomas to bring the carriage round?'

'When are you going to see how useless that old man is?' Luke replied sulkily. 'The old fool's taken to his bed again.'

Taking a deep breath, Oliver eyed him wearily, saying impatiently, 'I think you were there when I went through this with Teresa, were you not?' He did not wait for a reply but went on angrily, 'Thomas is neither old nor useless. He works a long hard day, always on hand, ready to be called out at any time. And if he's presently under the weather, then he's done right to take to his bed. We may all have to take to our bed at some time or another.' He lowered his voice, adding, 'And, by the same token, there will always be some people who are more useful than others, wouldn't you say, Luke?'

'Ackroyd is bringing the carriage round,' he answered, deliberately keeping his eyes averted.

'Good. Then I trust we're all ready to depart?' He looked from Luke to Teresa, who had returned to the mirror and was preening herself again. 'You look bewitching,' he said generously.

And she did. Her tall elegant figure was clothed in a gown of blue, and around her shoulders was the prettiest dark cape, trimmed with an abundance of fur that matched the muffler on her arm. Her brownish hair was piled into curls on the top of her head, the surplus of which spilled down to form a cascade round her face. At her father's words, she turned about, her brown eyes glittering. 'Thank you, Daddy,' she purred, at the same time stepping forward, ready to link her arm with his. He didn't see her intention as he went hurriedly towards the front door. But

Luke saw, and infuriated her by laughing softly in her face.

'We've a few minutes yet,' Oliver remarked, peering anxiously into the darkness beyond the window. 'All the same, we don't want to make a bad impression by arriving late.' He glanced at the grandfather clock down the hall. It was almost ten minutes to seven. The distance between this house and Jeffrey Banks's abode on Billenge End was nothing to speak of. In fact, it would probably be quicker to walk it than to wait for a carriage. But of course that was out of the question.

'If we're very clever, and everyone's the merrier for his best brandy, we might see an opportunity to talk Banks into selling the foundry after all.' Luke knew that if he were to shine in his father's eyes, he would have to achieve something very worthwhile, and what could be more so than bringing about his father's dearest ambition? 'You can't tell me you've *really* had a change of heart where that foundry's concerned?' he asked slyly.

Oliver confronted him with a grim face and forbidding eyes. 'No. I haven't had a change of heart,' he confessed. 'Of course I would like to put my own name over his foundry gates.' His eyes glittered as he paused to let the words sink in. 'But if and when I resume talks with Banks is a matter for *me* to decide, and I say that the matter is not for discussion at the moment. And even to contemplate raising such a delicate business proposition in a gentleman's home, especially when we have been kindly invited to celebrate Christmas Eve with him and his daughter, is unthinkable.' He waited for Luke's apology. When all that greeted him was a dumb silence, he said sharply, 'There will be no talk of business this evening. Is that clear, young man?'

'If you say so.' Luke realised he had gone too far, and he was wisely anxious to make amends. 'Of course you're right, Father,' he said. 'And I do apologise.'

'Good!' Oliver patted his son on the shoulder. 'You're learning,' he said with a little burst of pride. 'I'm convinced you

175

have the makings of a good businessman. It's all a matter of timing . . . knowing when to make a move, and when not to.' He glanced at the clock again. 'Young Ackroyd should have been here by now. Oh dear, I do hope Thomas hasn't taken a turn for the worst.'

Grabbing the bed-head on either side with two hands, Thomas hoisted himself up against the bolster. The effort took a good deal out of him and he lay there a moment, panting and breathless. 'Get off to the house, lad. They'll be kicking their heels,' he wheezed. 'Leave me to meself. I'll be fine.' His face was the shade of parchment, and his whole body was trembling. 'Don't keep the master waiting.' He shoved at Johnny's chest with the flat of his hand. 'Go on!' he said gruffly. 'Away with yer, else we'll *both* find ourselves outta work.'

'Are you sure you'll be all right?' Johnny had seen the old fella worsening slowly over the past few hours, and was deeply concerned. 'If you ask me, I'd say you want a doctor.'

Thomas was horrified. 'I'll have no doctor messing me about,' he declared angrily. Then, realising that Johnny meant well, he assured him kindly, 'Truly, I'm fine, lad.' He shook his head impatiently. 'Or I will be when you've gone away with that there carriage.' He coughed into the bedclothes. 'It's a chest cold, that's all. When you come back, you can brew me a strong mug o' tea and we'll drop a measure o' the good stuff in it.' He chuckled. 'That'll do the trick, you'll see. Now get off with yer . . . or I'll have to rise from me bed and do the job meself, bugger it!'

Knowing that Thomas was not one for making idle threats, Johnny did as he was bid, leaving the old fella with the warning, 'If I find you've been out of that bed while I'm gone, I'll fetch a doctor whether you want one or not.' And Thomas knew that this was no idle threat neither.

'Yer a hard man, Johnny Ackroyd,' he muttered, but there was the merest gleam of a smile in his eyes. 'So, I reckon I'd best do as I'm told, eh?' Though he had kicked and fussed and put up every kind of argument, Thomas had been unable to dissuade Johnny from staying the night. He had already told his mother that he wouldn't be home until the morning, and the bed was made up in the spare stable beneath Thomas's quarters.

'Aye, I reckon you'd better,' Johnny said, slowly moving his head up and down and thinking what a tough old bird Thomas was.

'Come on, Teresa, hurry now.' Oliver Arnold was not surprised when his son climbed into the carriage before him. But he was irritated when his daughter took too long in following. She seemed more interested in the horses than she did in making haste away from there. Or at least he thought it was the horses that held her interest, when in fact it was Johnny she was eyeing with such passion. For his part though, and sensing that she wanted him to turn his head and gaze on her, Johnny deliberately kept his attention on untangling the reins.

'Sorry, Daddy,' she said sweetly, hurrying to his side and allowing him to help her into the carriage; and thinking how she would much rather it was *Johnny's* hands that were round her waist, *Johnny* urging her to come away with him on this starlit night. 'I was just asking after Thomas,' she lied.

'Well then, you needn't have bothered,' Oliver remarked, dropping himself into the seat beside her. 'If you had been paying attention, you would have heard me ask about Thomas the moment we came out. Apparently he's got a chest cold, but it's nothing serious.' He beamed on her, saying with a surprised voice, 'All the same, my dear, it's good to know that you're concerned about Thomas.' He nodded his head and settled back as the carriage moved away. 'Yes, indeed. I'm pleased to see it,' he muttered with satisfaction. 'Very pleased indeed.'

In his heart, Oliver Arnold was convinced that all of his children would make good. His highest hopes were for Luke. A man needed his son to make his mark on the world. He glanced across the carriage interior at Luke's face; such a handsome face, although perhaps it could be softer, gentler, when all too often it was set like stone against the world. There were still a few rough edges to his character, together with a slight insensitivity with regard to the men who worked his father's foundries, and though he had not yet quite grasped the essence of good business, he was impatient to learn, too impatient sometimes. But still, that could often be a good thing, because it showed a keenness to get on.

There was nothing wrong with Luke having his sights set on being in full control of health and safety matters throughout his father's empire; indeed, Oliver had been very impressed by his son's enthusiasm. As a matter of fact, he was on the verge of entrusting immense responsibility to Luke because lately he had been inspired by the managers' reports on their protégé. From these reports, Oliver had unwisely read only what he wanted to read. By all accounts, gone was the immature and useless rebel who had caused him so much heartache and shame. In his place was now a young man with potential. And every day, growing ever more weary and inevitably older, Oliver was nearer and nearer to relinquishing more of the workload to his only son.

The iron-clad horses' hooves played a rhythmic tune over the jutting cobbles as they went across the road and wended their way in between high stone pillars. The wide entrance to Billenge House was not easy to negotiate off the road, although it was much easier on the way out because there was room for the carriage to turn and straighten before coming back onto Billenge End. 'Whoah . . . whoah there.' Johnny eased the horses to a halt before jumping down to help the passengers out. First came the master, then his son. 'What time will you want me to collect you, sir?' he asked Arnold senior. He was thinking about Thomas. He was a stubborn old bugger, and would never admit that he needed anybody.

'Make your way back about eleven o'clock,' Oliver told him. 'We'll be ready by then, I think.' The invitation had been open-ended, but it was Christmas Day tomorrow and he wanted to be up early in order to spend every minute with his beloved Ida.

'Right you are, sir.' Johnny sensed Teresa's eyes on him as she came slowly out of the carriage. When he leaned forward to help her down, she slid her gloved hand into his, deliberately squeezing his fingers and holding on even when she was safely to the ground. With her father and brother looking towards the house, she thrust herself towards Johnny and cupped his hand over her small firm breast. 'Do you see what you are missing?' she whispered wantonly, gently laughing when he swiftly withdrew his hand. 'You can't refuse me for ever,' she murmured. 'I will have you, Johnny darling. I always get what I want eventually.'

'Teresa!' Oliver was growing impatient. 'Quickly now.' He was a few steps ahead, but now he turned to wait for her.

'Coming, Daddy.' She hurried to his side, glancing back only once to watch as Johnny climbed into the driver's seat. The more he refused her, the more she wanted him. And the more she planned her days to that end. Even now, a plan was forming in her devious little mind. 'Daddy?' she said in a low voice designed so that neither Luke nor Johnny would hear. 'Don't you think it's unwise to leave poor old Thomas alone all night long?' She cast a surreptitious glance at Johnny, and her meaning was unmistakable. 'I'm sure Ackroyd wouldn't mind keeping an eye on his old friend?'

'Why, how thoughtful,' he declared. 'But you're a little behind the times, my dear, because it has already been arranged. Young Ackroyd saw the need before any of us, and asked my permission to make up a bed in the stables.' He looked at her in the moon-glow, and thought he saw something in her he had not seen before. Perhaps she was not altogether unfeeling after all.

Without any more ado, he went towards the front steps and up to the door. Here he lifted the heavy brass knocker and let it clang hard against the wood. At once there came the sound of footsteps from inside. He felt a little nervous. For so long now he had looked on Jeffrey Banks as a rival to be fended off or bought out. Tonight though that 'rival' had extended the offer of friendship by inviting the enemy into his house. It was a magnaminous gesture, and Oliver felt the onus was on him to make it a pleasant evening.

When the door was opened and they were ushered into the house, Teresa entered with all the grace and poise of a lady. But her thoughts were far from ladylike. They would have shamed any loose woman from the streets. Dark and dangerous thoughts, thoughts of lust and nakedness. Thoughts that warmed and thrilled her beyond her wildest imaginings. Now, as the party was taken along the hallway, she was actually smiling to herself. In her mind's eye she could see Johnny's strong body writhing on top of hers, she could almost feel his nakedness against hers, and the thought of his dark brooding eyes burning with passion at her touch was almost more than she could bear. Tonight! There would never be a better time to make her move. With that old fool Thomas out of the way, and Johnny unsuspecting, there was nothing to keep her from him. Oh, the evening could not go quickly enough for her.

The guests were now congregating in the drawing room. Cicely was at the door, waiting to greet the Arnold family. 'I'm delighted you could come,' she said, extending greetings first to the father, then to his children, male first. When it was Teresa's turn, Cicely found it hard not to stare. She was astonished by the young woman's dark beauty. 'This is my very dear friend, Miss

Miller . . . Miss Ruby Miller,' she said, and drawing Ruby forward, proudly presented her to the Arnold family, just as she had presented her to every guest who had entered the house on this Christmas Evening.

By this time, Ruby was used to being thrust forward and regarded by curious eyes. Yet she was not prepared for the envy in Teresa Arnold's, and she was shocked by the intimate smile bestowed on her by Luke. 'Your friend is very lovely,' he told Cicely, while holding Ruby's hand and staring at her with blatant admiration. 'No doubt we will have time to talk later?' The question was addressed directly to Ruby.

'No doubt,' she agreed, her ready smile lighting up her beauty until it dazzled him. But she had taken an instant dislike to this arrogant young man, and they would not have 'time to talk'. Not if she could help it, they wouldn't!

The formalities were over. Guest mingled with guest and the aperitifs were brought round. Soon the announcement was made that dinner would be served, and the guests assembled in pairs, with Jeffrey Banks and his daughter leading the procession to the dining-room. Somehow Ruby found herself linking arms with Luke Arnold. He held her too close, and smiled too often, and when he drew out her chair – before taking up position opposite from where he could watch her every move – he deliberately brushed her bare arm with the palm of his hand. She shivered. Even the touch of him was obnoxious to her. Some-thing else, too, worried Ruby; she and Cicely had gone through every eventuality for this evening, and because of her own experience at waiting table, Ruby had become suitably familiar with etiquette and proper manners. So she was assured that nothing could possibly go wrong. At first, she had been dreadfully nervous. Every time the master looked her way, she was convinced he was waiting for the slightest opportunity to expel her from the room, perhaps even from the house. But he had kept his distance,

Cicely had guided her well, and as a result her confidence had grown.

Now, though, one intimate smiling glance from Luke Arnold had threatened it all. She wondered whether he might somehow have guessed that, far from being what Cicely would have them believe, she was no more than a paid servant in this house. Riddled with doubt, she asked herself whether in some way he had discovered her secret. Perhaps he'd seen her in that subservient role at some time or another? Although she could never remember seeing him here in this house. If not, then why was he secretly smiling at her like that? It was an unnerving smile, too curious and too wicked altogether. Had she done something to provoke his suspicions? Had she given the game away by some slight mannerism? She began to panic. What was he playing at? Why was he staring at her like that? Why were his eyes on her every time she glanced up? He was a devil!

'Calm yourself, Ruby,' she muttered. 'The bugger can't know anything. He's just a rake looking for a bedmate, I shouldn't wonder.' She grew angry then, bolder. No, he couldn't possibly know. There was no way he could have guessed. In which case, why should he be allowed to spoil her big night out? Well, she wouldn't let him. If he had something to say, then he'd have to come right out and say it, instead of playing cat and mouse with her.

Her fighting spirit had returned now and she began boldly to return his surreptitious smiles. 'You little sod, Ruby Miller!' she chuckled under her breath. 'You're nothing but a hussy.' All the same, she was actually enjoying herself, and Luke Arnold was all the more bewitched by her.

All evening he could not take his eyes off this vibrant young thing who had caught his imagination. Ruby Miller was everything he admired in a woman. She was incredibly lovely, with her wild brown hair so thick and rich about her heart-shaped face, and eyes that were the deepest blue then black. All the while they teased and twisted his emotions, like nothing he had ever experienced. She was coy, then she was bold; she was smiling, inviting and pleasing him, then she was ignoring him altogether. All evening long he was tormented by her, and the meal seemed neverending.

The dinner began with soup, then came the fish and side dishes of succulent meats, then the entrées and the roasts, and on to the savouries and sweets, followed by the dessert of sweetmeats, fruit, nuts and bonbons. Finally the moment came when Cicely caught the ladies' eyes, signalling that it was time for the men to be left to their port, and the ladies to depart to the drawing room.

From the drawing room, the connecting doors to the 'great room' which was reserved for occasions such as this, were opened out to create a wonderful setting for entertainment. In one corner stood a huge Christmas tree, beautifully decorated and sparkling with tinsel stars. The splendid fireplace boasted heaped logs which merrily blazed, sending out a cheery glow over the whole room; the candles in the chandelier flickered and danced and altogether the whole ambience was delightful. At the farthest end the casement doors opened out into the conservatory, and from there the night sky could be seen, black and shifting, with the moon hanging low, and the stars glittering far off. To one side of the casement doors, the string quartet played a medley of gentle tunes. Altogether it was the most wonderful setting for a pleasant event.

Cicely had arranged the furniture to ensure that there were seats for everyone, providing secluded little corners for those who wished to talk privately, circles for those who felt the need to converse widely, and even an area where those who had the urge to dance could indulge to their heart's content. 'Please make yourselves comfortable, ladies,' she said as they filed into the room. Soon coffee was served and the buzz of conversation rippled through the air. Cicely breathed a sigh of relief, and Ruby stayed close to her. But then came the inevitable questions. 'Where did you say you live, my dear?' An old dowager peered at Ruby and everyone held their breath, all eager and waiting for her answer. This attractive young lady had made them all curious, and they were impatient to learn of her background. Teresa in particular watched her intently.

Ruby took a deep breath and tried to remember what Cicely had told her. 'Manchester,' she replied, and Cicely nodded approvingly. 'My family come from Manchester.' She had been warned that this inquisition would start the minute the ladies were divided from the men, and though she was well prepared, she didn't like it. Not at all.

'Ah!' A second lady leaned forward and addressed Ruby in a loud voice. 'Then you should know of the Morrimers . . . a very well established, extremely wealthy family. Came down from nobility, I believe.'

Ruby swallowed hard. 'I've never personally made acquaintance with them,' she replied tactfully. Glancing nervously at Cicely, she was reassured by her warm smile. 'Sorry,' she said lamely, and the woman grunted, immediately settling back into her seat and muttering under her breath.

The questions came thick and fast. 'Where did you attend school?' . . . 'What business is your family in?'

Without actually lying, Ruby answered as best she could, and though her answers were deliberately vague, they appeared to satisfy. At last, and much to both Ruby and Cicely's relief, the doors opened and Jeffrey Banks brought the men into the room. The women were soon on their feet, and little groups began to form. One or two daring couples took to the dance floor, and it wasn't long before gentle laughter floated through the buzz of conversation.

Cicely and Ruby withdrew to the conservatory. It was more

peaceful in there, no candles or lamps, and only the stars and moon to light it, together with an incoming shaft of lamplight from the adjoining room. This had always been Cicely's favourite place. 'I'm proud of you,' she said, hugging Ruby with all her might.

Ruby sighed aloud. 'I couldn't have done it without you,' she said, gently breaking away and falling heavily into an ornate wrought iron seat. 'I was scared to death in there just now. Did you see that awful Teresa Arnold staring at me? I'm sure she saw what a fraud I was.' Just like her brother, she thought bitterly.

'Nonsense!' Cicely sat beside her. 'You fooled them all. It's like I said, Ruby . . . you are as much a lady as any one of them.' She might have said more, but her duties as hostess called for her to return to the other room. 'I won't be long,' she promised, adding with a little laugh, 'I have orders from Father to be particularly nice to the Arnold family.'

'Rather you than me,' Ruby answered, thinking of the son and the way he made her feel nervous. 'But you go ahead. I'll be all right.' After Cicely had gone, Ruby pressed herself tighter into her shadowy corner. Noise and laughter filtered through the great room where everyone appeared to be enjoying the evening to the full. She was much happier where she was, here in this quiet shadowy place. Suddenly she felt dreadfully alone. Above all else, she missed her mam. She missed that homely busy figure flitting about; she missed Dolly's constant chatter, and she missed the children's arguing. It was Christmas Eve and this was the very first time she had not spent it at home with her family. Right now the children would be dreaming of tomorrow morning, and what Father Christmas might bring. And she wouldn't be there to see their faces when they opened the tiny parcels beneath the modest tree in the parlour.

On top of all that, it was her birthday tomorrow. 'Oh, Mam, I'm sorry,' she murmured. And suddenly, she wanted to go home.

Being a 'lady' wasn't all it was cracked up to be. Oh, she still wanted to be rich, and she wanted to dress in fine clothes. And her burning desire to lift her family to the heights burned just as brightly as before. But she had seen enough here tonight to know that there wasn't one woman out there who could match up to her own mother. In her heart, Ruby knew she could never be one of them, and wondered why it was that money and power made some people believe that they were a cut above the rest.

Lost in thoughts of home and family, she didn't hear the soft footsteps that brought Luke Arnold to the door of the conservatory. 'All alone are we?' The low resonant voice reached into the shadows and suddenly the room was dark and forbidding.

Startled, Ruby glanced up to see the outline of a man silhouetted against the light from the other room. Almost at once she recognised the thick-set figure of Oliver Arnold's son, and a faint rush of fear rippled through her. He was one of those people who gave the impression that he could see through and into the soul. She stiffened as he came forward. 'I had no idea there was anyone in here,' he lied. 'Although, of course, I did wonder where you'd got to.' Easing himself into the seat beside her, he murmured, 'Besides, I haven't had a chance to talk to you all evening.'

'Really, Mr Arnold?' She feigned surprise, although she suspected he was lying and had known all along that she was in here. No doubt he had seen Cicely come out and realised Ruby was alone. 'I wouldn't have thought we had anything to talk about,' she replied. 'So if you'll excuse me?' she added in that stately voice which had carried her successfully through tonight's adventure. 'I was just about to return to the other room.' His nearness bothered her. He was so close she could smell his clothes – not the rough harsh smell that enveloped her father but a rich tweedy aroma mingling with a faint perfume. It filled her head and made her giddy. And when he leaned forward to place his hand on hers, her throat almost closed and she found it hard to breathe. Strange how in that moment she thought about Johnny, with his honest handsome face and strong dark eyes; she shivered with delight in remembering the way he had kissed her. She wished he was here right now. Johnny would soon have this bloke on the run, she thought. 'I'd better get back,' she insisted with a gracious smile. But when she made to rise, he laid the palm of his hand on her shoulder and gently pressed her down again.

'Oh now, *please*. Don't walk out on me, Miss Miller . . . Ruby,' he pleaded, adding as an after-thought, 'I hope you don't mind my calling you Ruby?' She didn't answer. 'You're not shy, I know that,' he went on regardless. 'In fact, during dinner I got the impression that you were interested in me. Was I right?'

'You couldn't be more wrong,' she told him sharply.

'I don't believe you.' He was deeply aroused. All evening she had raised a need in him, and now that he had her here, just the two of them in this darkened room, he wasn't about to let her go that easily. He was also pleasantly amused, believing in his arrogance that she was merely toying with him. But there was no harm in playing her game. It entertained him, and the reward would be worth it, he was sure. Ruby had attracted him like no other woman he could remember. In fact she was nothing like the young ladies he had met through these dreary social events. Yet he couldn't put his finger on it. Certainly she was more gutsy and, unlike the cotton-headed butterflies he had previously encountered, she seemed an intelligent little thing. Put her alongside Jeffrey Banks's daughter, and the comparison was startling; where Cicely was delicate and fair, without fire and substance, Ruby Miller was real and alive. You could almost touch the unique aura that surrounded her. All the same, she was less genteel than Cicely, not quite 'polished', and yet Ruby had a certain style, a particular substance that lifted her above the crowd.

There was something odd though. Something that had kept

him guessing. *She was out of place here!* And yet she was not. It was puzzling. Oh, but all that aside, her dark beauty fascinated him, stirred his loins and made him careless. He wanted her, here and now. Even with all those people in the next room, he desperately wanted her. 'Why is it that we've never met before?' he persisted softly. 'I've been to more than a few social gatherings, but I can't recall ever seeing you.' The frown in his forehead deepened. 'I know I would have remembered someone like you.'

Ruby sensed his doubt and was on her guard. 'I expect we don't move in the same circles,' she said casually.

He was leaning towards her, his eyes searching her face. Seeming not to have heard her answer, he went on, 'You really are refreshingly different . . . innocent, I suppose,' he remarked. He was flushed with brandy and the smell wafted towards her. There was something about him that was frightening, and yet he was devastatingly charming. He looked at her a moment longer, and wondered how old she was. Her skin was pure as cream and there was a delightful honesty about her that appealed to him. She seemed almost like a child. Yet she was no child. In her daring ocean blue eyes he saw only a woman, a beautiful, desirable woman. 'Miller?' he studied the name. 'Miller? . . . No, I can't say I've heard that name.' His curiosity was heightening by the minute. But then he sensed her intention of leaving, and he couldn't let that happen. 'You're the loveliest creature I've ever seen,' he murmured, sliding his arm round her shoulders and pushing his face close to hers. 'What say we take a carriage somewhere . . . just you and me?'

'We'll do no such thing!' Ruby told him, staring into his face and prising his hand from her shoulder. Bloody cheek! she thought indignantly. He must think I'm easy game. There was no doubt he was handsome. And there was no doubt he had supped too much brandy because his face was warm and pink and he was leaning too heavily on her.

'You and me could have a wonderful time,' he insisted. When he saw that his words were only making her struggle all the more, he thrust one hand into his jacket pocket, searching for his wallet. He laughed softly. 'I see,' he said knowingly. 'Your favours come dearly, do they? Well, if it's money you're after, I'll dress you from top to toe in it.' When she pulled away, he was further aroused. 'You little wild-cat!' he growled. Suddenly, his hands were all over her. One minute he was fondling her breasts and the next tugging at her skirt, sliding his hand up to her thigh and groaning, 'Come on, don't tease. You can see the way it is with me.'

In the heat of the moment, and incensed by his treatment of her, Ruby forgot herself. 'Get your hands off me, you drunken bugger!' she snapped, lashing out at him. 'I don't want you and I don't want your money neither.' In her anger she had lost the fine edge to her voice and he stared at her in astonishment. Her heart sank as she realised that she'd given the game away.

Suddenly he was laughing out loud, rocking back in his seat. Incensed, she scrambled out of her seat then she lifted her hand and slapped it hard against his mouth. 'I may *only* be a lady's maid,' she said in a trembling voice, 'but I won't be handled like no woman off the streets!' With a snort and an angry twist of her trim shoulders, she marched away. 'Men like you want dunking in a tub of cold water!' she called after her.

Luke was stunned and enraged. Never in the whole of his experience had he been smacked across the mouth by a member of the opposite sex. It was a new and humiliating experience, and hell would freeze over before it ever happened again! 'Little bitch,' he snarled, delicately patting his painful jaw. He dabbed at his mouth with his fingertips then held them up. He was shocked to see that his mouth was actually bleeding. 'Cheap little vixen,' he hissed, taking out his handkerchief and mopping at the offending spot.

It was a while before his temper cooled. And when it did, he leaned back in the seat and recalled the entire incident. He'd been right to think her fiery. Suddenly, he began to chuckle.

'A lady's maid?' he said aloud. 'Well! Well!' Then he fell silent. No wonder she was different, he thought. 'A wild and prickly rose among the orchids, eh?' he murmured. It struck him that here was a little drama he could no doubt turn to his own advantage. In spite of her volatile temper – or perhaps because of it – Ruby Miller excited him. She was still the most desirable and real woman he had ever come across.

'Lady's maid or not, you haven't seen the last of me,' he threatened. 'What's more, you'll regret the day you ever raised a hand to Luke Arnold!'

He had been livid, but now he was deadly calm. His voice was chilling, 'No woman has ever refused me, and no woman ever will. You can count on this, Ruby Miller . . . there'll come a time when you'll *beg* for me.'

When he set his sights on something worthwhile, he usually pursued it to the end, by fair means or foul. But then he recalled how she had beaten him off, turned away like he was so much dirt. Much as he wanted her, as yet she obviously had no taste for him. 'But you will,' he promised darkly. 'You will.'

He rose from his seat and searched the other room with hostile eyes. 'So you think I'm not good enough for you?' He laughed sourly. 'A lady's maid, eh?' He caught sight of her then, and his smile was chilling. Deep in conversation with Cicely, she had not seen him, and so he was free to study her. For a long moment he gazed at her with mingled emotions. He was angry with her, but he still craved her. She was incredibly beautiful, alive and passionate. He found it hard to believe that such a low-bred woman could be so stunning. In a moment, his gaze shifted to the woman beside Ruby. Cicely Banks paled in comparison, he thought.

He watched them a while longer. They seemed so deep in conversation he wondered whether Ruby was telling her mistress what had happened in the conservatory with him. A thought crept into his mind. 'The lady and her maid . . . a strange conspiracy,' he muttered, light dawning in his mind. He remembered his real purpose for coming here tonight, and chuckled then.

Standing there, unseen in the shadows, he thought of Cicely Banks and he thought of her father, the eminent gentleman who was so reluctant to part with his foundry. He remembered how desperately his own father had wanted that same foundry. Tonight was to have been his chance to prove himself in the eyes of Oliver Arnold, and because of Ruby Miller, he had almost forgotten that.

'Well now, Cicely Banks, I can see I've neglected you. And that was a very foolish thing to do,' he told himself. With a determined flourish, he smartened his tie and tucked his soiled handkerchief into his pocket. 'It would never do to neglect such a fine lady,' he murmured, going towards the door. 'Especially when that lady could well be the means to an end.'

He was interested to see how very close Cicely and Ruby appeared to be. Who knows? he thought to himself. Tonight may well bring *two* delightful rewards . . . the foundry for my father, and the reluctant maid for me.

The prospect was enough to bring the smile back to his face. He was no fool, and knew that it would take time to bring it all about. But then, nothing worthwhile ever came easy. 'And I must not forget how you've shamed me, Miss Miller,' he murmured. It was obvious to him that Ruby had a great deal of affection for Cicely, and he intended turning this to his own advantage. 'Lovely though you are, Ruby dearest, you will have to be punished. Just a little, I think.' The thought was delicious.

By the time he came back into the room, he was fully composed and even sobered by what had happened between himself and

Ruby. Music was playing, there were still couples dancing, and thankfully no one seemed to have noticed the little upset in the conservatory. By this time Ruby and her mistress had moved away and he couldn't see them. His anxious eyes travelled the length and breadth of the room, searching for one face in particular. When his gaze alighted on Ruby, he began to make his way forward. At the same time Cicely had seen his approach and hurried towards him. He saw her intention and so he stayed where he was, close to the conservatory doors, his amused gaze going from one woman to the other. Cicely's face was set in a serious expression, while Ruby glowered at him with angry eyes.

'Could we talk, Mr Arnold?' Cicely's anxiety betrayed itself in her voice.

'But of course,' he replied. Stepping to one side he gallantly ushered her into the conservatory, surreptitiously slipping an arm round her waist and glancing backwards, deeply satisfied when he saw how alarmed Ruby was at this deliberately intimate gesture. 'I assume you want to explain how your maid comes to be here disguised as a lady?' he said pointedly.

'I would rather you didn't mention anything about it to anyone else.' Cicely didn't know him, and so could not tell whether his intention was to cause mischief.

'I shan't,' he agreed. 'Don't worry your pretty head. I may look like a villain, but I'm a gentleman at heart.' He put on his very best manners, thinking he would soon have the little fool eating out of his hand. It was all part of his two-fold plan, the foundry and Ruby. While the two of them talked and she explained how she loved Ruby like a sister, he was thinking, the foundry and Ruby. When she went on to outline how the harmless little deceit was no more than a way to show her affection and pride for Ruby, whom she claimed was her 'only true friend', he saw how painfully vulnerable she was, and became more determined than before.

'You mean you have no friends other than your own maid?' Luke was genuinely astonished.

'I'm content in my own company,' she explained. 'And Ruby is a darling.' By this time she was seated on the same bench where Ruby had fought him off. Luke was sat beside her, his arm stretched across the back of the bench. From this position, he could see Ruby. At that point a young man approached her and they went on to the dance floor. Luke was jealous, but managed to contain his feelings by concentrating on his devious intentions and flirting outrageously with Cicely.

'From what Ruby said, I thought you must be a monster,' she apologised. She believed that Ruby was either mistaken or else had exaggerated in her account of what happened, because in the few minutes she'd spent in his company, Cicely had found Luke Arnold to be amiable and charming. More than that, he had promised to say nothing about her and Ruby's charade.

Soon he had purposely moved the conversation away from Ruby, and now, to Cicely's delight, was showing a keen interest in her. 'Are you saying you have no beau?' he asked in feigned surprise. 'What! So pretty and intelligent? I'm surprised there isn't a whole chain of young men waiting to take you out.' He leaned towards her and her eyes twinkled at his flattery. 'I for one would be proud to walk you down the street.' As he spoke, he was thinking he would rather walk a dog. But she was his way to the other one, and it was the other one he wanted. Oh, but he wasn't forgetting the foundry. By the time this night was over, he would as good as have them both in his pocket.

'It's very kind of you to say so, Mr Arnold,' she said shyly. No man had ever spoken to Cicely in that way, and she wasn't certain how to respond.

'Oh, I'm not being kind,' he stressed, moving a little closer. 'I find you very attractive.'

Cicely actually giggled. 'Really, Mr Arnold.' She inched

away. 'Perhaps we had better return to the other guests?'

'Not yet, surely?' he said in a hurt voice. 'And please, don't call me Mr Arnold. It sounds so unfriendly. My name is Luke.' One look at her blushing face told him that he had her in the palm of his hand. He'd had no idea she was so naive. A little flattery, a suggestion here and a sprinkle of charm there, had been all it took to bowl her over. He'd had plenty of practice, and with smarter females than her.

Suddenly the evening had taken a real turn for the better, and Luke was thoroughly enjoying himself. The fact that he was deliberately setting out to deceive this gentle young woman did not diminish his pleasure. In fact, it only added to it. Cicely Banks was a means to an end. No more than that.

Whisked first this way then that, Ruby was breathless, and growing irritated. For two weeks now, Cicely had taken her painstakingly through her dance steps, and she was proud of the way Ruby had managed to master the simpler skills of dancing. But they were all wasted on the gangling young man who had partnered her on this particular occasion. Not only was he arrogant and full of his own importance, but he was totally out of step with the music and Ruby had lost count of the times he had stamped on her toes.

'Oh dear, I'm so sorry,' he told her, swinging her round and grinning down at her.

'So am I,' she muttered.

But then he tangled his feet with hers and the pair of them almost went headlong into a rather fat and completely bald gentleman who was nudging his way across the floor with an equally large and flowery woman. When the two of them glared and moved away, Ruby suggested hopefully, 'Perhaps we'd better sit this one out?'

She was concerned about Cicely. Every time her partner

swung her round, she peeped into the conservatory, and each time she was concerned to see that both Cicely and Luke Arnold were still huddled in the shadows there. All her instincts warned Ruby that he was up to no good. She knew also that Cicely was no match for Luke Arnold's cunning. 'You're up to summat, you sly bugger!' she murmured. And she hoped it wouldn't be Cicely who would suffer as a consequence.

'Sorry. What was that you said?' Her companion bent his head to hear the better.

Ruby had suffered enough. Squaring her shoulders, she stared up at him. 'I said, you can trample somebody else's feet from now on,' she returned sharply. 'You've shown me what a splendid fellow you are, and I'm a great deal wiser after the performance. But I wish you'd told me that you dance like a cart-horse! I'm not partial to having my feet flattened to the floor, so kindly take your limp arm from round my waist and lead me back to my chair this minute.'

Her feet were hurting and this young man was getting on her nerves with his clumsy twirls and smug expression. But her real reason for wanting to get off the floor was so that she could keep an eye on what was going on in that conservatory.

'Well! Really, my dear,' he pouted, taking her by the arm and pushing a way through to the row of chairs against the wall. 'I was under the impression that I was dancing with a lady, but I was obviously mistaken. I'll have you know I'm widely renowned for my foxtrot.' He was deeply injured by her remarks.

'Well, good for you!' remarked Ruby, falling into the chair with relief. 'But you're not foxtrotting all over *my* poor toes, I'll tell you that for nothing.' She might have told him to sod off in that gruff voice her mam often used when the rentman got a bit mouthy, but the young man scurried away before she got the chance. 'And good shuts to you,' she told him under her breath, leaning down to rub her mangled toes. In that moment her gaze lifted to the conservatory and what she saw made her heart leap into her mouth.

Cicely and Luke were entwined against the moonlit sky, one dark shadow, lost in a long and passionate kiss. A moment later, the two of them came into the room, Cicely looking up at him with stars in her eyes. But he didn't notice her admiration because he was smiling across the room, smiling at Ruby, a slow cruel smile that told her many things. It told her how he was punishing her for having dared to lift a hand to him. It told her that, in spite of it, he still wanted her. And, worst of all, in that awful smile he was showing how he had wormed his way into Cicely's lonely heart. There was no love in his face when he turned to glance at Cicely. No love or affection. No warmth, no gentleness. Instead, there was only a dark wickedness there. Ruby saw it. But the vulnerable Cicely was blinded by other emotions. With a shocked heart, Ruby watched as that dear soul seemed to light up when she returned Luke's smile. He placed her hand over his and guided her on to the floor where they were soon lost in the strains of a romantic waltz.

All the while they danced, he constantly glanced at Ruby. And she knew there would be no end to his vindictiveness.

'They make a fine couple, don't you think?' Startled Ruby looked up to see Teresa Arnold seating herself in the next chair.

'I suppose so,' she replied. She didn't like Luke, nor did she care much for this spoilt beauty who was his sister. Cicely had told her a tale or two about this one. Tarred with the same brush, I shouldn't wonder, she thought bitterly.

'How long have you and Cicely Banks known each other?' came the unexpected question.

'I've known Cicely for over a year now,' Ruby answered truthfully. All evening she had been on her guard against such curiosity. But now, after all that had happened, her guard was down and suddenly she felt threatened.

'She's pretty, isn't she?' Teresa admitted with some reluctance. But then added viciously, 'A little insipid though . . . and delicate, like a china doll.' She studied Ruby for a moment before inclining her head towards Cicely and Luke, two accomplished dancers who seemed to glide effortlessly across the floor. 'I should warn your friend about him,' she laughed lightly. 'My brother is known for his womanising.'

'Oh, don't worry. I intend to!' Ruby promised. It struck her that there was no love lost between brother and sister, and this only confirmed her suspicions that Luke Arnold was bad through and through.

Teresa turned at that, her eyes wide with surprise. 'Be careful you don't give the impression that you're jealous,' she warned, a faint look of amusement on her face.

When Ruby appeared to ignore her advice, she remarked, 'Most women find it hard to resist Luke's obvious charms, and I dare say Cicely Banks is no exception. In fact, if what I hear is to be believed, she's wide open to being swept off her feet.' She paused before adding in a low thoughtful voice, 'All the same, I wouldn't have said she was Luke's sort. But there! He never wastes time on women unless it serves a purpose. And I think I see what his purpose is here.' She laughed, a coarse unlovely sound. 'Jeffrey Banks has refused to sell his foundry to my father. My brother, on the other hand, has very *different* powers of persuasion. It wouldn't surprise me if Luke didn't succeed where my father has failed.'

'I wouldn't count on that!' Ruby felt like giving this one the same treatment she had given her arrogant brother. Between Oliver Arnold's son and daughter, she wasn't sure who most deserved a smack across the mouth. 'Cicely is no fool,' she retorted. 'And she won't be taken in by your brother's glib tongue.'

Teresa was amused. 'How quaint,' she remarked, eyeing Ruby

with narrowed eyes. 'You're fiercely protective of her, aren't you?' Ruby had held her attention for most of the evening, and she had seen Luke corner her in the conservatory. Now she wanted to know a great deal more about this 'dearest friend' of Cicely Banks's. 'Are you walking out with a young man?' she asked with some amusement.

Ruby sensed she was getting into deep water here, and so she did the unforgiveable: she answered a question with a question. 'I notice you yourself didn't arrive with a companion?' she said coolly. The music stopped then, and Ruby saw how Luke, having left Cicely seated on the other side of the room, was striding away towards the drinks table. 'Excuse me,' she said abruptly. In a moment she was making her way to Cicely's side.

But two things happened before she got there. First the music struck up again and Luke returned to Cicely's side. He bent to whisper something in her ear. She smiled and nodded, and they each looked up to smile at Ruby. When she was still only a few steps away, Luke strode across the floor towards her and, sweeping her into his arms, took up step to the music. 'Relax,' he murmured close to her ear. 'Don't let dear Cicely suspect anything.'

'What do you mean?' Ruby was bristling with anger. 'There's nothing to suspect!' She would have broken away from him but his fingers were wound tightly about her hand, and his arm reached right around her waist. Her toes were hardly touching the floor.

'You leave her alone!' she warned in a low threatening voice. 'She's done you no harm.'

'And I've done her none,' he was quick to point out, 'Can I help it if she finds me irresistible?'

'You intend to make mischief, I'm certain of it,' Ruby insisted. 'Even your own sister says you're only out to use Cicely in order to get the foundry.' She loathed him yet she couldn't help admire the way he danced, taking her with him across the floor, causing her to dip and step to the music as though she was born to it. 'She'll know how bad you are when I've finished.'

His smile fell away then, and he squeezed her so hard that she couldn't even cry out. 'Oh, I doubt that,' he sneered. 'I have a feeling that Cicely won't believe a word you say.' He laughed softly, making her flesh creep. 'I haven't met a woman yet who would believe anything bad about me.'

'Well, you've met one now,' Ruby snapped. 'Because I'm on to you all right. And I'll do my best to show Cicely what you're made of.'

'Oh, now, that's a real shame, Ruby, because I've taken a liking to you. In fact, I might even have changed the rules for you.'

He spoke in a light-hearted way, but having held her close, having touched his mouth against her rich brown hair, and after seeing those magnificent blue-black eyes looking up at him from beneath thick dark lashes, he feared she had stolen his heart. For the first time he believed himself to be head over heels in love. It was a sobering thought. For one mad moment he was even prepared to give up the idea of securing the foundry by using Cicely.

'I'll tell you what,' he whispered, trying not to let her see the true depth of his feelings, 'be nice to me and I might even let your friend down lightly. I admit I had it in mind to use her. But I'll gladly trade her for you. What do you say to that?' He was astonished to find himself trembling.

'I say you're a liar. And besides, who do you think you are, to trade one woman for another? You're wicked, and Cicely will come to see that for herself. As for me being "nice" to you, don't think I don't know what you mean by that. Men like you have used low-bred women like so much dirt . . . hiding them in back rooms and visiting whenever it suits you. I've heard the women in our street talking, and I wouldn't spit on your sort. Besides,

I don't want no man to carry me through life. I won't always be a lady's maid. I've got ambitions, and one day I'll be a woman of consequence with more money than I'll know what to do with. Men like you will be two a penny. Oh no, Mr Luke Arnold, sir!' she said sarcastically. 'I wouldn't be "nice" to you if you were the last man on God's earth!'

'You'll regret saying that,' he promised. Her fierce outburst had shaken him. If it had come from any other woman, he would have laughed in their face. But Ruby Miller was different. She was strong, and he knew that every word had been spoken from the bottom of her heart. Yet, for the second time in as many hours, she had rejected him, and he couldn't forgive her for that. Hatred bubbled up in him.

'Tonight, you've made yourself a deadly enemy,' he told her vehemently. He pulled her closer and swept her across the floor smiling all the while yet deliberately hurting her, digging his arm into her back and bending her fingers to his own. In that moment she saw that Luke Arnold was capable of murder. And somehow she knew this would not be the last time their paths were destined to cross.

'Go on, lad. You've left it late enough. Eleven o'clock he said, and it's nearly that now.' Thomas was bone weary. The chill had taken its toll and all he wanted to do was sleep. He pushed the foul-smelling liquid from under his nose. 'Take it away. I've no need of that,' he grumbled. 'Are you sure it ain't the stuff we rub the horses with? Lord knows it stinks like it.'

Johnny wouldn't be put off. 'You'll drink it or I'll not go,' he threatened. 'And stop being a babby. You know it's only tar and herbs. Mam said it would have you better in no time at all.'

'Aye?' Thomas peered at him through small tired eyes. 'That's if it don't kill me off first,' he moaned.

'Come on. Let's have you.' Johnny pushed it towards the old fellow's tightly closed mouth. 'It's *you* that's keeping the master waiting, because I'm not shifting 'til you've finished every last drop.'

Thomas grunted and pulled himself further up the bed, remaining there, hunched and reluctant, grimacing at the thought of allowing that black awful-smelling brew to slide down his throat. But he knew how determined Johnny was, and was desperate that the master shouldn't be kept waiting. 'Quick then,' he gasped. Pinching his nose between his finger and thumb, he screwed his eyes tightly shut and opened his mouth wide. When he felt the stuff slithering over his tongue, he made himself swallow deeply, gulping and noisily smacking his lips, until only the disgusting taste lingered in his mouth. At once he was coughing and spluttering, swearing and cursing. 'You bugger!' he ranted. 'It tastes as bad as it smells . . . bull's piss.'

'Give over. It's marvellous stuff.' Johnny laughed out loud. 'I'm proud of you, that I am.' Getting up from the bed where he'd been sitting, he assured the old fellow, 'I'll be away now. I'll not waken you when I come back. If my dad was anything to go by when he was taken badly last year, that medicine will make you sleep like a newborn.'

'Or a dead 'un!'

Johnny gave no answer, but gently drew Thomas deeper into the bed and covered him to his shoulders with the bedclothes. 'Rest now,' he said, and without another word left the room, softly closing the door behind him. One last backward glance told him that his mam's medicine was already beginning to work, because the old fellow had closed his eyes and turned his head to one side. 'That's it,' Johnny murmured. 'You sleep well, old 'un. When you wake up tomorrow, you'll feel like a spring colt.'

On the way through the stables, he checked the horses as usual, and satisfied that there were no problems, continued through to the outside yard where he had already harnessed the big bays to the carriage. They were fretful to be away, snorting and scraping the ground with their front hooves, and shaking their large heads from side to side with anticipation as he approached. It was only a few minutes later when he edged the cumbersome team out onto the road.

It was a glorious evening. The moon was high and a trillion stars shimmered, like brilliant jewels scattered across a velvet sky. To Johnny's mind there was nothing more beautiful unless it was another jewel which he cherished above all others. That jewel was Ruby. Earlier that evening, when he'd gone to collect the medicine from his mam, he'd also called round at Ruby's house, hoping to snatch a few precious minutes with her. When Lizzie told him that she had been called in to work, he was bitterly disappointed; not only for himself, but for Ruby too. He knew how much her family meant to her, and being taken from the children on Christmas Eve must have seemed so unfair to her. It struck him then that if the master wasn't yet ready and waiting, there might just be a chance for him to sneak into the kitchens and have a quick word with her. In his mind he pictured her there, up to her armpits in potato peelings, and Cook storming about, giving orders in that bombastic manner of hers. Still, he was sure that Cook wouldn't refuse him a few minutes with Ruby, especially on Christmas Eve.

Billenge House was soon in sight. On arrival, Johnny realised that his carriage was the first one there. Normally, after these social events, carriages would be lined up in the yard, and even partway down the road. I'm sure it was eleven when I was to fetch them, he pondered. He parked the carriage in the yard, keeping to one side so as not to hinder any other vehicles that might enter. Clambering down from the driver's seat, he stretched his limbs and yawned. One way or another it had been a very long day, but the thought of seeing Ruby was invigorating. Spying the narrow gate which led to the back of the house, he hurried on, over the meandering path and towards the lighted kitchen.

It was dark at the rear of the house with only the glow from the kitchen window to light his way. The layer of stones and gravel crunched beneath his boots, echoing into the night with a frantic rhythm. Going at a fair pace towards the kitchen door, he stretched his neck to see through the window. It was steamed up on the inside, and so he gingerly tapped on the door. When there was no answer, he tapped again, this time with a deal of determination.

The door was slowly inched open and a woman with round eyes declared in a nervous voice, 'Good heavens, young man! Whatever do you want, disturbing a respectable household at this time of night?' She clung to the door, keeping her foot firmly against it while staring at him disapprovingly.

Johnny had called at this house on only one other occasion, and that was on a fine afternoon last summer when he had hoped to walk Ruby to the tram stop. Sadly, she had already left, and when she saw him later that same day, had given him strict instructions never to come to Billenge House again: 'Or Cook will give me what for.' He never did, but on that day he had seen at first hand what a formidable woman Cook really was. She had made a lasting impression, and he knew at a glance that this woman was not she. He wondered whether she had been replaced. 'I'm sorry,' he said lamely. 'But – well, I wonder if I could have a word with Ruby?'

'Ruby?' She leaned forward, thinking how handsome the visitor was and feeling sorry that she was not the one he sought. 'There's no one of that name here, young man.'

'But there must be. She works here . . . in the kitchen.'

'Ah, then I'd better explain. Those of us who are employed here in this kitchen tonight, are only temporary. I believe the usual staff have taken Christmas Eve off. To visit family, I think. I expect your Ruby must be one of them.'

She would have shut the door then, but he put out his arm and thrilled her with a touch, 'No. She is here. She must be. Could you please make sure?'

His insistence frightened her. 'There's no need. Your friend isn't here so you'd best be off.' She slammed the door shut then, leaving him confused and bewildered. 'If she's not here, then where is she?' he asked the night. With a bowed head and heavy heart, he began to make his way back down the path. 'Happen she went home earlier and I missed her,' he mused. 'Aye, that's what happened. It's funny though, because her mam said clear enough, "Our Ruby's been called to work, and she'll be staying the night."' He didn't know quite what to make of it all. But one thing was certain: somewhere along the way plans must have changed and he'd missed her.

Out of sight of the kitchen, he leaned against the wall, hands thrust deep into his pockets while he absent-mindedly kicked at the gravel, spraying a clutch of small stones into the air. 'Damn and bugger it!' he groaned. Seeing Ruby would have lifted his spirits no end.

After a while he came back to the front of the house. Still there was no one in sight. Lonely now, and impatient to be away, he strolled round the carriage, stroked the horses' manes, sat on the narrow strip of grass beneath the hedge, where he looked across at the bright lighted house, and warmed himself with thoughts of his Ruby. 'I expect she's abed now,' he murmured. When the big bay gelding turned its head to stare at him, he told it, 'Don't lose your heart to any woman. She'll only break it.'

Suddenly the front door of the house opened and he scrambled to his feet, hoping it might be Oliver Arnold. But it was only an old man come out to breathe the night air. He didn't stay long in the cold. Instead he drew on his cigar, looked up at the stars, sighed aloud as though he was pining for something long gone, and then ambled back into the house.

Concerned now, because he thought it must be going on for midnight, Johnny toyed with the idea of knocking on the door and letting someone know that Mr Arnold's carriage was waiting. He went towards the house. The lights were blazing and the music was playing. As he came nearer, he could clearly see the guests inside. Curious, he came up to the window, looking inside the room. There were people dancing, and other couples standing around. There was laughter and chatter and a good deal of flirting going on, he thought, spying an elderly fellow with his hand firmly planted on a pink bustle. In a high-backed chair beside the fireplace, Teresa Arnold was toying with a young man's affections. Tall and thin, with a pasty face and narrow moustache, Tony Hargreaves bowed and scraped and laughed embarrassingly at her every word. It would have done Oliver Arnold's heart good to see his daughter married off to this young man; not only because Tony's father was a wealthy mine-owner, but because Tony was a good and harmless man who would make her a better husband than she deserved.

The window was high up, and Johnny had to stand on tiptoe to see the whole panorama. His eyes travelled the length and breadth of the room, and there, in deep conversation with a short and somewhat portly gentleman, was Oliver Arnold himself. 'Hmm! Looks like I've a long wait before *you're* ready to go home,' Johnny observed. He shivered. The night air was growing bitter, and the breeze cut spitefully through his clothes. He hoped it wouldn't be too long before he was tucked up in the comfortable makeshift bed in the stables. Drawing his jacket tighter about him, his attention was drawn by two young women seated beside the fireplace. They too were deep in conversation, and the one he could see more clearly appeared to be growing agitated. From Ruby's fond description of her employer's daughter, he thought this one must be Cicely Banks. She certainly looked pale and fragile.

The second young lady was partly turned away from him, but she was so slim and perfectly shaped, and her hair of that same rich autumn brown, that she might have been Ruby herself. In that moment a man came on the scene, and when he saw that it was Luke Arnold, Johnny instinctively recoiled from the window. If that obnoxious fellow was to see him staring through the window at the guests, there was no doubt he would have him instantly dismissed.

At first Luke spoke to Cicely, obviously asking her to dance. She blushed and fluttered her eyelids in embarrassment, then she gently laughed and pointed to her feet, implying that she had danced enough for the moment. He then turned to her companion, smiling and debonair, his arm extended towards her.

The young lady shook her head and put up her hand in refusal. Kindly Cicely was obviously disappointed, and, leaning towards her friend, appeared to be making an effort to persuade her. It took a few moments, but between Cicely and Luke Arnold it was only a matter of minutes before the other woman rose from her chair and was escorted to the floor by the triumphant Luke. Although the young lady's face was still turned from him, Johnny could clearly see the smug expression on Luke's face. His sympathies lay with the woman who had been bullied into accompanying him on to the dance floor.

As the music floated into a slow and romantic waltz, Johnny's thoughts turned to Ruby. If she was here with him right now, he would take her in his arms and dance her right around this yard. He closed his eyes and imagined her near him. He could see her in every lovely detail; the heart-shaped face, the wild brown hair that curled and teased about her forehead, and those magnificent eyes that could be dark as the ocean or blue as ripe cornflowers. Oh, how he ached for her. Opening his eyes, he looked into the room again, envying the couples there. He began to hum with the music. Ruby came to him then, and he stretched out his arms as though he was holding her close. Twisting and turning on the spot, he slowly danced in time to the melody, with Ruby safe in his arms and his heart soaring with joy.

Inspired by his antics, the horses grew impatient and started to move forward, taking the carriage with them. 'Whoah!' he called out, coming to an abrupt halt and almost falling into the low shrubbery when he unbalanced himself. 'It's no good you being fretful,' he laughed. 'You'll have to be patient, the same as me.' They stopped then, snorting and fidgeting, and throwing their large heads high in frustration. 'It won't be long now, my beauties,' he coaxed softly. Returning his attention to the scene on the other side of the window, he waited and watched. Gentle music was still playing, the couples were still dancing, and Luke Arnold appeared to be entranced by his partner, drawing her close and holding her as though he would never let her go. Johnny was fascinated. These two danced well together, he thought.

Although he himself was no expert, he could do a jig and enjoyed a good barn-hop, but these fancy dances were only for the toffs. Somehow, Johnny couldn't take his eyes off Luke and his partner. Now and again Luke would lean his head towards her, and she would look away. Shy, Johnny thought. But together they twirled and moved about the floor with confidence and grace. He began to grow curious about the woman who had so captured Luke Arnold's attention. From her slim shape and the lively manner in which she moved, it was obvious to him that she was young. He wondered if she was also beautiful. He hoped she would have the good sense to recognise Luke for the rogue he was.

'You hate me, don't you?' Luke hissed beneath his breath.

'I *loathe* you!' Ruby didn't even look up. The sight of his face leering at her was more than she could bear. Luke Arnold could go to hell for all she cared. Just now, when he had deliberately caused a 'gentlemanly' fuss in asking her to dance, Ruby had seen it as a veiled threat to expose her as a fraud. On top of that, poor misguided Cicely had taken his side, insisting that she should accept his kind invitation.

'Really, Ruby, you mustn't be so anti-social,' she had chided. Ruby realised that it would be easier to accept than to antagonise the pair of them. Later, she could talk to Cicely and reveal what Luke's own sister had said about him. Surely then Cicely must realise she should stay well clear of him. She hoped so. Thank God the music was coming to an end and soon the evening itself. Afterwards she would have Cicely all to herself and they could talk to their hearts' content.

As Luke swung her round, Ruby caught sight of his sister Teresa. She was dancing only an arm's reach away, partnered by a tall handsome man with greying whiskers and dark penetrating eyes that swept over Ruby with interest. Unaffected, she shifted her gaze to Teresa and was deeply disturbed to find herself being carefully studied. It was only a moment before Teresa turned away, but she had left Ruby with the awful feeling that Teresa Arnold had marked her well.

As she raised her eyes, Ruby saw that Cicely was also watching her. When their eyes met, Cicely excitedly waved her hand and smiled a wide angelic smile. Ruby took a deep breath and returned a bright happy smile that belied her true feelings. Any minute now it would be over and she could escape from this man who had thrown a dark and evil shadow across her life.

What Ruby didn't realise was that a *third* person was watching from outside the window. Deeply curious, Johnny had followed her and Luke as they wound their way across the floor, every step bringing them closer and closer to the window. Suddenly, Luke had swung his partner round and Ruby was in full view. Horrified, Johnny stared with disbelief. He gasped out loud, recoiling as though a huge fist had hit him full in the stomach.

'RUBY!' Her name burst from his lips without him knowing, echoing in the cold night air and sounding strange to him. 'IT'S RUBY!'

He closed his eyes, his mind reeling from what he had seen. Dressed in finery and looking every inch a lady, his Ruby was dancing in there, closed in Luke Arnold's arms as though she belonged. He couldn't believe what his eyes were telling him. *Ruby was in there with the toffs. Dancing and smiling and done up like she was one of them!* Suddenly he was laughing out loud, shaking his head and promising himself, 'You're seeing things, Johnny boy. It's just somebody that looks like her, that's all.' He felt breathless, sick to his heart. He couldn't, wouldn't accept what he had seen.

Climbing on to the low wall once more, he pressed his face to the window. All of his fears were confirmed when he stared across the room. The music had stopped and everyone was making their way back to the seats. Cicely Banks was on her feet now, a look of delight on her face and her arms stretched out towards the young woman who had danced with Luke Arnold. There was no denying it. The young lady with Luke Arnold was Ruby. And Johnny still could not believe it.

'Are you ready, Father?' Teresa Arnold was agitated, anxious to leave. Having found her father, she had managed to draw him away from a deep discussion regarding the dockers and Ben Tillett, who had fought on their behalf for a minimum four-hour day at sixpence an hour, and overtime paid at eighteenpence an hour. Across the country, in every industry, this astonishing success was seen by all employers as the thin end of a very painful wedge.

Oliver Arnold looked tired. 'I'm ready whenever you are, my dear,' he said. 'What about your brother?' He raised his head and looked about, and she did the same. But while he caught sight of

Luke, Teresa glanced towards the window and saw Johnny there. At once she was intrigued. He looked grey and shocked. She followed his gaze and it led her straight to Ruby. She was puzzled. He seemed to recognise that young woman, to *know* her. But how could he know her? Stable-hands and genteel ladies would hardly meet in social circumstances. Work then? She reasoned how Johnny might have worked for that young woman's family at some time or another. But *when*? Surely, Johnny had worked for her father ever since he was old enough? Still, there had to be an explanation. It occurred to her that perhaps Johnny's mother had taken her with him while she was in service at a household in the past, and this was where he had encountered the young woman. Yes, that would be it, she was certain. But then, why did he seem so shocked to see her?

She smiled. 'A little puzzle,' she murmured. She enjoyed a 'little puzzle'. Later when the household was asleep and they could be alone without anyone knowing, she would ask him herself. Oh, but then she might have other things on her mind, she thought wickedly. In her mind's eye was the image of Johnny as she had seen him at the pump, half-naked and bronzed by the sun. A thrill rippled through her.

'Quickly, Father. It's time we were away,' she said impatiently. And it was only a matter of moments before they had collected Luke, and the three of them were thanking Jeffrey Banks and his daughter for 'a wonderful evening'.

Outside, Johnny gave no indication of the trauma he had suffered on seeing Ruby in that house, with those people. Though devastated and confused, and even a little angry, he smiled at the master as he opened the carriage door, and when he was asked about Thomas, replied in a steady voice, 'I left him sleeping soundly, sir. Don't you worry about Thomas. I'll take good care of him.'

'I'm sure you will.' Johnny's responsible behaviour and keen sense of duty had made a deep impression on Oliver Arnold. 'If you need anything, you have only to ask,' he assured him, simultaneously ushering his children into the carriage, before he himself climbed in.

There was a hint of rain in the air and the night had grown pitch black. All along the hedgerows the wind whistled and played, making weird howling sounds that rose above the clatter of the carriage wheels. Johnny's thoughts were dark and brooding. As he drove the horses along the lane, his fists were clenched on the reins and his head was bent to the wind. There was a hard knot of rage at the base of his chest. All he could think of was Ruby. *She had been in that house, smiling and dancing with Luke Arnold.* His heartbeat was frantic, and he struggled to make sense of how Lizzie Miller's daughter could have come to be there, so bold and daring, done up in a fine silk dress and behaving as though she was one of the gentry. 'Been called in to work tonight,' Lizzie had told him. 'Staying over.' He wondered what she would say if she knew the truth. 'By God!' he muttered. 'It doesn't bear thinking about.'

The rain started then, great splashy drops that fell against the road and bounced in the carriage lights. It came down with a vengeance, sweeping the skies and falling upon him until he was drenched to the skin. He heard the master call out something, but his voice was taken by the wind. 'It's all right. I'm okay, sir,' Johnny shouted, guessing that Oliver Arnold was concerned about him being exposed to the weather. 'We're almost home.'

Drawing the carriage as near to the front door as he could, Johnny ushered his passengers out one after the other, each one running into the house under a hail of thunder. Only Teresa lingered, leaning towards him to whisper teasingly, 'If you ask me nicely, I'd be only too delighted to dry your back.'

'Goodnight, miss,' he said firmly, enraging her when he surreptitiously brushed her aside.

She didn't answer him. But her smile said it all when she looked at him demurely from beneath dripping lashes. At the door she turned and watched him drive away. Desire for him burned within her. 'Don't think you can escape me so easily this time,' she murmured into the darkness. Then she hurried inside, eager to soak in a hot bath and mentally go over the finer details of her little plan.

After he had taken off his outer garments, Johnny wiped down the horses, then fed and watered them before going upstairs to check on the old fellow. Thomas was hard and fast asleep. With tender fingers, Johnny covered him over with the blanket which he had thrown off in his dreams. That done, he softly tiptoed from the room, leaving the door ajar, in case the old fellow called out for him. After that he went down to the stables. Here, he lit the ancient stove and put a half-filled kettle on it. Soon the water was boiling, and once the tea was brewed he poured himself a generous measure of the strong black liquid. For a long time he sat on the trestle, rolling the mug between his capable hands, his tortured mind dwelling on the events of the night.

Johnny had long known of Ruby's dreams: dreams of being rich, dreams of taking her beloved family out of the slums and into a 'better' world. He could remember the first time she made it known. One summer's day about five years back he had been in the street when his attention was drawn by the children's laughter. Ruby was standing in the middle of them, unashamed and proud. Her strong dark eyes swam with tears as she faced the taunts and laughter.

'Laugh if you like,' she told them defiantly, 'but one day, when I'm a woman, I *will* be rich and famous. You'll see!'

On that day, Johnny realised he would have to be a special kind of man if he was to win her heart.

He couldn't blame her for having such powerful ambitions. But until this night he had never known how deeply they had affected her. He raked his mind, searching for reasons. Ruby was young yet, but poverty and the responsibility of being the eldest in a large family had matured her too quickly. Ambitions could be a terrible thing, he thought. They could shape a person out of all recognition. He adored Ruby, loved her with every inch of his being. For many a long day and night, he had imagined himself and Ruby as man and wife, travelling through each God-given day together, raising a family and spending the rest of their lives together.

Even though she gave him little quarter, he had never lost sight of his own dream. Now though, after what he'd witnessed tonight, he was desperately afraid. What he had seen was etched too deeply in his mind; Ruby, lost in the arms of a man with dubious character, smiling and dancing and wearing that beautiful dress as though she was born in it. Was that her ambition . . . was that what she really wanted out of life? To be gentry, and to fall in with a devil such as Luke Arnold? Surely not. He couldn't believe that Ruby would deliberately encourage a man like that. Yet hadn't he seen it with his own eyes? In heaven's name, what was she thinking of? Didn't she realise she was playing with fire? And how was it that a servant could mingle with the guests and not be noticed? There was only one answer to that.

'Cicely must have encouraged her,' he realised aloud. Otherwise it would have been impossible. He wondered whether Jeffrey Banks was aware of the deception. Perhaps not. After all, even *he* hadn't recognised Ruby straightaway, and he knew her almost as well as he knew himself.

Going to the cupboard where Thomas kept a fresh supply of linen, Johnny collected a towel, a clean shirt and a change of undergarments, all of which he had brought from home. He placed the clean clothes beside his bed, ready for the morning. Then he rubbed himself down with the towel until he was dry and comfortable. Spreading the towel over a timber post, he ran his fingers from forehead to neck, smoothing his tousled mop of hair. Somewhere there was a comb, probably in his jacket. But he wasn't thinking about things like that.

He was thinking of Ruby. Did she have any idea what she might be letting herself in for? Where did she think it would all lead? One day a lady, and the next a servant. Then what? Where did she go from there? How could she continue working, carrying on her duties, as though nothing had happened. Where would it all lead? He dared not think. It was all so incomprehensible. But then, Ruby herself could be incomprehensible. She was like no one else he knew. She was unique, daring and impulsive. Qualities that made him proud, yet filled him with frustration.

The initial shock had subsided, and now he was angry. Darkly, wildly angry. What awful thing was in her that made Ruby crave the unattainable? What was it that made her so restless? Didn't she realise that she was special, the way the Good Lord had made her? Strong and warm, she was the most naturally good creature he had ever known. Wasn't that enough for her? Would she go on and on until her ambitions strangled her very soul?

Something else occurred to him in that moment. Something that deadened his heart and brought him out in a cold sweat. Tonight she had widened the distance between them. In his bones he knew she loved him. And yet he knew instinctively that he would never be enough for her. Even now, he was more of a man than Luke Arnold would ever be. He would scour the world to satisfy her every need, and as far as he was able, would nurture and cherish her as no other man on earth could. He was strong and powerful of limb, a willing provider, and had more loving in him than Ruby could ever use up. But she wanted more. Far more than he could ever give. And that crippling knowledge was like the weight of the world across his shoulders.

Disillusioned and torn every which way, Johnny blew out the lamp and climbed into bed. But his mind was still too active to let him sleep. There was rage in him, burning and bubbling and spitting beneath the surface of his weariness until there was murder in his heart. Yet who would he murder? Luke? Ruby? Cicely? *Who?* Himself maybe? Yes, he would murder himself, and Ruby would never torture him again.

Ashamed, he thought of his mother and weak-willed father, and knew he could never be such a coward. In his mind's eyes he saw his sister's pale thin face and large honest eyes, and his heart swelled with love. That love soothed him, and he settled beneath the clothes with a calmer heart. Soon he was sleeping but not empty of anger. It made him turn and fret. The gentle rhythmic sounds of Thomas's snoring rumbled through the stables. Horses scraped at the straw with the edge of their hooves, and sly old rats scampered through the food racks, filling their stomachs before curling down in the hay until the dawn. Johnny slept too eventually, unaware that, already making her way towards the stables, the lady of the house was bent on making mischief that would rebound on them all.

Outside a barn owl screeched, winging its way home, a lifeless mouse caught in its talons, snatched up from the earth even before it had time to cry out. The moon was low now, subdued by the previous fall of rain and criss-crossed with grey scurrying clouds. It was a grim and lonely night, heralding strange shadows and moving shapes which laid low during the daylight and emerged under the cover of darkness.

Into this darkness crept another lonely creature. A dangerously beautiful creature. She too had lain in her bed, naked and restless, aching for Johnny, just as he had ached for Ruby. There was anger in her too. Anger that he hadn't come to her easily. Anger that she was made to sneak about like a thief in the night in order to lie in his arms. But she would lie in his arms, because overriding the anger of rejection was a fiercer emotion – lust. She lusted after him, and she meant to have him. In all of her short pampered life, she had never been refused. And she would not be refused by Johnny. Not tonight. Not any more.

When she came through the big doors, they creaked beneath their own weight. Remaining quite still, she held her breath, listening for any sound from inside. All was silent. Carefully pushing the doors to, she came forward again. In the darkness, she wasn't sure which way to go. Through a chink in the old woodwork, she was shown the way by a shaft of watery moonlight. Gripping the timbered rails, she ventured deeper into the great place, her toes touching the ground without a sound and her eyes peering into the dimness.

Teresa knew the stables would be full because hunters and cobs were always brought in from the fields at night, and on this evening, Johnny would have sensed the storm that was already brewing. With the stables filled, and Thomas fiercely possessive about his own quarters above, she reasoned that there could be only one practical place where Johnny might have made his bed. She was smiling as she felt her way along the rails towards the tack-room. She was sure he would be in there.

A moment later she almost stumbled over the bed. It was not exactly where she had imagined it to be. Johnny had placed himself close to the steps which led to Thomas's rooms, yet not too far from the stables. In that way he would hear any disturbance coming from either quarter. But he hadn't heard her approach, and he wasn't aware that she was staring down at him, her avaricious eyes sweeping over his naked chest. He moaned, turning on to his side, and when his hair tumbled over his forehead, Teresa stooped to stroke it gently from his face.

She remained there a moment longer, secretly observing him, her greedy eyes travelling that broad muscular chest, the carpet of thick dark hairs, and pink round nipples poking through. His upper arms were thick and honed by his labours, his hands were strong, fingers long and finely shaped. Now, as he turned on to his back, his head pressed into the bolster, the muscles on his neck and shoulders tightened, thick and magnificent. His chiselled features were incredibly handsome; dark beautifully shaped brows above clean pale eyelids, a straight slim-nostrilled nose and lips that were full and inviting. His chin was square and powerful, and his coal-black hair like an unruly waterfall spilling over his ears and temples. Even in his sleep, Johnny exuded a powerful animality. She had always known how much of a man he was, how rough and raw, how darkly handsome. Now he was hers for the taking.

Ever so softly, she undid the buttons of her mantle and shrugged her shoulders out of it. As it slithered to the floor she laughed softly and continued to look down on him.

For a long delicious moment she enjoyed her own nakedness, preening herself, drawing her long tresses to the front of her shoulders and stroking them. Her trembling fingers touched her breasts, caressing the nipples. Her sighs rippled through the darkened room. She had waited so long. So very long. To wait one moment longer would only heighten the pleasure when at last he wrapped his arms around her.

Gently she plucked the blanket from him. His nakedness made her gasp. His powerful legs were stretched out, slightly parted. Gingerly, she leaned down, letting the tips of her fingers roam his thighs. The touch of his bare skin excited her so that she could hardly breathe.

Suddenly, he was startled awake. With a loud cry, he sat up, dark suspicious eyes still heavy with sleep. When they saw her in the half-light, they widened in horror.

'YOU!'

The anger was still on him. He had been dreaming of Ruby. Dreaming that she had gone from him for ever, walking away on the arm of Luke Arnold. When he'd called out to her, she only laughed in his face. He wanted to drag her away from Luke, to smash his fist into the man's smiling face. But it wouldn't do any good. Ruby had laughed at him. She had made her choice, and she was leaving for good. His whole body was covered in a film of sweat. He was trembling. He was awake, yet still enmeshed in that nightmare. Ruby had left him for ever. That was all he could think.

'Don't send me away,' Teresa pleaded softly. In the half-light she was stunningly beautiful. Her tall slim figure was softly rounded; small pointed breasts, long shapely limbs, that dark shadow between her thighs, her own hands touching, teasing him.

She reached out then, brushing her hand over his face, tracing the contours of his mouth with soft fingertips. 'I do love you,' she murmured. And, in the heat of that moment, she did.

Her soft persuasive voice tormented his senses. 'Don't send me away.' It echoed against the walls of his mind, making him half-crazy. 'Don't send me away.' But Ruby had sent *him* away. And now it was his turn.

In an instant he was out of the bed and standing before her. 'I want you out of here!' he said in a rough voice. When she stretched up her arms and put the flat of her hands against his chest, he groaned, wrapping each of his hands about her wrists. In the semi-darkness her face was too familiar, her nakedness too close. He could feel the tips of her breasts beneath his ribs, gently rubbing, awakening dangerous feelings in him. Her hair was touching his arm, soft as rainwater. She was Ruby. She was not Ruby. Then she was. He loosened his grip on her wrists. She reached upwards. On tiptoe she wound her arms round the back of his neck and pressed his face down to hers. When their lips fused, it seemed to dissolve the anger in him. She pushed herself against his nakedness, moaning, sighing, touching him everywhere. Desire flooded through him. And a terrible fury. Ruby. Always Ruby! The fury unleashed a passion that stormed through him like a torrent.

'Love me,' groaned Teresa. He gripped her by the shoulders and pushed her away, propelling her back towards the timbered rail. He was hard, angry hard, wanting to hurt. Desperate to love. Ruby. Always Ruby!

He lifted her from the ground and bowed his head, kissing her neck, her face, her mouth, exciting her until she trembled from head to toe. He bent her backwards against the rail. Lowering his hands, he grasped her thighs, forcing them apart, forcing himself into her. She was panting, then groaning, then softly laughing, wanting too much of him. Clinging with all her might, she thrust herself upwards, raising her legs and wrapping her body right around his. She was frantic now, clawing at him. She wanted him deep inside her. The rail was hard against her back, he was hard against her front, and she would have turned herself inside out to be closer to him. When he drove into her again and again, she cried out with joy.

Their sweat mingled, dripping from his face onto hers. His mouth was over hers, then it was teasing her breasts, then his tongue was in her mouth, filling her with unbearable pleasure. They fell to the ground. They couldn't stop. Not now. Not when the tidal wave was engulfing them. He hardened inside her, throbbing now, spending the last of his energy. She cried out. The pain was delicious, taking her breath away. She broke over him, crying out like a wild animal. He groaned and rolled away. He hated her. He hated himself. It was Ruby. Always Ruby!

'I'll be back,' she threatened, slipping the robe over her bruised limbs.

'No!' he told her in a harsh voice.

She laughed, a hard coarse sound. 'Surely you don't think I can let you go now?' She had come into his arms a virgin. Now she was a woman. *He* had made her a woman. She would not forget that glorious experience. Neither could she let *him* forget it.

'I'm sorry,' he said, 'but don't ever come back.' He had done her a great wrong, and for the second time that night, he was ashamed.

'Oh, I'm not sorry,' she replied, her narrowed satisfied eyes raking his face. 'And I meant what I said. After all, you wouldn't want Daddy to know what took place here, would you?' The thought of her father discovering what she had done sent a tremor through her. What she had threatened just now was a daring bluff. But Johnny wasn't to know that.

He was shocked. 'Are you saying you'd risk your own well-being by telling him?'

Her answer was coolly to button her mantle and saunter towards the doors where she turned again, peering into the darkness with a slow and deliberate smile. She could not see him. But he could see her, and cursed himself for the fool he was. 'I'll be back,' she promised. Then, like a fleeting shadow, she went into the night.

Just for a moment, in the dark and quiet, it seemed to Johnny that she had never been here at all. But then her presence was all over him. He still burned from the wild insane passion that had taken his reason. His loins throbbed. Rivulets of sweat trickled down his back like a small waterfall. She had been here all right, and he knew she would be back. With great sadness, he realised that he might have to leave this place, leave Thomas and the horses. His anger had turned inward.

'You bloody fool, Ackroyd!' he cursed, sinking on to the bed and bending his head into his hands. 'You hot-headed bloody fool!'

Crippled with remorse, and still naked, he went out to the pump where he washed himself head to toe, scrubbing at his skin as though it was so much filth. Afterwards he dressed and strode out into the night. There was no sleep in him. Only anguish. And a sense of deep regret.

At first Thomas had imagined himself to be dreaming when he heard a noise from below. Dragging himself out of bed, he rubbed the grime from his bedroom window and directed his gaze to the stables beneath. It was too dark. He couldn't see anything.

Shuffling to the door, he came out on to the platform. He heard Teresa's threats from the doorway and he shook his greying head. 'So you've cornered him at last, you little trollop!' he murmured in disgust.

He watched her go, and heard Johnny reproach himself before going out to the pump. He listened while Johnny called himself all kinds of a fool, and guessed how that young man was feeling. Teresa Arnold was a beautiful creature but it was common knowledge that Johnny wanted only one sweetheart, and that was Ruby. All the same, he was only a man, and what man could refuse when a woman such as that offered herself to him? Yet Thomas knew Johnny well enough to know that now he would consider leaving here for good.

'I can't let that happen, Johnny lad,' he whispered, 'I'll not let you leave me, not because of a little witch like that, I won't!' He searched his mind for an answer to this awful dilemma, but he was tired and ill.

What had taken place here tonight was madness. Tomorrow he must think of a way to keep Johnny here with him, and safe from that one's clutches.

221

Chapter Seven

Luke Arnold didn't know whether to laugh or cry. In the end he stared at her, then dropped his head to his chest and said in a flat voice, 'He'll kill you when he finds out.'

'What am I going to do, Luke?' Teresa was frantic. 'You've got to help me.'

He swung round, eyes blazing. 'You can forget that, little sister,' he said sarcastically. 'You've had your fun, and now you can bloody well pay for it, because I'm not getting involved. Do you hear that?' He strode across the room and thrust his face close to hers. 'I AM NOT GETTING INVOLVED!'

Grabbing his coat cuff, she hung on. 'You've *got* to help me, Luke. There's no one else I can turn to. I'm afraid I'll be turned out without a penny. Oh, I couldn't bear it, Luke. I couldn't bear to be disowned and have to live from hand to mouth. Father would do that to me if he found out. I know he would.' She was sobbing. 'I can't live without fine things and servants, you know that, Luke. I'd die if he shamed me by turning me out. I would just die.'

Viciously shaking her loose, he snapped, 'You should have thought of all that, shouldn't you, eh? When you were writhing beneath him, with him poking at you like one of the stallions with a mare, you should have thought of the consequences.' His expression was one of disgust. 'How could you, Teresa?' he demanded. 'How could you lie with a stable-hand?' He turned and spat into the fire, as though ridding himself of a nasty taste.

She had been desperate, coming to him against her better judgement and pleading for his help. She should have known better than to expect anything from her hard-hearted brother. In that moment, she recalled something he had confided in her some time back. Now, incensed by his condemnation of her, she told him angrily, 'My fascination with a stable-hand is no more disgusting than your obsession with this lady's maid!'

'Shut up, you little fool!' He lifted his hand to strike her, but then thought better of it. 'I must have been mad to tell you about her.' Thank God he hadn't revealed Ruby's name or her place of employment.

'You were *drunk*.' She laughed in his face, savouring the moment. 'There's no difference between us. Oh, the things you told me that night,' she goaded. 'How you thought she was the devil, come to bewitch you . . . the way she smiled, and how you fell head over heels in love the first time you saw her.' A thought suddenly occurred to her. 'When did you first meet her? And who is she, this dark-eyed beauty? You never told me that!'

'It's none of your business!' Luke had never revealed Ruby's little deceit on the night of the party, three months ago. Besides costing him an opportunity to use Cicely, he suspected that to betray their little charade would have closed the door with Ruby for ever, and he couldn't bear that. Even now, after all this time, he longed for her, dreamed of her. But she wouldn't bend towards him, and though he still secretly, frantically, wanted her, there were times when he loathed her. The more she ignored him the more he needed to hurt her. He had discovered a way. *Cicely*. He had that foolish, pathetic woman dancing from a string, and he meant to tighten the knot. She was the route to the foundry, and she was the means by which he might yet win the elusive Ruby.

'And there is a difference,' he replied to his sister's earlier comment. 'The difference being that I have not slept with the maid.'

More's the pity, he thought bitterly.

'Ah! But you would if only she'd let you,' taunted Teresa. 'Perhaps the maid thinks herself above you? Probably seen the badness in you, I shouldn't wonder.' She flinched at the hatred in his eyes, and realised she had gone too far. He could be merciless when the mood took him. 'Please, Luke. Tell me what to do.'

He couldn't forgive her. 'You'll have to marry him. Go and live in a stable somewhere.' Suddenly the thought of it was too much. He collapsed into a chair, laughing helplessly. 'I hope the two of you will be very happy amongst the horse-muck,' he spluttered.

'You bastard!' She lunged at him, clawing at his face with her long nails.

He struck her then, a short hard blow across the face which sent her reeling. 'Don't ever do that again,' he warned. Springing out of the chair, he glared at her, feeling a sense of power as she curled into the chair, holding her face and softly weeping. 'You've got yourself into this mess, and you must get yourself out of it. One thing's for sure – you're not bringing his bastard into *this* house, I can promise you that.'

His fists were hard clenched and his eyes were like black slits in his white angry face. 'When Father finds out, he'll no doubt whip him all the way down the road and you with him. And I for one won't be sorry! To hell with you both. You deserve each other.'

She looked up and their eyes met. She searched for a little compassion, but there was only loathing. For as long as she lived, she would never forgive him. 'He won't whip him all the way down the road,' she remarked coolly, 'because he will never know the name of this child's father.'

'He will when I tell him.'

'I wouldn't advise you to do that, Luke. If you tell Father about Johnny Ackroyd, I'll have to tell him that you're only courting Cicely Banks to get the foundry. That you deliberately set out to entrap her . . . that you don't love her one bit, but that you'll marry her just so you can get your hands on her father's business. At first, you wanted the foundry to give to Father as a peace-offering, a prize, to show him what a splendid fellow you are.' She was growing braver by the minute. 'But all that has changed, hasn't it? Now that Cicely Banks is eating out of your hand, and you can see yourself as the owner of Banks's, you want it for *yourself*, don't you? You see yourself as the big man, and you intend to cause a little mischief and make life difficult for Father. Isn't that right? In the end, you want it *all*! But along the way, you mean to make Father pay for what he's done to you over the years. Isn't that what you have in your evil, warped mind?'

'Your guesses are a little wild, aren't they?' He tried to laugh, but it stuck in his throat. She was right. Everything she had said was right, and he could easily have strangled her for it.

'Not guesses. Dear me, no. All of it is what you yourself have told me. You'd be surprised how the drink loosens your tongue.' She sat in the chair opposite and crossed her legs, looking up at him with irritating sweetness. They were two devils, one as weak and wicked as the other. 'Oh, yes. Father would be most interested to hear what I've got to say. He might also be interested to know that once you've got the foundry, you'll discard that gentle kind woman just as fast as you can . . . perhaps even setting up home with your precious lady's maid. There's no doubt that your reputation, which you have cunningly retrieved these past months, will be irrevocably tarnished in his eyes. If there's one thing we both know about our father, it's his sense of duty and his tiresome principles.'

She paused in her tirade, before going on with a vindictive smile that made him realise she would do anything to put him out of favour with their father. 'I promise you, Luke, those same principles that would put *me* out on the street, will damage you every bit as much.' She said something then that made his blood run cold. 'You're a bad one, Luke. You've *always* been a bad one. You may have begun to fool Father, but you can't fool me. It wouldn't surprise me if you were up to no good with the small amount of responsibility Father's already entrusted to you. After all, I do believe you have a considerable say in how the money is spent with regard to safety at the main foundry.'

She watched his face for signs of guilt, but he was clever. He merely stared at her in disbelief. 'To this day, I don't believe he realises how much you hate him.'

'Not as much as I hate *you*, I think.'

'So you won't help me?'

'No. Even if I could see a way, I would not want to help you. You're a fool. I have no time for fools.'

The tears ran unheeded down her face. If Johnny Ackroyd had money or prospects, she would have seen to it that he was made to marry her. As it was, she had no intention of coupling her name with that of a penniless young man. 'You're right. I *am* a fool. But let me tell you this: if the day ever comes when I can make you suffer, I will,' she vowed.

'Oh, I'm not altogether cruel, sister dear.' He smirked, 'You have only yourself to blame when I end up with all Father's money. But I won't see you destitute. I think I could manage a small allowance. Perhaps enough to buy you a decent meal now and then. After all, I wouldn't want it to get about that I let my sister and her bastard starve to death, now would I? But as for keeping you in finery and feathered hats, you can forget that, my dear. Low-bred women have to do without these things, and you must learn to do the same.' He smiled and bowed from the waist

226

making a little click with his heels. 'Forgive me, but I really must leave you now. I'm sure you have a great deal to think about.' He straightened his back and the smile fell from his face. Without another word he strode from the room, leaving her staring after him with murderous eyes.

Coming out of the drawing room, Luke almost collided with his father. 'What the devil are you two arguing about? I could hear you from the other end of the hall?' Oliver demanded. Lately, his children were a real trial, and there were times when he thought they would be the death of him.

Luke was all charm. 'Oh, I'm sorry, Father,' he said. 'I thought you were still resting in your room.' He was never one to miss an opportunity. 'If you're still unwell tomorrow, you know I can be trusted to attend to things in your absence. I hope I've proven my ability these past months?'

Oliver nodded. 'I'm pleased with you, son, I won't deny that. You've shown yourself to be very capable, and it won't be long before you and I will be having a little talk,' he promised.

Luke feigned surprise. 'But that's wonderful, Father,' he exclaimed. 'Have you thought any more about putting me in full charge of the men's safety? Legislation is demanding more and more along these lines,' he pointed out.

'I'm well aware of it,' Oliver reminded him sharply, 'I don't need you to tell me these things.' Only last week an employer had been heavily fined and one of his factories closed down, when two of his workers had been killed because of out-dated and rusting machinery. Already Luke was showing admirable concern and considerable talent for matters of safety. The time was nearing when he would be trusted with the overseeing of these matters. 'As I say, you and I have things to discuss.'

'When?'

'Soon.'

'I shall look forward to it, Father.'

Oliver inclined his head towards the drawing room door. 'Is my daughter still in there?'

'She is.'

'You were arguing.'

'I'm sorry if we disturbed you, Father. It won't happen again.'

'What were you arguing about?'

'Something and nothing.' He so much wanted to betray Teresa. He felt she deserved it. But he was a coward at heart, and was afraid of the explosion that would follow if he was to tell his father that his eldest daughter was carrying the groom's child. Besides, his sister's threat was still ringing in his ears, heightening his fears. Teresa must confess to her own mistakes. She was the one who had brought it all about. 'I have to go now, Father,' he said swiftly. 'The new machinery's being installed, and your own orders are that I have to be there.'

'I asked . . . what were you arguing about?'

'Teresa will tell you.'

'*You tell me!*'

It had been on the tip of his tongue, and now when his father spoke to him in that formidable voice, it spilled out. '*She's with child.*' Astonished by his own outburst, he was instantly mortified, consoling himself only with the fact that he had not revealed the name of the father.

Oliver had been standing tall and straight, a proud man, even in the onset of illness. He faltered, his gaze fixed on Luke's face and his lips quivering – with rage or shock, it was hard to tell. Presently in a strong hard voice he told his son, 'Get to your work.' And the cowardly man lost no time in departing the house, leaving his sister to face their father alone.

The manager was expecting him. 'I've instructed the gangers and they're installing the new platforms now.' He sat at his desk, his shifty eyes levelled at Luke and his great spade-like hands spread across the desk surface. 'Do you want to talk?' he asked meaningfully.

He rose from his seat and went across the room where he slyly closed the door. Going to the cupboard, he collected a bottle and two glasses. 'I've closed off the main area, but we shouldn't lose too much production while the machinery's being put in.' He poured a measure of whisky into each glass, and after handing one to Luke, was about to take a sip of the other when it was viciously snatched from his hand.

'I've told you before, Marshall, leave the booze alone when you're working.' Luke had already learned to his cost that it loosened a man's tongue, making him spill out too many secrets. Grabbing the half-filled bottle, he tipped it upside down over the sink and drained it dry. Then he threw that and the glasses into the rubbish bin. 'No more booze. Understand?'

The fellow nervously wiped his greasy hands on the front of his overalls. 'Whatever you say,' he agreed. 'You're the boss.'

'I'm glad you remembered that.' Luke glanced down to the foundry floor, where the men seemed like tiny ants scurrying about. 'Have you done what I told you?' He didn't look at the fellow but kept his gaze downwards, watching the men at their work, thinking how dispensable these lowly creatures were. The heat from below reached up and almost suffocated him.

At once the fellow went to the cabinet. 'It's all done. Do you want to check it?' he asked, drawing out a thick leatherbound ledger which he thrust in front of the other man.

Luke made no attempt to check it. Instead he continued to watch the men below, asking in a quiet meaningful voice, 'Do I *need* to check it?'

'No, sir. You don't,' the fellow replied proudly. 'I've followed your instructions to the letter. It's all set out exactly as you wanted it.'

'And the invoices?'

'One set manufactured and the others kept safe, just as you said.'

'Get them.' He turned then, his greedy eyes following the fellow's every move. He saw Marshall go to the far wall where he dipped his hand into a crevice. Then he watched while the fellow hurried to the cabinet and unlocked the bottom drawer. Furtively, he grasped a small blue file and came forward with it. 'It's all here,' he said in an urgent whisper, handing it over.

'There's no need to whisper, my good man,' Luke told him with a patronising smile. 'We can't be overheard up here. Can we?' he added, quickly looking round.

'No, sir.'

'Good.' He came away from the window and sat himself at the desk, leaving the other fellow to stand on the opposite side, his mouth opening and shutting like a fish out of water. He was thirsty. He was always thirsty when Luke Arnold came into the foundry. Fear made a body thirsty.

Luke went through every note and every figure. It was exactly as he had instructed. 'You've done well,' he remarked, glancing up.

'Oh, you'll find that I'm a man to be trusted,' the other fellow declared with a sideways nod of his head.

'But then I should, shouldn't I?' Luke told him with a frown. 'After all, I pay you well enough, wouldn't you say?'

'Oh, yes indeed, sir! Yes, you do, and that's a fact. You're most generous, that you are.'

Luke looked him up and down, slowly nodding. Presently he said, 'You do realise what would happen if this ever got out?'

'I do.'

'I could never admit to being involved. It would be your word against mine, and I can afford the very best lawyers.'

'Yes, sir. But it wouldn't get out.'

'At best you would be put away for years.'

'Yes, Mr Arnold, sir.'

'At worst, I would have you murdered.'

The fellow gulped and began to tremble. 'There's no one will ever know what goes on, you've got my word on it.'

'Good fellow.' Snatching a batch of invoices from the file, Luke perused them once more then ripped them from top to bottom. There was a small stove in the office and the fellow ran towards it, lifting the top and standing back while Luke rammed the papers deep into the flames. 'You do understand what I've just been saying to you?' he asked, staring into the flames.

'Oh, I understand well enough.'

'Then I'll leave you.' He strode across the room. 'I think it might be wise if I showed my face to the gangers, don't you?'

'Whatever you say, sir.'

'You're a good man, Marshall.'

'Thank you, Mr Arnold, sir.'

Luke bestowed on him a smile before stepping outside and leaving the fellow to close the door behind him. As he travelled along the gangway, he kept his handkerchief to his nose. The heat was intense, and the fumes seemed to reach right inside his head. He wondered how people could work in such distressing conditions. Still, he wouldn't stay. Just long enough to display his 'interest' in what was going on. After the men had caught sight of him, he would be on his way.

There was another duty to perform yet, and its name was Cicely. In the process he hoped to catch more than a glimpse of Ruby. The thought made him quicken his steps. It didn't occur to him that he might be risking his life by walking along this recently installed structure. All he could think of was Ruby. And what he wondered was how long it might be before he could entice her into his bed.

* * *

Ruby had been sitting in the chair, her dark head bent and her quick fingers running the needle and thread through the brim of Cicely's favourite hat – an exquisite turquoise creation with narrow ribbons and pert little feathers. Ruby had mended it so many times that given the materials, she could have made an exact replica.

Every now and then she glanced up, sighing aloud when Cicely went to the drawing-room window for the umpteenth time, her anxious eyes searching the path to the front door. 'There's no sign of him, Ruby,' she moaned. 'He said he was coming to see me today.' She glanced at the clock on the mantelpiece. It was almost ten minutes past five. 'Five o'clock, he said. He's late. Perhaps he's not coming after all?' She shifted her gaze to Ruby. 'He wouldn't let me down, would he?'

'Who knows?' she replied, shrugging her shoulders and wishing Cicely had never set eyes on him. Since the Christmas Party three months ago, the obnoxious Luke Arnold had been a regular visitor to this house. Ruby knew what he was up to, but Cicely could see no wrong in him. In fact, she spent her days just waiting for his visits. If he allowed her a moment of his time Cicely was elated, and if he chose not to visit, she sank into a deep depression. Cicely's once mellow and gentle nature had changed so much that there were times when she was like a different person. But Ruby made allowances because she knew how cleverly Luke had woven his spell round her. She still hoped it would be only a matter of time before he made that one mistake which would show him in his true light. 'Anyway, if he did let you down, who would care?' she said crossly.

'*I* would care.' Cicely rounded on her. 'I know you don't like him, Ruby, but I think you should remember that while he is here, Luke is a guest in this house. He's a good man, and I respect him. Please have the decency to do the same.'

'If you say so.'

'I do.' Turning away, Cicely pressed her face close to the window, watching and waiting. Still there was no sign of him.

It was a moment before she swung round to demand, 'Why do you hate him so?' Irate because he had not yet arrived, she turned her anger on Ruby. 'He's always behaved like the perfect gentleman. Besides, he kept his promise, and he has never spoken one word to anyone about our little deceit at the party. I think that should tell you what an honourable man he is.'

Ruby kept her attention on her work. Without looking up, she replied, 'You're wrong, Miss Cicely.' These past weeks, Cicely had been so distant and aloof, that Ruby felt obliged to address her in a proper manner. 'If you don't mind me saying so, Luke Arnold is not a good man. Nor is he honourable.'

'I *do* mind, and to be perfectly honest, I'm beginning to think you might be jealous.'

Ruby was horrified. 'Jealous?' She leaned back in her chair and stared up at Cicely with shocked eyes. 'Oh! Surely you can't think that?'

'What am I to think then?' Cicely insisted. 'I've seen the way you linger when he enters the room, and I've seen the way he looks at you . . . probably wondering why you're taking such an interest in him.'

Ruby was on her feet then, eyes ablaze as she explained, 'If I linger, it's because I know he means to hurt you. And if he looks at me, it's only because he knows I'm onto him.'

'Utter and absolute nonsense! I've heard all your arguments . . . about Luke wanting to get at the foundry through me. You couldn't be more wrong. I've already asked him, and he emphatically denies it. It's me he wants. I believe him, so why can't you?' She paused, regarding Ruby with angry glittering eyes. 'Or don't you think a man would want me for myself?'

Ruby was mortified. 'Oh, of course a man would want you for yourself, Miss Cicely. *Any* man would think himself lucky to

233

have you for his wife.' She shook her head. There were tears in her eyes. 'But not *him*. Not Luke Arnold. He's bad. Like I said before, his own sister told me things about him. Even she called him a scoundrel. She said that he was only using you to get his hands on your father's foundry.' Cicely's face stiffened and Ruby feared she might have gone too far. 'I'm sorry,' she apologised. 'Happen I should mind my own business. But I love you, and I don't want to see you hurt.'

'If anyone is hurting me, Ruby, it's you.' Cicely folded her dainty hands across her narrow waist and in a low trembling voice she told Ruby, 'You are never again to mention his name. I forbid it.' Then she said something that startled Ruby. 'Lately I've begun to wonder if I made a mistake in promoting you as my personal maid. Perhaps it might be better for you to return to your work below stairs.'

'Is that what you really want, Miss Cicely?' Ruby asked in a shaking voice. She had been so happy in her new post. No Cook to order her about. No dirty fire-grates to empty, or great heavy rugs to shake. Her hands had become soft and white, and her 'uniform' was a pretty blue dress with white patterned lace at the collar and cuffs. She had become accustomed to having nice things about her. Fine clothes to sew and press, dainty shoes to polish, and more precious than all of that, she'd had Cicely as a companion.

There was something else too. Since becoming a lady's maid, Ruby had learned so much about how the gentry behaved. Such knowledge would carry her far in the future. Even her mam had complained that her daughter was 'beginning to talk like the bloody gentry!' Cicely had given no answer to Ruby's tremulously delivered question, so she softly rephrased it. 'Are you saying I must report to Cook, Miss Cicely?' She crossed her fingers behind her back, holding her breath, while Cicely continued to stare at her. Her mam had warned her all too often that her impulsive tongue would get her into trouble, and it looked as though she had been right.

At the sight of Ruby's deep blue eyes looking up at her, and knowing what a special friend she had been, Cicely felt a slight regret at her harsh words. She visibly relaxed. 'We shall see,' she said in a warmer voice. She smiled, instantly putting Ruby at ease. 'I know you mean well,' she admitted, 'but you *are* wrong about him, Ruby.' She lowered her gaze and Ruby was surprised to see her blushing. 'He has great affection for me.'

'And do you feel the same for him?' Ruby boldly put the question, but in her heart she already feared the answer.

'Have you forgotten so quickly?' Cicely sharply reminded her. 'I meant what I said, Ruby. From today, you are forbidden to murmur his name in this house.' She turned away, going to the window where she resumed her vigil. In a voice so low that Ruby could scarcely hear her, she confessed, 'I think I love him with all my heart.'

The silence that followed was charged with emotion. Saddened that Luke had not come to see her as promised, Cicely closed her eyes and leaned her forehead against the window.

Realising that nothing she could say would change Cicely's misguided love for a man who would use her without mercy, Ruby remained silent though in her heart she was crying. Cicely was so good. She was such a trusting and affectionate creature. For someone as devious as Luke Arnold, she was an easy conquest. All manner of things ran through Ruby's mind in that moment. Perhaps it *would* be better if she returned to the kitchen where she wouldn't see him destroying the person she loved? But no. Dear God, no! It would be tantamount to throwing Cicely into the lion's den. Ruby realised she would never rest, down there, away from her beloved Cicely. At least if she stayed here, she could keep a proper eye on her.

What then? What else could she do to protect someone who

wouldn't protect herself? She had tried to warn Cicely, but her words had fallen on deaf ears. She had even waylaid Luke Arnold and accused him of setting out to destroy Cicely's life. All he did was laugh. 'If you want me to be nicer to her, then you will have to be nicer to me,' he told her. Ruby knew well enough what he meant. And she loathed him all the more.

As a last resort, she had even toyed with the idea of asking to see the master when she would repeat exactly what Teresa Arnold had told her. What was more, she might even reveal something to him that she had kept from Cicely in order to spare her any anxiety. Ruby had not yet described how Luke had almost forced himself on her that night, and on many occasions since when he had come upon her at the house. Perhaps if she told the master all of these things he would know what to do.

But then Ruby recalled how delighted Jeffrey Banks appeared to be with regard to Cicely's blossoming courtship. There was no doubt that he craved a grandson and heir, and perhaps it was that which blinded him to Luke's treacherous character. Luke Arnold had charmed them both, and if Ruby was to speak out to the master, she might easily find herself sent packing altogether, and then how could she keep an eye on Cicely?

Suddenly there was a tap on the door and Cicely jerked round. 'Come in,' she called excitedly, her small fists clenching and unclenching. 'He's here, I know it,' she muttered glancing at Ruby. 'I told you he wouldn't let me down.'

The door opened and a small fair-haired woman stepped inside. She had recently been hired to take Ruby's place below stairs, and Cook had reported sullenly that the new recruit was 'passable'. Looking directly at her mistress, the maid said in a firm clear voice, 'You have a visitor, ma'am . . . a Mr Arnold.'

Rushing forward, Cicely told her, 'Show him in.' As the maid prepared to turn away, she reprimanded her, 'In future you will not stand on ceremony with regard to Mr Arnold. He's to be shown in without delay. Do you understand?'

Going red in the face and bowing from the neck, the woman uttered a hasty, 'Yes, ma'am,' and then was sent on her way. Ruby felt for her because she realised how the poor thing would be wondering whether she would be dismissed before the day was out. Later Ruby would tell her not to worry because Miss Cicely's bark was worse than her bite.

In a moment Luke Arnold swept in through the door, his arms outstretched in greeting and his smile as devastating as ever. 'Cicely! How charming you look,' he purred. And she blushed a soft shade of pink.

'I was afraid you might have forgotten me,' she said, her face uplifted in a dazzling smile and her blue eyes shining.

'Forget you, my dear?!' He looked suitably taken aback. 'Never!' He lifted her small white hand and placed his lips over her slender fingers, knowing she would believe anything he chose to tell her.

When Cicely's gaze went beyond him to the far end of the room, he swung round and found himself staring straight into Ruby's condemning eyes. 'Well, well! The maid who fancies herself as a lady!' he exclaimed in a burst of laughter. He might have gone on but that would have been foolish because to utter one more word would have told Cicely far too much about the way he really felt towards Ruby.

'Leave us.' Cicely's voice was unusually sharp as she turned on Ruby.

Without delay, she gathered the pieces of the hat she had been working on and left the room. She didn't look back. If she had done so, she would have seen Luke looking questioningly at Cicely. When the door was closed, he remarked, 'That was a little abrupt, my dear. I understood that you saw Ruby as your dearest friend?'

237

She chose not to remark on this observation, because it was hurtful to her. Ruby *was* very special, and she was already regretting the harshness with which she'd addressed her. Yet she did not see it as her fault. If only Ruby would stop trying to damn Luke in her eyes, she would have forgiven her anything. As it was, she was still a little cross. 'Did I misunderstand your message?' she asked him, deliberately changing the subject. 'I was certain you said five o'clock.' She checked the time by the mantelpiece clock. It was now twenty minutes past the hour.

'No, you didn't misunderstand,' he confirmed. 'But I had to oversee a delivery at the foundry. All day long I've been there, since six o'clock this morning, and I might tell you, I'm very weary.' He lied magnificently. 'I should have gone straight home to bathe and change, but I couldn't wait to see you, my lovely.' He leaned towards her and smiled deep into her eyes. 'Unfortunately, I can't stay long because Father is expecting a full report on his desk. He will want to discuss all manner of things. No doubt it will be the early hours before I get a wink of sleep.'

'Oh, dear.' Cicely was obviously disappointed. 'And here was I thinking we might have a cosy evening together. There would be no one to disturb us because Father won't be home until quite late.'

He sighed and kissed her hand again. 'An evening together? Just the two of us? Oh, what a shame. That would have been wonderful. I am sorry.'

Cicely led him to the settee where they sat and looked at each other, he with a fixed smile and she with mooning eyes. 'All the same, I'm grateful that you chose to come here before going home.' She looked towards the pull-bell beside the fireplace. 'You must be longing for a cup of tea and something to eat?'

He panicked then, sensing a delaying tactic. 'Oh no. I would rather spend the short time we have together just talking and holding hands.' He had known other women such as this gullible creature and knew that a little flattery would go a long way. They were so susceptible to a few chosen romantic words. 'As I said, my first thought was that I must come and see you, regardless of how tired I was.' He glanced at the clock. 'My! Is that the time?' It was almost five-thirty, and he knew that Ruby would be about to finish for the day. 'A few minutes more then I really must leave.'

For the next few minutes he pampered and wooed Cicely, and she blushed and giggled and before long was completely under his spell. At precisely five-thirty he kissed her lightly on the mouth, and while she was recovering, stood up, saying, 'I daren't stay another minute, or my father will send out the hounds after me.'

'Will I see you tomorrow?'

'I can't promise.'

'But it's Saturday tomorrow!'

'A man's work is never done,' he reminded her.

She was proud of him. No wonder her father approved of this young man. He was so conscientious, so dedicated. 'I understand,' she said warmly. 'So *when* will I see you?'

'Soon,' he assured her. 'Perhaps we could take a ride in the park on Sunday?' The very idea filled him with dread, but if he was to achieve his plans, there was no choice but to suffer her company. First the courting, then the customary long engagement. Next the wedding. Then the prize. A reward well earned, he mentally congratulated himself. It might be a year or two but in the end he would have it all. It would take all of his cunning to bring the ownership of Banks's foundry into his hands. Besides, even if that stubborn old man proved a hard nut to crack, his daughter Cicely would inherit everything when her father passed on. The inheritance would then become his. The thought made him smile: she was foolish enough to believe that he was smiling at her.

'Until Sunday then?' he teased.

'Oh, that will be lovely,' she said shyly. She fussed and blushed and thanked him for being so kind and thoughtful, then she reluctantly escorted him from the house, waving her little white handkerchief at him from the doorstep as he climbed into the waiting carriage.

In a moment he was being driven away, leaving her to return to the drawing room where she paced back and forth, her hands to her mouth. 'Oh, Luke, I do love you so,' she murmured. In years to come, those words would return to haunt her many times.

'Oh. Lowered yourself to come and see us, have you?' Cook was hanging the big copper pan on the wall above the great range when she heard the door swing to. She seemed surprised to see Ruby. 'Well, now,' she said, looking from the new maid to the wretched girl, both of them cleaning silver at the table. 'Look who's ventured below stairs.' She made a stiff little bow from the waist. 'What can we do for you, m'lady?' she asked sarcastically, looking pleased with herself when the other two began giggling.

Ignoring the jibe, Ruby came into the room and seated herself at the table. 'Can't I come and see you when I like?' she asked. After Luke had left the house, she had crept back to the drawing room, where through the half-open door she had seen how agitated and lovestruck Cicely was. It worried her more than she could say. What was more, she had missed her tram. It always left at precisely five-forty and not one minute later. It was now almost quarter to six. 'I thought I might be offered a cup of tea,' she said hopefully. 'I've missed the tram, and the next one isn't for fifteen minutes.'

'Oh? So that's the reason for this little visit. I don't suppose we should have seen you at all if you hadn't missed your tram then?'

'That's not fair, Cook,' Ruby told her, 'I come and see you as often as I can.'

'Well, that ain't too often neither,' came the haughty reply. 'Since you've been got up to lady's maid, you can't seem to drag yourself away from up there.' She clenched her fist and jerked her thumb upwards to the ceiling. 'Too good for us now, that's the truth of it, I dare say.' Cook was a spiteful woman when she set her mind to it, and she had set her mind against Ruby.

Suddenly another voice interrupted. 'Ruby *does* come and see us.' It was the wretched girl. And so astonished were the others that she had spoken out, all eyes were turned on her.

'She's allus coming down to see if we're all right, and she helped me the other morning when I dropped the tray outside Miss Cicely's door . . .' She clapped her hand to her mouth, her colour deepening when she realised how she had let the cat out of the bag. Ruby had been shaking her head all the while the wretched girl had been speaking, but the poor little soul didn't have the brains to know that she was trying to warn her.

Cook was on her like a mad dog. 'WHAT!' She leaned over the table. 'You dropped the tray?' she thundered. 'You little idiot. Can't I trust you to do anything?'

Terrified, the wretched thing ran off into the scullery, whimpering and squeaking, 'I didn't mean to. There weren't no harm done.' The new recruit didn't know what to make of it all. She stared from one to the other with round frightened eyes.

'She's right,' Ruby confirmed. 'There was no real harm done. The tea-cups were drained and the pot was half empty.' There had been a time not long back when she would have run a mile rather than argue with Cook like that. But she couldn't stand by and see the wretched girl frightened half out of her wits for something and nothing.

Cook was not impressed. She had suffered a long hard day, and her temper was up. She had been waiting for a chance to vent her feelings and this little episode was perfect. Woe betide anyone who got in her way now. 'I don't want you interfering in matters that don't concern you, Miss High and Mighty,' she snapped. 'Either get back upstairs where you belong, or get yourself off for the tram. I don't care which. But I would be obliged if you'd get out of my kitchen this very minute.'

When she banged the table with her fist, making all the crockery leap up and down, Ruby remained in her chair, but the new recruit gave a startled cry and jumped up, rushing to the pantry cupboard and disappearing inside where she could be heard frantically tidying the shelves. It occurred to Ruby in that minute that the poor thing wouldn't last long in this household, what with the telling-off she'd got from Cicely and now Cook throwing her considerable weight around.

Ruby glanced at the big round clock over the door. It was gone quarter to six. If she wasn't careful she'd miss the next tram, and her mam would be worried out of her mind. 'I'm sorry you feel like that, Cook,' she replied. 'I might be maid to Miss Cicely, but I'm no different than I was before. I still have to work for a living, the same as you.'

'Happen you do,' Cook conceded. 'But you *ain't* the same. You've got ideas above your station. You've *allus* had ideas above your station. But let me tell you this – fancy ideas won't win you any friends, and they'll get you in trouble before too long. There's nothing surer than that.'

Ruby had seen Cook in this awful mood many times and knew from experience that the only solution was to put a distance between them. 'Goodnight then,' she said brightly, anxiously glancing at the clock again. All Cook saw was a flurry of movement as Ruby rushed through the door. 'By! What's the world coming to when the young 'uns rise up agin the old?' she asked herself. Then she yelled for the other two to: 'Come and get on with your work, else feel the weight of a rolling pin round your arse!'

It was enough. Even before she stopped yelling, the new recruit and the wretched girl were seated at the table, heads down and arms going like shuttlecocks as they rubbed and polished at the silver.

'That's more like it,' Cook beamed from one to the other, then went to the cupboard and poured herself a sizeable measure of port. 'Medicinal!' she barked when the new recruit dared to look up.

The day had grown bitterly cold and the grey skies heralded a stormy night. Ruby pulled her coat tighter about her as she came up from the house and on to Billenge End. The walk to the tram-stop on Preston New Road would take but a few minutes and already she was thinking of that cosy little house on Fisher Street. In her mind's eye she could see her mam trotting from the scullery to the table, clearing the plates away and muttering to herself because Ruby was late. No matter, she thought. She should be home in time to enjoy her meal while it was still warm. Afterwards she would make her mam and dad a fresh brew of tea, then she'd wash the dishes and Dolly could dry. On leaving Cicely earlier she had been downcast, and then when Cook ended the day on a spiteful note, Ruby was made to feel miserable. Now, though, with her family in her thoughts, her spirits were lifted and she went down the road with a brisker step.

Normally there would be others walking down Billenge End to catch the tram. This evening though, apart from a carriage parked a short way ahead, the road was deserted. It puzzled her until she reminded herself that she had missed the earlier tram and the other folks were already on their way home.

She was nearing a dip where the trees overhung the path, camouflaging the entrance to a dark and narrow lane. The lane cut off to an isolated hamlet and from there to the open fields. She shivered as she came up to it. 'Spooky,' she murmured, glancing down the cobbled overgrown alley. There were two dogs confronting each other with their fangs bared and hair standing up. Each was threatening the other, emitting low throaty growls and occasionally darting forward combatively. Alarmed, Ruby pushed on, her head down against the rising breeze and her hands jammed deep into her coat pockets.

'My, my! Don't be in such a hurry.' The voice broke in on her thoughts, causing her to jerk her head up. Her heart turned somersaults and a scream almost burst from her lips when she saw that it was Luke Arnold. As she made to push by him, he put out his hand to restrain her. 'I've been waiting for you,' he said gruffly. 'Waiting to take you home.' Leaning forward, he pressed his two hands to the wall, pinning her between them. 'You and I should talk, I think.' His smile was evil. In the background, the two dogs could be heard savagely fighting.

'We have nothing to talk about.' Ruby kept her voice calm. Here was a man who would relish the knowledge that he had frightened her. 'As for you taking me home . . .' She gave a small laugh, 'One sight of you and my mam would send you down the street so fast you wouldn't know whether you were on your head or your heels!'

'Oh?' He seemed amused. 'She sounds like a wise woman. A woman who knows the virtue of keeping gentry away from rabble.'

'It's *you* who's the rabble.'

'That's what I like about you, Ruby. You say what's on your mind, and you don't give a damn.' Holding her fast, he stared at her for a while before remarking in a sly voice, 'If your mother is so opposed to the idea of you mixing with the gentry, what did she have to say about your little game on Christmas Eve, I wonder?' Ruby's fleeting downward glance told him all he wanted to know. 'Ah, so you haven't told her? Well, well. That *was* deceitful, Ruby. Perhaps it should be *you* she should chase down the street.'

'Get out of my way.' She thrust her hands against his chest but he was like a solid wall.

Inclining his head towards the waiting carriage, he told her, 'We could go for a ride?'

'I'm going nowhere with you.' The minutes were ticking away and she was frantic that she would miss her tram. She began to struggle then, but it only excited him the more. Suddenly his hand was gripping the back of her hair, wrenching her head back as he closed his mouth over hers. His kiss was fiery and brutal. Helpless, she could feel herself propelled up the alley into the shadows there. Her feet were off the ground and his arms were wound tight about her. Partway along the alley, he put her to her feet and pressed his body against her.

'You must be a witch,' he moaned breathlessly. 'I can't sleep for thinking of you. I want you all the time.' He was perturbed by her stony expression and hard condemning eyes. 'I'm no monster,' he pleaded. 'I'd rather you came to me of your own free will.'

Sensing his confusion, she didn't answer. Instead she remained silent and passive against him. He was infuriated. 'I could take you here and now,' he threatened. She gave him no encouragement, no sign that she was willing. He let out a long sigh but still he held her fast, his arms like iron bands about her and his body pressing her hard into the wall. 'I don't want *her*,' he groaned. 'It's you I need. When I have her where I want her and everything is mine, you and I could have such a good time, Ruby.'

Still she made no move.

'What is it? What do you want from me?' he demanded. 'A place of your own? Fine clothes? You can have them all. Just keep yourself for me and I promise I'll provide whatever you want.' She turned away and he boiled inside. 'Bitch! What other man can offer you all that? It isn't as if I'm old and ugly. You must feel something?'

He lowered his head and pressed his open lips against hers, his tongue probing the inside of her mouth.

Suddenly a huge black shape ran at them, knocking Luke sideways. He yelped and lost his balance as the two dogs raced out of the alley. Grabbing her chance, Ruby took to her heels and followed them. 'If you hurry,' she yelled with a chuckle, 'you might just get to that bitch before the dog!'

When she came to the bottom of Billenge End, her ribs felt as though they were coming out of her chest, she was hot and breathless, and to her horror the tram was just pulling away.

'WAIT!'

Her cry sailed out, alerting the conductor who rang the bell and delayed the tram's departure while she ran full pelt down the road.

'Oh thanks,' she gasped, leaping on to the platform. 'You saved my life.'

Whether he had or not, she would never know. But this much she did know: all her suspicions about Luke Arnold had been proved correct.

On the journey into Blackburn centre, Ruby relived the ordeal in the alley. She recalled his words. 'You can have everything you want . . . a place of your own . . . fine clothes.' He had meant every word, she knew. All the things she had ever wanted, had been offered to her on a plate. But at what price? she asked herself.

It was one she would never pay. Even though Cicely had threatened to send her back down below, and though lately she had been harsh and even cruel when Ruby had tried to make her see what a villain that man was, she still loved her mistress dearly.

Luke Arnold was the worst kind of man, a base and greedy creature without conscience or compassion. A man who would trample over others to get what he wanted. Desperate as she was to get out of Fisher Street, she could never deliberately hurt anyone. Oh, but she *would* get what she wanted. In time. In her own way. And she would get it by working, not by cheating and making others miserable.

Several times she wiped her mouth with the back of her hand. The taste of his kiss was still on her. Soon, much to her disgust, she found herself deliberately reliving the experience. Her feelings were a strange mixture of distaste and curiosity. Surely to God she wasn't attracted to him, was she? No! Heaven forbid! She loathed him.

Yet she had to admit that he did have a certain dark persuasiveness about him. She was shocked rigid by her own emotions. All this time she had never been able to understand what the foolish Cicely had seen in such a low creature. Suddenly, in that moment, she understood. And it made her all the more determined to be on her guard against him.

to get out of Irtime Street. She could never hold on to anything much. Oh, but she enjoyed what she wanted to time. In her own way. And she would eat into working, not by cheating and making others unhappy.

Several times she wiped her mouth with the back of her hand. The tastc of his kiss was still on her lips, might to her disgust she found herself deliberately reliving the experience. Her feelings were a strange mixture of disgust and curiosity. Surely to find she wasn't attracted to him. Was she? No! It soon found. She found him.

Yes she had to admit that he did have a certain dark brooding attractiveness about him. She was attracted right by her own emotions. All this time she just had been able to understand what had bothered Crest, and seen in such a new feature. Suddenly, in that moment, she understood. And it made her all the more determined to be on her guard against him.

Part Two

1892

WHISPERS

Chapter Eight

On Sunday 24 August 1892, Maureen took her second trip outdoors in a month. 'Oh, Ruby, I'm so excited, I can hardly keep a limb still!' she laughed. 'Last week a wander round the Saturday market, and now – oh!'

She clasped her hands to her face and stared into the mirror, her brown eyes sparkling as she watched Ruby's every move. 'That's enough,' she cried impatiently as her friend went on brushing her long brown hair. She couldn't wait to get out into the fresh air and sunshine.

'Stop moaning, and be patient,' Ruby scolded kindly. Last week when they had gone to the market Maureen had insisted on having her hair pinned back, and had adamantly refused when Ruby asked if she could wash and brush it.

'You've got such pretty hair,' she had argued, but Maureen was so nervous about her first outing in a long time, she couldn't wait another minute. When they arrived at the market, she was actually trembling from head to toe. Later, though, she had enjoyed her freedom and seen how, instead of staring at her as though she was a curiosity, folks really cared. Just as her mam and Ruby had said they would.

This morning it was Maureen herself who had suggested that Ruby should wash and brush her hair. 'Make me look really

251

pretty, Ruby,' she ordered. And that was exactly what she had done. So now Maureen had to do as she was told and suffer for the end result.

'Stop fidgeting! You're not ready yet,' Ruby ordered. Momentarily resting her hands on her friend's narrow shoulders, she sighed. 'Oh, Maureen, I want you to look wonderful. When we go out of this house and down the street, I want people to faint with admiration at the sight of you. I want them to whisper to each other and say, "Well, would you look at that! Whoever said Maureen Ackroyd was poorly must have come straight from a night on the booze. Why! The lass is lovely. She could turn any young man's head."' Gently shaking those pathetic little shoulders, Ruby went on, 'That's what I want. For the whole world to know how really pretty you are.'

'You'll have a long wait then.'

'I won't, you know,' Ruby retorted. Undeterred by Maureen's cynical attitude, she continued to whisk the brush down her brown hair, feverishly trying to coax a shine into the long limp strands. 'You'll be the most handsome girl in the street.' She so wanted Maureen to look special. Though her friend had been declared well enough to take the odd outing, the long debilitating illness had left its mark. Her cheekbones were high and jutting, and her large eyes seemed unusually dark in that narrow pallid face. Her arms were twig-like, and her hair hung lifeless down her shoulders.

'It was good of Cicely Banks to let me have that dress.' Maureen's gaze shifted to the wicker chair and the lovely emerald green dress that was draped over it. 'It's beautiful,' she breathed. 'You did thank her for me, didn't you, Ruby?'

'What do you think?' she answered. 'Of course I thanked her.'

'And those pretty shoes. Isn't it strange how me and Cicely Banks have the same shoe size?' The black patent leather shoes were dainty yet sturdy enough, with narrow cross-over ankle straps that fastened with a little pearl button. The heels were small but chunky.

'Not really,' Ruby said cautiously. 'Plenty of ladies have a size five.' She lowered her head so Maureen couldn't see her blushing face. Ruby was ashamed because for the first time ever she had lied to her friend. Knowing she could never have persuaded Maureen to let her buy the shoes out of her own hard-earned savings, Ruby had let her believe that they were a present from Cicely. 'To go with the dress,' she'd fibbed, and they were accepted with gratitude.

On this glorious Sunday morning, she had been getting her friend ready for two hours. She had even 'borrowed' some of Cicely's best shampoo, rubbing it into Maureen's fine hair with painstaking care. This past twenty minutes and more she had brushed and brushed until her arms felt like lead weights and her shoulders ached all over. But she'd been determined, and now her determination was rewarded when a faint sheen began to creep in. A little more vigorous brushing, then she placed the brush on the dresser and picked up a pretty hair band which she slid over Maureen's forehead and on to the sweep of hair, drawing it from the temples. She then turned Maureen slightly in the chair so that she could view the results of her handiwork. 'See the shine?' Ruby asked, smiling at the girl in the mirror. Her heart swelled with love when Maureen's face lit up.

'Oh, Ruby. It's lovely!' she gasped, her long thin fingers lovingly caressing the silky strands. 'How did you make it shine so?'

Ruby grunted, rolled her eyes to heaven and back again. 'Hard work, how do you think?' she demanded with a chuckle. Her reward was an upturned face waiting for a kiss. Afterwards the two girls cuddled and laughed, and Maureen asked with a delicious little giggle, 'Do you think I might catch myself a boyfriend?'

'*Two* I shouldn't wonder.'

253

'And will they be handsome, do you think?'

'So handsome it's a crime.'

'It's no good you asking to share, because you'll have to find your own.'

Ruby feigned astonishment. 'Why, I wouldn't dream of sharing.'

'Good.' Maureen waved her hand in the air, a haughty expression on her narrow face. 'It's time we were off. Hurry, girl. Fetch my carriage.'

Trying not to laugh, Ruby bent forward at the waist and bowed and scraped and was delightfully servile. 'At once, madam,' she said in a shaking voice, and the two of them collapsed in a helpless fit of laughter. Suddenly Maureen began coughing and gasping, and Ruby had quickly to run and fetch a glass of water from the jug on the bedside cabinet.

Startled into silence, she watched while Maureen took dainty little sips, catching her breath in between and smiling at her reassuringly. It was only a moment before Maureen had composed herself, but they were both subdued by the attack. Ruby sensed that her friend had been frightened more than she would say. She also knew from experience that Maureen wouldn't thank her if she made a fuss, so instead she attempted to bring the smile back to that poor little face. 'Shame on you, Maureen Ackroyd,' she said. 'You did that on purpose, didn't you?' Her voice was firm and accusing, but there was a little twinkle in her eye. 'After I promised not to steal your fellow and all!'

Maureen took a deep breath and let it out slowly. Her smile was loving as she raised her eyes. Taking Ruby's hand into her own, she murmured, 'I'm so lucky to have a friend like you, Ruby. I honestly don't know what I'd do without you.'

Too choked to answer, she just squeezed those long thin fingers and returned the smile. It was a moment before she said softly, 'We'd better get a move on. Your mam and Johnny will be growing impatient.' Her heart leaped at his name. But, as always, she pushed her emotions into the deepest recesses of her heart. When she compared that magnificent young fellow to the cowardly Luke, she was made to ask herself why she didn't up and marry Johnny at the first opportunity.

Yet even as she asked herself that persistent question, Ruby knew what it was that kept her and Johnny apart. She only had to look at Maureen to know that her dreams of one day becoming rich and powerful must stay ever strong. If the Ackroyd family had money, Maureen might have had better medical care. Oh, the doctor who visited was a good man, and he cared deeply about his patients. But there was a limit to what he could do. Ruby had not forgotten about the centre in Switzerland where wealthier T.B. sufferers had found respite from that terrible illness.

And then there was her own mam, a woman with a stout heart, who carried her family through every trauma and hardship. A kind and good woman who deserved better.

Sometimes at night Ruby would lie in her bed and ruminate on her life, haunted by a horror of the future. It was fear that strengthened what had been in her for as long as she could remember: the daydreams, the wishing and the wanting – and the questions. They were always there, and so was the answer. Money and influence. These things alone could open doors that would otherwise stay closed against her for ever.

Maureen's excited voice interrupted her then. 'Oh, Ruby. Won't they be surprised to see me all dressed up, with my hair shining and everything?'

She nodded, putting her two hands one on either side of Maureen's shoulders. When she felt the sharp bones there, shock rippled through her. 'Let's get you dressed,' she suggested brightly. 'Then we'll give them a real treat.'

Going across the room she collected the dress and quickly returned to where Maureen was making a determined effort to stand up. Ruby was frantic when she saw how the girl's pathetically thin limbs seemed to crumble beneath her. 'No, no, sweetheart,' she coaxed, her calm voice belying the panic inside her. 'Just wait a minute. There's no use wearing yourself out before we even start.' She rolled the dress over her arm then, with her other supporting Maureen, she slid the hem of the dress over her head, gradually feeding the whole garment down until it sat snug to the waist. 'Now then, let's have you on your feet,' she suggested. 'But mind you lean on me,' she warned.

It was a slow and painful procedure, and Maureen was so delicate that Ruby feared she would break in two. Now an accomplished needlewoman, Ruby had spent many a long hour altering Cicely's dress and the fit was good, the clever folds disguising her reed-thin figure, while the colour fetched a glow to her face. The pretty garment had a white lace collar, a narrow waistband of the same material, and a flounce of white lace at the hem. It was perfectly lovely. The floral band that held her hair from her face drew attention from the pallor of her features. Altogether she looked delightful and Ruby was deeply proud.

Exhausted by her own efforts, Maureen gladly leaned her slight weight against Ruby. Soon the dress was fastened about her thin form, and Ruby eased her back into the chair while she did up the top buttons at the neck. 'There!' She pressed Maureen deeper into the chair and stood away to survey the finished creation. 'You look so different,' she said, her elfin face wreathed in a smile and the tears bright in her dark blue eyes. What a tonic it was to see her friend like this, pretty as a picture and so excited about the coming picnic in Corporation Park. 'Oh, Maureen, just look at yourself,' she urged. 'Look in the mirror and see how lovely you are.'

Maureen turned her head and surveyed her own image. Her eyes popped open in astonishment. She didn't speak. She just stared and stared, and then dropped her head on to her chest, her eyes closed and her hands folded together on her lap. At first Ruby feared she was crying, but a glance in the mirror told her different.

'Well, that's a fine thank you!' she chided good-humouredly. She sensed it was all too much for Maureen, and she was saddened. 'You don't like my handiwork, is that it?' she asked, laying her hand on the girl's shoulder. When there came no answer, only a shuddering beneath her touch, Ruby promised in a brighter voice, 'It's going to be a wonderful day, Maureen. A day to remember.'

Moved by Ruby's enthusiasm, she looked up then. 'It's such a pity there won't be many more, isn't it?' she murmured. There was no self-pity, only painful resignation.

Ruby was horrified. 'I don't know what you mean,' she said, gently shaking the shoulders. 'And I won't listen to you when you talk like that.'

'You *do* know what I mean,' Maureen insisted. 'Everyone knows I won't make old bones.'

'Who knows?'

'Everyone.'

'They've said that to you, have they?'

'No. But I know what they're thinking.'

'Oh, I see. So now you're a mind-reader, are you?' Ruby had to shake off this mood that had settled on her. It wasn't often the girl let anyone see beneath that veneer of bravado. Suddenly though this special occasion had touched her deep enough to expose her inner thoughts. 'Has the doctor said anything about you not making old bones?' she demanded.

'No.'

'Your mother? Johnny? Perhaps your dad?' She was relentless.

'No.' Maureen shook her head. Her eyes were brighter and she was beginning to have doubts.

'In fact, didn't the doctor say he was extremely pleased with your progress?'

'Hmh.' It was true. He had.

'There you are then, Miss Know-all. Stop feeling sorry for yourself, and sit still while I fetch Johnny.'

'You're a bully.'

'Happen I am,' Ruby admitted, thankful that she had coaxed Maureen into a lighter frame of mind. 'But I'll not have you say such things . . . won't make old bones indeed! Only the good Lord can say who goes and who stays, and don't you ever forget that. What! I've never had a day's real illness, but I could walk out the door right now and get knocked down by the milkman's horse.'

Maureen laughed out loud. 'Not at the speed *our* milkman's old horse goes,' she spluttered.

Ruby laughed too. 'Away with you,' she said gaily. 'I'm off to fetch Johnny, so while I'm gone you could pinch your cheeks a few times to bring up the roses, eh?' Halfway across the room she glanced back to see Maureen doing just that. 'Shan't be long,' she promised, leaving the room and the door wide open.

Downstairs in the back parlour, Johnny was pacing the floor. He was more excited than his sister at the prospect of spending the day with Ruby. 'For goodness' sake, will you sit down?' his mother groaned. 'You're making me nervous.'

'Sorry, Mam,' he answered, flinging himself into the nearest chair. 'What in God's name are they doing up there?' he wanted to know.

'Woman's business,' came the coy reply. But it wasn't his mother who spoke. It was Ruby. Bouncing into the room and lighting it with her presence, she smiled proudly from one to the other. 'Wait 'til you see the result,' she told them. Then to Johnny, who had sprung from his chair at her appearance, she said warmly, 'You won't recognise your sister.'

'She's ready then?'

Ruby nodded. For the briefest moment she had been stunned

by Johnny's good looks. When she arrived that morning, he was nowhere to be seen. 'Gone to find his father,' Mrs Ackroyd explained. 'But he'll be back in time to take you and Maureen to the park.'

Now here he was, looking amazingly handsome in his dark brown cords and light blue shirt. This was open at the neck and little clusters of dark hair peeped through. In a minute he was across the room and standing over her, his black eyes shining down on her. 'You've been like a tonic to our Maureen,' he murmured. 'And I don't know how to thank you.' He instinctively put his hand on her shoulder, sending little thrills down her back.

'She's my friend,' Ruby replied simply.

'He's right though.' They both looked up at Mrs Ackroyd's quiet voice. 'You've been a godsend to her. Bless you for that.' Seeming to suppress her emotions, she took a deep breath then told Ruby, 'We shall have to make sure she's wrapped up warm. I know it's a glorious day but she's got no fat on her. I don't want her catching a chill.'

Johnny answered, 'Don't worry, Mam. We'll take great care of her, you know that.'

'Aye, lad.' Her smile was tempered by the knowledge that Maureen couldn't get to the park on her own two feet. 'I know you will.' She turned her head and gazed at the figure of her husband, prostrate on the settee, his mouth wide open, emitting deep rumbling snores that told her he would be unconscious for most of the day. 'It's a shame your father can't see the lass on her way, and her all done up to look pretty.'

'Not to worry, Mam,' Johnny said. 'Happen he'll see her when we get back.' He looked at his father and his feelings were a blend of disgust and compassion. 'I wish you'd let me take him to his bed, Mam,' he told her. He still had his hand on Ruby's shoulder and she made no move, even though she sensed the undercurrent of emotion in this little parlour. She had seen

Johnny's father stretched out on the settee, but tried to keep her gaze averted. The whole street knew of Mrs Ackroyd's burden where he was concerned, and that was on top of her heartache for Maureen. They knew also that if it wasn't for the love and strength of her son, she would likely have given up long ago.

'You're right, son,' she conceded. 'It's just that – well, I thought if he was down here with me, I could bring him round and we could talk.' She looked at her husband again, then shook her head and sighed. 'He reeks of booze, but at least he's come to no real harm.' She glanced at Ruby. 'Never wed a drinker,' she warned, and behind the light-hearted comment was a well of sadness. She laughed then, saying in a round warm voice, 'He's not a bad man really, and I can't help but love him.'

'We all love him, Mam,' Johnny answered. He didn't mind Ruby being here. In his heart he knew she understood. 'I'll take him to his bed then, eh?' he asked his mother.

'Aye. Take him up, and I'll keep an eye on him best I can,' she agreed.

Johnny crossed the room and lifted his father into his arms with such ease the man might have been a child. Without another word he carried him upstairs with Ruby following, her thoughts taken up entirely with what she had seen and heard. Mrs Ackroyd's warning echoed inside her head. 'Never wed a drinker', she had said. She might as well have added, 'Never wed into poverty', because to Ruby's mind that was just as much of a life sentence.

At the top of the stairs, Johnny stopped. 'Ruby, would you please open the door for me?' He stepped back on the confined landing while she pushed open the door. 'Thanks,' he muttered turning sideways to squeeze his awkward burden in through the narrow opening. 'Give me a minute,' he winked at her, 'then you can show me this vision of loveliness you've been creating.'

Just to have Ruby in this house was enough to turn his heart over. But to be standing so close and not able to do anything about it, was sheer purgatory.

'I'll wait here for you,' she assured him. If she needed a test of Johnny's worth, she had witnessed it here today. But her ambitions were not weakened. His goodness and strength only made it that much harder for her to say no to him.

Soon enough they were in Maureen's room, and Johnny was lost for words as he looked on the beauty that was his sister. In that green dress, with her long hair brushed to a deep shine and her eyes glowing, she seemed like a stranger to him.

'Well? What do you think?' Maureen was impatient to hear.

He went to her then and laughingly swept her into his arms, 'If I tell you what I think, it'll only make you swell-headed,' he teased.

'No, it won't,' she complained, breathless with laughter when he swung her round against his chest. 'Do you think I look lovely? Do you?' She beat at him with her small fists until he stopped.

For a long moment he stared down at her, thinking how like a feather she was in his arms. 'You'll have all the fellas sighing after you,' he said gently. 'You do look lovely, our Maureen.'

'She's a devil to keep still though,' Ruby chipped in. The picture before her eyes stirred her heart. These two had a very special love between them. And for no reason she could fathom, Ruby suddenly felt lonely. 'Your mam says you're to put your shawl on,' she told Maureen. 'She doesn't want you catching a chill.' To Johnny she gave the instruction, 'Sit her down in the chair. She still hasn't got her shoes on.' By the time she had collected the shoes, Maureen was seated. All the time she was strapping them to Maureen's feet, Ruby felt Johnny's eyes on her.

Snapping shut the last button on the ankle-strap, she clambered to her feet, deliberately keeping her eyes from Johnny's. 'If you can take Maureen downstairs and settle her into the bath-chair, I'll run along home and make sure Dolly's ready,' she suggested.

And even when he appeared beside her to gather Maureen into his arms, Ruby still dared not look at him.

Having carried his father up the stairs, Johnny now carried his sister down. This time Ruby insisted on going ahead. With every step she knew he was watching her, loving her with all his heart. A peculiar silence settled over them. They were each lost in their own thoughts; Johnny thinking of Ruby, Ruby thinking of Johnny, and Maureen deeply regretting Ruby's impossible dreams that kept these two apart. She believed Ruby to be wrong. Yet she had given her word, and she would not betray Ruby's confidence. Besides, if she *was* to tell Johnny why Ruby couldn't be persuaded to be his sweetheart, it would only hurt him. He would be made to feel inadequate and, with Ruby so adamant, there would be nothing worthwhile to be gained by it. So many times she and Ruby had talked about it, and each time Maureen was more convinced than ever that Ruby was making a rod for her own back. Yet nothing she could say would make her see that. 'I will make something of myself, you'll see!' was her answer. And Maureen despaired.

Ruby left the delighted Mrs Ackroyd fussing over her daughter while Johnny went to the cellar and brought up the big old bathchair which Thomas had found in the back of the Arnolds' stables. 'Take it home with you, lad,' he'd told Johnny with foresight. 'When the time comes for your sister to see the world this 'ere chair will do a good turn. It belonged to Mr Arnold's mother, but since she's been gone to her maker these many years, she ain't got no use for it now.'

When consulted, Oliver Arnold made the same observation. Later that same evening, Johnny was refused a place on the tram because of the cumbersome vehicle, so undeterred, pushed it all the way home into Blackburn. Maureen was thrilled when she saw it, and her mam was convinced that because of that old bathchair her daughter had suddenly gained a new lease of life.

The minute Ruby opened the front door, the noise flew up the passage to greet her. The twins were the loudest as they yelled at Lenny to, 'Stop messing with our Snap cards!' Then came the sound of Lenny's unkind voice, 'And if I don't, who's gonna make me, eh?' Now the baby was crying, and Lizzie's voice sailed above it all: 'So help me I'll swing for the lot of you if you don't behave yourselves!'

No sooner had Ruby pushed open the parlour door than Dolly rushed to grab hold of her hand. 'Oh, Ruby, I thought you weren't coming for me,' she cried, looking up adoringly at her big sister.

'I promised, didn't I?' Ruby reminded her. All was quiet now as everyone's eyes turned to look at her.

'Well, at least it'll be one less to aggravate me when you take Dolly,' Lizzie sighed. She had the bawling infant in her arms and was rocking it from side to side. 'It's been bedlam in here. Any minute now I'm throwing this lot out onto the street,' she threatened. When the child screamed louder, she walked it into the scullery, all the while cooing at it and patting its back to fetch up the wind.

Ruby was angry. Striding across the room to the table where the boys were seated, she confronted Lenny. 'Instead of being a nuisance, why don't you give our mam a hand?' she demanded. 'You're the oldest after me.'

Slicing his arm across the table, Lenny sent the playing cards flying, causing the twins to scramble down after them. 'Oh, dearie me, our Ruby,' he sneered. 'Now see what you made me do.' He grinned at her, cocking his head to one side and retorting in a cunning voice, 'So you think I should help our mam, eh? And how should I do that? Go out and shake the mats? Wash the dirty dishes? Take the awful twins out to play?' The smile fell from his face. 'That's all women's work.' He was enjoying taunting her. 'Or d'you think I should feed the babby?' He laughed, a harsh cruel sound that shocked her to the core. 'I'd have a job, wouldn't I, eh? 'Specially as I ain't got no withered wet titties like its mammy.'

He sniggered, glancing from one astonished face to the other, searching for a crumb of appreciation. But he yelped like a dog when all he got was a swipe across the face.

'Don't be so smutty,' Ruby warned him in a furious voice. 'You'd think twice about talking like that if our dad wasn't abed.'

Lenny glared at her, his short stubby fingers caressing his cheek. Ruby had hit him so hard that her fingers had left an imprint. 'Don't you ever hit me again,' he growled, 'or you'll be sorry.'

For a long disturbing moment they glared at each other. Ruby sensed that he was itching to hit her back, and all she wanted was an opportunity to fetch him another across that big vindictive mouth. 'Why don't you go for me?' she taunted. 'And it'll be you who's sorry.' She had never been so incensed.

When Lizzie returned from the kitchen with a quieter babby she was mortified to see her two eldest squaring up to each other. 'What's going on 'ere?' she demanded, quickly putting the child into its makeshift cot and coming to stand, arms folded, between her son and Ruby. 'Come on. Out with it!' she snapped.

She continued to stare, even when the twins cried out in unison, telling her how Lenny had said something bad and Ruby had slapped his face. 'I didn't ask *you*,' she returned sharply. One stony glare silenced them.

Afterwards she faced her son, her pretty brown eyes hard as glass. She knew he was the main culprit. He must have been more wicked than usual because she could not recall Ruby ever lifting her hand to anyone before. 'What have you got to say for yourself?' she demanded. He remained silent, so she turned to Ruby. 'What did he say?' she wanted to know. 'What's this all about?'

'Leave it, Mam. I don't think he meant it.' Ruby bitterly regretted having slapped him.

Lenny jumped up from his seat, shouting, 'I *did* mean it! And I meant what I said about *her* too.' He poked a stiff finger at Ruby. 'If she ever hits me again, she'll be sorry, that's all.'

Lizzie turned on him. 'GET TO YOUR BED!' she said through her teeth. When he made no move, she pinched his ear-lobe between her finger and thumb, and physically propelled him across the room. At the open door, she thrust him out into the passageway. 'And don't come down 'til I tell yer.' She waited there, listening to his footsteps deliberately thumping up each step. He could be heard cursing and moaning until at last there came an almighty bang when he shut the bedroom door. 'The little sod!'

Lizzie swung round to face the others, an expression of concern on her face. 'That'll wake your dad, and Lord knows he needs his sleep after working the extra shift.'

Together with her mam and the twins, and little Dolly clinging to her arm, Ruby listened. Sure enough, the muffled sounds coming from overhead told her that Lizzie was right, 'Oh, Mam. What gets into our Lenny?' she asked.

Lizzie shrugged her shoulders. 'I'm beggared if I know, lass. But I'll tell yer this . . . if he don't soon mend his ways, I'm asking your dad to come down real hard on him.'

Ralph had something to say about that. 'Dad won't do nowt,' he said sullenly. ''Cause Lenny's his favourite.'

Lizzie came and fondly tousled his hair. 'Stuff and nonsense!' she declared. 'There ain't no favourites in this house, my lad.' It seemed to appease him. But deep down Lizzie knew he was right. Lenny *was* his dad's favourite. He'd been allowed to get away with murder since the day he was born. And this was the end result, she thought sadly.

Lizzie looked at Ruby, and she was made to remember how she herself had committed the very same sin where her eldest child was concerned; happen because of her own guilty secret, and the fact that the lass had been deceived about her true father. All the same, Ruby and Lenny were two very different people, and Lizzie silently thanked the Lord for that darling lass. 'Don't let him spoil yer picnic,' she pleaded. 'Go off and enjoy yerselves, luv.' She motioned towards the scullery. 'You've made a lovely basket. The sun's shining, and your friend'll be wondering where you've got to. Off with you. And mind how you go, eh?'

For the first time Frank piped up, his eyes big and round as he looked at Ruby. 'Lenny's been at your basket, Ruby. He offered us some, but we said no, didn't we, Ralph?' he appealed to his brother, who was pretending not to have heard.

'What!' Lizzie hurried towards the scullery door. 'If he's ruined your basket, I'll flay his arse 'til he can't sit down!' she cried.

'I'll see.' Ruby brushed past her mam, and going swiftly to the corner where she had left the basket, lifted one corner of the lid and peered in. She'd bought the strong wicker basket from the market especially for today. The pretty blue frilled cover was twopence extra.

'Has he ruined it? Has he?' Lizzie was hovering, making an effort to see into the basket. 'You bought them things with your own hard-earned spending money, and he'd better not have interfered with it.'

Ruby put on her brightest smile and swung the basket on to her arm. 'It's all right, Mam. Nobody's touched it,' she lied.

Lizzie shook her head, but her whole face was bathed in relief. 'I'm glad,' she admitted. 'I don't hold with smacking the childer, you know that, lass.' Then she recalled how Lenny had been insolent with her just now, and knew the others were listening from the parlour. Her face hardened a little and she raised her voice so they could hear. 'That don't mean to say the buggers won't get a tanning if they deserve it, though.' She winked at Ruby who had to hide her smiles because she was in full view of young Ralph who too often viewed the rebellious Lenny as his idol.

'Are you going to be all right, Mam?' Ruby felt guilty at leaving her to cope with the family, especially when baby Lottie was playing up.

'Give over,' Lizzie chided. 'Yer not telling me I can't manage four childer are yer?' She hugged her daughter, saying with a wink, 'Go on with yer. What meks yer think I can't do without yer, eh?'

She appreciated Ruby's concern, and if it was any other time she might have asked the lass to stay behind and give her a hand. But Lizzie knew how much Ruby had looked forward to this picnic with Maureen. 'Thanks for taking Dolly,' she said, directing a smile at the younger girl. 'That's one less mischief-maker. And anyway, your dad will be down now. He'll keep the buggers in their place, that he will.'

She would have talked a little while longer but Lottie began crying again, her lusty uplifted voice piercing the air. Throwing her arms above her head in frustration, Lizzie turned tail to run back down the passage, crying out as she went, 'Enjoy yerselves. And don't be too late back now.'

They made a fetching sight as they went along the Preston New Road and up towards Corporation Park. Johnny was pushing the heavy bath-chair, with Ruby strolling along on one side and Dolly running to keep up on the other. Maureen was like a child, filled with wonder at everything she saw; each time a carriage went by she would clap her hands with excitement and, stretching her neck to see, would follow the graceful ensemble until it was out of sight.

As they turned in through the great entrance of Corporation Park, a genteel couple strolled by. Maureen gasped at the exquisite finery the young lady was wearing; a cream-coloured dress with huge frilly flounces, and a glamorous pink bonnet decorated with extravagant silk roses. She was carrying the daintiest parasol, and strutting alongside at her white booted feet was a tiny little dog with a pretty pink bow round its collar. 'Oh, look, Ruby!' she gasped. Realising she was the centre of attention, the young lady smiled sweetly and her handsome companion doffed his hat with a sweep of his well-tailored arm.

'She's not as pretty as you,' Ruby whispered in Maureen's ear, and the well-meant compliment brought a smile to her face.

As usual on a Sunday morning the Park was busy, with couples and families and well-behaved children all enjoying this beautiful place. The Park was one of the finest in Lancashire with fountains and cliffs, flower beds and shrubberies, narrow walkways and wide meandering avenues, all overhung with spreading boughs heavy with blossom. There was even a lake, populated by ducks and frequented by each and every one who sought refuge in this delightful oasis.

It was incredible but true that here the air smelled sweet and fresh, when only twenty minutes' walk away the atmosphere was choked and sooty, the smoke from the mills leaving its grime and odour on every house, street and thoroughfare in Blackburn.

The happy little party carried on, up to the lake and the lawns beyond. Nearby the great conservatories housed all manner of exotic and heavenly plants. 'Can we go in there? Can we?' Dolly was beside herself. This was the third time Ruby had brought her here, and each time was a new adventure.

'In a little while, maybe,' she answered. She was more concerned that Maureen was all right. It was a steep climb to this spot, and though she had been pushed in her bath-chair all the way, the sun was beating down and there was no breeze to relieve the heat.

'Aw, Ruby. Can't I go *now*?' Tugging at Ruby's skirt, Dolly was insistent.

Securing the brakes on the chair, and seeing how Ruby was

attending to his sister, Johnny swung the girl into his arms. 'No. You *can't* go now,' he laughed. 'We'll all go together like Ruby says, in a little while. But first we're hungry and thirsty, so we'll have our lunch first. What d'you say to that?' He tickled her ribs and she squealed with delight. When he put her on her feet, she fled to Ruby and hid behind her skirt. She didn't see the affectionate look that passed between Ruby and Johnny. She only knew there was something very special about today, and she loved Johnny almost as much as she loved her sister. She didn't know Maureen very well, but she liked her all the same. She thought Maureen was pretty, and she said so. Thrilled, Maureen returned the compliment.

It was the hottest August Ruby could remember. Maureen threatened to take off her shawl, but Johnny dissuaded her. 'You know what Mam said . . . you're to keep the shawl on so you don't catch a chill.' When she complained that she was too warm, he pushed her and the bath-chair out of the sun, beneath an aged willow whose branches dipped to the ground. From here she could see everything. A short distance away the lake shimmered and sparkled in the bright sunshine, and the whole panorama lay before her.

'How's that?' he asked.

'It's wonderful,' she whispered in awe. Satisfied, he returned to help Ruby who was setting out the picnic nearby.

Frank was right. Lenny *had* raided the contents of Ruby's precious basket. There was an apple missing, together with a small pork pie, and he'd taken a huge bite out of one of the cheese butties; Ruby surreptitiously hid this one in the basket so it couldn't be seen. Fortunately, Maureen's mother had packed a parcel containing some tit-bits and four slices of home-made fruit cake. Johnny laid them out on the tablecloth beside Ruby's generous offering. In addition to Mrs Ackroyd's contribution there was an abundance of cheese butties, four dark ripe plums, an orange each, four fat round muffins, and a tiny earthenware jar of raspberry preserve. There was also a stone bottle of sarsaparilla, and a fleshy chicken wing for Johnny.

'A spread fit for a king,' he told her. 'You must have saved weeks to pay for it.' His smile became a dark brooding gaze. 'You're not only beautiful but a real home-maker,' he murmured, and she blushed to the roots of her hair.

Still blushing, she kept her gaze averted while taking both crockery and cutlery out of the basket. 'Mam helped me with the cheese butties,' she admitted.

'I'm hungry,' wailed Dolly, who had eagerly helped to unpack the basket and now couldn't contain her appetite any longer.

'You'll have to wait,' Ruby scolded when the girl tried to take a muffin.

Seeing the disappointed look on her face, Johnny moaned, 'And I'm hungry.' But when Ruby glanced up to see his mischievous expression, she knew he meant something else entirely, and she had to laugh.

The lunch was a real treat. Johnny collected his sister out of her chair and, much to her delight, took off her shawl and asked Dolly to spread it on the ground for her to sit on. Both Ruby and Johnny kept a close watch on Maureen; the first sign that she was cold and she would be wrapped in her shawl whether she liked it or not.

As it happened, Maureen did not grow cold. The heat of the August sun shone down and kindly warmed them all. Ruby was thrilled to see that Maureen actually had the faintest tinge of roses in her cheeks. Everyone enjoyed their lunch, and after they had each partaken of a cup of sarsaparilla, it was time to clear away. 'I want the lavatory,' Dolly was moaning again. Johnny laughed out loud and suggested they should walk up towards the conservatories. Ruby knew it was his polite way of telling Dolly that there were lavatories there.

Afterwards, they strolled along the pretty walkways, up hill and down, until they came to some flat land. 'Let's stay here awhile,' Ruby said. Like the others she was reluctant to go home yet. 'It's so lovely here.' Her sparkling eyes scanned the horizon as she spoke. To the left of them were the high raised gardens spilling over with blooms, and over to the right was an expanse of green lush lawn, stretching as far as the eye could see. Shading her face with her hand, she looked in every direction. It was breathtaking.

When both Johnny and Maureen gladly agreed to rest here for a time, Dolly complained, 'I wanted to push Maureen for a while.' Looking at Johnny, she sternly reminded him, 'You said I could.'

Maureen interrupted, telling the girl affectionately, 'Johnny and Ruby can stay here if they like.' She had a feeling they might want to spend a few minutes together. 'If you go very slowly and don't tip me out, I might let you take me along that little path.' She pointed to where the footpath curved in towards the flower beds. 'We can sit on that bench awhile and watch the swans through the railings.' They had come the whole way round the lake and were now on the other side.

Dolly was ecstatic, but Ruby wasn't so sure. 'You're only little, Dolly,' she warned. 'When Johnny said you could push Maureen, he didn't mean on your own.'

Maureen argued, 'It's only a short way, and we'll be in sight all the time.' She appealed to her brother, 'It's all right, isn't it, Johnny?'

Like Ruby, he was reluctant. 'I don't know, Sis . . .'

Maureen was insistent. 'The chair can't tip over, not on flat ground, and you did promise Dolly she could push me.'

'You're a pair of bullies,' he said warmly. He looked at Dolly, who was patiently waiting with her fingers wrapped round the handle of the chair. She was a sturdy child, big for her age, and very sensible. 'All right then,' he conceded. 'But only a short way.' He motioned to the chestnut tree. 'As far as there and then back again. All right?' He watched them go, satisfying himself that they would be safe. 'What chance do I stand against two women,' he laughed then, coming to sit on the grass beside Ruby.

'They'll be fine,' she assured him, adding with a little smile, 'I think Maureen wanted us to have a few minutes together.'

'Sensible woman.' There was a pause then he asked, 'Will you tell me something, Ruby?' Suddenly his voice had a serious ring to it.

'What is it?' She shielded her eyes from the sun as she turned to look at him, his expression equally serious.

He seemed embarrassed. 'I haven't said anything before because I know it's none of my business.' Even now the memory shocked and infuriated him.

'Oh?' Ruby was intrigued. She was also a little afraid.

His gaze was dark and penetrating as he told her in a low firm voice, 'I saw you . . . that night at the Bankses' dance. I saw you there.' He watched her eyes turn down towards the grass, and knew she was ashamed. 'Why did you do it, Ruby? What in God's name made you do it?'

'Were you spying on me?' She raised her eyes then and boldly looked him in the face.

He shook his head. 'No, I would never do such a thing,' he explained. 'Thomas was ill so I was obliged to drive the carriage that night. It was chilly out there, and I was impatient to be gone. All I did was glance in the window to see if the party was winding up, that's all.' He laughed scornfully. 'I never dreamed that you were there, dressed like a lady and mingling as though you belonged.' He shook his head. He still hadn't got over the shock. 'Laughing and dancing with that scum Luke Arnold. I couldn't believe my own eyes!'

'You had no right looking in the window.'

'And you had no right being there like that.'

272

'You're not my keeper, Johnny Ackroyd, and don't ever forget that.' At first Ruby had been alarmed and a little ashamed. Now, though, her anger was rising. 'I don't want to talk about it.'

'I don't suppose you've told anyone what you did?'

'No, I haven't.' She tossed her head defiantly. 'I suppose you can't wait to tell?' Even as the unkind words fell from her lips she regretted them. Johnny wasn't like that, and she knew it. All the same, she was disturbed by the fact that he knew about her little deception.

'Aw, Ruby . . . RUBY!' He looked away, so frustrated he could have shaken her. 'Don't you think if I was going to tell, I would have done it by now? After all, I've had plenty of time, haven't I?' he reminded her fiercely.

'I know,' she admitted. 'I'm sorry.'

He looked at her then, a warm forgiving smile breaking over his handsome features. 'Won't you tell me why you did it, Ruby?'

'It was a prank.'

'A very dangerous prank.'

'I don't want to talk about it.'

He didn't answer. Instead he studied her a moment longer while she stared down, twiddling a piece of grass between her fingers. He knew her when she was in this mood. There was no use pursuing the matter. One thing he had to ask though. 'Does Luke Arnold mean anything to you?'

He was taken aback by the vehemence of her reply.

'I loathe him!' She wound the blade of grass round her fingers and broke it. 'You were wrong if you thought I was enjoying dancing with him. It was for Cicely. She's the one who's taken in by him.' Suddenly afraid that she had said too much already, Ruby warned, 'That's all I'm going to say. It was a prank, and that's an end to it.'

'He's a bad lot.'

'You don't have to tell me that. I know it already.' She was losing control and it showed in her voice. 'Now . . . can we leave it alone?'

'If that's what you want.'

'It is.'

There was an awkwardness between them now, and she deeply regretted that. He was right to warn her against Luke, and she should be grateful. Yet all she felt was irritation that he had seen her that night.

'I shouldn't have said anything.' He still felt the urge to shake her though.

She looked up and smiled at him. The subject was closed, and the day mustn't be spoiled because of it. Heartened, she turned her eyes to the sky, watching the small white clouds bumping into each other. A pleasant breeze was beginning to rustle the air. 'It is lovely here, isn't it?' she murmured. The air between them was clear now, and she was glad.

'Yes. It is lovely,' he agreed softly, glancing sideways at her. 'But only because you're here with me.' He sensed that if she could turn the clock back, she would change the events of that night and was grateful for that at least.

She looked at him then, and when he bent towards her and kissed her lightly on the mouth, made no resistance. In fact, it gave her a delicious thrill. Even with the heat of the sun on her face, she was trembling. In her heart she was afraid, desperately afraid that her own emotions might overwhelm her.

When he went to kiss her again, she deliberately turned away and looked over to where the other two were going at a snail's pace along the footpath. 'It's so good to see Maureen out and about,' she said. She wanted him to kiss her. Wanted him to hold her in his arms. But it wouldn't be fair. Not to him and not to her.

'What are you afraid of?' he asked.

'I'm afraid of nothing.'

'You're afraid of me . . . afraid of letting me love you,' he insisted. 'Why?'

'I'm not ready for love.'

'Don't lie to me, Ruby.'

'And don't you tell me how I feel,' she retorted. 'Love can't happen between you and me. Somewhere there's a girl waiting just for you. It isn't me, that's all I'm saying.' In a frantic attempt to remove herself from his dark quizzical gaze, she clambered to her knees and pointed to Maureen and Dolly, 'Look,' she cried, 'Dolly got her there safely. We were worrying over nothing.' He didn't reply. There was a moment of unbearable silence as he continued to gaze at her while she kept her eyes on the two girls.

When he spoke it was with great tenderness. 'Happen you don't love me, Ruby. Happen you *do*. I don't know. You blow hot and cold so I never can tell. But this much I *do* know, there'll never be any other woman for me.' Each word touched her heart and turned it over. 'If I have to wait for ever, I'll wait for you.'

The sincerity of his quiet voice was more than she could bear. 'Don't, Johnny,' she pleaded softly, 'I'm not the one for you. You're a good man, and you'll make a fine husband. Don't waste yourself on me. I'm not worth it.'

His smile was sad, but his voice was resolute. 'I meant what I said. There'll never be anyone else but you, Ruby.'

For some inexplicable reason, she wanted to cry. The tears clogged in her throat and hovered in her dark blue eyes. She tried to choke them back, but they brimmed over to tremble on the long sweeping lashes. There was so much she wanted to say, but it wouldn't be said. Instead she murmured lamely, 'It's time we were making for home.' He didn't argue. He had opened his heart to her. It was enough.

All the way to the main gates, Dolly and Maureen chatted and laughed. Johnny pushed the bath-chair while Ruby walked alongside. In spite of their emotional exchange, there was a strange contentment between them. Each knew the other's thoughts. There was no need for words. Not now. Ruby wanted Johnny, yet she didn't. She loved him, yet she didn't. All she knew for certain was that if she never saw him again, it would be a great sadness to her. But she must never tell him that. She had things to do with her life, and though she might regret it, Johnny was not part of it.

As they came out of the great gates, his attention was caught by the carriage which had just pulled up. He recognised it as belonging to the Arnold family. Sure enough, the door was flung open and out stepped a familiar figure, a tall thin fellow with a pale narrow face and pencil-slim moustache. 'Well, well!' He was visibly surprised, but not pleased.

Ruby had seen the look on Johnny's face and was curious. 'Do you know him?' she asked, looking towards the carriage and thinking she too had seen the young man somewhere.

Nodding, Johnny told her in a low voice, 'That's Tony Hargreaves, the son of a wealthy mine-owner. According to Thomas, he and his family live in a great mansion in Cornwall.' He glanced down at her. 'You know he and Teresa married?' He had celebrated the occasion for two reasons. First, he was downright ashamed because he'd made love to her that night when he had seen Ruby, and second, he was grateful that she would be moving so far away. Like Ruby he too had a secret. Which meant he had no right to judge her.

The young man stood by the carriage door, holding out his hand to the emerging lady. Ruby gasped when she saw that it was Teresa Arnold, looking splendid in a pale blue outfit, her hair piled up in coils and partly covered with a small veiled hat. Ruby's attention was caught by the hat, because Cicely had one very similar. It was her favourite and Ruby had mended it many times.

'I always wondered why they got wed in such a great hurry,' she told Johnny. Almost as though in answer, a second young lady appeared, carrying an infant in her arms. By the uniform she was wearing, it was obvious to Ruby that the woman was the child's nanny. This was confirmed when the driver of the carriage produced a perambulator from the rear and, after placing the child into it, the young woman proceeded to push the vehicle along the path, keeping a pace or two behind her employers.

'They got wed quickly because they love each other,' Maureen remarked innocently. Dolly looked on with interest.

'I expect so,' Ruby replied. At the same time she recalled how some of the women down Fisher Street had talked about the 'grand wedding'. It was common gossip from one end of the street to the other that Teresa Arnold had been with child when her father rushed her into marriage with that eligible young man. Still, she thought wryly, it wasn't the first time there'd been a slip up before wedding bells rang out, and no doubt it wouldn't be the last. 'How long are they staying at her father's house?' Ruby wanted to know.

'I didn't even know they were coming,' Johnny admitted. 'Although, come to think of it, Thomas did say something about how it was the lad's first birthday, and Oliver Arnold wanted to see him.' He looked at the infant, a happy, handsome boy with dark hair and big brown eyes. 'He's a bonny lad, and no mistake.' At the back of his mind he wondered whether there was a chance that he and Ruby would ever raise a family.

Suddenly, Teresa turned and saw them. For a long moment, while pretending to listen to her husband's chatter, she stared at Johnny in a certain way. A knowing and intimate way, which stirred Ruby's curiosity. She did not acknowledge them, nor did she stop. At the point where the path swerved away, she smiled. It was a smile that spoke of secrets. Dangerous, thrilling secrets.

Chapter Nine

'By! That's cold out there. October's a funny old month,' Ted Miller remarked thoughtfully as he went through the parlour and into the scullery. 'It's either the tail end of summer, or it's the dead end of winter.' He chuckled as he took off his coat and hung it on the nail behind the scullery door. 'I know which one it is *tonight*, and that's a fact, lass. Freeze a man's bones inside his skin, it would.' He groaned loudly, rubbing his hands together to get the blood flowing again. Then he swilled his hands and face in cold water at the sink, gasping when it took his breath away. 'It's grand to be home and no mistake,' he called out, vigorously rubbing at his face with the towel.

A few minutes later, blowing and shuddering, he came into the parlour where Lizzie and the childer were waiting for him to get the meal started. He took a moment to spread his large work-worn hands in front of the fire. The cheery flames gave out a delicious warmth. He thawed his front, then he thawed his back. Then he stretched himself and gave a long sigh. 'I pity the man without a fire to come home to,' he said, winking at Ruby who was watching his every move. 'And a family to be proud of,' he added grandly. How he could have produced such a striking beauty as that lovely young woman, he would never know. It had always been a mystery to him. Bursting with pride, he glanced around the table before his joyous glance came back to Ruby. She smiled at him and his heart was lifted through the roof.

'Come on then. We're all waiting for us tea.' Lizzie raised her face for a kiss. When it was given, she told him, 'Sit yourself down, man. There's a good rabbit stew on the table.'

The thick rich aroma had filled the little house, and when he gingerly lifted the lid of the earthenware dish, the sight of the chunky pink meat soaked in globules of fat and smothered in all manner of vegetables sent a wave of 'oohs' and 'aahs' round the table. The childer's stomachs sent up a chorus of groans, and Dolly took a sneaky bite out of her dollop of bread.

'That'll warm yer old bones,' Lizzie said, waggling her head at Ted and looking pleased with herself.

'Here!' he protested, his homely face creasing into a smile at Lizzie's remark. 'Not so much of the "old" if you don't mind.' Pulling out the carver, he sat himself down in it and uttered a short thanksgiving. Afterwards he ordered everyone to, 'Tuck into that rabbit, before it grows legs and runs off.' The twins laughed out loud, and Lizzie had to scold them. She gave her husband a reproving look and he quickly bent his head to his meal.

It was a while before anyone spoke, and then it was Lizzie who said, 'I expect you've noticed our Lenny's been fighting again?'

Ted raised his face to stare at his eldest son whose right eye was swollen and bruised. 'Aye. I noticed,' he acknowledged. Feigning annoyance, he directly addressed the boy, asking, 'What have you got to say for yoursel' then?'

Lenny remained sullen, mopping up the remains of his gravy with a folded piece of bread. He kept his gaze down until his father demanded in a firmer voice, 'Look at me when I talk to you, lad!' Putting his own knife and fork to the edge of his plate, he waited for the boy to sit up straight, and when their eyes met across the table, insisted, 'Well? What *have* you got to say for yourself?'

Lenny knew how to play his father against his mother. It was a skill he had worked at long and hard. He put it to the test now. 'Mam's got it wrong, Dad.' His voice was appealing, and he looked as though he was about to cry. 'I told her what happened but she won't believe it weren't my fault. She's *allus* ready to believe it's me that starts the fighting, and it ain't, I tell you. IT AIN'T.'

'Oh?' Ted glanced at Lizzie and she shook her head. He looked away. 'Why don't you try telling me what happened then, son?' he ordered, his voice noticeably softer. Positioning his elbows on the table and resting his chin in his hands, he leaned forward so as to concentrate on the boy's story. It was the same that had been told to Lizzie, about how he was: 'Minding my own business . . . just walking home, when that scab Arnie Dixon set on me.'

'Arnie Dixon?' Ted sounded shocked. 'I had a run in with his dad when I weren't much older than you are now. *He* were a right bad 'un too.' He flicked his gaze to the bruise on his son's eye, asking in an incredulous voice, 'Are you telling me that Arnie Dixon gave you that?' He stared at Lenny's black eye with disgust. 'By! I should'a thought you could take that lad with no trouble at all.' He was visibly disappointed. 'From what I've seen of him, a good wind would blow him over.'

Lenny was delighted at the way he had managed his dad. He could see that Lizzie was annoyed, and knew he had won the day yet again. 'Oh, he weren't on his own, Dad,' he declared, suitably wide-eyed and surprised. 'There were four of 'em. They all set on me at once. Come at me from all sides, they did. If Arnie Dixon had been on his own, he never would have dared to set himself up against me because he knows I can floor him any time. That's why he had to have them others. He's a coward, Dad.'

'Aye. His old fella were a coward an' all,' Ted remonstrated. He looked at his son, and he looked at Lizzie, and he was caught between the two of them. He grunted, then cleared his throat and instructed Lizzie in a fierce voice, 'They're a bad lot, them Dixon fellas. Allus wanting to argue and fight. I didn't tell you but there was a rumpus in the King's Head the other night and it was Arnie Dixon's old man that started it . . . used a knife too, so I'm told.'

When Lizzie angrily pursed her lips and continued to glare at him, he turned to Lenny. 'You did well, son,' he chuckled. 'Took on *four* of them, eh?' He looked at everyone in turn, his face betraying a certain misguided pride. He didn't get much response though, because they had heard it all earlier before their dad came in.

The twins were still tucking in, Frank drinking the gravy from the dish like it was a cup until Lizzie gave him one of her looks and he sheepishly put it back on the table. Ralph, as usual, was revelling in Lenny's every word, and wondering how he could imitate him. Dolly was more interested in making pretty patterns in the spilled gravy on the tablecloth. Ruby was listening though, and she despised the way in which Lenny could wind her dad round his little finger.

'And did you send 'em away with their tails between their legs?' he was asking now.

'I gave them a good thrashing before they got me on the ground.' Lenny glanced at Lizzie, and she could see the sly triumph in his face. 'Me mam don't believe I didn't start it. Will you tell her, Dad?' he asked with an air of innocence. 'Tell her I wouldn't do that.'

Lizzie retaliated. 'I don't want yer to tell me *nothing*,' she said stiffly. 'I already know what Mrs Dixon told me when she came banging on the door this morning.'

'And what was *her* account of the story?' Ted was already on Lenny's side and Lizzie knew it.

'She said as how Arnie was going to the shop for her when *your* son pushed him into a doorway, snatched the money she'd given him, and thrashed him until he was black and blue all over.' Lizzie always referred to the childer as belonging to Ted when they'd pushed her too far. 'Meg Dixon's a good woman, and she's had a hard time since losing that last child. She ain't no liar and never has been.'

'So you believe her story above his?' Ted pointed a finger at Lenny who was biting his lip so he wouldn't laugh at the memory of Arnie Dixon cowering in that doorway. The snivelling little rat! Taking the money from him was the easiest thing Lenny had ever done. In fact, he knew now what he wanted to do with his life. He wanted to be a big-shot who pushed all the little fellas about.

Lizzie was adamant. 'Yes, I believe her.'

Lenny was mortified. 'Mam! You're calling me a liar then?'

Ted was shocked. 'Surely not, lass?'

Scraping her chair back from the table, Lizzie stood up straight, her face set hard as she told the three younger childer: 'Into the scullery with you, and get your wash.' Without further ado, they scurried from the table, and in a minute could be heard laughing and squabbling in the scullery.

With only Ruby and the two men remaining, Lizzie looked her son in the eye and told him, 'I'm ashamed to say it but, yes, you *are* a liar. Everything you've told your dad and me is a fabrication, and well you know it!'

'You're wrong, Mam. It's Mrs Dixon that's telling lies, not me.'

'The more you open your mouth, the bigger liar you are.' No one had seen Lizzie so enraged before.

'Now then, lass!' Ted was astounded. 'Aren't you being a bit too hard on the lad?'

'No.' She turned on him. 'It's you that's being too soft. He knows how to use you, Ted Miller, and you can't see the forest for the trees. You've a liar and a coward for a son, and I think it's time you knew it. He wants taking in hand afore it's too late.'

Ted was on his feet now. 'I'll not have you talking like that, lass. Our Lenny's no coward. And what d'you mean by "take him in hand afore it's too late"?'

Up until now, Ruby had listened in silence. Now, when she saw her dad and mam at each other's throats, and Lenny secretly gloating over it, she had to intervene. 'The childer are listening.' She noticed that everything had gone quiet in the scullery.

The sound of Ruby's voice, calm and dignified, was like a damp cloth on the heat of the moment. Ted immediately sat down and Lizzie went at a rush into the scullery, where the childer were pretending to wash. 'Let's have yer!' she cried. 'Get them clothes off, yer little scamps. How d'yer expect to wash proper if you've still got your clothes on, eh?' For the next ten minutes all that could be heard was a series of squeals and protests while they were thoroughly scrubbed, one after the other.

Later, while Ruby cleared the dinner things away, Lizzie took the childer to bed and Ted took his son into the front parlour. Whether it was to question him further or to pat him on the back for seeing 'four' of them off, Ruby couldn't be sure although she agreed with her mam wholeheartedly: if Lenny weren't taken in hand soon, he would be no good to man yet beast.

When the dishes were washed and Ruby came into the parlour, there was no sign of either her dad or Lizzie although Lenny was warming himself in front of the fire. 'Well done,' she said sarcastically, standing beside him with her head back and hands on her hips in much the same manner as Lizzie would have done. 'Are you proud of setting Mam and Dad against each other like that?'

He shrugged his shoulders. Already, even though he was only fourteen years old, his shoulders had grown wide and strong, and there was a certain brutish strength about him, ''Tain't my fault if they want to fight,' he said, looking at her sideways.

In two strides she was on him. 'You're going wrong, our Lenny,' she said in a low, hard voice. At the same time she pushed him so hard he fell against the mantelpiece. 'You should be thrashed, just like you thrashed little Arnie.'

'Huh! He was a baby, that's all. A snivelling little baby, and there ain't *nobody* who can do that to me.'

'Don't be too sure,' she warned. 'Bigger bullies than you have met their match.'

His answer was to laugh at her.

'Where's Dad?' She hadn't heard him go out, but suspected he must have done or Lenny wouldn't be so loud-mouthed about the truth.

'Gone to the pub, I expect . . . to boast about how his favourite son took on four villains and thrashed 'em into the ground.' His whole face turned downwards in a sneer. 'It'll be *him* that's the liar then, won't it?'

Ruby tried a different tack with him. After all, he was her brother and it would break their mam's heart if he kept going down the same road. 'Why don't you stop and think about what you're doing?' she pleaded. 'Don't go bad on us, our Lenny.'

'Bad's exciting.'

Ruby shook her head, her face sombre. 'No, Lenny. Bad is prison.'

'*This* is *prison!*' His eyes blazed into hers, then with a sharp turn of his heel, he went out of the room and down the passageway where he slammed shut the door behind him.

Thinking on his words, Ruby's heart sank. 'This is prison.' It struck her that her brother's sentiments about Fisher Street were not too far from her own. The only difference between her and Lenny was that she intended to work her way out of Fisher Street, while he was determined to fight his way out. 'Keep going the way you are, our Lenny,' she murmured after him, 'and all you'll be doing is swapping one prison for another.'

For the next half hour Ruby busied herself about the little parlour. When everything was tidied, a spill of cinders collected from the grate and taken to the yard outside and the kettle filled then placed on the coals to be nicely bubbling when her mam came down, Ruby sat beside the cheery fire to wait for her. They hadn't had much of a chance to talk lately, and there was a deal to catch up on.

It was a while before Ruby realised she couldn't hear her mam moving about upstairs. 'Whatever is she doing up there?' she murmured. Normally it didn't take long for the childer to be tucked up in their beds. She glanced at the mantelpiece clock. It was nearly eight. Lizzie had been upstairs over an hour.

Springing from her chair, Ruby went at a run across the room and out into the passage where she fled up the stairs two at a time. From the top landing she went straight to Dolly's room, and sure enough, there was Lizzie, spread over the bed, one arm hanging across the pillow and the other securely wrapped round the sleeping child. 'Well, I never!' Ruby smiled to herself. Six childer were enough to tucker anybody out, she thought. But then she remembered the awful scene at the table, and knew how her mam took such things to heart. 'It's our Lenny that wears you out, isn't it?' she whispered, shaking her head forlornly, 'More shame on him.'

Backing out of the room, she closed the door and went downstairs where she sat in her mam's chair staring into the flames, deep in thought until the sound of the front door opening made her gather her wits. It was Lenny.

'You'd best get washed and off to bed before our mam comes down.' Ruby still hadn't forgiven him. 'Thanks to you, she's worn out, fast asleep next to Dolly.'

'I'm not ready for bed.' Flinging himself into his father's

chair he stared across at Ruby. 'I'll go when I'm ready,' he declared defiantly, raising his legs to put his feet on the fender.

Ruby was incensed. Flinging herself forward, she grabbed his arm and yanked him out of the chair. Thrusting him towards the scullery, she instructed, 'You'll get your wash, then up to bed. NOW!' When he struggled against her, she merely tightened her grip. As big as he was, she could handle him and he knew it. The three years between them was enough.

'Who d'you think you are?' he snapped as she propelled him into the scullery.

'I'm the eldest, that's who I am. And I say you get washed and up to your bed.'

'And if I don't?' She had him at the sink now, but he swung round to confront her. He was shaking with temper, and for a moment Ruby thought he was going to strike out.

'Well now, if you want to cause a fuss, that's up to you.' Her calm voice belied the turmoil inside her. She was angry too. Angry that once again he had deliberately set Mam and Dad against each other. Her dark blue eyes glittered as she told him, 'I might not be as big as you, but I promise I won't be as easy to thrash as poor little Arnie Dixon.'

It was as she'd thought. For whatever reason, he wasn't prepared to tackle her. 'Leave me alone,' he muttered sullenly, snatching himself away and bending his head to the sink, his arms outstretched.

'Five minutes,' she warned, going out of the scullery and into the parlour.

In no time at all he came skulking out, bare-chested and with his shirt over his arm. Without another word he went upstairs, leaving Ruby wondering whether she should have tried reasoning with him. But then, she had lost count of the times she had tried talking sense into him. But at least he still recognised her as being the eldest and as yet he hadn't challenged her position in this

household. 'And he'd better not!' she said aloud, glaring towards
the parlour door.

At eight-thirty, Lizzie came downstairs, bleary-eyed and
drunk with sleep. 'Why didn't yer wake me?' she asked Ruby.
'Good God above!' she exclaimed, raising her eyes to the mantelpiece clock. 'Look at the time.' She began rushing about, going
into the scullery then coming out, falling into the chair then
clambering up again. 'I'm all at sixes and sevens,' she moaned,
dropping into the fireside chair again.

'Keep still, Mam,' Ruby chuckled. Her mam's antics had left
her breathless too. 'The kettle's boiling, and the teapot's ready.
I'll make you a brew, shall I?'

Lizzie welcomed that. 'Aye, lass. A cup o' tea and I'll be able
to think straight, eh?' She was on the point of getting out of the
chair yet again, but at Ruby's offer fell back into it, eyes closed
and hands folded across her stomach. 'Can't think what come
over me,' she went on while Ruby took the kettle to the scullery
and bustled about there. ''Tain't like your mam to fall asleep an'
leave you to do all the work. Sorry, lass.'

Returning with two mugs of steaming tea, Ruby gave one to
her mam and set the other into the hearth to cool. 'It's all right,'
she said. 'It didn't take me long to tidy.'

'All the same, lass, it ain't right that you should have to do it
all. Lord knows, you work hard enough as it is.' She gave a long
deep sigh. 'Lenny won't be long afore he's out to work, thank
God. It might keep the bugger outta mischief. Yer dad's keeping
an eye out for summat, but there ain't much work about, not
now.' She eyed Ruby with interest. 'There's rumours that Jeffrey
Banks is turning his foundry over to his daughter when she weds
Luke Arnold. Is that right, lass? Would he do such a thing? It
ain't usual for a woman to have such authority.'

Lost in thought for a moment, Lizzie saw Jeffrey Banks as a
younger man; handsome he was, and kind. 'Still, I expect it'll be

287

easier for him when he has a son-in-law to rely on, eh?'

The business of Cicely and Luke was a sore point with Ruby. Only yesterday she and Cicely had had words again. 'Oh, yes, I think he would trust Cicely with a deal more responsibility,' Ruby confirmed. 'She has proved herself to be a very capable young woman. She runs that house like clockwork, and is respected by the staff. Besides, Mr Banks isn't so well these days, and he doesn't really want to sell the foundry. So the next best thing is to let his daughter and her husband have the running of it.'

She hated the idea because she knew it was the very reason why Luke had proposed to Cicely. Clever and efficient though she may be, she was also lonely and aching for someone to share her life with. That made her gullible where the awful Luke was concerned, and he never hesitated to take advantage.

'Hmm. He's a trusting fella is Jeffrey Banks.' Lizzie still held a deal of affection for him. 'How does he feel about having Luke Arnold for a son-in-law then? Do they get on, the two of them?'

'More than that, Mam. He thinks the sun shines out of Luke's backside.' Ruby saw a lot of her own brother in Luke. And Cicely's father was just as much taken in by the wily Luke as her own father where Lenny was concerned.

Lizzie supped her tea and fell silent. She knew Ruby well enough to realise there were deep waters here. 'You don't like the fella, do yer, lass?' she asked presently.

'I just think he's wrong for Cicely,' she returned guardedly.

'In what way?' Lizzie leaned back and blew on the top of her tea, then she took a long gulp of the hot liquid. 'By! That's grand,' she said with an approving shake of her head. Realising that Ruby hadn't answered her question, she asked it again. 'What meks yer think Luke Arnold's wrong for Cicely Banks?' Lizzie sensed trouble. 'What is it, lass? You ain't worried about your place with Cicely once she gets wed, are yer?' A shocking thought occurred to her. 'Surely to God yer ain't let the fella see that you don't approve of him? 'Cause if yer have, then he might well show yer the door once he's got his feet well and truly under the table.'

She saw the anxiety on her daughter's face, and feared the worst. 'Oh, lass! Lass! Ain't I allus told yer to keep yer opinions to yerself? How many times have I said how you'd get yerself in trouble by speaking too straight?' Putting her mug to the hearth, she sat forward in the chair, her hands on her knees. 'Don't tell me you've been given yer marching orders already?' The idea was unthinkable.

Ruby put her mam's mind at rest straightaway. 'No,' she answered, 'so don't start worrying.'

Lizzie visibly relaxed. However, Ruby's next words made her sit up. 'All the same, I don't intend to be a lady's maid for the rest of my life.' Taking a deep breath, Ruby blurted out what had been on her mind these past weeks, ever since Cicely had threatened her with dismissal. 'You know I'm good at making and mending hats?'

'Aye. You've mended my old boater often enough. Lord knows how you've managed to hold it together, 'cause it's been threadbare more times than I care to remember.' The navy straw boater meant a great deal to Lizzie, because it was the one she was wearing the day she met her Ted. She even wore it the afternoon they got wed. She wore it on the tram all the way to Blackpool, and she'd lost count of the times she'd worn it since. 'What is it yer getting at, lass?'

'Cicely sent me to the milliner's last Friday. I was trusted to choose a new hat to go with her favourite blue dress, and do you know what?' She didn't wait for her mam to answer. 'Widow Reece who owns the shop – well, she's getting on in years now, and she says it's all too much for her.'

'What!' A light began to dawn in Lizzie's mind. 'Yer never

thinking of giving up yer post with Cicely to go and work in a hat shop?' She was horrified. 'Yer can't do that, lass. For one thing, the money won't be anywhere near as good. And, besides, you'd have to work all day on Saturday.' She didn't mention the other reason: that she herself wouldn't be able to boast down the market about how her lass was a lady's maid up at the Bankses' house. Still and all, it was only a little show of Lizzie's to impress the womenfolk. Deep down she would rather have seen Ruby serving some other household. It wasn't the same if your lass worked in a hat shop and that was a fact. 'I'm surprised at yer,' she chided. 'I can't imagine what yer thinking about, child.'

'Well, I'll tell you what I'm thinking about, shall I?' Ruby had half expected her mam to go off the deep end, but she wasn't deterred, because now she knew what she wanted to do. Making and mending hats came naturally to her, and it was a talent she didn't intend wasting. 'I'm not thinking to be an assistant, Mam.'

'Oh? What then?'

'I intend to have my own shop one day.' Ruby's dream didn't stop there. 'Before too long, I expect I'll have a whole chain of hat shops right across the country,' she said proudly.

Lizzie's eyes popped open. 'There yer go with yer dreaming and wishing!' she said angrily. 'I've telled you afore my girl . . . there's only grief can come from wanting what yer can't have. Put all that stuff and nonsense out of yer mind, and settle for what you've got.' Lizzie hated being harsh on the girl, but she felt so afraid when Ruby talked like that. 'Oh, lass, you've done so well, what with going from scullery maid to parlour maid, and now lady's maid. There's many a young lass would think that were good enough.'

'Not me, Mam,' Ruby insisted. 'If I've been made up, it's only because I've worked hard. I've earned every penny I'm paid.'

Suddenly, Lizzie realised. 'So, *that's* why you've been saving like a squirrel! Never going out. Allus working every minute's overtime yer can get.' She had been concerned, but now it all made sense.

'That's right, Mam. And I'll go on working and saving until I've got enough to get me started in a shop of my own.' She smiled lovingly at Lizzie, not wanting to raise old fears. 'Still, I've a long way to go yet, and besides it might never happen, eh?' she lied, knowing full well that she wouldn't rest until she had her own shop. She had even entertained the idea of Widow Reece's milliner's, but that seemed too far out of reach for now. 'So there's no use talking about it now, is there?'

'That's the first sensible thing you've said.' Lizzie was relieved. For so long now Ruby had seemed to be settled with Cicely Banks, and Lizzie was delighted that her daughter hadn't talked of being wealthy for a long time. To Lizzie, being wealthy meant gentry, and she could never forget that Ruby's real father was gentry too. Hearing her say all those things just now struck at Lizzie's humble heart, bringing back the old fears. She was just an ordinary woman and such fierce ambitions made her tremble. 'Cicely will need yer more after she's wed, you'll see,' she pointed out. 'And then, when there's childer, well, who knows, yer might be made up to take care of 'em.'

Ruby laughed, glad that she'd managed to lead her mam on to other things. She didn't know what was really on Lizzie's mind, but she was about to find out. 'So you think Cicely intends to have a big family, do you?' she asked with amusement. It didn't seem likely that Luke Arnold would want the same thing, she thought wryly.

'Oh, I do. What's more, she couldn't find nobody better than you to take care of 'em.' Lizzie rolled her eyes up to the ceiling and the childer above. 'Lord knows you've had enough experience with this lot, eh?' She really liked the thought of Ruby getting paid for doing what came naturally to her. In fact, when her time came, Ruby herself would make a wonderful mother. 'Happen Cicely will double yer wages. Then, when it's time for you and Johnny to get wed, you'll have a nice little nest egg.' Suddenly she was flushed with pleasure. 'By! I'll be that proud to see yer, all done up as a bride, with that fine young man standing aside yer.'

Ruby was astounded. So that was it! Her mam was nurturing secret ideas of her and Johnny walking down the aisle together. She had to put a stop to such ideas, and she had to do it now before it went too far. 'Don't count on me getting wed for a long time, Mam,' she warned kindly.

'Why's that? You're not a child no more, my girl! You're a grown woman,' Lizzie reminded her. 'Time to start thinking about your future.'

'I don't want to talk about it, Mam.'

Lizzie was disappointed, but she didn't show it. 'All right, lass. As you say.' And she settled back to finish her tea. Ruby did the same, and while each became lost in her own thoughts, the little parlour was silent.

It wasn't long before Lizzie had dozed off in the heat of the fire. Ruby took the two tea mugs into the scullery where she washed them and replaced them in the cupboard. No sooner had she come back into the parlour than her dad was coming down the passage.

Ted Miller seemed unusually thoughtful. What with the argument at the table tonight, he hadn't really had a chance to talk to Lizzie about something that was preying on his mind. And now she was fast and hard asleep. 'Poor bugger,' he remarked. Standing in front of the fire and warming his backside, he gazed down on his slumbering wife. 'I've allus said a woman's lot is worse than any man's.'

Through her quiet dreams Lizzie heard her man's voice, and she liked what he said. Peeping out of one eye she told him mischievously, 'I couldn't agree more, but it's good to know I'm appreciated, luv.'

Ted laughed out loud, a pleasant rough sound that told of his love for her. 'You little sod! You weren't asleep at all.'

Lizzie struggled to sit up straight in the squashy depths of the chair. 'I were,' she protested. 'But I've learned to sleep light in case the childer ever need me.'

Turning to Ruby, Ted asked, 'Aren't you going along to see your friend this evening?'

'I've already been. It's too cold for Maureen to go out, so Johnny came up and the three of us played Snap. Then we sat and talked a while, until Maureen's mam thought it were time she had her rest.' Ruby didn't mention how Johnny had walked her home and kissed her at the door. Nor had she forgotten the wonderful glow his kiss sent through her. But she was anxious about the way things were going between her and Johnny. The more she told him she didn't want anything serious, the harder it became for her to believe herself. Lately, it seemed she was only happy when he was close. That frightened her. Johnny meant Fisher Street, or a street very much like it. And that wasn't what she had planned at all.

'Well, if you're not going out, how about making your old dad a cheese buttie and a brew?' Ted was anxious to talk with Lizzie, and what he had to say wasn't for anybody else's ears, not even Ruby's although she was always the soul of discretion.

Sensing that her parents might have something private to talk about, Ruby went into the kitchen and returned a moment later with a half-filled kettle which she carefully lodged on the coals. Afterwards she went back into the scullery where she took her time in preparing the sandwich. So her parents would know she couldn't hear what was being said, she sang softly to herself. In the background she could hear their voices, low and intimate. She smiled. It was a good feeling to know that your parents were still in love after so many years.

'I'm worried, Lizzie. There's summat been on my mind, and

I'm not sure what to do about it.' Ted was perched on the edge of the chair which Ruby had just vacated. Leaning forward, he bowed his head and ran both hands over his face, as if he was washing it. 'If I speak out, it could mean trouble for me, and if I say nowt, men could be killed.' He was greatly agitated.

Lizzie was upright now, bending towards him, her eyes searching his face. 'Whatever's the matter, Ted? Is it your work?' She had seen him like this only once before, and that was when he was dismissed from the Arnold foundry.

'Aye, lass. It *is* my work in a way. Not where I work now, but where I used to work.' Taking a deep breath, he looked towards the scullery from where Ruby's voice could be heard raised in a soft melody. Satisfied, he fell back in his chair. 'I've learned summat that rankles me and that's a fact. There's word going about concerning the manager at the Arnold plant. The same fella as sacked me. Folks say he's crooked, Lizzie.'

'Crooked?' She was shocked. 'What d'yer mean . . . crooked?'

'Look, Lizzie, you know yourself I don't listen to gossip, but if it's true, something should be done.'

'I *don't* know what yer getting at. Are yer saying the manager's turning out bad steel, is that it?'

Ted shook his head. 'No, lass. What I'm saying is that he's not *turning out* bad steel. According to what I've heard, he's *buying it in*!' In his excitement his voice became raised and he glanced anxiously towards the scullery. Ruby was still singing so he went on, 'I've been told that he's using second grade steel to build them new platforms. If that's the case, Lizzie, they ain't safe.'

'Who told you this?' She wasn't one to listen to gossip. It was a sure way of landing yourself in trouble.

'Jack Armitage. It were him as told me.'

Lizzie pulled a face. 'Drunk was he?' She had never seen Jack Armitage when he *wasn't*.

Ted appeared embarrassed then. 'Well, happen he'd sunk a pint or two but . . .'

'No buts, Ted. You know as well as I do that Jack Armitage is a fool who lets his tongue run away with him. Besides, didn't he have a run-in with that manager some time back? Weren't he given a warning about fighting on the premises?'

Ted thought a minute before mumbling his agreement. 'Aye, that's right, lass.'

Encouraged, she went on, 'And have yer forgotten how he spread the rumour that Alice May had skipped off with some fella, when all the time the poor woman was lying close to death's door in the infirmary?' The entire episode had caused uproar and was still talked about. 'By! It's a wonder her old man didn't flay him alive when he found out who it was spreading the tale.' She leaned forward and fondly patted Ted's hand. 'Think on that, luv,' she suggested kindly. 'And think on this . . . how could the manager buy bad steel in without Luke Arnold knowing about it?'

Ted hadn't thought of that. It did put a different complexion on the matter, that was for sure. 'You're right, lass. Everything has to go through the boss . . . orders, accounts and the like. No, it couldn't be done without him finding out, I'm certain. And the manager, for all his faults, isn't stupid enough to risk losing his own livelihood.' He was visibly relaxed, even smiling. 'That bloody Jack Armitage!' The cloud had lifted from his face and now there was only anger visible. 'Get somebody hung one day, he will.'

'So long as it ain't you.' Satisfied that the matter was closed, Lizzie called out, 'Ruby! Where's them sandwiches? You'd best fetch 'em in afore yer faither starves to death.'

As she made her way into the parlour with a plate of chunky sandwiches, someone else made their way back upstairs unseen. Going on tiptoe into his room, Lenny stood by the window awhile, turning over in his mind what he had heard.

'So it's bad steel, is it?' he murmured. 'And the manager couldn't do it without the boss knowing, eh?' He smiled deeply as a delicious thought occurred to him. 'And who's to say the boss ain't in on it as well, that's what I'd like to know? After all, Luke Arnold and the likes of him ain't above corruption, any more than the rest of us.'

As the disgruntled Lenny climbed to his bed he wasn't quite certain what to do with this useful snippet of information. But it was certainly something to keep in mind for the future, he thought cunningly.

Chapter Ten

The March wind cut across the high ground, whistling and howling like a demented soul and bending the tree boughs almost to the ground. For two days now it had blown relentlessly, and Johnny began to wonder when it would let up. 'No matter, my beauty,' he told the powerful stallion as he led it out of the top field and towards the stables. 'Nature has its own way, and we have a job to do all the same.'

He and the great bay hunter made a striking silhouette against the grey shifting sky as they pressed on determinedly, heads bowed to the wind. 'She's in the paddock waiting for you,' he teased. 'And we wouldn't want to disappoint her now, would we, eh?'

From the mouth of the stables, old Thomas watched while Johnny and the hunter made their descent. Behind him in the small railed paddock, the mare caught the stallion's scent. Excited, she began rearing and pawing at the ground, impatient for her lover.

'Whoah, there!' Thomas called, ambling towards her. 'Behave yerself, yer little hussy. It won't be long now.'

'Throwing a tantrum, is she?' Tony Hargreaves leaned against the rail on the far side, his curious gaze going from Thomas to the mare, and back again. 'She's a magnificent creature,' he said, regarding her with awe. He was a little afraid of horses. 'Worth a bit, I'll be bound.' Since a boy, he had learned all there was to know about tin mines, but even though he had been wed to Teresa for almost two years now, and had visited these stables on the many occasions he and his family had stayed at her father's house, he still knew next to nothing about horses.

'Worth a bloody fortune more like,' Thomas replied sharply. He was never one to change his ways, not for peasant nor gentry. It was this stubborn attitude that both endeared him to Oliver Arnold and alienated his spoiled daughter Teresa. 'That there mare comes of top breeding stock. Belongs to a farmer the other side o' Darwen. It's cost him a pretty penny to put that mare with our stallion, but the offspring will be priceless. Especially if it's a filly. Oh, aye, it'll have blue blood running through its veins from both parents, make no mistake about that. That there stallion comes from a long line o' champions.'

He turned to look at the mare. 'Oh, but she's a grand 'un, that she is.' He let his gaze wander over her magnificent lines, from the muscular straight neck to the strong finely curved limbs. She was darkest bay in colour, with huge saucer eyes the shade of ripe chestnuts. 'Fiery though,' Thomas warned now. 'When that stallion comes to serve her, you'd best stay well clear. They get too excited, y'see. Sometimes they'll nuzzle and mate with the stallion in a matter o' minutes, and sometimes they'll panic and fight just like a wild woman.' He chuckled at his many memories. 'What! I've known a mare to clear an eight-foot fence an' run like the wind afore she'd let the big fella mount her.'

At the gate, Johnny was having a job to hold back the great horse. Seeing the mare, it began fidgeting and fighting, eager to be let loose. 'Get back, you bugger!' It took all of Johnny's strength to hold the animal while Thomas quickly slipped the mare inside the stable. With the top half of the door open the two of them could regard each other before mating. It was important not to let the stallion straight at the mare. With their senses heightened, and the mare in full season, that could often prove to be dangerous, and Thomas was never one for taking chances.

'In you go then.' As soon as Thomas had the gate wide open, Johnny brought the stallion into the paddock. 'Easy now. Easy.' Leaving the halter in place, he deftly slipped the rope out of the ring and let the animal have its head. 'Get clear, Thomas,' he instructed, and the old fella obediently crawled through the railings to watch from the other side.

'Be careful, son,' he warned. 'They can be unpredictable. Especially when it's the stallion's first time, like now.'

At first the beast seemed unsure. It was all a new experience for him. He stamped the ground and threw his head high, shaking it from side to side, wild white eyes rolling. There was a strange silence, almost eerie, as he slowly encircled the paddock, tall and proud, every muscle taut, his limbs quivering in anticipation.

From the stable, the mare began to whinny, frantically tossing her head then sinking her teeth into the door. She was greatly agitated. 'Go round, Thomas,' Johnny whispered. It was on the tip of his tongue to add, 'Be careful. Don't send her out until I say,' but Thomas had taught him everything he knew, and though he was a good deal slower in the body, the old fellow still had his wits about him.

Staying close to the rails, Johnny kept his eye on the stallion. Like any man in the full anticipation of passion, that magnificent creature was eager to serve his mate; his great chest was swelled with pride, and he was immensely erect, though was still uncertain, still hesitant.

Out of the corner of his eye, Johnny saw Thomas scurry round to the back door of the stables. From there he would turn the mare out when it was considered safe.

'Is it all right for me to be here?' Tony Hargreaves was nervous. All he wanted was an excuse to leave without seeming too much of a coward. 'I think I'm making him wary.' Besides, the very idea of watching these two creatures actually mating was abhorrent to him.

Johnny didn't like the idea of a stranger being near at a time like this. 'It might be best if you weren't,' he answered. 'Like Thomas said, they can be unpredictable, and I wouldn't want you to get hurt.' That was all the encouragement the young man needed. In no time at all he was striding away, back to the house, thankful that his father's fortune was made in tin mines and not through the breeding of horses.

From the upper window, Teresa watched her husband enter the house. It was what she had been waiting for. With the skill of long practice, she came out on to the landing and waited until she heard the study door close behind him and then came swiftly down the stairs out into the open. Once away from the house, she went speedily towards the stables. Careful not to let either Thomas or Johnny see her, she positioned herself by the aged weeping willow. From here, and camouflaged by the long drooping branches that swept the ground, she watched and waited, her small evil eyes following Johnny's every move.

The stallion was displaying himself, rudely exhibiting his full and glorious manhood. Still a virgin, but obviously ready for his first sexual encounter, he trembled with excitement. Reaching his thick broad neck over the stable door he nuzzled the mare, making small guttural noises in the back of his throat when she began to respond.

'*Now*, Thomas. Send her out *now*. She's accepted him.' Johnny's voice was controlled. Too loud, too intrusive, one wrong move, and it could all be spoiled.

'There, lass . . . Shh, my lovely.' Thomas edged himself

nearer. The mare knew him. She trusted him. 'Out you go.'

Slowly, he swung the door open. At first she was reluctant to leave the safety of her enclosure. But then, suddenly, she was out, free in the paddock, head high, nostrils flared, her every limb ready for flight. 'Easy now. Easy, girl.' Thomas pushed the stable door to, but he didn't throw the bolt. If she took panic, it was best for her to retreat into the stable rather than jump the fence and injure herself.

There was a deal of snorting and nuzzling, breathing into each other's nostrils and putting eyeball to eyeball. Now the stallion was stalking her, his huge black eyes wide and staring. He was big and hard, ready to take her. She pushed him with her nose, a winsome smile on her handsome face, but still he wasn't quite sure. He stalked her again and brushed against her lightly, then stepped proudly round the paddock, pretending not to notice her. She called out to him. He went to her, nuzzling nose to nose at first then gently sniffing her rear end. Shivering with delight, she raised her tail high, inviting him, persistently calling. Suddenly he was up in the air, throwing himself over her, thrusting his huge body forwards. He fell and thrashed about, climbing on and falling off, growing more and more frustrated, his hooves clawing at her back, making long jagged marks.

'He's a clumsy bugger!' Thomas called out. 'Yer can tell he ain't done it afore.' He watched as the stallion tried and tried again. The confused animal had no trouble mounting but couldn't penetrate, and while he fumbled the mare was being cut and torn. 'You'll have to help him, Johnny,' he cried. 'Afore she's cut to buggery.' In his younger days Thomas had been called on more than once to help a young stallion in distress, but it was a dangerous job and a man needed to be strong and quick. These days he was no match for the brute if it should turn nasty. Johnny could do it, though. He knew how.

Johnny didn't need telling twice. He had seen with his own

eyes that the mare was not only being cut, but that she was growing impatient. Any minute now she would turn on the stallion and that could lead to all hell being let loose. 'Stay back,' he warned, and Thomas instinctively stepped away a pace.

Slowly and carefully, Johnny made his way to the centre of the paddock where the two animals were wildly thrashing about. Exhausted, the mare would tear away, then the stallion would follow to try again. He was confused now, and growing angry. From behind Johnny could hear Thomas warning him to 'Be careful, lad. For God's sake, be careful.'

He had to let it be known that he was advancing. Horses in particular do not like being taken by surprise. 'It's all right,' he murmured. 'Shh, easy does it now.' The mare turned her big soulful eyes on him, but the stallion clung to her back, thrusting his powerful bulk against her haunches and growing more and more frantic. The sweat was teeming down his body, glistening like dew against the darkness of his coat.

'It's all right, my beauty. Easy now.' Johnny waited until the stallion had seen him before coming in from the side, all the while murmuring soothing words, coaxing and encouraging the great handsome beast.

He was so close now he could feel the animal's warm breath fanning the back of his neck. His skin crept with fear. If the stallion was to fall on him, he would be crushed like an egg-shell.

'Easy, boy. It's all right.' His voice was like a caress, soothing the irate creature who looked sideways at Johnny as though he knew the man was there to help. 'All right, fella. It's all right.' The stallion snorted, flicking his tail angrily. Skilfully, Johnny guided him into position. The next thrust struck home and the mare cried out. But she stood her ground, throwing her head high and pushing against her mate.

Quickly now Johnny sprang out of the way. Even before he

got back to the rails, where he washed his hands at the trough, it was all over. 'He'll know how to do it next time,' Thomas chuckled.

'I hope so,' Johnny replied, relieved. 'I wouldn't want to do that again.'

'Sometimes we have to do the unpleasant,' Thomas said. 'He's young yet, but he'll learn. All we can hope is that there'll be a lovely foal for all our troubles.'

Soon the mare was safely stabled, settled with a bucket of beet until her owner came to collect her. The stallion was released into the field where he could run off any excess energy, and Thomas and Johnny set about their other many duties before retiring for a well-earned break.

From her vantage point beneath the willow tree Teresa watched until the two men were out of sight. Afterwards, she strolled back to the house, a devious smile on her handsome face. What she had seen was still vivid on her mind, and she ached for a man. She ached for Johnny. He was still in her blood. He always would be.

At the front of the house, she paused to look back. In the distance she could see the two familiar figures: Thomas was going into the stables, while Johnny strode off in the direction of the spinney. She was sorely tempted, and might even have followed him, but just then her husband came to the door with the child in his arms.

'Oh! *There* you are, my dear,' he said with a broad smile. 'We've been looking for you.' He glanced at the child, a fine healthy boy with dark eyes and a bright lively face. 'We should spend a little time with our son before your brother and his intended come calling.'

'Oh, hell!' She stamped her foot. 'I'd forgotten all about Luke and that dreadful Cicely Banks.'

'Don't be churlish, my dear. If you ask me, they make a

303

splendid couple.' He held the boy out to her, and the child reached up his arms, waiting to be taken.

'Nobody's asking you!' she snapped, brushing past the pair of them. 'I'm going to my room, and *don't* disturb me until you have to.'

At the foot of the stairs she crossed paths with her father. 'I've got a headache,' she said in a pitiful voice, at the same time tenderly stroking her fingers over her brow. 'I have to lie down for a while.' Looking at him with beseeching eyes, she pleaded, '*Must* I come down when Luke arrives?'

Oliver Arnold had seen it all before, and he was not moved. 'Of course you must,' he insisted. 'Isn't this the very reason I asked you and your family here this weekend . . . to celebrate the fact that your brother is shortly to wed? There are all manner of things to be discussed. And besides, I have a little announcement of my own to make.'

He wasn't surprised when she turned on her heel and rushed up the stairs without another word. Teresa was sullen. He had come to expect it of her.

At the sound of running feet, he swung round. Ida flung herself into his arms. 'Daddy! Do you think Luke and Cicely will let me be bridesmaid?' she asked, nestling into the curve of his arm.

'I shall insist on it,' he joked, and she flushed with happiness. 'Tony's in the drawing room,' she said. 'He told me that Teresa had gone to bed with a headache.' She made a face. 'I don't believe it. I think she's hiding from Cicely and Luke.'

'Now why would she want to do that?' It wasn't right that Ida should think such things, even if they were true.

'Because she's already told me she doesn't like Cicely.'

'Nonsense. She hardly knows the poor girl.'

Ida giggled. 'Teresa doesn't have to know anyone to dislike them.' She looked up at him with adoring eyes. '*I* think

Cicely's sweet. And I think she's too good for Luke.'

'That's a harsh thing to say.' He was careful not to admit that the very same thought had crossed his own mind. They were coming to the drawing room now, and when she drew away from him, he went directly to the settee and plucked the boy from its depths. 'And how is my grandson then?' He hadn't got used to being a grandfather, and spoke to the child as he would to a business colleague. Ida giggled again, and Tony looked on with amusement. He was a good man, but his love for Teresa put him at her mercy.

No one heard the boy's nanny enter until her crisp voice announced: 'I'll take the boy upstairs for his bath now.' She crossed the room with long strides and bundled the child out of Oliver's arms. There was no resistance – not from the father, and not from the grandfather. This capable woman's authority was unquestionable and essential to the boy's well-being, especially since his mother took little or no interest in him.

When the door closed behind her, Ida informed the men, 'I'm going to ask if I can help. If she won't let me help, then I'll just watch.'

'Go ahead, child,' Oliver told her. 'Tony and I have things to talk over.' For two days now, ever since his daughter and her family came to stay, he had been quietly mulling over two matters in particular. First, he had seen how despicably Teresa treated both her husband and son, and intended to rebuke his son-in-law for allowing it. Second, he had a mind to settle a few business issues, and as Tony was a sensible young man, thought to seek his opinion; although having already spoken to his own solicitor, his mind was made up and could not be changed. He knew that Teresa would not like what he had to announce that evening, but then she was altogether a contrary person. Besides, he believed that what he was about to propose was fair to all parties concerned.

* * *

At six-thirty, Luke arrived, dishevelled and unusually merry. It was obvious to all that he had been drinking.

'Good heavens, man, you ought to have more sense!' Oliver was furious as he propelled his son straight upstairs. In fact, he began to wonder whether he had made the right decision after all. Perhaps he should postpone the planned announcement? 'Where in God's name have you been since yesterday? Have you forgotten your future wife and her father are joining us for dinner in less than two hours?'

'Don't worry, Father,' Luke said charmingly. 'By the time our guests arrive, I shall be both sober and handsomely turned out.' Falling against his father he giggled like a schoolboy. 'I promise you'll be proud of me.'

Disgusted, Oliver gave no reply. Instead, he opened his son's bedroom door and pushed him in, ordering in a hard voice, 'You're a fool! I'll send up a pot of black coffee. *Drink it!* After that you'd better get some sleep. I'll see to it that you're woken in good time.' He swept a disgusted glance over him. 'I thought I would never again see you like this.'

Even with his mind fuddled, Luke realised he had gone too far. These past months he'd been careful not to bring his drinking home with him, staying overnight wherever he could lay his head, and presenting a responsible and sober image to his father the next day. Last night, though, the thought that he would soon be marrying one woman when he desperately craved another was suddenly too much for him. He had tried to escape the reality of it by skulking off to Manchester where he had availed himself of the first whore who offered. After that he sought solace in drink, then another and another, until he fell into a stupor. All night and all day today he had lain in that hotel bed, thinking and cursing, not wanting to come back, yet knowing he had no choice. Finally, he dragged himself down to the bar where he gulped down two hairs of the dog that bit him, then another, and another, until he had enough courage to face the celebrations.

'I'm truly sorry, Father,' he lied. 'It's the thought of wedding bells, I expect.' He grinned. 'I've never been a husband before.'

He could see his father softening, and he played on it. 'I'm nervous,' he admitted. 'I expect you were, when you got married?'

For a moment Oliver was taken aback, thinking he might have been too hard on his son. After all, Luke's behaviour had been exemplary of late. He was showing a surprisingly responsible attitude where the business was concerned, and had found himself an eminently suitable woman. Cicely Banks was a good catch by any standard.

'All right, son,' he said, placing a friendlier hand on his shoulder. 'I do understand. Marriage is a big step in a man's life, and I can see how it would make you nervous.' He laughed. 'Come to think of it, yes, I do believe I felt the very same.' His face grew grim then. 'However, I can't recollect going away to get quietly drunk.'

'It won't happen again.' Luke was secretly gloating. He had won, and it was his father who was the fool.

'See that it doesn't,' Oliver warned. Yet again he had found a reason to forgive his only son. But he comforted himself with the knowledge that a man usually only wed once. It might be as well for Luke to sow any wild oats now, before he was finally committed to the sanctity of marriage.

When Cicely and her father arrived at precisely eight o'clock, Luke greeted them at the door. Just as he had promised, he was both sober and well presented, looking quite debonair in a dark suit with silk waistcoat and white embroidered shirt.

'Oh, Cicely, you look lovely,' he murmured, kissing her dutifully on the mouth. The fact that she did indeed look very pretty in a new soft grey dress with little pearl buttons at the throat, was of no interest at all to him. He was playing a part, and he played it with practised skill. 'How do you do, Mr Banks?' he said, extending a friendly hand to his future father-in-law. 'It's good to see you. I'm sure we're going to have a wonderful evening.'

'Thank you, son.'

Jeffrey Banks felt suitably proud that his daughter had the good sense to find herself such an agreeable and accomplished young man. The word was already out that, on the occasion of this forthcoming wedding, Oliver Arnold intended making part of the business over to his son. If that was the case, then Cicely's future was indeed secure, because where Jeffrey himself had one foundry, Oliver Arnold had many more. In fact, only this year he had secured the deeds to yet another, not in Blackburn but situated in the heart of the Midlands.

Maids came and went, carrying in a tray here, taking out another there, emptying the ashtrays into long funnel-like objects and hovering discreetly, ready to pander to the smallest whim. This was their place in life and they prided themselves on their talent for cossetting the gentry. As for the gentry themselves, waiting for dinner to be served was a pleasant enough pastime, a short interlude for aperitifs and small talk in the drawing room, a time when barriers were broken down and everyone put at ease.

Luke and Cicely were seated on the settee, Teresa and her husband occupied the two armchairs, and the two older men stood with their backs to the great fireplace. The general conversation ran through the state of the nation, the problems of running a large household, business in general and the workforce in particular. Wedding plans were at the fore, and yet another key issue was lightly touched on when Jeffrey Banks outlined his plans for a complete overhaul of safety and welfare at his plant.

'Oh, I agree,' said Oliver, feverishly nodding his head. 'It's becoming more and more important to stay ahead of all these blasted rules and regulations which seem to overwhelm us these days. But then, of course, it is an employer's *moral* responsibility to look after the men in his building.' He went on to describe how he himself had instigated an expensive programme whereby: 'Starting with the main foundry, which will be the essential prototype, every aged beam and platform in all my foundries will be replaced within two years. Like yourself, I produce only the finest steel.' He sighed long and deep. 'Steel is only as good as the metals you introduce into it, and you must know it costs a fortune to buy in nickel, tungsten, manganese and the like. However, these elements are essential, are they not? So it goes without saying that if you want to produce good strong steel, you have to pay the market prices for the ingredients.'

Much to everyone's embarrassment, Cicely interrupted. 'Much like baking a cake, I think,' she said, growing quiet when her statement drew blank faces. 'I mean, your cake is only as good as the ingredients you put in,' she finished lamely.

Oliver broke the uncomfortable silence. 'Quite, my dear,' he said with an encouraging look. Continuing, he addressed himself to Jeffrey Banks, 'Of course, all our best iron and steel is being put aside to provide a whole new interior structure.' He glanced proudly at Luke. 'Isn't that right, son?' On an affirmative answer from Luke, he went on proudly, 'These days I come to rely on this young man more and more.' He beamed at his son and Luke went up in Jeffrey Banks's estimation by the minute.

During dinner there was an underlying air of conspiracy, particularly between Teresa and her brother. In spite of her husband's bid to draw her into the social spirit of the evening, Teresa sulked from the moment she sat down. Embarrassed by this hostile reception, yet eager to make it apparent that she was open to friendship, Cicely smiled sweetly at one and all. The two elder men were soon deep in conversation, and Luke busied himself by heaping attention on his intended, making her blush and giggle in turn. To all intents and purposes he was in love, and there was no doubt that he was the perfect gentleman.

Only Teresa knew his little game, and she watched him with amusement all evening long, occasionally catching his eye with a sly little grin that sent shivers of fear down his spine. He knew what a predatory animal she could be, and cursed himself for having confided in her when he had been the worse for drink. Consequently she knew his inner thoughts: how he was marrying Cicely only for monetary and power gains. She knew also that he still nurtured a dark loathing of their father and that he was obsessed with taking revenge. That was partly why he had connived with other weak and deceitful creatures to rob his father by selling out the top-grade steel which was earmarked for the interior construction work, then buying in second-rate pig-iron and skimming off the money that should have gone to pay for vital quantities of other metals needed to produce first-grade steel.

It wasn't only revenge that prompted Luke to commit such a foolhardy and dangerous act. Nor was it the fact that he had cunningly betrayed his father's trust. There was another motive and that was insatiable greed. The more he had, the more he wanted, and the more his loathing of his father ate away at him. He could not forget how he had suffered deep shame and humiliation when his father took him out of school and forced him to be educated at home, alongside his younger sisters. Marrying Cicely Banks would give him the means whereby he might prove his own superiority, and eventually strip his father of everything he owned.

Besides revenge and money, and the power that would come with it, there was one other need that drove him, and that was the need for a woman. Not the many women he had bedded and discarded; they were nothing but a pastime to him, something to keep him amused while he plotted and schemed. The woman he wanted was Ruby, and as yet she was unattainable. But already he was working and scheming to the day when she would beg him to take her. Unlike the indomitable maid, whose love and devotion for Cicely was her own weakness, *he* saw Cicely as only a pawn by which he might realise all his heart's desires.

Apart from Ruby's identity, Teresa knew all of this, and he could never be certain whether she might betray him. But then he suspected she had her own secrets – the child for one whom he knew was not Tony's son. If she ever made life difficult for him, he would see to it that she was made an outcast. The thought amused him as he returned her devious little smile. Such an air of confidence appeared to confuse her. Satisfied, he attended to his meal with a heightened appetite.

Dishes of steamed fish and succulent vegetables were served on the finest china plates. Then followed soufflés and a meringue that melted in the mouth. Best wine was poured into long crystal glasses, and as it flowed, conversation quickened, embracing everyone, even Teresa, who was mellowed by the drink. All in all, everyone had a splendid time, and soon it was time for the main announcement.

'Take up your glasses,' Luke called, rising to his feet, 'and drink a toast to my lovely Cicely.'

Everyone's eyes turned to Cicely, who was visibly shrinking with delight and embarrassment. 'Come, my dear,' he invited. 'Stand beside me.' In a moment she was pressing against him and he, pretending to enjoy her nearness, announced in a cool strong voice, 'Cicely and I have considered our respective fathers' wishes and have now chosen a date for the marriage.' He bent to place a gossamer kiss on her upturned face before going on grandly, 'The date is to be the fourteenth of June . . . less than three months from now.'

There followed a rush of congratulations. In anticipation, Oliver had already ordered the very best wine to be brought up from the cellars and made ready. Once this was poured, all glasses were raised and the toast was given by Oliver himself: 'To Cicely and Luke.'

When Luke saw that Teresa was slyly smiling, his own smugness fell away, and he wondered furiously what could be done about her . . .

'If you will all remain standing,' Oliver's voice rang out now, 'I have a special announcement of my own to make.' All eyes were on him as he continued, 'For some time I have been considering the prospect of taking life a little easier. Up to now, it has been unthinkable. Like you, Jeffrey,' he nodded in the direction of Cicely's father, 'my life is fraught with responsibilities. However, now that my son has achieved an age when he can be trusted implicitly to execute his duties to the full, I have come to a decision.'

He paused, gazing round the sea of faces that all stared at him; Jeffrey Banks's with surprised interest, Cicely with politeness, Teresa with amused curiosity, and Tony Hargreaves playing his fingers against the tablecloth until Teresa put a warning hand over his knuckles and shrivelled him with one dark look.

Luke gave his full and undivided attention to what was being said. His mouth was half open, his astonished brain rapidly assimilating his father's words and daring to believe that he was about to be put in sole charge of the business. 'In giving Luke a free hand with regard to these new safety measures at the first plant, I wasn't quite certain whether it would be something I might come to regret. In the event, I am more than delighted. He has proved himself to be keen and conscientious. He has a natural winning way with the men, and all reports show him to be immensely capable of stepping into my shoes, so to speak.' He turned to his son and raised his glass. 'You've done well.'

'Thank you, Father.' Luke sounded suitably humble.

Replacing his glass on the table, Oliver went on, 'I want it to be known that there was a time when I despaired of my only son. On more than one occasion after his mother died, I was summoned to his school and asked to take him off the premises. There was then no choice but to educate my son with his younger sisters . . . a grinding humiliation for any young man. But he rose above it admirably, and now I have a son to be proud of. I'm a very lucky man.' He glanced down at the tablecloth, reliving those bad days and thanking God they were over.

In that moment, Luke was also reliving the same memories. And because his father was making his humiliation known to strangers, his hatred for Oliver knew no bounds. When all attention was turned now to him, he was outwardly calm and smiling. Inside, though, he was seething. However, his father's next words made him stiffen with excitement.

'On the day of his marriage to the lovely Cicely, I intend to take a back seat and hand over a greater proportion of the business into Luke's hands. In fact, it wouldn't surprise me if he didn't find himself in sole charge before his first wedding anniversary. I think I'm about ready to hand over the reins.' He had been standing proud and uptight, but now his whole body seemed to sag as he relaxed; Oliver had been feeling his age for some time now, and with the announcement that he was about to relinquish a deal of responsibility, it was as though the weight of the world had fallen from his shoulders. 'Of course, if Luke had not made the announcement with regard to his forthcoming marriage, I would not be making this announcement either,' he confessed. 'He is still young yet, but, when a man takes on the responsibility of a wife, he shows himself to be mature.'

Teresa addressed her father then, goading him as always. 'What you're saying is . . . no marriage, no directorship?' An awkward silence settled over the party.

'Yes.' Oliver was wise to her. 'That is precisely what I'm saying, my dear.'

'And what about *me*!' She laughed lightly, but her dark eyes glittered. 'Do I have a share?'

'You're a woman,' he replied. He too was smiling. It was like a game being played out. 'Besides, why would you want to bother your pretty little head about such things when you have a husband to care for you?'

Impatient to assert his manhood, Tony spoke out. 'Quite right, sir,' he acknowledged. Addressing Teresa, he told her, 'While I'm alive, and even if I were to die tomorrow, you and our son will always be well cared for, my darling.'

She gave no reply, but glared at him. Later she would have her say, and he would regret putting her down in that way in front of everyone.

Teresa nursed her bitterness until it was time for the guests to leave. While Oliver and Jeffrey led the way into the hall, with Cicely and Luke trailing behind – Luke inwardly sickened when Cicely clung to him like a limpet – Teresa drew the affable Tony to one side where, out of earshot of the others, she laid into him with a vicious tongue.

'Goodnight then, Oliver.'

The maid held out his coat and Jeffrey Banks shrugged his thick shoulders into it. Then, extending a hand in farewell, he informed his host, 'It's been a fascinating and enjoyable evening.' Behind him, Luke dutifully saw to it that Cicely was wrapped against the night air. When she raised her face for a kiss he cringed inside. By making this marriage a condition of his being given greater authority, his father had made him a prisoner and Luke blamed Cicely for it.

'I'll walk you to your carriage,' Oliver told his guests. 'It's been a pleasant evening all round, I think,' he added benevolently. The atmosphere was altogether congenial. The two men sauntered through the open doorway and out to the waiting carriage. Cicely and Luke followed at a discreet distance. 'I'm proud that my son and your daughter are to be man and wife,' Oliver confessed. 'There was a time when I thought we might be bitter enemies, you and I.'

Jeffrey reflected on that and knew how true it was. 'Ah, but fate has a way of intervening,' he said profoundly. Oliver nodded in agreement and they proceeded in silence.

In no time at all, Cicely and her father were seated in the carriage and being driven away at a sedate pace. From the back window Cicely waved, her shining eyes focused on the figure of her future husband. Instead of returning her wave he turned away, thankful that the awful episode was over.

'Good night, son. I'm a little weary so I'll go straight to my bed.' Oliver went up the wide staircase and was soon lost to sight. Luke went into the drawing room where he poured himself a stiff brandy. He drank it down in one gulp, shaking his head and gasping when it burned his throat. Tonight had been an ordeal. 'Thank God that's over!' he murmured. Yet he knew there would be many more ordeals like that, and he dreaded them.

'Poor little brother!' Teresa's voice emanated from a high-backed chair, startling Luke out of his wits. She had seen him come in, and had watched while he threw the drink down his throat. She had heard his comment, and it pleased her immensely.

'What the devil are you playing at?' he demanded, his face drained white. She merely continued to gaze at him, a half empty glass of gin in her hand and her eyes glazed over. It was obvious she was drunk.

'He's got you, hasn't he?' She laughed, a wicked sound that made him want to strangle her. 'Father has you pinned to the ground at last.'

'What are you talking about?' He looked at her with disgust. 'You're drunk.'

Shaking her head, she assured him, 'No, I'm not drunk, brother dear.'

He recalled her bitter words at the table. It made him smile. 'You're *jealous*, aren't you?' he demanded.

Inflamed by his manner, she sat bolt upright in the chair. 'Yes, I'm jealous, and rightly so!'

'Don't be silly, Teresa. You're well looked after. Your husband's a wealthy man. Besides, I'm the only son.' He enjoyed watching her squirm. 'Whatever comes to me, will be mine by right.'

She stared at him for a long moment, then said in a crafty voice, 'Suppose I were to tell him a few things? He might not be so trusting then, or so generous.'

Taking a threatening step towards her, he asked, 'What things? There is nothing you could say that would turn him against me.' He was bluffing. He still wasn't certain how much she knew.

'What would he do, I wonder, if he knew how much you hated him? And don't you think he would lose faith in you altogether if he was to find out that you mean to use the gullible Cicely only so as to lay your hands on her father's business, then use that to get back at Father? Once you had that kind of money and power, you wouldn't stop until you had everything he owned. You would even take the shirt off his back, and see him out on the street beggared. Isn't that so?' She lay back in the chair, keeping her eyes fixed on his shocked face. 'As a dutiful daughter, I should warn him against you, don't you think?'

'You stupid little fool!' Luke had no doubts now. She did know enough to ruin all of his plans. 'Why would I want to do all that? You heard him say that he intends to turn more and more over to me. In time I'll have it all. Doesn't that make a nonsense of your vicious lies?'

She laughed out loud. 'Really! You must think I was born

yesterday.' Her dark handsome eyes flashed a warning. 'You know as well as I do that Father won't turn *everything* over to you. It will be a long time before he steps out of the picture altogether. And besides, even the greater responsibility he might put on you will be subject to your marrying Cicely.' She curled up, hugging herself and laughing at his misfortune. 'That's what I meant when I said he's got you where he wants you,' she reminded him. 'You heard me ask him was it no marriage, no directorship, and you heard his answer. The plain truth is, dear brother, if you don't wed your little mouse, you won't get any part of Father's business.'

She could see how her every word cut him deep, and she revelled in his pain. 'You're stuck with her, aren't you? What a great pity . . . to be stuck with someone you hate almost as much as you hate Father.'

'What makes you say I hate Cicely?' He was trembling now. 'I'm marrying her, aren't I?' At least she knew nothing of his plan to use Cicely as bait in order to have the lovely Ruby.

'Huh! You haven't got any choice now, have you? Besides, you forget how drink loosens the tongue. You yourself told me that you love someone else. But whoever she is, she doesn't want you, does she? You told me that too.' She struggled from the depths of the chair and sat unsteadily on its edge. 'Wise woman,' she laughed, staring up at him with evil eyes. 'You shouldn't have told me all these things, Luke. You know what a wicked bastard I can be.' Taunting him further, she wanted to know: 'This woman who appears to have stolen your wicked heart . . . who is she?'

'A better woman than you. That's all you need to know.'

'Father would get it out of you.'

'Breathe a word to him, and I'll kill you!'

She regarded him in a different light then, her gaze going from his head to his toes. 'I believe you would,' she said presently.

'Especially if I were to tell him of my suspicions regarding the *other* matter.'

His heart was pounding. For God's sake! How much had he told her that night when he was drunk? 'What the hell are you talking about now?'

'You,' she replied carefully. 'I'm talking about you and the responsibility he's already foolishly given you.' She paused, making him wait. She wasn't as sure of her facts as she would have him believe. So far, all she had were suspicions. She tutted and shook her head, making him think she knew a great deal more than she actually did.

'You're such a deceitful young man, aren't you? I mean, here you are, being trusted with a very important task, and you can't even do that without robbing him blind.' She grew excited when Luke went a pale shade of grey. So! She was nearer the truth than she'd first realised. 'Wouldn't Father be outraged if he thought you weren't carrying out his instructions to the letter? You're playing a dangerous game, Luke.' She might have said more but wasn't sure of the facts, although she was now convinced that he was up to something.

'What dangerous game?' He began to sense that she was fishing, and he had to call her bluff.

'What does it matter?' she asked evasively. 'All that really matters is that I'm duty bound to relate all of this to Father.'

'Do that.' He put on his boldest front. 'And while we're at it, I'll tell him a few home truths about you.'

'Such as?'

'Such as the fact that his grandson is a bastard.'

It was her turn to suffer. 'LIAR!' She sprang from the chair to confront him. In her haste she spilled her drink. 'You've no right to say such a thing! Tony is the boy's father, and you can't prove otherwise.'

'Don't deny it,' he told her, adding cautiously, 'Tony is *not* the father. You know it, and I know it.' He bent forward and smiled into her face, saying cunningly, 'Wouldn't that make juicy gossip now? Oliver Arnold's daughter being bedded by a groom, and passing the bastard off as the respectable Tony Hargreaves's?' He widened his eyes until they were round and astonished. 'What! If that was to get about, your devoted husband would turn his back on you like you were so much dirt. And if he was foolish enough to let you wrap him round your little finger, *old* Mr Hargreaves would pauper the pair of you.'

She was frantic. 'It's not true!' she yelled, thumping at his chest with clenched fists. 'Tony *is* the father.'

'Really?' He grabbed her wrists, squeezing them so hard that she actually cried out. 'I suppose that was what you told Father?'

'Because it's true.' She was struggling but he wouldn't let go.

Suddenly, contemptuously, he threw her backwards into the chair. In a moment he had departed the room, leaving her with the threat: 'Open your mouth with one bad word against me, and I promise your name will be sullied from one end of Lancashire to the other. You'll have *nothing* by the time I've finished with you.'

'Bastard!' she muttered. But his secrets were safe for the while, because she knew he meant every word. If he set his mind to ruining her, he would do it without the slightest compunction.

Hurrying to the door, she slammed it shut and leaned against it, regaining her composure and letting his threat turn over in her mind. Suddenly, she began laughing. Crossing the room on unsteady footsteps, she went to the dresser where she poured herself a large measure of spirit.

'Cheers, you bastard!' she said, raising her glass to the door. A second drink, then another, before she slumped in the chair. Dark vengeful thoughts pervaded her mind. Laughter turned to tears. Not because of the shocking scene which had happened here, nor of the awful exchange that had passed between herself and Luke, whom she secretly admired. She was crying for that which she had lost: her freedom, her secret need of a *real* man. And that man was Johnny.

Every minute of every day and night he was on her mind. He was on her mind now. And he was in her dreams when her anxious husband came down the stairs to look for her.

'Oh, sweetheart,' he moaned, taking her sleeping form in his arms and helping her gently to their room. 'When will I ever understand you?'

Chapter Eleven

Cicely swept into the room. 'It's a lovely day outside,' she told Ruby. 'Oh, I do hope the sun is shining when Luke and I are married.' She ran to the window and looked out across the lawns to the horizon. It was a warm and glorious day. The sun was high in the heavens, the blue sky was clear, and just outside the windows a robin could be heard trilling a delightful melody. It was 6 June and the day of her wedding was almost upon them.

'It's going to be all right, Ruby,' she said, swinging round to stare at the figure bent to her sewing. 'Luke and I are going to be so happy, I know it.' Her face grew serious. 'I really can't understand why you don't like him, Ruby,' she remarked sadly. 'He's a fine man, and I love him.'

'He's devious.' Ruby kept her gaze on her work. Even when she sensed Cicely's horror at her words, and even though her mistress was already making her way across the room towards her, she still did not look up.

All these weeks, ever since Cicely had revealed the date of the wedding, Ruby had tried to dissuade her. She had lost count of the number of times Cicely had threatened her with dismissal, and she was sent from the room in disgrace on more than one occasion. As a punishment, Ruby had been returned below stairs for two days where Cook took great delight in making her suffer.

'Outta favour, are you?' she taunted. 'Serves you right, you little madam!' It seemed to infuriate her when, far from rising to the cruel jibes, Ruby merely set about her work with new determination. 'Mark my words, you'll come unstuck,' the envious woman predicted with glee. 'It ain't natural for a servant to be so friendly with the mistress. Tears'll come after the laughter, and it's only a matter o' time before she sends you on your way.'

'One more word, Ruby, and you'll drive me to do something I might regret,' Cicely warned now.

Her answer was to concentrate intently on her sewing, not even flinching when the needle jabbed her thumb and brought blood. Like her mam had so often said: 'Know when ter keep yer mouth shut.' Ruby tried to follow that good advice, but it was hard.

Lately she had been greatly tempted to betray Luke's real nature to the love-blinded Cicely. The awful truth had trembled on the tip of her tongue: of how Luke had not denied that Cicely was only the means to an end, and of how he'd deliberately waylaid Ruby in that dark alley. To this day she was convinced that if the dogs had not been there to distract him, he would have forced himself on her. She was under no illusion about what might have happened then; however much she detested him, and even though she would have fought him with all of her strength, she was no match for a man like Luke.

All of these things she was tempted to tell Cicely, yet she was also deeply reluctant, not least because her mistress would be shocked and hurt to discover the truth. It was a dilemma. If she spoke up, Cicely's heart would be broken, and if she said nothing, and the wedding went ahead, her heart would no doubt be broken soon enough. Ruby had hoped and prayed that somehow, Cicely might somehow discover these things for herself, and the wedding would be called off. She even entertained ideas that Luke himself might call it off. It was only now, in these final days before the ceremony, that Ruby knew it would go ahead exactly as he had planned. And she was frantic.

'You're not to say things like that about him!' Cicely was trembling with anger. 'Luke and I are to be married shortly, and I will not have you defaming his character.' She was standing over Ruby, her small fists clenched by her sides. 'Why are you so set against him?' she demanded. 'Are you jealous? Is that it?'

Shocked to the core by Cicely's accusation, Ruby looked up. 'Jealous?' she asked incredulously. Placing her sewing on the chair arm, she forced herself to remain calm. 'Oh, Cicely, you don't know what you're saying,' she murmured fondly. 'It's *you* I'm concerned about. He means to hurt you, I know he does.' She stood up, her dark blue eyes beseeching as she asked, 'Please, Cicely. Think hard before you go through with it. He's using you, and you can't see it.'

'Oh?' She gave a small wry laugh. 'Using me now, is he?' Her vivid blue eyes were piercing, but as she spoke they were bright with tears. 'Well, go on then!' she snapped. 'You've been trying to tell me something these many weeks. You've already warned me he's all kinds of a scoundrel, that he's bad.' She demanded in a sarcastic voice that grew louder with every word, 'So, *please*, don't stop there. Tell me the worst. What are these dreadful things he's supposed to have done? Why is he bad? What makes you say he's using me? Has he told you that? HAS HE?'

She paused, seeming surprised by her own wild emotions. She made a sound like a sob, but then she straightened her shoulders and blinked the tears away. When she spoke again, it was in an uncertain voice and her eyes were softer, almost like those of a wounded animal. 'No, don't say anything,' she pleaded. 'Because, whatever you tell me, it won't make a scrap of difference to how I feel about him.' Her gaze momentarily faltered. 'I love him, do you see?' Holding her head high, she announced in a proud voice, 'Luke and I will be married in eight days' time, and there isn't a thing you can say that will stop it.' There was dull pain in her eyes now. She was too proud. Too certain. And somehow too afraid.

At first, Ruby was stunned. In all the heated arguments she and Cicely had exchanged with regard to Luke, never once had Ruby seen beneath that cool exterior. She saw beneath it now though, and suddenly the truth came to her like a bolt out of the blue.

'You know?' she murmured, disbelievingly. 'You know he's bad, don't you?'

Ruby wondered whether her own insistence over these past weeks had made Cicely think hard. Or had she somehow discovered for herself that the man she was to marry was a cheat and a womaniser?

'I wouldn't lie to you,' she promised. 'Everything I've said about him is true.' If ever there was a time to show Cicely just how evil he was, it had to be now. Now, while she was vulnerable and uncertain, while she was open to the truth at last. 'And yes, he *did* as good as tell me that he was using you to get at your father's money. There's a lot of hate in him, don't you see? There's something wrong with him. Something dangerous. Oh, Cicely, send him on his way. Be rid of him once and for all. There'll be a young man for you one day, good and worthy of you. Not him, though. Not Luke Arnold.'

'Is that all?' Cicely's voice was cold now.

For a long awful moment, Ruby wondered whether she should tell of that night in the alley. It was a strange and inexplicable thing, but she felt dirtied by that incident. Time and again she had looked back over it and searched her heart. Was there any time when she might have given a glance, one look, that could have given him the impression that she was easy game? Always the answer came back: No. All she had ever felt for Luke was a certain revulsion. But wait, she reminded herself. Wasn't there just one moment, one fleeting instant when she thought him deeply attractive? She closed her mind against such disturbing thoughts. Cicely was waiting. Would she tell or wouldn't she?

Ruby faced those startling blue eyes with a fierce strength. Reluctantly, she spoke out. 'I know he doesn't love you, Cicely.' Every word was bitter on her tongue. 'I know it because he's even made approaches to me. One evening some time back, when I missed my tram . . . he . . .' She hesitated, but if she didn't thrust that last awful truth home, Ruby knew that the moment would be gone and it would be too late. 'It was dark. He waited for me . . . pushed me into the alley.' She hated herself, but if she could make Cicely see sense, it would be worth it. 'He said he wanted me. If I hadn't managed to get away,' she closed her eyes at the memory, 'God only knows what might have happened.'

While Ruby was speaking, the tears were flowing down Cicely's face. She didn't doubt Ruby's words because she had seen the way Luke's eyes were drawn to her when he thought no one was watching. Deep down, Cicely knew that he was a womaniser, and possibly that he did have ulterior motives for marrying her. But, like all women in love, she tried not to see the obvious. It was far less painful to pretend. And anyway, she had high hopes that, once they were married, he would make a good and loyal husband. To her mind, a life with Luke was better than the lonely existence she suffered now. She could not send him away. Nor could she let the world know her humiliation; especially not Ruby, who was unusually perceptive, and would fight tooth and nail for her friends. The last thing Cicely wanted was for Ruby to come between her and Luke. And so she fought for at least a semblance of dignity. 'You're a liar.'

'You know I'm not.'

'Leave me. I want you out of my sight . . . out of this house.'

'You're dismissing me?' Ruby could hardly believe her ears.

Her only intention had been to show Cicely what she was letting herself in for, and somehow it had all rebounded.

'Get your things and leave. Your wages will be sent on to you.'

It was painful for Cicely to send Ruby away, but she had been left with no choice. If it was all to come right between her and Luke, it was better for Ruby to be out of the way. Out of his way. Ruby loved her, she knew that. She knew also that she would never find a truer friend. But it was Luke she wanted now, and only him. These past months he had crept up on her like a disease, until suddenly there was no room in her life for anyone else. She was shocked to find that also included her own dear father. In that moment she realised just how much she was sacrificing for this man whom she hardly knew. But then, where love was concerned, the heart dictated and all reason flew out the window.

'Do you really want me to go . . . and never come back?' Ruby's dark eyes were like a blue turbulent ocean as she looked up at this woman who had been so close to her.

Cicely couldn't bear to see Ruby's face, and so she turned away. 'I never want to see you again,' she murmured. 'And if I hear you have spoken to my father about any of this, I will never forgive you.' Behind her the hush was deafening. She heard the soft footsteps going across the room, and it took all of her will-power not to turn about and call Ruby back. Then she thought of Luke, and he was all that mattered now. The door closed. She went to the armchair and sank into it.

'I'm sorry, Ruby,' she whispered. 'I can't lose him because of you.' There were no tears now. Her face was set like stone. She closed her eyes and gave herself up to thoughts of her wedding. Somehow, though, all her excitement was gone. Instead she felt only anxiety, and a determination to be so good a wife to him that he would never want to part from her.

* * *

At the bottom of the stairs, Ruby paused to look back. The full implications of the scene in Cicely's room had only just sunk in. 'I never want to see you again', that's what Cicely had said! Stunned, she sat on the bottom step, her head bent into her hands. It was really true. She was dismissed, and she was never to set foot in this house again.

'God almighty, what have I done?' she asked herself. Now she would not be able to keep an eye on Cicely as she had planned. At one time there had been mention of her going with Cicely, should she and Luke find themselves a new house. Now she would be at his mercy. 'You're a big mouth, Ruby Miller,' she told herself. 'When will you ever learn?' Another thought struck her so hard that she sat up straight and cried out loud, 'Whatever will I tell me mam?'

Jeffrey Banks was rounding the corner from his study when he heard her. 'Is everything all right, Ruby?' he asked, striding towards her.

Flustered by his sudden appearance, she sprang up to face him. 'Sorry, sir?' she muttered. She was thoroughly miserable, and it showed. 'I were just thinking out loud.'

'You're upset about something, I can see that, Ruby.' There was something not quite right here, he thought. His glance went up the stairs in the direction of Cicely's room before coming back to examine Ruby's face. 'Do you want to talk about it?'

'Not really, sir.'

He smiled in that kindly way she had come to know. 'I might be able to help,' he suggested. 'Whatever it is, I'm sure it can't be all that bad.'

Ruby took a deep breath. 'I've been dismissed, sir.' He would know soon enough anyway.

Visibly shocked, Jeffrey told her to: 'Make your way to my study. I'll be along in a moment.' He waited until Ruby had done

327

as she was bid, after which he went up the stairs and into Cicely's room.

Outside, the wretched girl scurried along the landing, gaily flicking her feather duster over the many paintings that lined the walls. When she came to Cicely's room and heard the raised voices, she glanced furtively about. Then, satisfied that she was alone, bent her ear to the keyhole. 'Well, I never!' she declared, 'Well, I never!'

A few minutes later she was tripping her way down the stairs and into the kitchen, where she related the entire episode to Cook. 'Ruby's been sent packing,' she said, all wide-eyed and excited. 'The master's upstairs now, taking Miss Cicely to task, but she won't give way. "I can't have her around any more." That's what she told him. "Ruby's become too full of herself, and it's no good sending her below stairs because she's been spoiled, and there's no longer anywhere she can suitably fit into this household."'

Cook was ecstatic. 'I knew it!' she cried jubilantly. 'I knew that young woman would overstep the mark.' She returned her attention to rolling out the pastry. 'I told her, didn't I, eh?' she demanded. '"It'll all end in tears," that's what I said. And now it has.' She was so pleased that she could hardly contain herself. In fact, the wretched girl was startled out of her wits, when Cook suddenly instructed her to, 'Sit yourself down, girl. We'll partake of a drop o' brandy together.'

Jeffrey Banks waited for an answer. When none was forthcoming, he repeated his question. 'What happened between you two, Ruby?' He was standing in his study, with Ruby facing him. 'You've always been such good friends.' He couldn't understand it. Just now when he spoke to Cicely, he had been distressed to see how adamant she was.

'I'd rather not say, sir.'

'I'm deeply disappointed, Ruby.' She was barely an arm's

reach away, and he was amazed at her beauty. The night of the party, when he had foolishly allowed that little charade, there had been many comments from the other guests. Astonishing comments that had made him think for a long time afterwards. To save face and deter the curious, Ruby had been introduced as being close to the family. Strangely enough, not once, but many times the observation was made to him that she bore a strong resemblance to himself.

At the time he had taken little notice. But later, when he had time to think, he wondered. And the more he thought on it, the more likely it seemed. He looked at Ruby now: that sweetheart face and those strong dark eyes that twinkled blue in one light and black in another. He let his gaze surreptitiously rove to her hair, abundant brown hair the colour of rich chocolate. It stabbed at his heart when he realised that it was true what those people had said. *Ruby did have the look of him!* Certainly, though his hair was now streaked with grey, there had been a time when it was the same colour and texture as Ruby's. And those eyes, those blue eyes that were speckled black. Why! He might have been looking in a mirror.

Seeing her there, in these circumstances, he had the strongest urge to take her in his fatherly arms and comfort her. After all, it would have been the most natural thing in the world, because now he was convinced. *Lizzie's daughter was his daughter too.*

'Won't you tell me what took place between you and my daughter?' he asked fondly. Thinking, my *other* daughter. It wasn't the first time a master had fathered a child out of wedlock, and it wouldn't be the last. But somehow he held himself above all others, and was determined secretly to do his best by Lizzie's girl. 'You don't want to leave, do you?'

'It's for the best, sir.' Ruby didn't like lying to this man, but she felt cornered. She had not forgotten Cicely's warning: 'If I hear you've spoken to my father about any of this, I will never forgive you.' If she was to tell him the truth, then any faint chance of a reconciliation with Cicely would be gone for ever. She daren't risk that.

'Why do you say it's for the best?' he wanted to know. 'I don't understand. You and Cicely have been so good for each other.' He gazed at her for a considerable time during which Ruby felt decidedly uncomfortable. Presently he said, 'Whatever it is that's caused you and Cicely to fight, I'm sure it's no more than a storm in a teacup.'

'Cicely has dismissed me, sir, and I think it's best if I go now.'

'But *I* don't want you to go.' When Ruby looked at him with clear steadfast eyes, he folded his two hands behind his head, then raising his face to the ceiling, sighed. 'Women!' he muttered. 'There's no fathoming them.' He sighed again, as though there was a great weight upon him. He felt trapped, and angry, and truly believed that here was his own daughter, yet he had no right to claim her as such. All the same, he found he couldn't let her go so easily. 'Ruby, I want to know what happened between you and Cicely.' His voice was firm and he stared at her with serious eyes. 'I have asked her and she won't speak of it. So now I'm asking you.'

'It's best left alone, sir.' She felt threatened. The more he probed, the more she felt the need to run. 'If Cicely wanted you to know what we disagreed about, she would have told you.'

'Ah! So you *did* disagree about something. I knew there was more to this than met the eye.' Something occurred to him then, though for the life of him he couldn't think why it should. 'Was it because of my future son-in-law? Did you disagree about him?' He was inwardly shocked that such a thing should come into his mind.

Ruby was also shocked – so much so that the truth slipped out. 'I don't like him, sir.' The minute the words left her lips she cursed herself.

He answered in measured tones, 'You don't like him? Now why would you say a thing like that, child?' He asked himself much the same question. Why would *he* think the two young women had fought because of Luke Arnold? He watched Ruby closely, and realised that she was already regretting her admission. He was afraid there might be a deeper motive for the fight between her and Cicely. 'You love my daughter, don't you?'

'Very much, sir.'

'Yet you say you don't like her husband-to-be? I can see now that you were brave, or foolish, enough to tell this to my daughter. She was deeply offended, and that was why she dismissed you.' He waited for Ruby to confirm this, but she remained silent. Her silence told him a great deal. He decided not to press her further. 'Very well, Ruby. I won't badger you,' he promised. 'Perhaps in time, you and Cicely will mend your differences?'

Her eyes shone then. 'Oh, I do hope so, sir, I really do.'

For one dreadful moment there, she'd believed he would not let her go until she had confessed everything. She was tempted to. There would have been great satisfaction in telling him about the villainous Luke, how he meant to steal all of Cicely's inheritance, and how he felt nothing for her but contempt. Ruby was fearful of what the master would say if he knew Luke had propositioned *her*. She so much wanted to spill it all out and wholly discredit him in this man's eyes. Only the knowledge that Cicely would hate her for ever made her hold back. Still and all, wherever she was, she would do her utmost to keep an eye out for Cicely's well-being. If it ever became known to Ruby that Luke was ill-treating Cicely, she would move heaven and earth to punish him.

Without realising it, Ruby had stirred Jeffrey's suspicions, but on seeing the set of her pretty mouth, and knowing how reluctant she had been to speak all along, he realised that Ruby had said as much as she was going to. He admired her loyalty to Cicely.

'Yes. Perhaps the two of you will do better without interference from me,' he agreed. 'But what will you do now? Have you work that you can go to?' He knew Lizzie's family lived from day to day, and it worried him.

'No, sir. I have no work. But I'll find it soon enough.'

'Where will you look? There isn't much to be had.' He felt responsible for her.

'Don't worry about me, sir. I have a good strong back, and I can turn my hand to anything.'

'Hmmm.' He was mentally weighing the situation. 'Tell me something, Ruby?'

'Yes, sir?'

'What would you *like* to do?' He added swiftly, 'I believe you would prefer to stay here with my daughter, but other than that, what would you like to do?'

At first, she was surprised and puzzled by his question. 'What? You mean, if I had a choice and I wasn't poor?'

That hurt him. She shouldn't be poor. Lizzie shouldn't be poor either. 'Yes, that's what I mean,' he confirmed.

Ruby didn't have to think twice. 'Why, I'd like to have my own milliner's. Later, when I've saved enough, that's what I mean to do. I'm good at making and mending hats, d'you see, sir.' In fact, it had already crossed her mind to approach Cicely's own milliner, to ask Widow Reece if she needed an assistant.

He smiled then. 'Your own milliner's, eh? I didn't realise you were so ambitious.'

He had unwittingly stumbled on to Ruby's dream. 'Oh, yes, sir,' she said, and her whole face was aglow. 'One day I mean to get my mam and dad and the childer out of Fisher Street and into a nice place. A place where there ain't no bugs to suck your blood when you're asleep, where the rats don't run about in the yard and the rain don't stream down the bedroom walls.'

Realising she was getting carried away, she clamped her mouth shut and dropped her gaze to the carpet. By! If her mam was here, there would be hell to pay. Fancy opening her heart to the gentry like that! 'I'd really like to leave now, sir.'

'Of course.' He strode to the door and watched her walk towards him. She moved gracefully and he was proud to think he had fathered her. When the two of them were facing each other, he kept the door closed, telling her, 'I'll try my best to make Cicely see reason. Meanwhile, I'll arrange for your wages to be sent to you.' He touched her arm and she stared at him in astonishment.

'Thank you, sir.' He drew away, and it was as though the incident had never happened. 'But I'd be grateful if you didn't upset Cicely on my account. It might make things worse between us,' Ruby warned.

He nodded. 'I understand.' Opening the door, he allowed her through, quietly closing it behind her. Going to his desk, he sat heavily in the chair and leaned back, his forehead creased in thought as he mulled over what had transpired.

'So perhaps Ruby has seen something in that young man that I've missed?' he mused.

He was both intrigued and disturbed. Cicely was very precious to him, and he would hate to think he had misjudged the young man who had asked for her hand in marriage. Though he himself had seen Luke as a presentable and eligible fellow, hard-working and devoted to his father's business, Ruby had other ideas. But then he reminded himself, 'Isn't it natural that she should feel perhaps a little jealous? After all, she and Cicely have been so close, and now Cicely is to be married.'

No! Whatever was he thinking of? It wasn't Ruby's nature to be jealous of Cicely's happiness. Quite the contrary – she would be delighted if it was the right man. *If it was the right man!*

He couldn't rest. In a moment he had crossed the room. Flinging the door open, he went out in a hurry, then up the stairs to Cicely's room. He must satisfy himself that all was well, and that Ruby's dislike of the young man was at worst passing female envy, and at best a simple misunderstanding.

Ten minutes later, he came down to the drawing room. Cicely was with him and they were happy together. She had assured him that the disagreement between herself and Ruby was of a personal nature and had nothing whatsoever to do with Luke.

'What could she know of him?' she asked innocently, and Jeffrey was obliged to consider her point.

All the same, he had not altogether forgotten Ruby's sincere confession: 'I don't like him, sir.' In spite of everything, it preyed on his mind.

Ruby didn't go straight home. If she arrived early there were bound to be questions and she wasn't ready for them. Instead she went into Blackburn town where she wandered about, gazing in the shop windows and searching her troubled mind for the best way to explain what had happened. If only she could find work before she went home, the shock to her mam wouldn't be so bad.

With this in mind, Ruby made her way to Widow Reece's shop. It was a sizeable place, right at the top of King Street, straddling the corner and almost facing The Sun public house. This was a busy thoroughfare and Widow Reece did a thriving business here.

Pausing outside, Ruby looked in the window, admiring the splendid display. At the back, the larger wide-brimmed hats, boaters and boas made a colourful collage from one side to the other, while smaller hats took up the foreground. These were cleverly positioned on stands of varying heights, each hat carefully chosen so that one colour complemented another. There were hats that were fancy and extravagant, exquisitely bedecked with feathers and veils, then there were small round hats with a variety of chin-straps – some as fine as gossamer that might snap in a high wind, others as wide as a woman's neck, and beautiful silk straps that came over the hat to culminate in a beautifully tied ribbon at the throat. The colours were breathtaking: blue like a summer sky, pink as heather, and white as the winter's snow.

The shades and styles reflected Widow Reece's many years of experience. She knew instinctively what kind of hat a woman would want to be seen in, and it was no wonder that her expertise was sought far and wide. It was even more astonishing that she did everything herself, with her own two hands, from design to creation. She chose the material, dyed it, cut and shaped it, moulded it into a hat, and finally dressed it with silk and feathers. According to the older inhabitants of Blackburn, Widow Reece had never been known to have an assistant.

'What would I do with one?' she had been heard to ask. 'I'd only spend valuable time training her, and then likely as not, off she would go at the first sign of marriage and children.'

It was fourteen years since her own husband had gone from this life, and she had thrown herself into her work to forget the loneliness. Now, at sixty-two years of age and no longer handsome, she was a private woman, accustomed to living and working alone, and preferred it that way.

It was this thought that caused Ruby to hesitate. Somehow, she couldn't really see Widow Reece changing her habits after all this time. Disillusioned, she toyed with the idea of not going into the shop at all. But then she reminded herself that there was only one other milliner's in the whole of Blackburn. It was a miserable little place down Nab Lane, and the woman who owned it was even more miserable. No. Ruby told herself that if she really wanted to work in a milliner's, she had to summon up courage and have a word with Widow Reece. After all, she could only say no. But Ruby hoped with all her heart that she would say yes.

* * *

Widow Reece stayed behind her counter, eyeing Ruby with curiosity, while Ruby did the same to her. The woman looked much older than when Ruby had last seen her, nine months ago when a selection of hats was brought to the House for Cicely to choose from. Widow Reece was now snow-white and her fine-featured face was creased with a multitude of deep meandering wrinkles. She seemed smaller too, and when she rounded the counter to examine Ruby more clearly, she walked with a slight limp. 'I don't know what makes you think I'm looking for an assistant,' she remarked. 'To tell you the truth, I've been con-sidering selling up. Did someone send you here?' She was not unfriendly.

'No. I came of my own accord,' Ruby answered. She thought that at one time Widow Reece must have been a real beauty. Her nose was straight and very slightly tipped at the end, and her pale eyes were round and smiling. There was an air of graciousness about her, although sadly overwhelmed by the onset of old age.

'I've seen you before, I think.' The woman peered through narrowed eyes at Ruby, at the lovely face and those rich blue eyes – dark striking eyes that a body would not easily forget. 'You're Cicely Banks's lady's maid. Am I right?'

'In a way,' Ruby affirmed. 'I *was* her maid.' It hurt her to say it in the past tense like that. 'But now I'm looking for work in a milliner's.' Shame washed over her as she anticipated the next question. Ruby couldn't bring herself to say she had just been dismissed, and so went on hurriedly, 'I just wondered whether you might have need of an assistant? I've been told I have a natural talent for mending and making hats.' She was so anxious not to be turned away that she hardly paused for breath. 'I wouldn't want a big wage, and I'll stay as late as you like. I don't mind how much sewing and mending I do, 'cause my fingers are used to it. Later, though, I would like to help make the hats. I don't mind getting dye on my hands. In fact, I'll do anything and everything with a good heart . . .'

'Goodness me!' Widow Reece put her hands to her face and rolled her eyes. 'You're making me breathless!' she cried.

Ruby drew in a great gulp of air. 'Sorry, ma'am,' she replied. 'It's just that . . . well, I really do need work, and I have such an interest in the making of hats.' She saw how the other woman's face fell, and her heart fell with it. 'You're telling me you ain't got no work then?'

There followed a long pause while Widow Reece looked Ruby up and down. Ruby stood stiffly to attention, her heart in her mouth and the faintest of hopes stirring inside her. She daren't speak, was almost afraid to breathe. Presently she was told, 'Come with me.' As the other woman turned and made her way into the back room, Ruby followed.

'Look around you,' Widow Reece said, waving her slim gnarled hand in an extravagant gesture. 'Tell me what you think.' She went to the window, grabbing the curtains with both hands and thrusting them all the way back. The afternoon light flooded in, illuminating every corner of that little room.

Ruby was astounded. Her mouth opened and her eyes grew round like two ocean-blue pools. 'It's wonderful!' she said in a hushed voice. 'Why! I ain't never seen the like.' There were trestles and tables, shelves and cupboards, a set of drawers and an oak wardrobe with its doors open; every available space, every shelf, every surface, and even most of the floor, was piled high with hats in varying stages of development. The colours were blinding, every one imaginable, all shades of pink and blue, green and brown, yellow, red and orange.

Like a rainbow, Ruby thought. I'm standing in the middle of a rainbow! She was exhilarated.

Over by the window a long shelf stretched right across the wall, and here, displayed in all their glory, were the finished articles, resplendent in veils and feathers, extravagant neck-ties and silken roses. 'Oh! They're so beautiful!' Rushing to the window, Ruby couldn't resist reverently running her fingers over them. In all of her life, she would never forget this glorious experience.

When she turned, Widow Reece was smiling. 'You'll do,' she murmured, nodding her head. 'I wasn't sure at first, but now I know.'

Ruby daren't believe what her instincts were telling her. '*Are you saying I can work with you?*' she asked in a trembling voice.

The other woman came to her then. Placing a gentle hand on Ruby's shoulder, she said warmly, 'To create a thing of beauty, you have to *think* with beauty. You need a certain love and reverence for the thing you are creating.' She relaxed into the nearest chair and keeping her eyes on Ruby's face, went on, 'Any woman can appreciate a beautiful hat, but there are only a very few who can actually create it with their own hands. Though it isn't the hands themselves that create it, because they are only the tools. It's the heart that creates it, the heart that weaves the magic. You need to have a particular imagination, a certain passion for what you're doing.' She smiled wistfully. 'Do you understand what I'm saying? You have to have the magic in your heart in the first place.'

'I can see how that might be, ma'am,' Ruby admitted. She understood everything that was being said, and she knew it was right.

'Just now, when you came into my work-room, I watched you closely for a reason. Seeing you enthralled, seeing how your eyes lit up and the way in which you caressed the finished creations, I knew then . . . *you* have the magic in your heart. And, yes, I can find work here for you. If you still want it.'

Ruby could hardly believe her ears. 'IF I STILL WANT IT?' she cried. 'Oh, you can't know how much.'

'Very well then. One month's trial. You may begin on Monday morning. You'll start at seven and finish at six for six days a week.' She was delighted to see that Ruby didn't flinch at the mention of these long hours which might have daunted a less enthusiastic person. 'Your wages will reflect the fact that you're on a trial period. To start with, I'll pay you ten shillings a week. Is that satisfactory?'

The first thought that struck Ruby was that she would be earning less than before. Yet she set that disappointment against the fact that she would be doing what she had always wanted, and it would stand her in good stead for the future. 'Very well, ma'am,' she agreed. 'And thank you.'

'Don't call me "ma'am". There are no servants here. I am your employer and you my employee. You can address me as Mrs Reece. By the way, what's your name, young lady?'

'Ruby Miller.'

'Miller, eh?' That amused her. 'Miller. Well, would you believe it! You're already partway a milliner, aren't you?'

'I never thought of that.' Somehow it pleased her. Perhaps the good Lord meant her to be a milliner after all.

'And where do you live?'

'Fisher Street.'

The smile momentarily fell from her face. 'Oh?' She saw the disappointment in Ruby's dark eyes and was instantly ashamed that she should have shown her distaste for that particular area. 'We all have to start somewhere, I suppose.' Beaming from ear to ear, she saw Ruby to the door. 'Of course, you'll be required to wear one of my straw boaters to and from these premises. A form of advertising, do you see?'

'I would like that.'

Regarding Ruby with quizzical eyes, Widow Reece revealed, 'It's odd, you coming here today, because until this morning I had no intention of ever letting anyone else touch my precious hats. I suppose it's been creeping up on me, but like the foolish old woman I am, I chose to ignore it. It's my hands, do you see?' She held out her gnarled fingers showing their bony crooked knuckles. 'I'm losing my grip . . . and when a milliner begins to lose her grip, she begins to lose her livelihood.'

'I'm sorry.' Ruby thought it very sad.

'Oh, you mustn't be sorry. Especially when it's got you into my work-room.' She laughed out loud and startled Ruby by actually shaking hands with her. 'I'm counting on you to be my fingers,' she murmured softly. In a brighter, stronger voice she added, 'Well, good day then, Miss Ruby Miller. I shall expect to see you at seven on Monday morning.'

'And I'll be here, Mrs Reece, ready and willing to get to work,' she promised.

'Hmmm.' She looked Ruby up and down and was pleased with what she saw. This young woman was unusually lovely, trim and smart with a certain flair that would attract the customers. Oh, yes, she was good material, and eager to be trained. More than that, the young lady had a decidedly pleasant and engaging nature. Lately, Widow Reece had been afraid that she would be forced to close her shop. That would have broken her heart. Now, though, she saw a new lease of life for herself, through engaging Ruby, and it occurred to her that it must have been the hand of Fate that had guided the girl here today. Her gratitude shone through as she spoke. 'I'm glad you came, and hope this is the beginning of a very fruitful association.'

'So do I,' Ruby answered. 'Oh, so do I.' And she could think of nothing else as she made her way back to Fisher Street. At least she could tell her mam she had secured other work. What was more, it was work she had always longed to do.

All the same, as she pushed open her front door, Ruby was already missing Cicely. Even the thought of working in Widow Reece's shop couldn't take the heartache away altogether.

* * *

Lizzie threw up her hands and wiped them down her face, peeping at Ruby over her fingers. 'God bless and love us, gal!' she cried anxiously. 'I knew there were summat yer wanted to tell me. All night long you've been fidgeting and fussing . . . hardly touched yer tea . . . and now, when yer dad's out and the childer abed, yer after giving me a heart attack!'

She had come into the parlour from putting Lottie upstairs and was seated in the horse-hair chair by the fireside when Ruby told her that she wouldn't be going back to her place with Cicely. In an instant her mam was on her feet and pacing up and down. 'What in God's name have yer done, eh?' she demanded. 'I warned yer not to get too friendly with the gentry. And now it's cost you yer job.' She slewed round to see Ruby's sad eyes staring up at her, and was filled with remorse. 'Oh, sweetheart, I don't mean to go on,' she apologised. 'I expect yer feeling bad enough, without me nagging at yer, and I know yer were that fond o' Cicely.' She sighed long and deep. 'But we'll all be worse off without that second wage coming in.'

Ruby held out her hand. 'Mam, come and sit down. It's not as bad as it seems because I've got something else to tell you.'

Perching herself on the edge of the chair opposite, Lizzie waited, her pretty brown eyes focussed on Ruby's face and her hands nervously folded on her lap. 'Summat else?' she asked. 'Well, go on then, lass. *What* else?'

'I'll still have a wage coming in,' she said proudly. 'Widow Reece has set me on at her shop, and I'm to start on Monday.'

Lizzie was agape. 'Widder Reece? What . . . the milliner's at the top o' King Street?'

'That's right, Mam,' she said proudly.

'Well, I never!' A reluctant little smile turned up the corners of Lizzie's mouth. 'Is that right, lass? Widder Reece has taken you on, when she allus swore she'd never let anybody within a mile of her workshop?' This was a real turn up. But then, Ruby was allus interested in that kind of work, and no doubt the widder saw what a fine helper she'd be getting in Ruby.

'There's only one drawback, Mam,' she admitted. 'I won't be getting the same wages as I was with Cicely. I'm to be given a month's trial, and started at ten shilling a week.'

'Ten shilling!' Lizzie shouted. 'I'm buggered if she ain't taking advantage. Yer not accepting that, are yer?'

'I've already given my word. And, to be honest, Mam, I'm really looking forward to it. You know I've always wanted to do that kind of work. Even though I think the world of Cicely, I knew there would come a time when I'd want to move.'

She could hardly contain her excitement. 'Widow Reece has given me the opportunity I need. I'll work hard for her, and I'll learn all there is to learn. I'll save and save until I can start a shop of my own.'

Lizzie was angry. 'There yer go again!' she snapped, 'Dreams. Big impossible dreams. It ain't right that a lass of your sort should be entertaining such grand ideas.'

'They're not impossible dreams,' Ruby protested. 'I can make them come true. It will take a long time, but I know I can make them come true.'

To her mind, what she planned had never been a dream. All her life she had wanted something of her own, something that would bring her the kind of independence and respect that Widow Reece had enjoyed. Something that would raise them all out of this place. It hurt her when her mam spoke like this, dismissing her ambitions as though they were a sin. 'Oh, Mam, don't you believe in me at all?'

Lizzie stiffened. 'Well, o' course I do,' she declared. Though she would never admit it out loud, Ruby was her darling and her favourite. She was her first-born and, more than that, Ruby was herself when she was young. But the other side of her character belonged to her father, a man educated in the skills of business, a man with a razor-sharp mind and fine intellect. Lizzie was convinced that Jeffrey's blood in Ruby's veins caused the driving ambition that wouldn't let her rest.

There had been a time when Lizzie herself had entertained ideas above her station, when she too wondered what it would be like to be a lady of consequence, to be someone other folks would look up to. To her never-ending shame she had been drawn to Jeffrey Banks, a rich and powerful man above her station, a man whose attentions had set her foolish young heart racing. But for all that, he was a good man, and to this day Lizzie had no doubt that he had loved her. Yet she could never forgive herself for what took place on that night. To her dying day she would see it as a terrible sin and a shocking weakness in her past. Ruby was a constant reminder of that awful, wonderful episode. Now, in her, Lizzie saw a dangerous need that could only end in heartache. 'I've told you afore, I don't want you talking about not being content with what the good Lord gave yer!'

Lizzie truly believed she had to reprimand Ruby for her own good. It never occurred to her that she might be punishing Ruby for the sin she herself had committed. All she could see was the wrong of it all. Mixing with the gentry was wrong, wanting was wrong, looking beyond the street in which you lived was wrong. Deliberately drawing the conversation away from Ruby's new work, she asked suspiciously, 'What happened at the big house, our Ruby?' Up to now, all Ruby had told her was that she and Cicely had parted.

Believing it was best to tell the truth, Ruby answered, 'I was dismissed.' And, before her mam could explode, she went on in a sad voice, 'I didn't want that, Mam. I thought if Cicely moved house, I would be going with her.' Her eyes were bright with tears as she looked at Lizzie. 'I'll miss her, Mam. And I'm so afraid for her.'

'What d'yer mean, afraid? And whyever did yer get dismissed? Was it the mistress or the master who put yer out?' At the back of her mind, she had the numbing notion that Jeffrey Banks might somehow have discovered that Ruby was his own daughter, and that was why he had shown her the door. 'Oh, Ruby lass, whatever did yer do to get dismissed?'

Her answer satisfied both questions. 'It was Cicely who dismissed me. She was angry because I tried to warn her against Luke Arnold.' She went on to explain how she didn't trust him, and believed that he would make Cicely's life a misery. Yet she dared not say how she knew these things because then she would have to confess about that deceitful little charade at the party, and would also have to describe how Luke had pushed her into that dark alley, wanting his way with her. If Lizzie knew all of that, there would be no holding her. And so, in order to justify her suspicions of Luke, Ruby told her mam, 'It's well known that he wants to wed Cicely only so he can get his hands on the foundry, and Mr Banks's money. What's more, I've heard it said that he's a womaniser into the bargain. If Cicely takes him for a husband, she'll rue the day, I just know it. Oh, Mam, he'll make her so unhappy.'

Lizzie was furious. 'Yer mean to tell me that you've said all these things to Cicely Banks? Well! No wonder she threw yer out. She's a grown woman, and who she chooses to take for her husband ain't none of yer business, my girl. How many times have I told yer it's dangerous to listen to hearsay and gossip? Come ter think of it, I ain't heard no such talk about that young man. And haven't I warned yer to keep yer tongue between yer teeth, else you'll dig yer own grave with it?' She tutted and shook her head. 'By! Why must yer allus want to speak yer mind, when it's often best to keep certain things to yerself?'

'Because Cicely's my friend.'

Lizzie sprang from the chair, her eyes bright with anger.

'CICELY BANKS IS GENTRY!' For some inexplicable reason, she was suddenly fearful. Yet she was instantly sorry for having yelled at Ruby like that. 'Oh, look, lass, I don't mean to be hard on yer.'

She came to stand behind this daughter whom she loved with a ferocity that frightened her. Placing her hands on Ruby's shoulders, she went on in a softer voice, 'You can't know anything of Luke Arnold. Most of the time there ain't no truth in gossip, and yer should never have told it to yer mistress. I know yer think the world of her, and I know yer hackles would be up if yer thought she were letting herself in for a lot of sorrow.' She patted her hand agitatedly on Ruby's shoulder. 'But it ain't your place to interfere.'

She returned to her chair and for a while there was a tense atmosphere between them. But then Lizzie asked something of Ruby that created a greater conflict. 'I want yer to promise me summat, lass?'

'If I can.'

'I want yer to say that even if Cicely Banks seeks yer out and asks yer to come back you'll say no. I have a feeling that when she calms down and has time to think on it, that young woman might regret having dismissed yer. Oh, don't think I don't know the affection you two have for each other, I'm not such a fool as to believe it was only one way. After all, it were her that got yer brought up from the kitchen to be her personal maid. And, God forbid, yer told me yerself that she treated yer almost like a sister.'

It was that more than anything that had frightened Lizzie, because it was too near the truth. 'Will yer promise me, lass? Will yer refuse if she comes after yer? I don't ever want yer working in that house again. In fact, when I come to think of it, I reckon it might be a real godsend that you've found a place with Widder Reece. At least she ain't gentry as such.'

She regarded Ruby for a moment, thinking how quiet she had

grown and realising that all of this must have been very hard on her.

'I ain't asking much, lass,' Lizzie persisted. 'Yer mam don't ever ask much of yer, but now I need yer answer. Promise you'll not go back even if she asks yer?' She waited anxiously for she knew it was indeed a lot to ask.

Ruby had to think deeply on what her mam had put forward. If the truth were told, she had not even anticipated that Cicely would come after her, therefore had had no cause to contemplate what she might do if that happened. If Ruby knew anything at all, she knew that Cicely's love for Luke Arnold had blinded her to everything else. It was highly unlikely that Ruby would ever be asked to set foot in that house again. Even the master had been unable to persuade Cicely to a change of heart.

'All right, Mam,' she conceded. 'You have my word.' To Ruby's mind it was a promise that she would never be tested on. 'I won't let Cicely persuade me to go back.'

Lizzie was delighted. 'Well, that's a relief,' she said. 'I'm glad you've got work with Widow Reece, and I dare say if we all pull us belts in, we'll manage well enough with a smaller wage.' She settled back in the chair and glanced at the clock. 'I hope yer father's staying clear of them troublemakers from Arnold's foundry. There's summat brewing there, I reckon, and I don't want Ted mixed up in it.'

Ruby got out of her chair and, kissing her mam on the forehead, told her, 'We can talk later if you like. I want to see Maureen before she's settled for the night.'

She needed to tell her friend all the news. Besides, Maureen was the only one who knew the whole truth: about Luke Arnold, the party, and everything. It was good to have someone she could confide in. The only thing Maureen disapproved of was Ruby's reticence with Johnny, why was it that while one opened his heart, the other closed hers?

Ruby was disappointed to find that Johnny was out but Maureen greeted her with a big hug and a warm smile. Within minutes Ruby was pouring out her heart: about Cicely and Luke, about Widow Reece and her new post, and how she meant to listen and watch until there was nothing she needed to know about the business of making and selling hats.

Maureen listened eagerly. She adored Ruby, and knew there would come a day when her name would be known far and wide. As always, Ruby's enthusiasm excited and thrilled her. Yet at the same time she was sad because she suspected that the price Ruby must pay was her love for Johnny. To Maureen's mind, Ruby would be losing something very precious. Far more precious than all the money and influence in the world. But nothing would ever be allowed to diminish Ruby's dream. It had grown with her until now it was as dear to her as her own life.

Now, while she listened as Ruby outlined her future at the milliner's, Maureen was afraid. She knew without a doubt how determined and ambitious her friend was, but what concerned her most was where this new step into unknown territory would lead.

As Ruby so rightly pointed out, Widow Reece had given her a wonderful opportunity. Put that together with Ruby's natural talents and consuming ambition, and it made a heady brew.

Chapter Twelve

On Thursday 12 June, something happened which was to shape Ruby's future for a long time to come.

She had been working at the milliner's for almost a week when a letter was delivered from Jeffrey Banks to the house in Fisher Street. Flustered by the unceasing demands of her two youngest, and aching all over from scrubbing the flagstones on the scullery floor, Lizzie groaned out loud when the knock came on the door, 'Who can that be at this time of morning?' she grumbled.

'Happen it's our Ruby forgot her pack-up,' Dolly suggested lazily. She had been washing her own little corner with a bit of rag and a bowl of water given to her by Lizzie, and imagined herself all grown up. 'It's a nuisance, isn't it, Mam?' she asked with a frowning face. ''Cause the water runs all in the cracks if you don't mop it up straightaway.'

'Aye, well, happen you'll mop it up for me, will yer, lass?' she asked with a chuckle. 'And keep an eye on that little scoundrel there.' Lizzie inclined her head towards young Lottie who was crawling over the carpet on all fours. 'Don't let the little sod get into any mischief, will yer?'

'I'll clip her ear if she don't behave,' Dolly said in a sombre voice, staring at the infant as though she had done something awful. When the bemused Lottie merely gurgled at her, Dolly giggled. 'See, Mam?' she announced. 'Lottie knows what you say, don't she, eh?' Addressing the infant again, she repeated in a firm voice, 'I *will*. I'll clip your ear if you start yer bawling.'

'You'll do no such thing,' Lizzie warned. Just then another knock at the door echoed loudly through the house. 'By! Some folks is that impatient,' she moaned. 'Watch the young 'un, that's all,' she instructed, 'I'll not be a minute.' Clambering to her knees, she slopped the cloth back into her bucket and wiped her hands on the tail end of her pinafore. That done, she took another glance at the two children and put the bucket up on the dresser out of reach of small hands. 'Be good now,' she warned, before going at a hurried pace along the passage to answer the door. 'Wait on!' she yelled as the knocks grew more impatient. 'Wait on, yer bugger. I'm on me way.'

When Lizzie flung open the door and saw the gentry carriage outside, her heart nearly stopped. The first thought that leaped to mind was that a contrite Cicely had come to collect Ruby. Yet there was no sign of her, nor of her father.

Regarding the uniformed driver with mingled fear and suspicion, Lizzie kept the door closed to within an inch. Peeping from within the safety of her own domain, she demanded in a shrill unwelcoming voice, 'Who are yer? And what's yer business at a decent woman's door?'

The tall moustached man held out his hand. 'I've been told to deliver this in person.' When she made no move to take it, he insisted, 'It's for a Ruby Miller. She does live here, doesn't she?' He had a strange-sounding voice, high-pitched and forced, like the wind that came from the bellows when Lizzie squeezed them to light the fire.

Convinced that Ruby was in some kind of trouble, she demanded, 'Who wants to know, eh?'

'Jeffrey Banks, that's who.' With growing impatience, he thrust the letter forward.

Lizzie would not be intimidated. Her round brown eyes shifted to the vehicle. 'Jeffrey Banks don't keep no carriages. So who's is that, eh? And how do I know it's him that's sent yer?'

'I don't see that it's any of your business, but the carriage is hired. The young lady of the house is to be wed on Saturday, and there's much toing and froing.' He stepped forward, causing Lizzie to shrink away. 'So, you see, I'm rushed off my feet. Either you take the letter, or I'll be obliged to leave it on the step,' he warned. 'I'm not particular,' he added sharply. He was feeling peeved. It wasn't often he was asked to run errands like a common messenger boy, and it went against the grain with him. What was more, he detested venturing into a street such as this, which to his mind was nothing more than a slum inhabited by people who had neither brains nor scruples.

'Give it here then.' Lizzie stuck her arm through the narrow gap in the door. 'I'll see she gets it.' Once the letter was in her fist, she slammed the door shut. 'Toffee-nosed git!' she muttered as she went slowly down the passage, turning the letter over and over in her hands. 'What's all this about?' she asked herself. 'Why would the master be writing to my Ruby?'

In the parlour she placed the letter high on the mantelpiece, propped up behind the clock, its two ends jutting out either side and frightening her with its formal appearance. 'I hope they ain't asking her to go back,' she murmured. 'I know our Ruby's given me her word, but all the same it would be a temptation, I know, being as how she thinks the world of that Miss Cicely.'

Dolly came to stand beside her and they both stared at the letter for what seemed an age. 'Ruby won't break her promise,' Dolly presently announced in a stern little voice. She knew about the promise Ruby had made their mam, because she'd heard her parents talking about it and her dad saying. 'Aw, Lizzie, it weren't fair to ask the lass to do that.'

'Hey!' Lizzie glanced down at the little figure beside her. 'Who asked you, eh?'

'She won't though. Ruby never breaks a promise.'

Lizzie stroked the girl's head. 'Aye, lass,' she admitted, 'you're right. All the same, I can't help wondering what's in that there letter.'

'Open it then.'

Lizzie was shocked. 'By! I can't do that, and shame on yer for thinking such a thing!' She propelled the child back to the damp patch on the scullery floor. 'Get on with yer work,' she instructed, 'and mind yer mop that floor dry, else yer mam'll likely upend herself on it.'

When the child was busy at her work, Lizzie dropped to her knees, dipping the cloth in the suds, wringing it out then slapping it on to the flagstones which she rubbed with increasing vigour until they shone like bright wet pebbles. And all the while her mind was on that letter and on Ruby. As Dolly had pointed out, Ruby would never break a promise, but it would be a pity if she were made miserable because of it, especially when she was getting on so well at Widow Reece's shop.

Time and again, Lizzie paused in her labours to glance at the letter. She glanced at it on her way into the scullery, and she thought about it when she swilled the dirty water into the yard; she stared at it on her way back into the parlour, and then again when she was feeding the infant at her breast. She peeked at it when she laid the sleeping bairn into its makeshift cot, and later on, when she was sipping her tea. Her frantic eyes kept going to it all the while she was telling Dolly a story about elves and fairies, and she felt it burning into her back when she was blackleading the range. The clock ticked away the minutes, and the minutes turned into hours, and the hours couldn't go quick enough. 'Come home, our Ruby,' she muttered beneath her breath. 'I shan't rest 'til I know what's in that there letter.'

351

Lizzie would not have been so keen if she'd known that the contents of that letter were bound to fuel Ruby's ambitions, taking her further down the very road her mother so feared.

At four-thirty the twins came home, starving hungry and noisier than a wagon-load of monkeys. Lizzie sent them into the yard where they could argue and shout to their hearts' content. Ten minutes later, Lenny dragged himself into the parlour, his torn shirt hanging round his shoulders in strips and his face a mass of bruises. 'God bless and love us, you've been at it again!' Lizzie complained, and once more he was sent to wash, change and 'Keep yerself in yer room 'til yer father comes home!'

When Ted came in just after six o'clock, Lizzie had relented and Lenny was sitting at the table with the twins and Dolly. They were all scrubbed and shining, and waiting patiently for their tea. Lottie was fast asleep in her box, with a full tummy and a contented smile on her face. 'I'm glad one of you is out for the count,' Lizzie observed with a little grin as she made her way into the scullery. There was cheese and bacon dumpling for tea, and a slice of jam pie afterwards. As she went to and fro, her eyes were constantly drawn to that long envelope which stood behind the clock and seemed to fill the room from end to end.

'There's a letter from Jeffrey Banks to our Ruby,' she told her husband as they ate their tea.

'Oh, aye?' He followed her troubled gaze to the mantelpiece. 'It'll be summat and nowt,' he said dryly.

Lizzie was astounded at his lack of concern, 'Well now, *you* don't seem worried, I must say,' she remarked, regarding him out of the corner of her eye. 'I wondered if it were a summons for her to go back to working there, and yer know I'm not in favour o' that, don't yer?'

'Aye, I know it, lass,' he admitted. 'But to tell the truth, I can't see no harm in Ruby being personal maid to Cicely Banks. They're a good family and Cicely's father's seen me all right. If it hadn't been for him, I'd be out of work and we'd not be sitting here enjoying such a nice spread at the table. You can't deny that, now can you?' He collected a large juicy piece of dumpling on to his fork and poked it into his mouth. For the moment he was unable to comment further, but his thoughts were racing ahead, and he had more on his mind than Ruby being offered her old place back. There was something wrong at the foundry where he used to work, disturbing murmurs about second-grade materials and 'money changing hands in high places'. He was no stranger to such rumours, but they were growing stronger. Until now he had dismissed them, because he himself had seen nothing untoward. Besides, it was dangerous to pay attention to malicious gossip. Still, there *was* something. And it was getting harder and harder to put it out of his mind.

'We'll know soon enough when she comes home,' Lizzie was thinking out loud. 'I do hope she won't go back to Jeffrey Banks's household. God knows, I don't want her in that house. I should never have let her go there in the first place . . .' She was startled when Ted cast her a quizzical glance. 'Well, I mean . . . she's doing so well at Widder Reece's, ain't she?' she added quickly. In her heart she shrank from the prospect of Ted ever discovering that he was not Ruby's father. And, worse, that Jeffrey Banks *was*! It was her worst nightmare.

'I can't think why you're so set against Jeffrey Banks and his daughter,' Ted remarked. 'And anyway, if Cicely has asked Ruby back, and things come right between them, it isn't for us to say anything. It must be Ruby's decision. She's not a child any more. She's grown and responsible. It isn't for us to say how she earns a living, so long as it's decent. We should be grateful that she fetches a wage in. What! There are women of her age already wed and pushing prams about.' He reached out and, to the amusement of the watching children, put his hand over hers, assuring her fondly, 'She's a good lass, and yer mustn't fret over her.' He

353

looked up at the mantelpiece. 'That's Ruby's letter, and it's Ruby's business. She doesn't even have to tell us about it if she doesn't want to.'

Lizzie didn't answer. There was nothing for her to say. Everything Ted had pointed out was true, and she could find no rational argument with it. At least, not one that she could say outright. Instead, she concentrated on slicing the jam pie. Afterwards she watched the clock, and waited with growing impatience for Ruby to come home.

Ruby saw the last customer safely away. 'You've made the right choice,' she told the aged dowager. 'You have excellent taste.' It had taken over an hour to satisfy this difficult person, but at last she was pleased with her purchase; a lovely cream, broad-brimmed hat with an abundance of precious blue feathers and a small discreet veil that gave her ageing face a soft pretty look. The tricky part had been persuading Lady Lloyd Briggs towards a hat that not only flattered her but gave her an air of importance befitting her social position. Even harder was the task of drawing her away from the desperately unsuitable, frilly fancy thing that would have better suited a woman half her age. Although it was twice the price of the one the customer had settled for, Ruby's conscience would not have allowed her to complete a sale on it.

The large white-haired lady nodded and smiled as Ruby helped her to the waiting carriage where the driver was patiently waiting. 'You really are a clever little thing,' she told Ruby in a warm admiring voice. 'You might allow me to think *I* chose the hat, when we all know it was *you* who chose it for me.' When she saw how Ruby's dark blue eyes grew round with astonishment, she laughed out loud. 'I'm grateful to you,' she admitted, much to Ruby's relief. 'What an absolute fool I would have looked, wearing that young frilly thing that took my fancy.' She shook her head. 'I don't know what came over me,' she confessed. 'I have a certain position to maintain, and my days of youthful fancy are long gone.' She sighed. 'But thank you, my dear. The hat I'm taking away is a beautiful thing, and to be honest it makes me look ten years younger . . . keeps the wrinkles in the shadows,' she laughed. As she looked beyond Ruby, she saw Widow Reece standing in the doorway. 'You have a real gem in this young lady,' she told her. 'From now on, I want her to attend to me, if you don't mind?'

'But of course.'

'Good.' Another warm smile bestowed on Ruby, and then she was seated in the carriage, one hand crossed over the other on her lap and her chin held high. Ruby thought she looked every inch the grand old lady she was. In a moment the carriage was going down the street and soon it was lost to sight.

Inside the shop, Ruby turned the sign round to read 'Closed', and then followed her employer into the back room to collect her coat and bag. 'I like her,' she said simply. 'And she's not half as difficult as she used to be.'

'That's because she's taken a liking to you, and she respects your judgement,' the other woman said. 'She's right, you know, Ruby. You really are very clever.'

'No.' She shook her head as she shrugged herself into her coat. 'The hat she took was the only one in the shop that would have done for her.' She went to the cupboard and collected her bag. 'Once I arranged it on her head, she could see that for herself.'

'Ruby?'

'Yes, Mrs Reece?'

'Have you got a moment?'

'Well, yes. I could catch the later tram if you like. Is there urgent work for me to do?'

'No, no. Nothing like that.' Widow Reece shook her head. 'As far as I can tell, you've caught up with everything.' She roved her gaze about the room. It was neater than she had ever known it. 'I never cease to be amazed at the amount of work you get through in the course of a day.' Walking across the room, she explained to Ruby. 'It's just a little talk I want, that's all, and then you can go. It shouldn't take a moment, and hopefully, you won't have to catch a later tram.' She seated herself at the work-bench, patting the nearby chair. 'Sit here with me a while,' she suggested. 'There's something I have to say.'

Ruby's face flushed with fear. 'Oh, Mrs Reece! It isn't something I've done, is it? I ain't angered you, have I?' As she sat on the chair, her troubled eyes never left the other woman's face.

'Angered me?' Widow Reece was amazed that Ruby should even think such a thing. 'On the contrary, I am delighted with you. In the short while you've been here, I've received nothing but praise and admiration for the wonderful way in which you handle the customers. You've made a very big impact on my sales, and the repairs are done in record time.' She paused, staring at Ruby with wonder. 'If it wasn't for you, Ruby, I might have been obliged to close this shop and resign myself to a lonely old age.'

'Oh, but you could have got someone to help you. There are any number of nimble-fingered folk looking for work.' Ruby was greatly relieved that she wasn't about to be sent on her way yet again. She was still smarting from Cicely's treatment of her.

'No, Ruby. It was you or no one. Like you say, there *are* any number of nimble-fingered folk out there, but as I've already explained, it's the *heart* that creates a thing of beauty. Not the head, nor the fingers. *You* have the heart, Ruby. The minute you walked into this shop, I sensed it.'

'I'm glad.'

'I want to take you into my confidence. That's why I asked you to stay behind for this talk.'

She was intrigued, 'What do you mean, Mrs Reece?'

'You know my hands are getting worse?'

Reluctant to acknowledge such a cruel thing, she remained silent.

'I know you saw me drop the box of cuttings the other day, and you must realise how much expensive material I've wasted by stubbornly trying to cut out the hat-shapes. You've seen these things, and you have never interfered. Instead, like the caring soul you are, you have discreetly gone behind me and put things to right. I'm grateful for that, Ruby.' When she saw the girl was about to protest, she put up her hand. 'Hear me out,' she insisted. 'The thing is . . . I've seen the doctor. There is nothing whatsoever he or anyone else can do. The disease in my bones will worsen until there will come a time, not too far off, when I won't even be able to lift a cup, let alone make a hat.'

Ruby was horrified. Seeing this kind woman facing such an unkind fate made her heart go out to her. 'I'm so sorry,' she murmured. The words seemed pitifully inadequate. 'I'll do whatever you ask of me,' she offered. 'Say the word, and it's done.'

The other woman smiled sadly. 'Bless you,' she murmured. 'I know you'll work harder if I ask you, and that *is* just what I'm asking you. So far I've been able to manage, but when the pain gets stronger and my fingers begin to wither, can I count on you, Ruby? Alternatively, I could take on another assistant, and between the two of us we could probably train her to a good standard. What do you say, Ruby? Either way, I'll be putting a deal of responsibility on your shoulders. I wish I could say it won't be for some long time yet, but the doctor tells me the disease is taking a terrible hold.'

Her eyes were suspiciously bright as she gazed on Ruby's concerned face, 'I don't want to close this shop.' Her voice was small and quivering. 'It's been my life for too long, do you see?' Suddenly she recalled the accountant's advice. 'Of course, I could sell a share of the business . . . take on a partner. But then things would never be the same, would they?'

The idea of a stranger coming in to give her orders was shocking to Ruby. Besides, she had a feeling that Widow Reece would be made even more unhappy by such a move. She was adamant. 'You and I can keep this business going, Mrs Reece. There won't be need of a partner, or another assistant, because then all your profits will be gone. I'll work harder and stay longer, and there are plenty of things you can do, even if your fingers are not so nimble any more. You're so skilled at choosing material and knowing what the customers want. Nobody designs like you, and every pattern in this shop is one you've created . . . you told me that yourself. If your fingers refuse to work, you've still got a quick and clever brain. You know how to buy, and you know how to sell. You only have to cast your eyes over a hat to know whether it's right or wrong. That's a gift, Mrs Reece, and you can't just waste it. You mustn't!

'If I stayed in the back room, and did all the cutting and making, it would work. It really would. Oh, and whatever would you do if you sold your shop? You'd be that unhappy.'

She stopped, ashamed at letting her thoughts burst out like that. 'I'm sorry. It isn't my place to say these things,' she said sheepishly. 'My mam always said I never knew when to keep my mouth closed.'

'Please don't apologise, Ruby. You've said what I hoped you would say, and I thank you for it. Of course, I'll raise your wages, that goes without saying. I had intended to do that anyway.' She raised her eyes to the ceiling, deep in thought, as though reading something written there. After a while, when the silence was thick and expectant, she lowered her gaze and stared at Ruby, saying softly, 'My accountant thinks I should sell up and see a little of the world before I become altogether immobile.' She took a long deep breath. 'He's a good man, and he's the best at his profession, but he knows nothing of human nature.'

'I think you should do what your heart tells you to.' Ruby was astonished that she should say such a thing, when all the while she ignored the urging of her own heart, which told her she should go to Johnny and accept the love that had grown between them.

'You're a strange young woman, so much older than your years.' Widow Reece looked at Ruby as though seeing her in a new light. 'I feel better for confiding in you.'

'And I'm glad you did.' Ruby rose from her chair and began to fasten the buttons on her coat. 'But, if I'm to catch that tram, I really ought to be going.'

'Of course.' Mrs Reece saw Ruby to the door, afterwards throwing the bolts home and returning to the back room, where she sat on the stool and gazed around. The room was meticulously neat, with every type and shade of material lovingly stacked on the many shelves. Hats in their different stages were arrayed on stands, and Ruby's large work-box was placed to one side of the table where she spent many hours bent to her joyous task. There was a great sense of love and devotion in that little room.

She bowed her head and stared at her hands. The fingers were already misshapen, with the joints butting upwards at a peculiar angle. 'Old age is a cruel thing, Ruby,' she whispered. 'And perhaps I'm asking the impossible. Who knows? At the end of the day I might be made to sell after all. But for the time being, Ruby Miller, you've given me hope. God bless you for that.'

Her arms fell heavily to her sides. Taking one last look around before closing the door, she then went on slow footsteps upstairs to her own comfortable quarters.

'RUBY!' Dolly's voice sailed up the street, bringing a smile to the approaching Ruby. 'Look at me . . . look at me, Ruby!'

The girl was seated on a makeshift swing that wound her

round and round the lamp post, before spinning her back the other way. She was laughing and screaming with delight as she counted the number of swings before the rope had wound itself, and her, tight to the post. As Ruby came nearer, she kicked out with her feet and sent herself whizzing high and wide. 'I can do ten swings,' she bragged. 'And our Frank can only do eight.' Whereupon Frank ran indoors in a sulk, Ralph followed, and by the time Ruby reached the front door, they were rolling about the passage floor, punching and yelling at each other.

'Hey!' She grabbed them by the scruff of the neck. 'If you want to fight, do it on the cobbles and not in here, thank you.'

Frank was the first to wriggle free. Ralph waited until he was well out of reach before he put out his tongue at Ruby. 'You little devils,' she called as they tumbled out the front door. 'I've a good mind to tan your backsides.'

Lizzie had heard it all. 'They've been a right pair o' sods, I can tell yer,' she grumbled. 'Yer dad's gone out, and Lenny's took his hook. It's time that lot were abed.' She nodded towards the doorway. 'There'll be hell to pay if they're still up when yer dad gets back.' She was seated in the fireside chair but seemed restless, picking at the sewing on her lap and occasionally glancing up at the mantelpiece. The letter wasn't easily visible now, because Lenny had been too interested in it so Lizzie had pushed it out of sight. 'I'll get yer tea, lass,' she said, beginning to clamber from the chair.

'No. You stay where you are,' Ruby told her. 'It sounds to me like you've had a bad day.'

Lizzie chuckled. 'Aye, well, I'll not deny it,' she confessed. While Ruby was hanging her coat on the nail behind the door, Lizzie regarded her with deep curiosity. 'When the childer are abed, you and me can have a little chat, eh?' She needed to be alone with Ruby when the matter of that letter came up.

'If you like.' She went into the scullery and came out with

the food her mam had kept warm. 'Do you want to chat about anything special?' she asked, seating herself at the table and beginning her meal. Her strong blue eyes searched Lizzie's face. 'This dumpling is good, Mam.' Lizzie never failed to put a wholesome meal on the table, and Ruby was always filled with admiration.

'Aye, well, you get that down yer. Afterwards yer can help me get the young 'uns to bed. Then we can sit and chinwag,' Lizzie declared, settling back into her chair. The bairn was fast asleep, and for the moment she had little to do. Soon, though, this little house would echo to the shouts and tears of the childer when she marched them off to the scullery for their bedtime wash. Outside she might seem a pillar of strength, but there were times when Lizzie felt bone tired from the day to day struggles.

It was gone nine o'clock before the last of the children was sent upstairs. Lenny had been late coming in, and arrived only minutes after his dad. There was a short interrogation and Ted told him he was to come home at the time his mam set. 'You're not old enough to stay out 'til all hours,' he reminded him. And all the way up the stairs, Lenny grumbled under his breath.

At last though, the little parlour was quiet, with Lizzie on one side of the fireplace and Ted on the other. The washing up was done, the crockery put away, and now Ruby could be heard busying herself in the scullery. After a while she came into the parlour, drying her hair with the big towel which was kept for the grown-ups, 'By! That water's stone cold,' she complained with a shiver.

'Yer should have put the kettle on then.' Lizzie was impatient to hear about the letter, but she was also afraid. All the same, it wasn't her letter and she had no right keeping it from the lass. 'When you're ready, there's summat for yer,' she said. Ted opened his eyes then closed them again. He had the feeling that something was brewing, and thought it best to stay out of it.

Ruby was curious. 'What is it?'

'When yer ready, I said.'

'You're being very secretive, Mam.' Ruby hurried back into the scullery, ran a comb through her damp hair and returned to the parlour where she sat on the stand-chair within arm's reach of Lizzie. 'Well? Are you going to tell me?'

Lizzie didn't smile. Instead, she got out of the chair and reached up to the mantelpiece. Taking the letter from behind the clock, she handed it to Ruby. 'This was fetched by a fancy carriage belonging to Jeffrey Banks.' Anticipating what Ruby was about to say, she revealed, 'The carriage is hired to run Cicely about afore her wedding. I expect there's shopping and the like, fittings and things to see to.' She made a guttural noise. 'It's all right fer some,' she scoffed. 'I don't get no fancy carriage when *I* have ter run about. By! There's times when I feel like an old donkey with only three legs.'

She was momentarily silenced, her heart in her mouth, when Ruby slit open the envelope. 'What is it, lass? Don't tell me they want yer back? Oh, yer mustn't go, lass. Yer doing so well at the milliner's!'

She was seated on the edge of her chair while Ted watched through one half-closed eye. Not for the first time, he wondered why Lizzie was so set against Ruby working at Jeffrey Banks's house. It wasn't as if the man had been a bad employer. In fact, as far as Ted could tell, up until this last business when Ruby was finished, both Jeffrey Banks and his daughter had been very good to her. What was more, Lizzie herself was employed there when he met her, and had stayed there for some time after they were wed. As far as he could recall, she had seemed happy enough. It was a mystery, and that was a fact.

Ruby's wide eyes scanned the page, going over it for the second time to make sure she'd read it right. Just as her mam had said, the letter was from Jeffrey Banks so that was no surprise.

But the *contents* were astonishing. There were *two* documents: the letter and an official-looking piece of paper.

'What does it say, lass?' Lizzie urged. 'Are the buggers asking yer to go back?'

Dropping the letter to her lap, Ruby shook her head, her fingers still clasped round the two pages. 'No.' The relief on Lizzie's face was immediately obvious. 'But he's sent me some money.'

'Oh, it's yer wages?' Lizzie visibly relaxed. The letter contained nothing more sinister than the lass's wages, and here she'd been working herself up to a pitch for nothing at all. 'There yer are then, lass, you've got yer week in hand, and now yer earning from Widow Reece, so yer can put a bit away toward yer nest egg . . . fer when yer gets wed, eh?' she added hopefully. More than anything else in the world, she wanted to see Ruby walk down the aisle with some eligible young man, preferably Johnny Ackroyd.

It suddenly occurred to her that something was wrong, however. Ruby was very still and seemed shocked, making Lizzie ask angrily, 'The buggers ain't short-changed yer, have they?'

At this Ted sat up and looked from one to the other. If Ruby had been short-changed, he would have something to say and that was a fact. Certainly her face was drained of colour, as though she'd suffered a shock. 'Is that what they've done, lass?' he asked in a kindly voice. A situation like this called for restraint, while Lizzie tended to over-react.

'See for yourself.' Leaning forward, Ruby gave the two documents to her dad. The letter was on top, and he proceeded to read aloud:

Dear Ruby,
   Both my daughter and I have valued your time here with us, and I particularly regret the circumstances under which you left this employ.

Sadly, I have been unable to persuade Cicely to change her mind about letting you go. Nevertheless, I would like to thank you for your loyalty and dedication.

To this end, I have enclosed a money draft, which constitutes a fair settlement. Take it along to Messrs. Armstrong and Leyton, at 14 Ainsworth Street. They are already informed and will honour it on receipt.

Meanwhile, I do know how difficult it is to secure employment at the present time. These wages in lieu will tide you over until something comes along. It is the least I can do.

Should you need references, please do not hesitate to contact me at once.

Yours sincerely

Jeffrey Banks, Esq.

Ted raised his eyes. They were round and vivid in his chalk grey face. 'Good God above, lass!' he exclaimed in a strange voice. 'It's a small fortune.'

Lizzie could contain herself no longer. 'Let me see that.' Taking the letter from him, she proceeded to read it with great difficulty. Presently she cast her eyes over the enclosed draft and what she saw there made her gasp aloud. 'Fifty guineas!' In an instant she was on her feet, her brown eyes blazing as she instructed Ruby, 'Yer not to take it!'

Ted interrupted. 'Don't talk daft, woman. Of course she'll take it. The lass has earned every penny. Why shouldn't she have that money, eh?'

Lizzie turned on him then. 'Because it's *gentry* money, that's why. And I don't want no charity from gentry coming into this house.'

Ted was also on his feet now, and staring at her in a curious fashion. 'What's wrong with you, lass, eh?' he wanted to know.

'Why have you got such a bee in your bonnet with regard to the gentry? And in particular Jeffrey Banks? Has he ever done you any harm?' When Lizzie hesitated he insisted impatiently, 'Well, has he?'

In her mind's eye, Lizzie could see herself and Jeffrey in that fancy bed, both of them stark naked, he on top of her and she with her arms clasping him close. Looking at her husband's face now, she trembled inside. 'No, he's never done me any harm,' she answered in a subdued voice, praying that he didn't already suspect.

'Well then. If you don't want the lass to change this draft, you'll need to give me a good enough reason. So if you've got one, you'd best get it off your chest right now.' He stood his ground, his eyes boring into her face.

Lizzie was growing more and more uncomfortable. He had her cornered and there was something in his manner that troubled her. 'I suppose if you say it's all right, then who am I to argue?' she reluctantly conceded. 'It's just that – well, it does seem such a great sum of money.'

Ted appeared satisfied. 'Stuff and nonsense! It happens all the time amongst the gentry. It's what they call a parting gift.'

'Aye, but *we're* not gentry,' Lizzie solemnly reminded him.

Ted merely nodded, giving both the letter and the draft back to Ruby. 'What will you do with it, lass?' he asked.

'I'll share it with you and Mam, of course,' she said without hesitation.

He shook his head. 'No, lass. It's your money and you've earned it. Me and your mam are managing fine. I dare say there'll come a day when you're ready to take a husband and you'll be glad of that money then. Put it away safe and sound.' He gave a loud noisy sigh that seemed to lift him off his feet. 'By! I ain't never seen that much money all at one time, and that's for sure.' He chuckled. 'Happen I should get myself a job as lady's maid, eh?'

He then settled back into his chair and fell asleep, every now and then shaking his head as though dreaming of the impossible.

'I'll send it back if you like, Mam.' Ruby hated it when her parents had harsh words.

Lizzie shook her head. 'Yer dad says yer to have it, so have it yer must.' She took a long hard look at her daughter. More and more she could see Jeffrey Banks in her. 'What *will* yer do with it, lass?'

While her mam and dad had been arguing, Ruby had been thinking ahead. She had already decided to follow their advice and put it away for a nest egg – but it wouldn't be for a wedding. Oh, no! That money, and every penny she saved herself, was towards her dream. She already had forty shilling put by, which seemed meagre when set against fifty guineas. She had seen her dream taking years and years, but now it was so much closer she could almost taste it. Uppermost in her mind was a thought that excited her so much she could hardly keep still. Suddenly she saw how to make that money work, and it had to do with the milliner's shop. But she would have to talk with Widow Reece before taking too much for granted. And she would do that first thing in the morning, straight after she had drawn on that money draft. First though, she had to be sure that her mam and dad were all right. 'Mam, do you mind what I do with this money?' she wanted to know. 'Was Dad right when he said you were managing fine?'

'If yer dad said that, then it must be right.' Lizzie could almost see Ruby's mind ticking over. 'All the same, I hope yer don't do nothing foolish with that there money.'

Overwhelmed with everything that had happened, and deeply moved by the anxious look on Lizzie's face, Ruby went to her mam and flung her arms round her. 'Oh, Mam, you mustn't worry about me. I'm not about to do anything silly.'

'I hope not, lass. All this talk of being rich and wanting the moon – well, it does upset me, I'll not deny it.' She clung to Ruby as though she had never held her before. 'I love yer, lass, and I don't want to lose yer.'

'Aw, Mam. How could you ever lose me?' Ruby looked into her mam's worried brown eyes and hugged her. 'You mean the world to me,' she murmured. For a while they were content in each other's embrace; Lizzie sorely troubled by the thought of what that money could take from her and Ruby greatly excited by what it could bring.

Presently, Lizzie pushed her daughter away. She also had an idea. Like Ruby, she was planning an errand in the morning. But it was a very different errand from Ruby's. 'Go on then, lass,' she said, 'I know you're itching to tell yon Maureen about yer good news.'

'There isn't much you don't know about me, is there, Mam?' Ruby remarked with a warm smile, thinking it was just as well her mam couldn't read thoughts, or she'd explode if she knew what her daughter was planning to ask Widow Reece in the morning. 'I shan't be long,' she promised.

'Yer wrong, lass,' Lizzie murmured to herself as Ruby left. 'There's a great deal I don't know about yer, and worse still there's a deal yer don't know about yer mam, God forgive her.' And she sat in the chair, letting the tears fall down her face. The night grew dark outside, and she lit another candle.

Ted slept on, his gentle snores echoing round the tiny parlour. And while he slept, Lizzie made her plans. Tomorrow, she would ask Ma Collins to take care of the bairn while she herself took the tram out to Billenge. From there she would go to Jeffrey Banks's house where once and for all she would get to the bottom of why he had sent such a great amount of money to someone who was only a lady's maid. If her suspicions were unfounded then she would keep her peace of mind, but if he was a threat she had to know.

She felt unnerved, excited and angry all at the same time. And to her great surprise, she found herself trembling at the thought of seeing him again. She felt like a foolish young girl when, of a sudden, she began wondering what she should wear. Happen that new frock she'd just finished, in preparation for the likely event of Ruby and Johnny getting wed. 'Aye. Happen I'll wear my best frock,' she murmured into the gloom. After all, she ought to look her best because, when all was said and done, a woman had her pride.

'Is your mam in?' Ruby followed Johnny into the parlour. There was an oil lamp lit in the centre of the table, and a small fire burning in the grate. The room was bathed in a soft romantic glow. As Johnny turned to gaze on her, Ruby's heart nearly stopped. Those dark eyes seemed to reach right into her soul. 'It's just that I'd like a word with her before I go up to see Maureen,' she explained.

In the half light, with his shirt open to his chest and his sleeves rolled up over strong brown arms, Johnny was unnervingly handsome. His brooding gaze fell on her and made her shiver to the tips of her toes. Disturbed, she glanced around the room. 'Upstairs, is she?' she asked, her voice firm and clear, belying the tumult inside her.

Johnny shook his head. 'They're out,' he murmured. 'And we're alone.' His hand touched her shoulder, sending shivers down her spine. 'Will you stay?' When she slightly turned, he thought it might be to leave. 'Just to talk,' he promised.

As always when she was near him, Ruby wanted to run. At the same time she desperately wanted to stay. 'For a while,' she said. 'What time will they be back?' She thought it strange that Maureen should be out so late.

'They won't be back tonight. They're gone to Bolton for a couple of days, to stay with an old friend of my mother. Mrs

Williams is a kindly soul, retired from nursing now. Mam asked the doctor whether it would be all right for her to take Maureen away for a couple of days, and he thought it would do more good than harm. I mentioned it to Thomas, and he spoke to Mr Arnold who insisted that I should take them to Bolton in his own carriage.' He smiled with pleasure at the memory. 'They were that thrilled, anyone would have thought they'd been given the crown jewels.' Cupping his hand beneath her elbow, he said, 'Sit yourself down, Ruby, while I get us a drink. Then we can talk.' He walked her to the armchair, and when she was seated, left her for a while during which time she could hear him opening and shutting cupboards in the front parlour. In a surprisingly short time he was back, holding two glasses and a bottle of home-made wine.

'One of my mother's latent talents,' he laughed. 'She hasn't made wine since our Maureen's illness. If Dad had known this was hiding in there, it would have been long gone.' He took out the cork and sniffed it. 'Smells all right,' he told her, pouring a small measure of the dark liquid into each of the glasses. Seating himself in the chair opposite, he asked, 'What do you think to it?'

Raising the glass to her lips, Ruby took a tiny sip. Warmth spread through her like a gentle tide. 'It's very pleasant,' she confessed. *Everything* was pleasant. Being here all alone with Johnny, the coziness of this tiny parlour and the cheery glow from the fire sending lazy shadows round the walls, the way it warmed her through and flickered over his straight strong features, creating sunshine and shadows in that marvellous face. There was a certain danger here, but even that was strangely reassuring. As she reached out to place her glass on the table, she was acutely aware of his dark eyes following her every move.

'I planned to call round later and tell you that Maureen was away for a while,' he said softly. His smile turned her heart over. 'I'm so glad you came here tonight.'

Suddenly, Ruby was unsure. 'I wouldn't have if I'd known Maureen wasn't here.'

'Are you sure?'

'It isn't right . . . you and me being here alone.' All kinds of images invaded her mind and she found herself trembling. 'I'd better go.' She stood up.

He walked with her to the door. 'Must you, Ruby?' he asked. His voice was low and resonant, sapping her will. 'Won't you stay?' He was behind her now, his hands gripping her shoulders. She visibly shivered when he bent his head to her neck and kissed the exposed flesh there. 'I love you so,' he murmured. Slowly, he turned her round, passion alight in those dark eyes as they fixed on her upturned face. 'Stay with me,' he whispered.

In the firelight glow, Ruby was more radiant than he had ever seen her. She was an enigma to him; she had the look of a child, yet exuded the fire and passion of a woman. Her perfect lovely face was like a pale jewel set in that wonderful spill of rich brown hair. It tumbled about her face and curled at the nape of her neck, glinting in the dancing firelight. 'Don't go, my lovely,' he murmured.

For one heart-stopping moment, he feared she would run away. But then he saw her eyes soften, and was encouraged. Gathering her into his arms, he pulled her close, kissing her full on the mouth and groaning deep inside himself when he felt her tremble.

She wanted to push him away, but here in his embrace she was safe and warm. Yet not content. Never content. All the same, when she was with him she didn't need to be anyone other than who she was: Ruby Miller from Fisher Street . . . Lizzie's lass. It was so easy, so straightforward. Life could be wonderfully simple. With Johnny, there was no awful urgency to raise herself in the eyes of the world. This wonderful man loved her, and that should be enough.

But it wasn't! 'I'd better leave.' Her small empty voice said one thing, her heart said another. His arms became loose about her. For one agonising moment their eyes met, his burning dark, hers looking up, beseeching him to understand. Suddenly she was caught to his chest, his arms like steel bands round her. Never in her life had she felt such fierce and all-consuming emotions. There was a need in her, a desperate longing that shook her to the roots.

Gently, he swept her up in his arms and carried her away. She didn't resist. Her passion was as fierce as his own. When he laid her on the rug before the fire and knelt between her legs, she slid her hands beneath the neck of his shirt, her fingers stroking the short thick hairs that covered his chest. The glow from the fire bathed and caressed them. She felt somehow distanced from it all. His hands ran over her, so tender, yet so fierce. When he stood before her, naked and magnificent, she was both ashamed and exhilarated. There was an animal beauty about him, a magnetism that made her gasp aloud.

It seemed like a lifetime but it was only a heartbeat before she too had stripped away the last garment. In their nakedness they blended one into the other. His mouth was warm and soft against hers, his whole body covering her, swallowing her into himself. The fresh warm smell of him permeated her senses. His skin pulsed firm and smooth against her mouth, and his hair teased her face. As she writhed beneath him, he moved his strong hands to the curve of her back, pulling her up towards him. In that glorious moment when he entered her, she uttered his name. The way she looked at him told him everything he needed to know.

He stilled the murmur with the most gentle of kisses. Willingly she arched into him, her blood fired by a shocking want. His deep and rhythmic movements inside her were immensely satisfying. She pushed with him, his mouth was on her neck, on her face. Half-open lips, moist and probing, found her every nerve ending.

The gentle movement grew frantic. His trembling tongue played on her nipple, making it stiffen in his mouth. Again and again he penetrated deep inside her. The ecstasy was unbearable. Thrills rippled through her body, causing her to cry out softly. He held her tight, tighter still, his arms closing round her slim form, binding their two bodies together. The heat from the fire was excruciating. The sweat gathered in tiny droplets on his nakedness, dripping on to her and settling in the pores of her own skin. She could feel his heart beating madly, at one with her own.

In his climactic fever she felt him lock into her. Her senses rose and fell in a glorious ebbing tide. Suddenly, it was over and he was holding her, rocking her like a mother might rock a child. Spent and fulfilled, she ached with love for him.

Silence settled over them. She was aware of his kisses, astonished that the love had not died with the passion. Her heart was overwhelmed with joy, and wonder, and pain. Softly, she disentangled herself and began to dress.

'Marry me, Ruby,' he murmured. When she turned away, he put on his clothes and came to her. 'Surely to God you can't deny our love now?' He was uncertain again. She always managed to do that to him. Even though he had held her as close as any man could hold a woman, she still eluded him; that precious essence that was Ruby stayed hidden from him. And he didn't know how to cope with that.

'I have to go,' she said. She could not bring herself to look on him then.

'Didn't it mean anything to you?' There was disbelief in his voice, but not arrogance. He loved her too much for that.

She looked at him then, a sad look that sent his heart to his boots. For a long dreadful moment she lowered her gaze to the floor, searching for the right words and hating herself because she knew she must hurt him. 'I'm sorry, Johnny,' she whispered.

The firelight lit the agony in her eyes. 'What happened just now – it can't ever happen again.'

'What are you saying, Ruby? That you don't love me. Is that it?'

She answered truthfully, 'No, I'm not saying that.'

'Then what *are* you saying, for God's sake?'

'I'm not for you, Johnny. I never will be.' The things she had to say would hurt her as much as they would hurt him, but she had to say them. 'All my life I've wanted something better than Fisher Street, better than a husband who works from dawn to dusk and half a dozen children who will never know what it's like to live in comfort, or have enough on the table to eat . . . going to school in hand-me-downs, and being laughed at by the better off.'

'But it doesn't have to be like that, sweetheart!'

'Yes, it does!' The tears spilled over her thick dark lashes, running down her face like silver threads in the half-light. 'I've been there. I know what it's like, and I've hated every minute. I've seen my mam and dad wrung with despair because of poverty. I've hidden behind the sofa with our mam, when the rentman's been at the door, both of us crouched out of sight, on our knees, because she hadn't got the money to pay him. When our dad was out of work we all went hungry, and even now, young Lottie still hasn't got a decent cot. So don't you tell me it doesn't have to be like that, because I know it does. And I won't live like it. *I won't!*' The tears flowed and she was sobbing loudly now. Distraught, he made a move towards her.

'NO!' She ran to the door and flung it open. 'Stay away, Johnny. PLEASE STAY AWAY. From now on, you and I must never be alone again.'

With her heart and soul poured out to him, she fled along the passage and out into the night. After the sultry warmth of that little parlour and the feel of Johnny's arms about her the air struck cold and shocking on her face.

He had started after her, but then thought better of it. She had made her feelings plain. She loved him, but she didn't want him. It was difficult to comprehend. But then Ruby was different from anyone he had ever known. Tonight, when at last he had caught a glimpse of her love for him, she had cruelly snatched it away. There was something awful haunting Ruby. Something she had to work out of her system, all by herself. There wasn't a family down Fisher Street that hadn't suffered deprivation and poverty to varying degrees, and yet they were not deeply affected by it the way Ruby was. He loved her but couldn't understand what drove her. He had asked her to marry him. She had rejected him. He was wise enough to know that she would only hate him if he pursued her. Time would tell, and he must be patient. And so, with a heavy heart, he watched her walk out of his life. And he knew he would love her always.

It was two o'clock in the morning when Ruby woke from the nightmare. Sweat ran down her temples and on to the pillow where she lay. In her dreams she was running towards Johnny, calling his name, wanting him, her two arms outstretched. The nearer she got, the further away he was. Something pulled her back, tugging at her, tearing her apart. Like a wishbone she was caught between two forces. Even when she woke, when the candle was lit and the window flung open to let in the cool night air, the nightmare still clung to her.

Leaning on the wall by the window, absent-mindedly gazing out, Ruby so wanted to relive the night's events, to feel again the strength of his arms about her. But she dared not. She thought of Johnny and her heart was sore. They were so right together. And they were so wrong. A searing confusion took hold of her. She was glad that she had put a distance between them. She was sorry too. Want him. Hate him. Love and fear. Powerful emotions that tormented her, throwing her this way then that until she longed to be free. Yet, always, there was another world out there, a world that she had only glimpsed and which was calling her.

Nervous and hesitant, Lizzie stood outside Billenge House. She had taken great care with her appearance, and now she looked bright and pretty, much younger somehow. Her greying brown hair was loosely curled about her round face, and her eyes sparkled as they hadn't for many years. Her new frock had given her confidence, and the long-line jacket that had hung in the cupboard since before Lottie's birth gave her a slimmer, taller look. From the back of the stairhole she had found her best pair of black patent shoes, the ones with the small slim heels and dainty ankle-straps. After searching the big box in the loft, she recovered her prettiest hat; she was wearing it now, a navy straw boater, with a wide brim and an upturned feather at the side. At first, when she'd seen herself in the old wardrobe mirror, she was both delighted and horrified. It struck her that if Ted was to walk in at that minute, he'd think there was a stranger in the house. That was the trouble with a long marriage and a lot of childer, she thought. After a while, the two of you grew heart-lazy, taking the other for granted. She had been thoroughly ashamed and struck with a terrible fear when she found herself wondering whether Ruby was right after all, to want more out of life.

The memory of her own past overwhelmed her now. 'Shame on yer, Lizzie Miller!' she scolded, reminding herself that she and Ted had been together for too many years for her to begin doubting things. 'You've got yourself a man to be proud of. He's loved yer through thick and thin, and you've loved him back – washing his socks, fattening him up with the meat dumplings he provided, and proudly bearing his offspring. What more could any woman want?'

She set her shoulders and put a grim expression on her face, her eyes raking the front of the big house. 'It ain't no good standing our here, yer foolish woman,' she muttered. 'You've come to have yer say, and the sooner it's said the better.' She took a step forward, then dodged behind the hedge when there was the sound of the back door being slammed shut. She knew that sound well for hadn't she herself worked in this house and slammed that same kitchen door many times? She emerged once again and made her way towards the front door. She had never before entered this house by the front door. 'God Almighty, what am I doing here?' she asked out loud. 'If he sees me, he'll likely set the constable on me heels!' It suddenly occurred to her that Jeffrey Banks would be highly embarrassed and possibly extremely angry at her for showing up here. After all, a man of his importance would not take kindly to being reminded of his indiscretions.

Her nerve began to give out again. This morning, when she had set out from her own humble abode, there had been a fierce determination in her. She had to find out whether her long ago lover had discovered her fiercely kept secret. She needed to know if he had guessed that Ruby was his. And more than anything else, if he *had* found out, she must know what his intentions were. One thing Lizzie was certain of. If he meant to claim that lovely lass, it would be over her dead body! The thought of Ruby spurred her on. 'Do what you've come to do, yer coward,' she told herself, and with that in mind, went smartly down the path.

'Yes?' The newly appointed housekeeper was a woman of immense proportions with a face like rolling thunder. She eyed Lizzie from a lofty height, wondering what a woman of such common appearance could want at this door.

'Is the master at home?' Lizzie held herself with pride. Now she'd made up her mind, she wasn't going to be put off by no stuck-up creature that weren't no better than she herself.

'Have you an appointment?'

Lizzie shook her head. Speaking in a firm polite voice, she

answered. 'No. I ain't got no appointment. Would you kindly tell him it's Lizzie . . . Ruby's mam.' When the woman seemed about to close the door, she added stubbornly, 'Yer can also tell him that I ain't leaving until I've spoken with him.'

'Wait there.' The door was closed and Lizzie was left outside, to ponder on how Jeffrey Banks might greet her after all this time. She wished she was prettier, smaller of body and less stretched by the bearing of all them childer. Riddled with doubts and conscious of her many failings, she peeped in the small window nearby, preening her hair and setting the navy boater at an angle that would shadow the ageing bags under her eyes. 'Do what yer like, Lizzie gal,' she chuckled, 'but yer still a faded old bloom, and there ain't no changing it now.' Her sense of humour rose to lighten her spirits, 'Silly old cow!' she told the image in the window. All the same, she brushed her coat and nervously glanced down to make sure her shoes were shining.

She was visibly startled when the door was flung open and the housekeeper appeared. 'Mr Banks will see you,' the woman announced. Her face told another story. It told Lizzie that she could not understand why the master would entertain such a lowly creature.

Lizzie swept past her with a broad smile. 'Sorry to disappoint yer,' she said. The two of them went at a brisk pace across the hall and on towards the drawing room. Lizzie was surprised to be shown into this room, because she truly believed he would prefer to see her in the more formal surroundings of his study.

As the door was opened, Lizzie craned to see inside the room. He was there, standing against the fireplace, looking towards the door. His eyes met Lizzie's and he visibly stiffened. His voice was authoritative as the other woman ushered Lizzie in. 'Thank you, Mrs Addison. Will you please arrange for tea and refreshments?' he asked. She acknowledged him with a small curtsey, afterwards reluctantly closing the door on them. It would have been nice to know what these two had in common, she thought.

The moment the door was closed and they were alone, Jeffrey's attitude changed. His features melted into a smile as he rushed forward with his arms outstretched. 'Lizzie. Oh, it's so good to see you.' His whole face was lit with delight.

She was astonished. She was standing with her back to the door, unsure and afraid. 'Yer don't mind me coming here then?' she asked with relief.

His hands reached for hers, grasping them warmly. 'Mind!' He shook his head in disbelief. 'I've wanted to talk with you, and I haven't known how,' he confessed. Before she could respond, he propelled her to the armchair by the fireplace. 'Come,' he ordered. 'Sit down and let me look at you.' When she was seated, he sat opposite and appraised her stalwart little figure, the long slimming lines of the dark jacket and the attractive angle of her navy boater. His gaze fell to her feet and the shiny patent shoes, then back to her pretty bright eyes. 'You haven't changed,' he said with too much affection. 'You're still the Lizzie I knew.'

She blushed deeply. 'Away with yer!' she remarked. 'I'm far from being the silly lass who once worked in this house.' Like a bolt from the blue, the picture sprang into her mind – the two of them naked, in his bed. Oh dear God!

A knock on the door caused him to leap to his feet. 'Yes!' he called. Whereupon the door opened and in came the wretched girl with a tray laden with a tea service and a plate of dainty sandwiches. 'Where shall I put them, sir?' she asked sheepishly. Gormless and dithering, she remained by the door until he told her, 'On the side table, I think.' Nodding feverishly, she scurried across the room and did as he ordered. That done she backed out of the room in the curious manner he had come to accept. 'Thank you,' he remarked, and as she disappeared out of the door, she gave a little squeal that made Lizzie think the foolish girl had stepped on the cat.

'I don't want no tea.' Lizzie eyed the silver teapot and china cups. They looked the same as when she used to fetch them for the master. Suddenly it seemed like yesterday. 'I didn't want to come here, yer know.' She thought she had best explain that she wasn't about to make a habit of paying him calls. 'I came this once because I had to.'

'Oh?' He resumed his seat and regarded her with a serious expression. 'Is anything wrong, Lizzie? Is it Ruby?'

'Ruby? Why do yer say that?' Her suspicions rose to the fore.

'Oh, it's just that – well, Cicely dismisses Ruby, and now here *you* are.' He couldn't take his eyes off her. All he could see was the lovely young girl who had enchanted him. 'It hasn't caused you any hardship, has it?' he wanted to know. 'In view of the way Cicely treated her, I did send Ruby a generous settlement.'

'I know, and that's why I'm here.' Lizzie's voice hardened. 'I can understand why yer wanted to put a little more in the lass's pay packet. But what I *can't* understand is why yer should pay her a small fortune.' She thought she saw a flicker of guilt wash across his face, and her fears were heightened. 'I wanted her to give it back, but her dad said no.' She deliberately emphasised the word 'dad'. It seemed to affect him.

It was a moment before he spoke, and when he did it was only to confirm Lizzie's worst fears. 'Why didn't you tell me, Lizzie?' His voice was almost a whisper, and his eyes were suspiciously bright. The whole story was written there.

At once she was on her feet. 'What d'yer mean?' she demanded in a trembling voice. 'Tell yer what?' She was clutching her bag so tightly that her knuckles were stark white.

He reached out to still those trembling hands. 'Don't be afraid,' he urged, 'I won't shame you.' He eased her back into the chair. 'You don't fool me, Lizzie. I *know* why you came here today.' There was such affection in his face that she had to look away. She had come to this house praying that her suspicions were wrong, but now she was desperately afraid. His next words drove that fear home, 'Ruby's my daughter, isn't she?'

A small breathless gasp burst from her, and she couldn't answer. She glanced up at him with tearful eyes. Biting her lip, she shrank back into the chair and her quivering fingers played with the clasp on her bag. But she didn't answer. She dared not.

'It's all right, Lizzie,' he murmured. 'I won't lay claim to her.'

She spoke then, gratitude glowing in her brown eyes. 'You won't?'

He shook his head slowly from side to side. 'No, I won't do that,' he promised. 'Oh, it's not that I wouldn't be proud to recognise her as mine. Ruby is a lovely girl, with an admirable character. She's the daughter every man dreams of. But no, I would never do anything that would hurt you or your family.' He asked her again, 'Why didn't you tell me, Lizzie?'

She searched deep inside herself, casting her mind back over the years. At first, when she found that she was with child by this man, she had been tempted to tell him, if only to clear her own conscience. But she was wed, she was a maid, and the father of her child was gentry. That was a recipe for disaster. 'I kept quiet then for the same reasons I'm begging you to keep quiet now. Besides, if I'd said anything, how was I to know yer wouldn't take the child from me the minute I brought her into the world?'

'If you think that, then you didn't know me.'

'I don't know you now.'

He smiled, 'I think you do, Lizzie. You and me, we had something very special. I haven't forgotten.'

'Yer not to talk like that!' she said in a loud whisper, at the same time glancing furtively towards the door. 'It ain't right yer should talk like that. What we did was shameful and bad. Besides, it were a long time since, and best forgotten.' When he remained silent, she was unsure as to what to do. She felt

380

suddenly vulnerable. Should she leave or should she stay? She discreetly regarded him. He was still a handsome man, still the same kindly caring soul she had freely given herself to. These past days she'd wondered how she would feel when she came face to face with him, and she wasn't all that surprised to discover that she still held him in affection. 'How did you know?' she asked.

The corners of his mouth curled up in the way she remembered. 'Oh, Lizzie, how could I not see myself in her?' Leaning back in the chair he let his gaze fall to the carpet. 'At first I never even suspected. I liked her because she was good, and she reminded me of you. But then Cicely persuaded me to let her come to a party . . . she passed her off as a close friend.' He saw the astonishment on Lizzie's face, and was mortified. 'You didn't know?'

'No. She never told me.' It hurt her to think that Ruby had deceived her. 'I never thought she'd keep something like that from her mam.'

'Oh.' Jeffrey cursed himself for revealing the truth of that night. 'And would you have let her go if she *had* told you?'

Lizzie's mouth was a thin hard line. She shook her head fervently. 'Never!' she snapped.

'Then it's easy to see why she didn't tell you. Young people are all the same, I think. They mean no harm, but there are times when they do the most foolish things. I mean, look how Cicely dismissed Ruby, and they such good friends. I know in my heart she will come to regret it. I expect Ruby regrets that night when she kept the truth from you. Don't be too harsh on her,' he asked. Then he demanded, 'And don't betray me, Lizzie. Don't let Ruby know I've told you.'

She saw how anxious he was, and realised that one good turn deserved another. 'Have I *your* word that you'll never reveal you're Ruby's father? Not to any living soul?' When he nodded, she went on, 'All right. Much as I'd like to, I'll not tackle the lass about her little deception.' She recalled his earlier words. 'And what was it that made you think Ruby was yourn?'

'On the night of the party several guests made the comment that she resembled me. Afterwards, when they'd all gone, I looked in the mirror and saw it for myself . . . the cut of her features more delicate of course but nevertheless there *was* a definite resemblance.'

Lizzie agreed. 'Particularly round the eyes,' she admitted, thinking how Ruby and Jeffrey had that same dark warmth in their smile.

'It got me thinking . . . about you and me.' He paused when Lizzie cast her gaze downwards. 'It all began to fit . . . how you ran from here and never came back. The news filtered through from downstairs, that you had given birth to a child some months later. Oh, Lizzie, I was so blind. It just never occurred to me. When I realised that Ruby was the right age, I felt as though I'd let you down badly.'

'There ain't nothing spoiled. Ted brought the lass up as his own. He never knew, and I pray to God he never will.'

'I promise he won't learn it from me.'

'Bless yer for that.' But Lizzie wanted more. 'I want yer to take the money back.'

'Why?' His astonishment betrayed itself in his face. 'Whyever would you want me to do such a thing?'

Lizzie told him of her fears that the money could open doors which she would rather stayed shut, and that his own blood in Ruby made the lass dangerously ambitious. 'She don't get it from me, and that's a fact.'

Reluctantly, he explained that he could not take away the gift he had sent Ruby. 'It wasn't conscience money, Lizzie. It was money that Ruby had earned and richly deserved. It belongs to her now, and I can't . . . *won't* ask for it back.'

As far as Lizzie was concerned, the meeting was at an end. She met his gaze with defiance. 'Then you're doing her an injustice,' she warned, 'Ruby is an ordinary lass, brought up in an ordinary way. Sadly for her, she sees a larger world beckoning, and it can only lead to pain. I thank you for the gift of my Ruby, and I thank you for keeping the secret between us. But I *can't* thank you for putting temptation in her way.' She gave a strange little curtsey which made him wince. To someone like Lizzie, old habits died hard. 'I'll be on my way now,' she said, going quickly to the door.

He followed her. 'Ruby is a level-headed girl. She'll use that money wisely, I know.'

'I pray to God you're right.' One tight little smile before Lizzie dismissed herself and made her way along the hall and out of the front door. At the bottom of the drive, she paused, took out her handkerchief and mopped the sweat from her brow. Even though she felt proud of the way she had controlled her nervousness, there was still something very disturbing about being face to face with the gentry. And if she lived to be a hundred she would never know how she came to be bedded by that man. She glanced back and a tiny smile lit up her pretty brown eyes. Jeffrey Banks was a good man though. For all that he had disappointed her on the issue that brought her here, he was a fine and caring gentleman with a warm heart. On second thoughts, remembering the way it had been between them, she *could* see how she had fallen into his arms. And, God forgive her, to this day she did not regret it. How could she, when Ruby was a living reminder who brightened her every minute?

Unhappy that he had refused to take the money back, yet content that she had sought him out and secured another promise, Lizzie went on her way. If she hurried, she would just make the twelve-thirty tram.

* * *

383

'It will work, I know it will!' The shop was shut, and Ruby had gone with Widow Reece into the back room. Earlier, she had dared to outline her plan. Widow Reece had been taken completely by surprise. She had asked for time to consider, and now it was the end of the day. The shop was closed and the two of them were in the back room. Ruby waited for the other woman's decision, one that could shape her life from now on.

She had her fingers crossed behind her back as she waited for the answer. Widow Reece paced the floor, from the window to the door and back again, turning Ruby's interesting proposal over and over in her mind. Presently, she paused. Then she turned to study Ruby. The thoughtful expression relaxed into a wide warm smile. 'All right, Ruby. I think it's a marvellous idea, and I say yes.'

Springing from the chair, Ruby flung her arms around the startled woman and danced her round the room. 'Oh, Mrs Reece, it'll be wonderful! You'll never regret it, I promise you,' she cried. When the idea first came to her, she never dreamed that Widow Reece would give it a second look. But now . . . Oh, now! This was her dream come true. And she couldn't wait to tell her mam.

It was quarter to seven when Ruby struggled through the front door with her arms full. The whole family gathered round, watching with excitement while she dipped into a large box-like object and drew out present after present. The twins got so carried away that they started fighting and Lizzie had to clip Frank's ear. Dolly jumped up and down and said it was like Christmas. Only it was better than any Christmas they had ever known.

Everyone got a parcel. There was a brown clay pipe for Dad, a new game of Snap for the twins, a bow and arrow for Lenny, and the most beautiful pair of red shoes for Dolly. Lizzie's face lit up when she saw her own present, a knitted shawl that reached down to her ankles. 'And this is for our Lottie,' Ruby announced, tearing away the wrapping from the box-like object. When the beautiful wooden cradle was revealed, Lizzie clapped her hands to her mouth and wept openly. 'Well, I never,' she kept saying over and over. 'Well, I never.' The tears ran down her face and plopped on to her blouse, and her old heart swelled with pride as she gazed at the polished cot with its big rockers and pretty covers inside.

A hush had settled over everyone as they saw the marvellous gift which Ruby had brought for the babby. 'Do you like it, Mam?' she asked softly.

'Oh, lass, what can I say?' Lizzie glanced at her husband, and pointing to the cradle, murmured, 'Look, Dad, ain't that the grandest thing yer ever saw?'

He gave no answer. His heart was too full. With great tenderness, he went to the sleeping child and raised her from the wooden box which had been her cot. 'You've a better place now,' he whispered into her ear. Ruby turned back the cream-flowered cover while he laid the bairn into its fold. She snuggled down and Dolly began gently rocking the cradle. Ted spoke to Ruby now, and what he said warmed her through and through. 'The Lord blessed your mam and me when he sent us you. There's only so much a man can do, lass, and I've been that worn down with putting the food into our mouths, and a roof over our heads that there's never been anything left over for fancy things. But, oh lass, you shouldn't have spent all your money on us.'

Ruby was on her knees, looking up at him. Now she stood up at his words and, looking from one to the other of her beloved family, said quietly, 'I haven't spent it all on you. I've bought myself a present as well.'

Dolly asked the question that was on everyone's mind. 'Where is it then?'

Ruby reached out and ruffled the girl's hair. 'It isn't that kind of present,' she explained. 'You can't see it. It isn't wrapped in paper, and you can't carry it home in a parcel.' She looked at her mam and she was a little afraid. 'This is the best day of my life, Mam,' she pleaded softly.

Lizzie's heart turned somersaults. 'What have yer done, lass?' She knew something had happened. She could sense the fear and the excitement in Ruby's countenance. 'You'd best tell me *now*. What's this present you've bought yerself that we can't see?' The whole family waited for Ruby's answer.

Taking a deep breath, she told them her news. 'Widow Reece has let me buy a small share in the milliner's shop.' There! Now the sparks would fly.

Everything happened at once. Ted let out a great whoop and grabbed her in his arms. 'By! You've done us proud, lass,' he exclaimed. 'Whoever would'a thought a Miller would rise to be a property owner?' Overwhelmed by the occasion, the twins started fighting again and Dolly rocked the cradle with such vigour that the bairn let out a loud shriek. Lenny shrugged and walked out. It was only a moment before Ted put on his coat and followed him. He made his way to the pub with quickening footsteps. By! He had summat to tell them tonight, and that was a fact.

Lizzie sat in her chair and stared at the carpet. 'This is the best day of my life,' Ruby had said. But, much as she wanted to, Lizzie couldn't see it that way. Deeply concerned at her mam's condemning silence, Ruby knelt before her. 'This is only the beginning, Mam,' she told her. 'Can't you see that?'

Without a word, Lizzie rose from the chair and went into the scullery where she looked out of the window to the yard below. She didn't see the high stone wall nor the grey flagstones glinting in the evening light. All she could see was Jeffrey Banks, and their daughter. It haunted her: the way Ted had been so proud just now; the way she felt herself curl up inside when he thanked the

Lord for giving Ruby to them. Lizzie could see all of these things. But Ruby, going to a party as gentry. Even now she couldn't believe that her daughter had kept that from her.

A strong persistent instinct told Lizzie that things would never be the same again. Suddenly, everything she had ever feared was staring her in the face.

Chapter Thirteen

It was Saturday 15 September in the year of Our Lord 1893. It was also Cicely Banks's wedding day. Thanks to Luke's insisting that the wedding should be delayed until the first phase of the foundry refitment was completed, Cicely's big day had been put back by many weeks. She had pleaded with him not to let the work at the foundry interfere with their plans, and was peeved when he resisted her pleas. She wasn't to know that the real reason was his great fear that his underhand and dangerous practices would be discovered. To his mind, once the platforms and gangways were completed, his crime would go undetected. And so, instead of being a June bride, Cicely was forced to be patient. The main work at the foundry was now complete, and the remainder could wait until Luke returned from honeymoon; he would have curtailed the length of that, but thought it wise to act the loving husband in front of Cicely's father.

Now, at long last, she would have her dearest wish. The local newspapers were filled with news of the event, and it was reported that the happy couple would spend their honeymoon travelling Europe and return sometime towards the middle of October.

Ruby could think of nothing else. There were times when she was sorely tempted to go to Cicely and persuade her that what she was doing would be the ruin of her. But then she remembered how Cicely had shown her the door for saying much less than that. It was plain that Cicely was hell bent on becoming Luke Arnold's wife. She had fallen under his spell, and nothing would make her change her mind. Ruby knew that any interference from her would only make Cicely dig her heels in even more.

Each day that week everyone who came into the milliner's commented on the imminent occasion, relaying with great relish and in graphic detail what they had learned about Cicely's gown and accessories. 'They say she'll be wearing satin shoes,' remarked Mrs Lacey. 'Oh, it's said her head-dress will be encrusted with tiny gems,' added the baker's wife. In her usual cynical fashion, the lady from the draper's next-door told Ruby, 'What a pity you were dismissed, dear. Just think, it might have been you preparing Miss Banks for her wedding day.' Widow Reece had been annoyed at the woman's insensitivity, but Ruby had made light of it. After all, the draper's assistant was only echoing what had been in her own mind for some time now.

'Why don't you go and watch?' Widow Reece's voice cut across Ruby's thoughts. She was standing at the door, craning her neck to hear the church bells ring out. In her mind's eye she could see Cicely, all done up like a dream, sedately walking down the aisle towards the man of her choice. Suddenly, in thinking of him, Ruby's joy was cruelly dashed. She prayed that she might be wrong and that Luke Arnold would make Cicely a good husband. Somehow, though, she couldn't bring herself to believe it.

'Oh, I can't do that,' Ruby protested. 'Lunchtime on Saturday is always busy, and besides it was me who persuaded you not to close each day for lunch. The least I can do is stay and do my share.'

'Nonsense!' Widow Reece bestowed a fond smile on her. 'You were right in persuading me to stay open at lunchtimes. My goodness! I never would have imagined people would flock in the way they do, although I should have thought of it myself. As you rightly pointed out, there are more women working these days, and the only time they can get to the shops on a weekday is at lunchtime. My dear, you've made us a great deal of money, what with one thing and another.'

She looked round the freshly painted shop, admiring the clean fresh lines and the open shelves filled with bright and colourful displays. 'You've given this old shop, and me, a new lease of life, Ruby Miller,' she confessed. 'I have to admit I was on the point of selling when you walked through that door over three months ago. You were a stranger, yet by the end of that first day when you came to work for me, it was as though I'd known you all my life.'

She took a moment to recall the occasion when Ruby had asked to buy a small share in the milliner's. At first she had been horrified. After all, she had known her for only a week. The idea seemed preposterous. But then, by the end of the day, three things had swayed her into going along with the proposal. First, there was her own diminishing good health. Second, Ruby had already proved herself to be a born businesswoman; she had a keen open mind and a natural instinct for serving customers. And then there was the question of the money which Ruby had offered in exchange for a small interest in the business; to someone from her background, that money must have seemed like a fortune, and yet she was willing to risk it all without hesitation. That alone was enough to tell her employer how highly Ruby regarded the business, and also that she had great faith in her own abilities. She was not afraid of the future, and that made the widow ask herself why *she* should be afraid. Right from the start, Ruby was bursting with ideas – ideas for improvement, for increasing sales, and with regard to the needs of the more modern woman. For a full hour she and the widow had talked, and the more Ruby outlined her ideas, the more the widow was impressed. She had never been a woman for taking risks, but where Ruby was concerned she'd followed her instincts. And it had paid off handsomely.

She looked at Ruby now, and saw not only a business colleague but a kind young friend. 'You know, Ruby,' she continued, 'the wisest thing I ever did was to take you on, and though I must admit I had reservations about selling you part of my precious business, I have never regretted it. You've raised our takings right through the week, you've streamlined the business with your direct approach, and you've made my disability seem lighter.' Her expression softened as she looked into Ruby's bright eyes. 'If anyone had told me that I would sell part of my little business, I would have said they were out of their minds.' She laughed. 'With my hands the way they are, I suppose I would have been mad not to say yes to you.'

'I'm glad you're not sorry,' Ruby told her, 'because I've never been so happy.'

'You miss being with Cicely though, don't you?'

'Sometimes,' she admitted.

'Then it's only right you should see her married.' The widow hurried away to the back room, returning with Ruby's coat. After handing it to her, she opened the door. 'Go on,' she urged. 'I know she was more than just an employer to you. Off you go, and you tell me all about it when you get back.'

'If you're sure?'

The other woman merely pushed her out of the door and closed it on her, smiling through the window pane as Ruby went at a run down the street.

By the time she reached the path that led up to the church, everyone was inside. The strains of organ music filtered through the air; a beautiful plaintive sound that touched her heart and made her want to weep. By rights Cicely's wedding day should be heralding a new beginning, a time of joy and hope for the future. Tiptoeing into the vestibule of God's own house, Ruby gave up a little prayer that Cicely would find the happiness she truly deserved. 'We all make mistakes, Lord,' she murmured. 'So don't punish her too harshly.'

Gently swinging open the great oak door, Ruby peeped inside. The church was packed. There were flowers everywhere and the intoxicating smell of blossom was all around. Cicely was at the altar, her face upturned to the tall handsome man by her side. He gazed down on her as though she was the most precious thing in the whole world. The music stopped and the ceremony began in earnest. Ruby watched for a while, but then, when one or two guests turned to glare at her, she softly closed the door and turned away.

Coming out into the bright sunlight of a September day, Ruby took up position by a big old oak tree that had stood the test of wind and weather for many long years. Leaning into its broad dark trunk, she waited.

A small crowd began to gather on the lawns. Chattering factory workers in their cotton turbans, plump smiling women with small children clinging to their skirts, a few inquisitive men, and a bevy of young giggling girls who dreamed of their own wedding day. None of them appeared to notice Ruby.

Suddenly there was an excited cry as music wafted through the air and the church doors were flung open. Almost immediately Cicely swept out, a vision of loveliness in a startling white gown; a straight-cut and stunning creation bedecked with pearls and trimmed with a scalloped hem sewn with the most exquisite tiny pink rosebuds. Her hair was swept up into a diamanté head-band, and dainty wispy curls had been arranged to tease her face. In the bright sunlight, her eyes seemed bluer than Ruby remembered.

To all who watched, Cicely was a young woman in love, so obviously captivated by the man at her side. And yet, as Ruby studied her face from the vantage point that hid her presence, she wondered at the faint shadowy circles beneath Cicely's blue eyes, and somehow her smile, though bright and wide, gave Ruby the impression it was painted on. You're looking too deep, Ruby Miller, she chided herself, before stepping forward with the intention of losing herself in the crowd.

In that moment, Cicely caught sight of her. Their eyes met. The smile slid from Cicely's face, and just for one fleeting second Ruby thought she detected a certain regret. But then she held her head high, a look of defiance on her features, a look that warned Ruby: Leave me alone. I know what I'm doing.

Ruby held Cicely's gaze long enough to mouth the words, 'Be happy.' Just a simple wish, but she meant it with all her heart.

Cicely gave the slightest nod, and then was lost in a shower of confetti and the crush of well-wishers. Ruby was delighted that Cicely had at least acknowledged her because, to her mind, it meant that her old friend had not forgotten the way things once were between them.

As Cicely climbed into the carriage, with Luke standing below, his hand dutifully cupped about his wife's elbow, Ruby came down the narrow path, discreetly keeping to the side. It was when he leaned out of the carriage to secure the door that he saw her. At once his eyes lit up. He didn't smile. Instead he stared for a moment, dark longing in his gaze. The merest nod of his head and a sly look of satisfaction. Then he was in the carriage and on his way, leaving Ruby in no doubt: Luke Arnold had not mended his ways. He never would.

It was more than a week after the wedding when Ted came home from work in a strange mood. He picked at his evening meal in silence, and afterwards went into the yard, where he paced up and down, furiously puffing on his pipe, his head bent deep in thought. 'What's to do with him, Mam?' Ruby asked. 'He hardly touched his dinner. Is he ill, do you think?'

The very same thought had been running through Lizzie's head. 'I don't know, lass,' she replied. 'Happen it's summat at work that bothers him. Yer know what yer dad's like. Keeps things to hisself most o' the time.'

Lizzie was more concerned than she wanted to admit. For some weeks now, Ted had been morose and secretive, and it was the first time in all the years she'd known him that he wouldn't confide in her. Because of it, she was unduly irritable herself, snapping at the childer and blaming all and sundry for her husband's strange moods.

'Will you talk to him?' Ruby pleaded. 'Find out what's wrong?'

Lizzie was indignant at that. She swung round. 'Leave that to me!' she snapped, 'I don't need you to tell me what to do where your father is concerned.' The minute the words were out of her mouth she could have bitten off her tongue. But she couldn't bring herself to apologise. She hadn't altogether forgiven Ruby for keeping secrets from her.

She was shocked at her mam's outburst. 'What's wrong with *you*?' she wanted to know.

'What d'yer mean?'

Ruby glanced out of the window to where her dad was still striding up and down, before returning her attention to Lizzie. 'Well, it seems to me that Dad isn't the only one to have things on his mind.'

'There's nothing on my mind,' Lizzie said.

Ruby wouldn't be put off. 'Oh, yes there is. You've been like a bear with a sore head these past few weeks. Is it because I used that money to buy into the milliner's?' She hated being at odds with her mam.

'It ain't none o' my business what yer choose to do with yer money. And besides, all that was talked through with yer father. If he says it's all right, then it's all right.' But it would never be all right with her, whatever Ted said.

'Well, *something*'s bothering you, Mam. Out with it. What have I done to upset you?'

This was Lizzie's opportunity to vent her true feelings. 'If yer must know, I don't take kindly to yer burying yerself indoors. Yer a bonny lass, and it ain't healthy to stay in night after night. Not when there's a fine young man down the street who's more than willing to take up courting with yer.'

'You mean Johnny?' Ruby had seen him on only two occasions since that wonderful night. It was curious how they could speak politely and coolly, as though they were strangers meeting for the first time. Ruby was torn between guilt and remorse, and somewhere in between there was a great ache in her heart. But she made herself accept the odd truce that had settled between them. It was simpler that way.

Lizzie went to the cradle and made sure that the child was slumbering. The other childer were outside playing. 'Yes, I mean Johnny,' she said sharply. 'Unless there's another fella that's been making eyes at yer?' She glanced at Ruby, waiting for some kind of response. When there was none, she grunted, 'It ain't right, I tell yer . . . working all hours and closeting yerself indoors like a hermit, sketching and cutting out patterns, and fetching home all manner of paperwork. I knew summat would go wrong when yer got that money. I told yer dad, and I were right.' She shook her head so frantically that her whole body rippled from top to toe, 'But he wouldn't listen. Oh, no. The pair on yer can't see no further than yer noses.' To Ruby's astonishment, Lizzie fell into the chair and began sobbing.

'What's gonna become of us, eh?' she whispered hoarsely. 'What in God's name's gonna become of us?'

Ruby went to her then. '*Nothing*'s going to become of us,' she comforted, bending low to cradle Lizzie's bowed head, 'You're not to worry about Dad,' she urged. 'If there's a problem, he'll sort it out in his own way. He always does, you know that.' As though to ease her mam's mind, she added softly, 'You're not to worry about me neither.' She hugged Lizzie hard. 'If I didn't know better, I'd say you were trying to marry me off and get rid of me.'

That made Lizzie smile. 'Hmh!' she snorted, wiping her eye on the cuff of her sleeve. 'I expect you'll wed when yer ready and not afore. What's more, I don't expect you'll ever make a grandma of me, more's the pity.'

Without knowing it, she had touched on something that had haunted Ruby these past months. 'Oh, I don't know, Mam,' she sighed. 'Who knows? One of these days I might surprise you.'

'Aye, and sparrers'll wear clogs,' Lizzie replied in a lighter voice. When she looked up sharply, she thought she saw a certain sadness in Ruby's ocean blue eyes. 'I'm sorry I yelled at yer, lass,' she said. 'But I'm not pleased at what's going on. I've allus been made to speak my mind, and I have to say I'm not sorry yer were sent packing from the Bankses' house, because you and that Cicely were becoming too fond of each other. But, oh, I do wish he hadn't sent you that money, 'cause money of that kind brings its own trouble. I can feel it in me bones.' Heaving a great big sigh she clambered out of the chair, saying wearily, 'Fetch the childer in, lass, while I go and talk to yer dad. It's getting dark, and I reckon I'm ready fer an early bed tonight.' She yawned. 'Age is creeping up on me,' she said ruefully. And with that she went out of the parlour, through the scullery and into the yard, where she and Ted were soon engrossed in conversation.

As she came out into the street, Ruby caught sight of Lenny striding towards her. Since acquiring work with the blacksmith, he had seemed to grow overnight; no longer the boy who looked for trouble at every corner and teased the childer for the delight of it, he was a young man with a responsible job, and even the odd girlfriend calling now and then. He was also quieter and proving to be a deep thinker like his dad. Ruby waylaid him as he approached. 'Tell Mam I'm going to see Maureen and I'll collect the childer in a while.'

He merely nodded. These days he had little to say. Anything important he saved for his dad. After all, he was a man now and men must stick together. Ruby watched him go into the house. Somehow, she still couldn't believe that the nasty side of him was altogether gone.

Maureen was enjoying the last of the evening sunshine. Seated in the high-backed chair that Johnny had bought her from the Saturday market, she was warmly wrapped in the soft brown chequered shawl that Ruby had given her as a present. She had a blanket over her legs and a mug of steaming tea in her hands. 'I saw you talking to Lenny,' she said. 'How's he getting on at his work?'

Ruby sat on the doorstep beside her friend with her knees tucked under her chin. 'Oh, he's all right, I suppose. At least it keeps him out of mischief.' She went on to ask how Maureen herself had been. She said she was better every day, then quickly diverted the conversation from herself, asked Ruby all about the milliner's, and whether she was rich yet, and what would she do when she was.

'I'll buy you a lovely new dress and coat to match, and a hat with big feathers that shiver in the wind,' laughed Ruby.

'I won't let you,' Maureen interrupted. 'You're always buying me presents.' When Ruby pulled a face, she went on, 'What else will you do? As if I don't know.' She knew all of Ruby's dreams and never tired of hearing them. Her own life was dreary and predictable, while Ruby's was growing more exciting by the day, and Maureen loved to hear her talk. A year ago, even a few months ago, Ruby's dreams seemed impossible, like a fairy-tale. Now, though, Maureen could see them coming true, and she wanted to share in it all. 'Go on, Ruby,' she urged, leaning forward in her chair. 'Tell me what you'll do when you're rich.'

Before Ruby could answer, another voice intervened and it turned her heart over. 'We all know what Ruby wants, Maureen.' Johnny came out of the house and stood behind them. 'She wants the whole world,' he said softly.

Ruby was caught off guard by the bitterness in his voice. 'And what's wrong with that?' she wanted to know.

His dark eyes roved her face. 'Who am I to say?' he murmured. 'But, remember, we can't always have what we want.' He resisted the urge to sweep her up in his arms, thinking no one could want anything as much as he wanted Ruby. But he was wise enough to know that often a man has to be patient. Turning to his sister, he told her, 'It's getting chilly, Maureen, we'd best get you inside.' Stepping down to the pavement, he clasped her by the shoulders and eased her on to her feet.

'Are you coming in, Ruby?' Maureen asked as she was gently lifted into his arms. Johnny turned his head, waiting for her answer.

'No. I promised Mam I'd collect the childer,' she said, rising from the step. 'But I'll be round to see you tomorrow, then we'll have a long talk. How about that?'

Maureen's answer was a big warm smile. 'Sounds all right to me.'

Shifting her gaze to Johnny, Ruby spoke in a quiet voice. 'Goodnight.'

'Goodnight, Ruby,' he answered. He wanted to say so many things but knew this was not the time. Perhaps there would never be a time for him and Ruby. The thought was unbearable.

Later, when the house was asleep and darkness filtered into every corner of her room, Ruby lay in bed, listening to Dolly's gentle slumbering and staring at the brown damp patches on the ceiling. The candlelight flickered and trembled across the room, making the patches creep along like awful monsters that would fall on her at any minute. She was bone tired but couldn't sleep. There were so many troubled thoughts pushing at the walls of her mind. She wondered what it was that made her father so quiet and moody of late, and her mam so quickly out of temper. Was she so wrong in wanting more out of life? Was it a sin to think about riches and wonderful things? Ruby didn't know.

The more she thought on it, and the more she pondered her mother's warnings, the more confused she became. Had she lost her way? Was her mam right after all? Certainly, where there had always been laughter and a simple life in this familiar little house, there was now a shadow over it. Was it because of her? Dear God, she hoped not.

Not too far away Lizzie also lay awake, tossing this way then that. She was deeply worried because Ted would not discuss what was bothering him. She guessed that it was to do with his work at the foundry, but he would neither deny nor confirm it, and so she was left wondering. In all the years they'd been together, he had never kept anything from her until now. Then there was Ruby, who seemed hell bent on wasting her young life.

'God above, what's happening to us?' she asked, heaving a deep sigh that swept through her and left her breathless.

Sad of heart, Lizzie reminded herself that a family was a living thing that grew and branched out, and she could never hold it together as she could when they were all bairns. Suddenly, for no reason that she could fathom, she was gripped with a rush of horror. In that moment the room felt so cold that she found herself shivering. It was as though the icy breath of the dark reaper had blown in through the very walls.

Chapter Fourteen

Not long after he made Cicely his bride, Luke Arnold made another heartless and calculated decision. On a freezing November morning, he arrived at his father's foundry. His mood was dark as he rushed into the manager's office. 'What the hell do you mean by this?' He opened his palm to reveal a crumpled piece of paper. 'I'm no messenger boy to be summoned by the likes of you!' he exploded, sending the paper across the desk with an angry flick of the wrist. 'Explain yourself, man.'

At once the manager sprang to his feet and captured the fluttering paper between finger and thumb. 'I'm sorry,' he apologised, the other man's hard stare forcing him momentarily to lower his gaze. 'Only I thought you should know what's been happening here.' He glanced towards the door and lowered his voice. 'It's trouble, I reckon.'

'Trouble?' Luke Arnold half turned his head, wondering whether there was someone behind him. 'What kind of trouble?' His whole manner changed as he waited for an answer. Gone was the arrogance. He was suddenly edgy and afraid. Guilty men were always afraid.

'You recall a fellow by the name of Ted Miller . . . the one you told me to get rid of?'

Luke searched his mind for a moment. The name was familiar.

He remembered. 'The troublemaker, you mean?' When the other man nodded, he went on, 'Well, what of him? If I remember rightly, I gave orders that he should be paid off.'

'Oh, he was paid off. I sent him on his way just like you told me.' He made a small chuckling sound. 'Funny, him being taken on at Banks's foundry soon after. So you see he's back in the family so to speak. But then, who would have thought that you'd end up wedding Banks's daughter, eh?'

Luke was not amused. 'Stick to the point, damn you!'

'You won't like it.' He took a deep breath and spat the words out as though they were bitter on his tongue. 'He's stirring up trouble again. If you don't put a stop to him, we'll *all* be for the high jump.'

'Go on,' Luke ordered impatiently. He was both surprised and disappointed to learn that Ted Miller was actually working for Cicely's father. As yet he had little influence in that direction, although he was determined it would soon be rectified. He could never lose sight of the main reason he married the pathetic Cicely. At night, when he used that insipid creature to satisfy his lust, he imagined it was the beautiful Ruby, and hated his wife all the more.

'These past weeks there have been rumblings,' the manager explained. 'Some of the men have been heard asking questions about the quality of raw materials brought in to make the steel. Oh, there's nothing to worry about . . . *not yet there isn't.*' His warning was unmistakable.

'What has Miller to do with it?'

'I'm not rightly sure. But the foreman reckons he heard two names mentioned. One was an idiot I know the men wouldn't pay too much mind to. The fellow's a fool to himself, drinks like a fish and thinks out of his arse.'

'And the other?'

'Well, that's just it. It seems that Ted Miller listened to the drunk's ramblings, and now he won't let it be. He's asking questions. So far that's all. But I'm worried. Soon ever I heard the name Miller, I thought it best to let you know. He's a sharp one is Ted. If he keeps probing, it won't take him long to put two and two together.' He rolled his eyes and glanced at the door again. 'He'll do for us both,' he whispered.

Luke strolled away from the desk, the tip of his finger tapping against his teeth and making an irritating noise. He thought long and hard before slewing round. 'Ted Miller? What family does he have?' At the back of his mind was the realisation that this man might well be Ruby's father.

'Well, there's a wife, of course, and twins. Then there's a lad. Oh, and there's two young 'uns. And of course, there's Ruby . . . used to be your own wife's personal maid, if my information serves me right.' Misunderstanding the other man's intention, he added, 'He has a deal of responsibility as you can see. But you're wrong if you think you can frighten him. Ted Miller isn't the kind of man to be warned off. He may not work here, but that won't stop him from being interested in what goes on. Besides, the men here know and respect him. They'll listen to what he has to say.'

Luke laughed, a low cynical sound that cautioned the other fellow to remember his place. 'A man with principles, is he?' he snorted. 'They're the worst kind.' He felt a certain sadistic satisfaction at knowing that this 'troublemaker' was none other than Ruby's father; with the same proud attitude and irritating concern for others, it was plain they were made out of the same mould.

'What can we do?' The manager's several chins were visibly shivering. 'I tell you, it's only a matter of time before he discovers what we've been up to. I don't mind admitting that I'm frightened out of my wits.'

'What do we do?' Luke came back to the desk and leaned

his face close to the other man's. 'We get rid of him, that's what we do.'

The other man looked confused. 'How do you suggest we do that?' Knowing Ted Miller, any suspicious moves would only light the fuse and send the whole rotten business, and them, sky high.

'We get rid of him. Only *not* like before.' He paused to let his words sink in. 'You see, *this* time, he won't be able to spread his nasty little rumours, because he won't be coming back.' He watched with amusement while the manager's eyes grew wider. 'That's right.' He saw how the other fellow was riveted with shock, and it amused him. 'I hope you're not squeamish,' he warned softly. 'It would displease me if I was to suddenly realise I couldn't count on you.'

The man swallowed so hard that his Adam's apple bobbed up and down. 'Oh, you can count on me, have no fear about that,' he said hoarsely. 'I understand what you're saying, and you can leave it to me.'

He was about to explain that he knew someone who would do anything for a price, but Luke was already on his way out of the office. 'See to it!' he snarled over his shoulder. 'But spare me the details. I know nothing whatsoever about it. Remember that.'

The other man was left listening to Luke's quick footsteps as they went down the stairs. When he thought on the task ahead, he fell backwards into his chair and the sweat ran fast down his temples. 'Murder,' he whispered. 'The bugger wants me to commit murder.' He couldn't believe it, and yet he saw the need. All the same, the thought of actually killing Ted Miller made him sick to his stomach.

Some weeks later, Ted came away from the marketplace, a happy grin on his face and a feeling of joy in his heart. Today was Christmas Eve. He was excited at the coming festivities and proud of his bargaining talent, because, in between having a celebratory drink with his mates in the nearby pub, and dodging the shoppers to find his way back to the stall, he had finally haggled the price of the best tree down to two shillings and threepence. 'By! Wait 'til I walk in the door with this beauty,' he chuckled, wrapping his two arms round the magnificent tree, and finding his way out of the marketplace.

The evening was drawing in fast as he made his way towards Fisher Street. Everyone seemed to be in a dreadful hurry to get home before dark, blindly rushing here and there and not looking where they were going. All day long the snow had fallen and now the chilly wind was hardening it to ice. The ground was dangerously slippery and Ted was forced to slow his pace as he picked his way along the pavements. Twice he had to swing the tree out of the way, when frantic folk insisted on careering into him. 'Watch where you're going then!' he called out when one man swore aloud as the prickly branches brushed his face.

He was only a few steps away from his own front door when the tragedy happened. It was pitch dark now, with only the lone street lamp at the top of Fisher Street to guide him. He heard the carriage coming at full pelt behind him, and remembered thinking what a fool the driver was, to rush around like that, especially in the dark and on icy cobbled roads. When it thundered closer, he slowed his pace and turned round. He didn't see the man spring out of the doorway, but he felt the jolt when he was pushed hard from the side and sent hurtling across the road – straight into the path of the oncoming vehicle. As his face crunched against the cobbles, he was aware of the driver standing up, yelling fearfully as the carriage brakes screeched and the whole ensemble seemed to veer away from him. There was a glancing thud, which rolled him backwards, flicking him sideways before his head cracked into the kerb and he lost consciousness. In the split second as his senses left him, he saw the dark shadowy figure running away. And then he knew no more.

All along Fisher Street the doors were flung open and folk came rushing out. 'What happened?' Ma Collins yelled. She had been coaxing Mrs Wentworth's first bairn into the world, and that poor young woman had given a good account of herself, yelling and crying enough to wake the dead. When all the noise broke outside, she was miraculously silenced and the bairn popped into the world without any further ado. Now that the newborn was lying safely on its mammy's breast, Ma Collins had taken the opportunity to investigate what dreadful happening had taken place in the street outside. While everyone stood around the huddled figure on the ground, she forced her way through. At once recognising Ted, she asked in a shocked and quiet voice, 'Where's Lizzie?'

Even as she looked up, the crowd parted and Lizzie stood there. At first she stared curiously at the faces around her, then she stared at Ma Collins, and what she saw there made Lizzie shift her gaze to the misshapen bundle on the ground. When she realised that it was her own dear Ted lying there, she cried out his name, falling to her knees beside him and gathering him roughly into her arms. She didn't utter a single word after that. She continued to stare at his face which seemed the colour of chalk in the light of the street lamp, her horrified gaze followed the thin red river surging down his temples, smudging her own arms. Burying her face against his, she rocked him back and forth, softly crying, and silently praying.

For what seemed an age, the silence all around her was impenetrable. Suddenly, Ruby was on the ground beside her, one arm round her mam and the other stroking her father's hair. 'He'll be all right, Mam,' she murmured. 'He'll be all right.' It was then that Ma Collins drew the two of them away. 'We'll get him to the infirmary,' she promised. 'After that, you must trust in the Lord.'

The carriage driver was frantic. 'It weren't my fault,' he moaned, wiping his hands down his face as though to shut out the sight before him. 'He just fell into the road in front of me,' he insisted. 'There weren't nothing I could do.' As the men gently laid Ted into the back of his empty carriage, he openly wept. It didn't matter that his seats were smeared with blood. All that mattered was that these people should believe it wasn't his fault. 'Will he be all right?' he asked Ma Collins.

'He'll have a better chance if yer stop bawling and get the poor sod to the infirmary as fast as yer can,' she answered. While he swiftly clambered back into his seat, Ruby helped her mam into the carriage and then climbed in beside her. Ted lay across the seat before them, unmoving and crumpled, his face like a mask and his eyes closed against the world. As Lizzie slid into the seat beside him to cradle his head against her breast, Ruby sat opposite, desperately afraid yet ever hopeful. 'Will you watch the childer?' she asked, leaning out of the window to speak to Ma Collins as the carriage pulled away. Dolly and the twins watched from the upstairs window. Lenny stood in the doorway. When she saw the tears glittering on his face, Ruby suddenly realised that he was still only a frightened child at heart.

'Aye, don't worry about them,' answered Ma Collins. 'They'll be tekken care of.' A chorus of agreement went up from every woman there. Thankful, Ruby returned her attention to the two inside the carriage.

All the way to Blackburn Infirmary she watched in anguish while her mam bent her own body close to this man whom she loved, desperate to instil her own warm life into his veins, and dying a little inside herself when he remained cold and still in her arms.

When they rushed Ted into the infirmary, one of the nurses told Ruby that there was 'a flicker of life'. And so they waited outside in the corridor, deeply anxious and deriving comfort from each other while the doctor and nurses urgently attended him.

When, after a while, the grey-haired doctor came softly towards them, Lizzie and Ruby each saw the truth written on his tired old face. 'I'm so sorry,' he murmured. He went on to explain how Ted's skull had been shattered, but neither Lizzie nor Ruby heard. Lizzie had collapsed in her daughter's arms, and the only thing they understood in that awful moment was that he would never come home again. It was a shocking thing to realise. And as she held on to her distraught mam, Ruby could only think that it was Christmas. It was Christmas Eve, and her dad was never coming home again.

It was early in the morning when Ruby brought her mam back to the house on Fisher Street. Inside, Ma Collins waited for news. She saw straightaway that it was not good. 'The childer are sound asleep,' she told Ruby. 'All but Lenny, and he's gone out into the night.'

Lizzie spoke then. Looking at Ruby with eyes that were red and sore from crying, she whispered, 'He idolised yer dad. Find him, lass. Find him and bring him home.'

Her voice broke on a sob, and Ma Collins led her to the chair by the fireplace. 'We'll sit here, you and me,' she suggested kindly. 'And we'll talk all night if you want.' She turned to Ruby, saw how devastated she was and asked, 'Or d'you want me to find your brother, lass?'

'No,' Ruby replied. 'Thank you, but I think I know where to find him.' She glanced anxiously at her mam who pleaded, 'Break it to him gently, lass, for he'll take it awful hard.'

Outside, Ruby stood on the doorstep, a solitary and lonely soul, trying to come to terms with what had happened. In spite of her awful grief she hadn't cried. For her mam's sake she had been a tower of strength. Now, though, she was numb all over. She felt so strange. All knotted up inside, yet floating, as though she was not in control of herself. 'Be strong for them,' she murmured into the darkness. 'They'll need you more than ever now.'

Johnny had come home late, and was shocked to hear about Ted Miller's accident. Now he came out of the house and saw her standing there. Hurrying the short distance between them, he stopped just an arm's reach away. He saw how she stood slumped against the door and feared the worst. 'Ruby?' His voice crept into her thoughts. She glanced up at him, and he knew her terrible grief.

'He's dead,' she murmured, and her voice was like that of a stranger. When he stepped forward and opened his arms to her, she tumbled forward, safe in the warmth of his embrace. Out of the corner of her eye she saw the crumpled Christmas tree propped against the wall. Someone had said Ted was carrying the tree when he was run down. Suddenly the tears she had kept back welled up inside her. Then it was like a dam opening as they gushed up, burning her eyes, spilling over to flow freely down her face. 'Our dad's dead,' she sobbed, over and over she told him. 'He's never coming home again.'

Johnny held her tight. 'Shh,' he whispered. 'Shh, my darling.' And his heart went out to her.

Together they went in search of Lenny. Just as Ruby suspected, he was sitting on the bridge over Blakewater, dangling his legs in mid-air and staring into the distance towards the foundry where his dad had worked. 'He always told me that one day he would get me a job there,' he told Ruby and Johnny. Then he broke down and cried. Johnny told Ruby it was the best thing that could happen. 'Grief is better out than in,' he said. And she knew he was right.

Part Three

1895

LONELINESS

Chapter Fifteen

'It might as well have been made for you, Mrs Lacey.' Ruby
smiled into the mirror at the woman's dainty image. Mrs Lacey
had been a regular client at the milliner's for almost two years
now; about the same length of time as Ruby had been there. She
was a pretty woman with an oval-shaped face and long fluttering
lashes. Every one of the four hats she had tried would have
flattered her, but the neat cream creation with its tiny lace veil
that reached just below the eyes was something very special.
'This one suits you best of all,' Ruby remarked truthfully, at the
same time tilting the hat at an attractive angle on the woman's
swirl of dark hair.

Reaching forward in her seat, the woman examined the hat
from every side. At length, she returned Ruby's warm smile. 'As
usual, you're right, my dear,' she declared. 'I'll take it.' And,
being a woman of decision, she quickly summoned her waiting
driver, who dutifully collected the cumbersome hat-box and
afterwards accompanied his mistress out to the waiting carriage.

After entering the item on Mrs Lacey's account, Ruby watched
them drive away down the road. Returning inside, where she
glanced at the small marble clock on the new elegant fireplace,
she was astonished and relieved to see that it was almost five.
With a sigh, she turned the door sign over to read CLOSED.

Normally, she would have remained open a while longer, but on this glorious June Saturday she felt unusually weary. Besides, she had other business to attend to, and was concerned that Widow Reece had not returned. These past twelve months, that poor woman had been in considerable pain, the delicate bones in her hands growing increasingly troublesome, and after a great deal of persuasion from Ruby, she had finally made an appointment to visit the doctor.

Ruby was clearing the counter, deep in thought, when the girl emerged from the back room. She was a slight fair-haired young creature with a nervous way about her, though she was a quick learner and Ruby was delighted with her progress. 'I've finished my work, Miss Miller,' she said in a peculiar high-pitched voice. 'Is there anything else you'd like me to do before I go?'

'No, thank you, Katie, it's already gone five,' Ruby answered. 'You get off now. You don't want to miss your tram.' At first, Ruby had been reluctant to take on a girl who was so young and inexperienced. But her wages were small, and already she was proving to be a godsend. She worked hard and she had a natural aptitude that ran through all her work. Besides which, she had a flair for colour and design that prompted Widow Reece to tell Ruby, 'The girl reminds me of you when you first came here.'

'Goodnight then,' she called out as she closed the shop door behind her. After locking the door, Ruby went into the back room. As usual it was left neat and tidy, much as she herself liked to leave it. She thought fondly of that first day when she came to work here. 'Was it really almost two years ago?' she mused aloud. It only seemed like yesterday to her.

So much had happened in that time; so many memories were made, some good and some bad. On the good side, Lenny was making a fine young man, and the other three childer were making strides at the Church school; Lottie was a fine sturdy infant, with an amiable and delightful nature. Thanks to Ruby's growing affluence and Lenny's considerable contribution, they were all well clothed, and hunger was a thing of the past in the Miller household. On the work-front, Ruby had eagerly absorbed everything Widow Reece had taught her, and more besides. She had grown competent and knowledgeable where the business side was concerned; so much so that Widow Reece had gradually relinquished the greater responsibility, until it was now Ruby who virtually ran the business. Profits had exceeded all expectations. Her savings had grown considerably, and she felt as though at long last she had achieved something. Yet, Ruby looked on it only as a beginning. More and more she felt in charge of her own destiny, and it was a good feeling.

Her only regret was Johnny. She loved him as much as she had always loved him, and she knew instinctively that he loved her; although he didn't tell her so any more. Instead, he smiled and talked with her. He congratulated her on realising part of her ambitions, and he was the perfect gentleman. But he rarely stayed when she was around, nor did he make any attempt to cross her path. Oh, there were times when she wanted him to, when she remembered that glorious night of love and longed to be held close in his strong loving arms. For a while after that night, Ruby had thought she was with child. But then it proved not to be. Often she wondered whether she would have been satisfied and happy with such an event, married to Johnny and raising their children. But the thought frightened her and so she launched herself deeper into her work. To her, Johnny still represented a life she wanted no part of.

On the bad side, her mam had been prematurely widowed and Ruby herself, along with the other childer, had lost a caring father. Since her man had been taken two years ago this coming Christmas Eve, Lizzie was a changed woman, less active, quick to temper and prone to deep silent moods. The atmosphere in that little house on Fisher Street was different somehow. This was one of the reasons why Ruby had finally decided it was time to move the family away. She had already paid an advance rent on a bigger property, and tonight she would break the news to her mam. In view of Lizzie's set ways and vehement opposition to any change for the better, Ruby didn't relish the idea of telling her.

Besides being deeply concerned about her mam, Ruby was disturbed about things she had heard with regard to Cicely. There were growing rumours that Luke Arnold was not the wonderful husband Cicely had hoped he would be, and it was claimed by some that he was blatantly unfaithful. So many times, Ruby had toyed with the idea of visiting her in that grand house on Preston New Road; a palatial place chosen by Luke and paid for by her father as a wedding present. But she thought better of it. Cicely had made her feelings plain long ago, when she cruelly dismissed Ruby; she certainly wouldn't thank her for turning up on the doorstep now.

Ruby was visibly startled when a voice spoke quite close to her. 'My, you *are* deep in thought, aren't you?' It was Widow Reece, and Ruby hadn't even heard her come in. She was even more startled, some moments later, when she realised that the other woman had not only been to the doctor's but had attended a meeting with none other than a representative of Gabriel's Fashions, a fast-growing chain of stores that was spreading throughout the North West and sold everything from pins to overcoats. 'They want to buy us out,' she told Ruby. 'And to be honest, I am greatly tempted.'

Ruby was horrified. 'Buy us out?' she gasped. 'We can't do that!' For one fleeting awful minute she saw all their good work going out the window.

Widow Reece took off her coat and with slow studied movements laid it over the back of the chair. Then she folded the front of the ankle-length skirt between her hands and seated herself, at the same time giving Ruby a long hard look. 'I'm sorry to spring it on you like this, Ruby,' she said softly. 'No one knows better than I how hard you've worked here. I know this must come as a shock, but Gabriel's approached me some four months ago and I've been at my wits' end ever since. They don't know that I've sold a share of the business to you, and I kept that to myself because I didn't want them talking to you. I didn't want to tell you then and I don't want to let you down now.'

'Then *don't*,' Ruby pleaded. She was no fool. She knew that if Widow Reece sold her larger share of this business, it would put her in a very vulnerable position. However, what she heard next tempered her anger.

'I have no choice, you see,' Widow Reece went on. 'As you know, I've been to see the doctor.' She made a little sob in the back of her throat, but her face remained remarkably impassive as she continued in a subdued voice, 'The news was worse than I'd feared.'

Seeing that the woman was distressed, Ruby came and sat on the chair opposite, 'What is it?' she asked gently. 'What did the doctor have to say?'

For answer, Widow Reece raised her hands and made an effort to stretch the gnarled fingers. They made a grotesque sight, twisted and thin, like brittle twigs that had been trodden underfoot. 'Even to lift a sheet of paper has become agonising.' She laughed, but it was a pitiful sound. 'Do you really want to know what the doctor told me?' Ruby nodded her head, her eyes intent on the other woman's face. 'He told me that it's only a matter of time before the crippling disease spreads to other joints. Then who knows?' She raised her wretched eyes. 'I've tried. You know I've tried, Ruby.' The sigh she made reached deep inside. Her head bowed a little as though a mighty weight was slowly crushing it down. 'It's time to rest now, I think,' she said. 'Time to say goodbye to this place and go to live in Scarborough with my sister. As you know, she's been badgering me for some time now.' She roved her quiet gaze around the shop. 'I shall miss it, you know. And I shall miss you.'

Ruby was ashamed. 'I'm sorry,' she said. 'I didn't realise your condition was worsening. Why did you never say anything?'

'Because I wanted to fool myself, I suppose,' she confessed. 'And I can be very devious when I want. I've become adept at hiding my ugly hands, and keeping my emotions from prying eyes.' Realising how cruel that might sound, she quickly retracted her remark. 'Oh! I didn't mean *you* . . . I mean . . . you've been so kind and understanding. Please, Ruby, understand now. The harsh truth is this . . . I simply can't go on.'

Ruby put her mind at rest. 'It's all right. I do understand,' she replied. 'We've been a good team, you and I.' Even as she spoke, the germ of a plan was taking shape in her fertile mind. 'Couldn't we remain partners? If I was to run the shop altogether, you would be able to take things easy, perhaps go on a long holiday. You know I'll take good care of things in your absence.' There must be a way to keep the shop, she thought frantically. THERE HAS TO BE A WAY!

Widow Reece merely smiled, a sad little smile that sank Ruby's hopes. 'I'm sorry, dear,' she said. 'I have tried so hard to hang on, but now I must burn my bridges. I'm not young any more. There can be no half measures, and the only money I have in the whole world is tied up in this business. You know I have to do this, don't you, dear? There is no alternative but to accept the generous deal offered by Gabriel's.'

'Have you given word?' Ruby wasn't finished yet.

'Not yet. But I promised to get back to them within the week.'

'And what if you found another buyer?'

'Oh, but I haven't.'

'Sell it to me!'

'TO YOU!' Widow Reece's mouth fell open as she continued

to stare at Ruby. 'I've been offered four hundred guineas, my dear,' she explained. 'I would be a fool to settle for less.'

'I'm not asking you to settle for less.' Momentarily taken aback by the amount involved, Ruby's thoughts were still racing. 'I'm willing to match Gabriel's offer.' She saw how the other woman was about to interrupt, and so she pressed on. 'You say they've offered you four hundred guineas for the entire business?'

'That's right.'

'And I now own twenty-five per cent, isn't that so?'

'You know it is.'

'So, according to our agreement, when the sale is complete, I should have somewhere in the region of one hundred guineas coming to me . . . twenty-five per cent of the purchase price. Am I right?'

'Yes. That's perfectly true,' Widow Reece confirmed. 'So you see, my dear, with the excellent value put on the business, you will be quite well off. And rightly so, because it's thanks to you that the accounts show excellent returns.'

'Please, I have something to propose. Will you hear me out?'

'I'm listening.' She settled back in the chair and, watching Ruby's face closely, paid particular attention to what was being said.

'I know that a hundred guineas is a great deal of money, and I know there are things I could do with it that I never imagined.' Ruby's voice was strong and firm as she continued to put her case. 'The plain fact is, I don't want the money. Your mind is obviously made up, and I can understand why. But if this business is on the market, as far as I'm concerned, there's only one buyer. And that buyer is me!' She took a deep breath. 'I can't pay you the entire amount all at once, you know that. But, taking my own share into account, I estimate that you yourself will end up with approximately two hundred and sixty guineas after solicitor's costs?'

'A little more than that, I think. I certainly don't intend paying my solicitor such an extravagant sum as forty guineas.' She was impressed by Ruby's business acumen. 'But go on, my dear,' she urged. 'Where is all this leading?'

'I have saved hard over these past two years,' Ruby explained. 'Oh, it isn't a great fortune, but it represents two years of hard scrimping and saving. It isn't anywhere near what you want, and I know there isn't a bank or money-lender in the world who would put up the capital for me to buy this business. But, scraping almost everything I have together, I can pay you a good lump sum straightaway, and the remainder on a monthly basis. What do you say?' With her heart in her mouth, she waited for an answer.

It took a moment for the other woman to recover. Here was an eventuality she had not prepared for. 'Oh, Ruby! Ruby! It would take a lifetime to pay off the debt.' She shook her head. 'No, I don't think it's feasible,' she reluctantly replied. To her mind, a burden such as Ruby wanted to shoulder was terrifying. But Ruby never ceased to amaze her.

She persisted, 'With respect, you're wrong. It wouldn't take me a lifetime. If you still plan on going to your sister in Scarborough, the earning potential in this business will be doubled virtually overnight.' Her quick mind was racing ahead and she felt as though she was fighting for her very life.

Widow Reece was curious. 'What do you mean?'

'Oh, I had such plans . . . expanding here, then in a couple of years, perhaps opening another milliner's in Darwen, then Preston. You know yourself it was within our grasp. I would still work towards that end, and promise you your money within the space of five years.'

'That's very ambitious, my dear.'

Sensing that Widow Reece was warming to the idea, Ruby described her immediate plans. 'If I had this business, and you vacated your flat above, what a marvellous salon it would make . . . the clients could come here to have their nails manicured, we could dress their hair and pamper them upstairs, then send them on their way with a new hat to suit their new hairstyle. Land has been earmarked for future development in this area. That means business is bound to increase. The opportunities for expansion will be limitless. Gabriel's are no fools. They know the potential. We're positioned well here. You can be sure they've done their homework.'

She paused for breath before asking beseechingly, 'If you really have to sell, please let it be to me. It can all be drawn up by your solicitor – the period of time over which you want the money repaid, and the amount each month . . . even a share in the profits if you'd prefer. You have my word, I *will* pay you back, every penny that I owe, and in the stated time. Will you? Will you do it?' she pleaded. While Widow Reece seriously considered what had been said, Ruby's heart was in her mouth. She hardly dared to breathe. Finally, after what seemed an age, the answer was given.

'If there was the slightest chance, you know I would want you to have this place, providing you could afford it.' The older woman regarded Ruby with admiration. 'But then, I shouldn't be surprised if you've saved a considerable amount. Especially when you've spent every hour God sends with your back bent to your work, forever striving to improve things, always searching for that elusive pot of gold at the end of the rainbow . . . no social life, nothing else but this business to fill your days and your nights.'

Many was the time she had come down at two in the morning to find Ruby still poring over the books, or sitting knee deep in repairs and half-finished hats. In all her life, she had never come across anyone like Ruby. She was totally inspiring. 'All right. I'll talk to my solicitor and see what he thinks about your proposition,' she promised, 'I owe you that much. But I'm promising nothing, you understand?'

'I understand,' Ruby declared, her eyes bright with excitement as she began pacing the floor. 'I haven't even begun to spread my wings,' she said, in a voice so low that it was barely audible. Oh, the things she had planned! How could she let it all fall away? Turning round, she said gratefully, 'If you can persuade him, you won't regret it, I promise. If all is well and you sell this place to me, you can rest assured that it will be cared for, just as you yourself have always cared for it, and the door will always be open to you.' She smiled then, and never was there more affection between these two women. 'You gave me my first chance and I won't ever forget.'

'Oh, if it hadn't happened here, you would have found a way, Ruby. There's fire in your soul and a hunger in your blood.' She'd always known Ruby was different. 'You were born to be successful,' she said whimsically. 'For my part, I'll do everything humanly possible to find a way. But, like I've said, I won't promise anything.' She was suddenly weary. Getting out of the chair she said, 'I think I'll make my way to bed. The day's events have tired me out.'

The sun was still shining brightly when Ruby put on her light blue coat and departed the shop, at once making her way to the tram stop. 'Montague Street,' she told the conductor. Once there, she clambered from the tram platform and set off at a fast pace.

Coming to the top of Derwent Street, she paused a moment looking down its considerable length. It was an ordinary street, flanked both sides by doorways and big square windows dressed with pretty net curtains. Its pavements were lined all along with fluted gaslamps. Some way down, a number of children played in the road, hopping across the cobbles and laughing with that carefree joy which should be natural to all children.

Ruby watched them for a short while before going to the second house on her left. The door was dark brown with six panels and the number four at the top. Fishing in her skirt pocket, Ruby took out a long iron key. Inserting it into the lock, she turned it and pushed the door open. Cold air made her shiver as she went along the passage and into the back parlour. 'Oh, Mam, you're going to love this house,' she murmured, standing in the doorway and casting her gaze around the room.

The parlour was almost twice the size of the one in Fisher Street, and the back window was high and large, letting the sunshine spill in. Strolling round the room, Ruby lovingly stroked her fingers along the wooden mantelpiece. She opened and shut the cavernous cupboards in the recesses either side of the fireplace, peeped inside the big oven in the fire-range, then went to the window where she gazed out into the daylight.

On Fisher Street the back parlour window overlooked a flagstoned yard. But here, you could look out of the window on to a small patch of green grass. There were even little pockets of soil that were once flower beds and could be again. At the bottom of the small square lawn stood the lavatory house. It even had a little window in the narrow wall, and what was more, the window was covered in the prettiest lace curtain.

As she went from room to room, Ruby's heart sang. There was a front parlour, a scullery with proper cupboards and a sparkling white sink situated beneath a wide window. There were four good-sized bedrooms; a bedroom big enough for the twins to have a bed each, another for Lenny to be on his own as a growing man should be; and two other large rooms, one for her and Dolly, and the best one at the front of the house for her mam and little Lottie.

Downstairs, there was room enough so that they wouldn't all be under each other's feet. 'So much room!' Ruby cried, hurrying upstairs then down, and upstairs again. 'Room enough to breathe,'

421

she said aloud, her heart painfully full. 'Room enough to grow.'

After a while she closed the bedroom doors and went downstairs. Here, she drew pictures in her mind, pictures of how it would be. Of course, she would want her mam to have new furniture, pretty curtains and everything she could never have before. There would be big soft armchairs and colourful rugs. Oh, and Ruby would pay an odd-job man to decorate every room, just the way her mam wanted it. Oh, she couldn't wait to see her face tonight when she told her about this lovely house on Derwent Street. And it was theirs. The rent was paid for three months in advance, and it was theirs. IT WAS THEIRS! Ruby could hardly believe it herself. At long last, her dearest wish was coming true.

Returning downstairs, she ensured that everything was secure then went quickly down the passage and out of the house. Halfway down the street, a woman and a man sat on chairs outside a front door. Their heads were bowed in earnest conversation. Suddenly they glanced up and saw her. There was a moment's hesitation at seeing a stranger, but then the woman put up her hand in greeting. The man stretched his back, took out his pipe and nodded in a friendly manner. They were too far away to converse so they exchanged smiles with Ruby. Her heart raced. Thoughts of the conversation she and Widow Reece had earlier raced through her mind and thrilled her. She believed with all her heart that the business would be hers. She felt it in her young bones. This wonderful day was a day she would remember for the rest of her life.

Ruby turned to look lovingly at the house once more before she left. It was a strong solid house, warm and welcoming. It seemed to be telling her that it would take care of them, that they would be happy in Derwent Street. 'Oh, Mam. You'll love it so,' she murmured. And, with that in mind, she hurried to the tram-stop. It was ten minutes to Fisher Street, but to Ruby, who couldn't wait to tell her mam all the exciting news, it seemed like a lifetime.

'I want no part of it!' Lizzie banged her fist on the table, sending the crockery into a comical jig. There was a time when she would have contained her anger before the young 'uns, but that was before her darling man was taken from her and she had grown sour with the whole world. Turning from Ruby, she addressed herself to the childer. 'Eat yer teas, then get out and play awhile.' When Ruby tried again to talk with her, she jerked her head sideways and said solemnly, 'I don't want to discuss it, d'yer hear? Not *any* of it!' And with that she set about her rabbit pie, her head bent low and a look of defiance about her whole countenance.

Ruby thought it best to leave her mam alone a while. At least until she'd had her tea and the childer were out from under her feet. Even with Lenny working and Dolly at Church school with the twins, there was still Lottie to tend to, and enough work in this little house to fray her mam's nerves. Besides, Lizzie was still missing her mate, and nothing in the world could compensate for a loss of that magnitude.

The meal continued in a strained atmosphere, with only the clatter of knives and forks breaking the awful silence. Presently, Lizzie got to her feet and told the childer, 'Take yerselves off and play in the street. I'll call yer when it's time fer yer beds.'

'Can I take Lottie out?' Dolly wanted to know. 'I'll sit her with me against the wall, and we'll just watch the others. I'll not let her come to harm, Mam,' she promised.

Thinking hard, Lizzie pursed her lips and scowled. These days her old familiar smile seemed to have been buried beneath a constant frown. 'Go on then,' she said. 'But mind yer stay with her now!'

Dolly collected the infant into her arms and went away with

her, all the while crooning and making the little thing chuckle out loud. The twins soon followed. But Lenny remained in his seat, slowly eating the remains of his meal and watching the two women with growing interest. He sensed trouble brewing here, and being man of the house, he thought he should be on hand. 'What's all this about moving, our Ruby?' he asked slyly. He took umbrage at not having been consulted.

Thinking she could warm her mam to the idea, Ruby explained enthusiastically, 'I've got us a lovely house on Derwent Street. It's got four big rooms upstairs, and it's closer to town. Our mam won't have far to walk to the shops.'

With the childer out of the way, Lizzie let her temper explode. 'That's enough talk o' moving!' she snapped. 'You'll not get me setting foot in that house on Derwent Street. Nor in any other fancy place you put your mind to.'

'It's not a fancy place, Mam,' Ruby protested. 'It's just a bigger house, with a window in the lavatory wall and a real little garden in the back.' She so much wanted her mam to understand. 'I got it for you. So you could have a place to sit when the sun shines, and a bigger parlour that's not so cluttered and where you won't keep bumping into things.'

'Unlike you, my girl, I can do without what I've never had!' Lizzie retorted. 'And I wouldn't know what to do with a garden if I had one. Besides, what's wrong with sitting out front in a stand-chair, eh? And if I bump into things in the parlour, it's *my* parlour, and the things I bump into are the very same that me and yer dad bought over the years.' She shook her head vigorously. 'If you've been entertaining ideas about installing yer mam in some strange place among strange folk, then you'd best think again. Are yer listening to what I'm saying?' she demanded angrily. 'You'll not be moving Lizzie Miller outta Fisher Street . . . not until she's cold and stiff and lying in her box!'

'But, Mam, won't you at least go and see it?' Ruby was certain

424

that once Lizzie saw the house, she would fall in love with it.

'No! I'll not go and see it. What's more, I'll not have another word said on the matter.' She slammed herself down in the rocking chair and began to rock herself furiously. 'Not another word,' she muttered, turning her head towards the empty fireplace.

Ruby had been worried for some long time about the way her mam was moping. Her grief seemed to have turned inward, and there was no reaching her any more. 'Surely you can come and see the house before you make up your mind,' she pleaded.

'Never!'

'What's the matter with you, Mam? Are you afraid you might like it? Can't you face the fact that there just might be life after Fisher Street? Tell me what's so special about this place?' She was desperate now. Flinging her arms wide, she pointed to the walls and the dark brown streaks where the rain trickled down in winter, and the damp rose up in the midst of summer. '*This* is what you're clinging to . . . a place where the roof's riddled with holes and the damp gets on your chest, making you cough until you ache. The landlord refuses to spend a penny on it, and he makes you pay the earth for the pleasure of living here! It's ripe for demolition, you know that, and yet you won't admit it. Why won't you admit it, Mam? And why in God's name won't you let me take us all to somewhere better before the winter's on us again?'

She was bitter now. All her plans meant nothing if they didn't carry her mam and the family along as well. 'Didn't you hear what I said? Widow Reece is retiring on doctor's orders and there's every chance I could buy the business. On top of that, I've got us a decent house on Derwent Street. *And you won't even listen.* Why, Mam? WHAT ARE YOU FRIGHTENED OF?'

Of all the things Ruby could have said, that was the worst. Without realising it, she had touched on the truth of the matter. Lizzie was frightened. She had always been frightened, ever since she had defiled her marriage vows and gone to another man's bed, she was frightened that the Lord would rise up against her. She was frightened that her daughter's fierce ambitions would split this family apart, and she was frightened that Ruby might somehow discover the truth of her own origins.

Deeper than any of that, Lizzie was frightened by her own emotions. Terrified of the affection she still felt for Jeffrey Banks, and guilty because she would never know which man she had loved the most. Ted had been her husband, and now she was sincerely grieving for him, but even as she grieved, the memory of what she did all those years ago tore her apart. Ted had not known how deceitful she had been, but in her heart Lizzie felt certain that he knew now. Up there, where souls could see into places where mere humans couldn't, Ted knew everything, and she was mortified by the thought that he was looking down on her, her shame bared to his eyes, and she with no chance to explain. She should have explained all those years ago. Now it was too late. She felt the need to punish herself. To deny everything that might better her station in life. It was a kind of penance. There were times, when she was lying in her lonely bed at night and the childer were all asleep, when she felt as though she was the only person still left alive in the whole world; those were the worst times of all. In her terrible guilt, Lizzie would imagine that Ted was standing before her in that cold dark room, pointing a finger at her. 'You cheated me, Lizzie,' he would murmur. 'And I can't forgive you.'

These were the things Lizzie was frightened of. And just now, with her innocent words, Ruby had unwittingly opened all the old wounds. In her pain, Lizzie was like a wounded animal. Springing from her chair, she screamed, 'Don't you tell me I'm frightened, Ruby Miller! I'm still the same woman I've allus been, and I've never been frightened of anything in my life,' she lied. 'It ain't *me* that's different. It's *you* that's changed. I don't know you any more. As far back as I can remember, you've always wanted more than the good Lord gave yer. Well, now it seems to me that you've got what yer want, so you'd better get yerself off to yer precious house on Derwent Street, because we're none of us coming with yer.' When Ruby stared at her in amazement, she strode across the room and flung open the door. 'Go on!' she yelled. 'Take yourself off. And I don't care if I never see yer again!'

It was a moment before Ruby realised that her mam meant every word. She turned to Lenny, 'Please, our Lenny, tell her I'm only doing it for her,' she pleaded lamely.

During the heated exchange between these two, he had sat dumbfounded. In all his life he could never recall his mam attacking Ruby in such a way. They had always been so close, so supportive of each other. Secretly, he was glad that Ruby had been brought down a peg or two, because to his mind she had always entertained ideas above her station. Oh, there were times when he too had ambitions of getting away from Fisher Street, but when it came down to it he hadn't the guts nor the drive, and now, like everyone else, had become trapped here. Not Ruby though. She had never lost sight of what she wanted. That irritated him. Now here was his opportunity to get the better of her.

'Mam says she wants you out,' he declared boldly. Rising from his chair and going to where Lizzie stood, he placed a protective arm round her shoulders. 'If that's what she wants, then you'd best go. I'm sorry, Sis, but it seems you've outstayed your welcome.'

Ruby's gaze fell on her mam's face but there was no response. Lizzie remained unmoved, her hand on the door-knob and the door inching open a little further. 'All right, Mam,' Ruby conceded. 'If that's what you really want?'

'It is.'

She brushed past. When she was alongside that little figure, she was sorely tempted to throw her arms round its neck and promise anything, just as long as the two of them made friends again. But, like Lizzie, Ruby felt that she was in the right. All she ever wanted was the best for her mam and the family. She could see nothing in that to be ashamed of. 'If you want me, Mam, you know where I'll be,' she said softly.

Lizzie's answer was to close the door against her. Afterwards, she remained where she was, her ears tuned to Ruby's departing footsteps, her old heart sore and aching. 'What have I done, our Lenny?' she murmured. 'Dear God above, what have I done?' Part of her wanted to run down the passage and fetch Ruby back. It was wrong to blame the lass for her own sins. Yet another, greater part of her saw how that same sin had made Ruby the woman she was; there was too much of her real father in her. Yet Jeffrey Banks was a good kindly man, and Ruby had inherited those traits as well. Suddenly it was all too painful. In a burst of sobs, she fell against her son. 'I didn't want that to happen,' she cried, clinging to him. 'It ain't her fault. God knows, it ain't her fault.'

'It's all right, Mam,' he said. 'It'll all come right, you'll see.'

But he had a feeling that a lot of water would run under the bridge before that happened. There was something here that he didn't understand. Something between his mam and Ruby that reached too far down for him to see. But then, he was only a man and didn't pretend to know what went on in any woman's mind.

Outside, Ruby hurried away. There was no consolation for her, no reason as to why this parting had happened, and she had seen a side to her mam that shook her to her roots. As she went along, the bitter tears ran down her face and she could hardly see where she was going.

When she climbed aboard the tram, everyone stared at her from the corners of their eyes. She wasn't aware of their curiosity. She only knew that today she had lost her best friend in all the world. And she didn't even know why.

Chapter Sixteen

It was the middle of November, and even though she now had *two* very capable assistants, Ruby was bone tired. The shop had never been busier. It seemed that every woman in Blackburn had decided they would have a new hat. Mrs Cartwright, the blacksmith's wife, was no exception. 'Have you heard from Widow Reece?' she wanted to know. 'My! She's been gone some five months now, hasn't she? And it hardly seems like a day!'

'I had a letter only last week,' Ruby replied. 'Her sister is laid low with a sudden illness, but Mrs Reece is very happy there. The sea air appears to be doing her a world of good.'

The woman tutted loudly. 'I should think it's shedding the responsibility of this business that's given her a new lease of life. Still, there've been many changes for the better since you became the new owner. Everything a woman wants, all under the same roof . . . first a pleasant hour downstairs, then it's off up top to have your hands and nails cossetted. I tell you, Miss Miller, this place has been a real godsend to the women in this town.'

'Thank you. We do our best.' Ruby wasn't in the mood for chit-chat, but the customer must never suspect it.

'It's awful hard, running a business, and I should know, because I hear it every day from my husband.' There was something else she was itching to say, and as she went on she cast her eyes to the mirror and watched Ruby's face. 'Your brother is doing very well. My husband says he's making a fine blacksmith under his tuition.'

Ruby's face gave nothing away. 'I'm glad to hear it,' she said.

'He confides quite a lot in my husband, did you know that?'

'No.'

'Oh, yes. My husband's taken him under his wing, so to speak. I must say, though, I was surprised to hear that you and your mother had fallen out.' When Ruby's hands became still, she was satisfied that she had struck a nerve. 'It's a common thing, I suppose . . . mothers and daughters at each other's throats.'

'We are not at each other's throats.'

'Of course not, dear. But you *have* fallen out, and that seems such a pity?'

With trembling hands, Ruby stretched the veil into position, thinking how much pleasure it would give her to stretch Mrs Cartwright's scrawny neck. Instead, she gently removed the hat and bestowed her very best smile on the astonished woman. Taking the hat across the room, she collected a round box from the top shelf and placed the hat inside. 'That will be four and sixpence, please,' she said crisply.

'Thank you, dear.' Mrs Cartwright ambled across the room, spilling the coins from her purse onto the counter, 'I didn't mean to speak out of turn,' she lied. 'Silly old woman that I am, I feel I've said too much.' She could see how her remarks had upset Ruby and suffered a pang of conscience. After all, Ruby was that rare breed of woman who had carved herself a place in the world of business. 'I really am sorry,' she said sincerely.

'Good night, Mrs Cartwright,' Ruby replied. 'Please, don't concern yourself. I'm not at all offended. It's just that it's been a long day and I won't be sorry to shut up shop and get home.'

'Well, of course. I expect you're looking forward to the holidays too? It won't be long now before Christmas arrives.

Another seven weeks, I think.' She counted the weeks on her slim white fingers. 'My! Doesn't time just fly?' she commented, unable to resist adding slyly, 'Of course, you'll be spending the holidays with your family?'

Ruby merely nodded, deliberately misleading this nosy character. Walking the woman to the door, she saw her safely outside then she quietly pushed the door to. 'With my family?' she murmured sadly. 'Oh, if only I was.'

Just then a slim red-haired young woman came down the stairs. 'Phew! What a rush,' she laughed. 'My legs feel like tree-trunks, and my feet have gone all numb. I'll be glad to get home, I can tell you.' She went straight to the cupboard and took out a bright red coat which she slung over her shoulders, 'So I'll be off for the weekend. See you Monday morning at eight sharp.'

Before Ruby could answer, another voice was heard. 'Everything's ship-shape upstairs, and I'm ready for home myself.' It was Katie, the girl whom Ruby had taken on first of all. Climbing down the stairs, she smiled at Ruby. 'It's been so busy,' she moaned. She was plumper now, but more sure of herself. She also went to the cupboard and collected her coat. When they saw Ruby going to the desk, the two young women came and stood close by, their faces bright with anticipation. 'Have a pleasant break,' Ruby told them, placing a long brown envelope into each of their outstretched hands. She never regretted paying these two their wages. They earned every penny. Both had been carefully chosen from a long list of applicants, and with each passing day, Ruby was more convinced that she had made the right choice.

When the young women had departed, Ruby made her rounds. It was now entirely Ruby's responsibility. There was no one else to answer to, and no one else to whom she could turn for advice. The success or failure of this business rested entirely with her, and she shouldered the burden well. Widow Reece had agreed to Ruby's financial proposal, and her own solicitor had sanctioned it. The seventy guineas were duly paid over, and the terms were set for monthly instalments to be made on the remaining balance. Although Ruby was loath to admit it, the debt was a great source of worry to her, but then, when she had accrued enough money, her plans were put into action; the upstairs was opened out and the business took a huge leap forward. It made life a little easier, although there was still a long way to go before the debt was satisfied and the business was truly hers.

She took one last look around the upstairs, noting with satis-faction the wide comfortable chairs and smart little footstools, the small handbasins and long narrow mirrors. It was all very satisfactory. Downstairs the same.

A few moments later, Ruby had locked the premises and was hurrying on her way. 'Goodnight, m'dear, and God luv yer,' a lonely old soul whispered as she passed by him. Drunk and glowing, with round cheeks and a vivid nose, he had his tattered old hat pulled down and his holey muffler tucked into the top of his scruffy overcoat. Ducking and dancing over the flagstones, he was obviously the worse for drink. 'Goodnight to you too,' Ruby returned, chuckling beneath her breath. 'Seems like you've started the festivities early, you old rascal.' His cheery spirit drove home her own awful loneliness.

As she went on her way, the night pressed down, like a dark cold mantle settling over everything beneath. It hadn't snowed yet, but it was in the air. Already, the signs of Christmas were everywhere; bright lights and coloured displays in the shop windows, a mighty tree especially planted right in the centre of Market Square, and children all eager and bright-eyed as they gazed at the toys in the shop windows.

The sharp cutting breeze whipped up and swirled the dust from the pavements. Ruby shivered and pulled her coat tighter about her slim form, pushing her way through the hurrying bodies bent against the wind and hastily making their way home to cheery firesides. Even at six-thirty, people were rushing here and there, some with their empty hands thrust deep into their pockets, and others with great shopping bags filled to the brim. In the growing darkness, boisterous children played round every corner, laughing and shrieking, and filling the night with a sense of joy.

Normally, Ruby would have caught the tram to Derwent Street, but on this occasion, Mrs Cartwright's comments played strongly on her mind. Her thoughts were in turmoil as she decided to walk home. She felt agitated, unsure of herself. Everything she had ever wanted was within her grasp, yet there were times of late when her heart was empty and unfulfilled.

Many times she had been tempted to go round Fisher Street, hoping to mend the rift between herself and her mam. But she was afraid; especially when Dolly and the twins came to see her on a Sunday morning and told her, 'Our mam's still angry with you.' Ruby felt there was more to it all than met the eye. On her many subsequent visits to Derwent Street, Dolly would ask innocently, 'Why don't our mam love you any more?' and Ruby's heart would break all over again. Lenny never came round, but the childer kept Ruby in touch, so she had to satisfy herself with second-hand knowledge of his blacksmithing talents.

During these past months, Ruby was so beset by her responsibilities that she found neither the time nor the energy to go visiting. But she had kept in touch with Maureen through Dolly, and messages were regularly sent back and forth. Ruby was delighted that her friend's health was stable, and Maureen was full of praise for Ruby's rise in the world. Johnny was often mentioned. It seemed that old Thomas had retired and Johnny was now in charge of the stables. His wages had trebled, and Oliver Arnold had come to greatly value him.

Ruby loved to hear about Johnny. She missed him. She missed her friend and ached for her family. She now had the finest clothes in her wardrobe. She was invited to speak at business functions and ladies' circles. Each month saw a little more of her debt paid off and a small amount put by. Her name was written in bold letters over the door of her own establishment, and she was looked up to by all who entered. She should have been deliriously happy but she wasn't. Looking for excuses, she put it down to the long demanding hours and the strain of building up her fortunes. This is what you've always wanted, she convinced herself, believing that in the end her mam would be talked round and all of this would be worthwhile. It will take time, that's all, she promised herself. And our mam can't shut me out for ever.

From what Dolly had told her, Ruby knew the first move had to come from Lizzie, for if Ruby was to go round to Fisher Street, Lizzie would only dig her heels in all the more. She tried not to dwell on the awful upset between herself and her mam. Instead she compensated by launching herself into her work and never allowing herself a minute to think. Now though, the upstairs at the milliner's was completed and things were beginning to run a little easier. Suddenly the days stretched before her like an endless road, and the awful loneliness crept up on her when she least expected it.

As she drew nearer to her home, the streets grew quieter and her thoughts grew calmer. Always, they came back to her mam and the family. And to Johnny. The memory of how he had loved her was somehow deeply comforting. There was talk that he had taken up courting one of the Lowther girls from Sharrock Street, but it was only talk. When Ruby made casual mention of it in her last letter to Maureen, she had dismissed it out of hand. 'He's never said anything to me,' she told Ruby. 'And I don't recollect him ever bringing a girl home.' Maureen's comforting words lifted a shadow from Ruby, yet she didn't dwell on it, because whenever she let herself think too long of Johnny, it always left her feeling desperately confused.

Letting herself into the house on Derwent Street, Ruby took

off her dark ankle-length coat and hung it on the peg behind the door. The house struck cold. Going straight into the parlour she located the oil lamp on the dresser, pumped it up and set a match to the wick. Almost at once the room was transformed. Flickering yellow strips of light licked the walls and illuminated the darker corners. The parlour was homely rather than grand, furnished in a style that would have pleased Lizzie. There was an oak dresser with a tall scalloped back containing four shelves which held an array of pretty floral plates with matching cups and saucers; there was a big round table with six stand-chairs about it, and a splendid crystal lamp decorating its centre. At the door a long green cord curtain kept out the draughts, and the windows were dressed with pretty tapestry curtains that reached down to the warm brown-patterned carpet. The mantelpiece was dressed with a green silk-tasselled cover, upon which were set a number of silver and porcelain ornaments.

Before going to work that morning, Ruby had arranged the paper and firewood in the grate, ready for lighting. She put a match to it now. Once the flames began bursting through, she carefully placed the smallest pieces of coal on the wooden pyramid. Soon the coals were glowing and the parlour was bathed in a rosy glow. Warmer now, she went into the scullery and placed a full kettle on the gas ring. Once this was lit, she took the wooden tray from behind the bread-bin and laid out a cup and saucer, the sugar bowl and milk-jug, and, after making herself a cheese and pickle sandwich, placed it on a plate and put the plate on the tray. While waiting for the kettle to boil she put two small spoons of tea into the brown earthenware teapot. Soon the tea was brewed and she returned to the parlour, where she placed the tray on the table.

Ruby didn't sit down immediately. Instead, when a terrible feeling of loneliness washed over her, she went to the mantelpiece where she reached up to probe her fingers behind the clock. From here she withdrew a small envelope. Taking out the picture of the sacred heart, she turned it over and read:

Pray for the soul of Edward Miller,
late of this parish, and laid into
consecrated earth, on this day
28 December
in the year of Our Lord,
1893

Crushing the picture to her breast, Ruby allowed the memories to flood in. 'I still miss you, Dad,' she murmured. The tears threatened but they didn't flow. Since coming to this house, Ruby had shed too many tears. And so she reverently replaced the envelope and its contents, saying in a soft voice, 'If you've got any influence up there, will you bring Mam and me back together, for I can't get to her no how?' She hoped the Lord was listening. And, with that thought uppermost in her mind, she sat at the table.

An hour later, when she had eaten, washed the dishes and then lazily bathed herself at the kitchen sink, Ruby wrapped herself in her night-robe and, nursing a cup of steaming cocoa, settled down by the fireside. The warmth made her feel tired. 'Shan't be long before I'm off to my bed,' she murmured. That was another habit she had started; talking to herself was something she had never done before. But then, she had never felt the need. There had always been someone to talk to; in fact there had been times in that little parlour on Fisher Street when the noise was deafening. Now it was the silence that was deafening.

Oliver Arnold saw how quiet and nervous Cicely had been all night and was genuinely concerned. Luke, on the other hand, was full of himself. Since Jeffrey Banks had suffered a small breakdown in health and had been persuaded by Cicely to take himself away on an extensive tour of Europe, Luke had been left in joint charge of the foundry, together with the general manager, a most respectable and conscientious fellow who had been in Banks's employ for some years. Unfortunately for Luke, he and the fellow had a mutual distrust of each other, and he could see no opportunity to further his underhand activities. But he wasn't too perturbed. He still had his father's trust and was continuing to rake in a very handsome profit from his false accountings. In fact, the fraudulent practice of buying inferior raw materials and doctoring the figures was now so cleverly accomplished that discovery grew less and less likely. Consequently he grew more and more confident.

It was true he was disappointed at not having been put in sole charge of Banks's in his father-in-law's absence. But then again, he could wait. If there was anything he had learned, it was the art of patience; especially when it had been intimated by Jeffrey Banks that he might not want to take up the reins again on his return. In which case, Luke's main motive for marrying Cicely might not have been in vain after all.

'Are you all right, my dear?' Oliver asked her. She looked so pale and worn it worried him.

'Why, yes, I'm fine thank you,' she answered with a smile. 'Although the child is particularly restless in this last month. I won't deny I'll be glad when it's born.'

'Of course. As you say, it will be a good thing when it's born.' He himself was hoping she would produce a boy to make him proud. But, looking at Cicely now, he couldn't help but wonder whether she was strong enough to bear any child. For all her assurances, he still wasn't convinced that everything was as it should be. At the dinner table she had barely spoken a word, and now, when the three of them were seated in the drawing room, he was compelled to voice his fears. He had grown very fond of his daughter-in-law. She was gentle and kind, considerate to a fault and immensely affectionate towards himself and his darling Ida. In fact, she was everything Teresa could never be. It was to Cicely that he addressed himself. 'I know it isn't any of my business, and I hope you'll forgive me, my dear, but . . .' He paused, still unsure about voicing his fears. Determined though, he took a deep breath. 'Is there anything wrong between you and my son?' From the corner of his eye he saw Luke stiffen.

Cicely was visibly taken aback and, before she could answer, Luke's abrasive voice cut in. 'Wrong?' he said in a shocked voice. 'Good heavens no. Cicely and I are perfectly suited.' He grinned. 'If that wasn't so, do you think we'd be making you a grandfather?' He leaned over from his chair and fondly stroked the back of Cicely's frail hand. 'We're still as much in love as on our wedding day, isn't that so, my lovely?' he asked in his most charming voice. The touch of his bare skin against hers was nauseating to him, but he forced himself to endure it a moment longer.

Cicely's answer was a polite nod which did not altogether satisfy either of the men.

The next hour was whiled away in small talk when Arnold inquired after Cicely's father and she in turn replied. 'He's enjoying the sights of Paris, I believe.' Luke had little to say but was busy in thought. And his thoughts were of Ruby. Only last night he had teased her home address out of her red-headed assistant. Since then he had spent a sleepless night and many an hour planning how he might show himself at her front door. This very night he meant to do just that, and was deeply excited.

Though his sexual needs were rampant and there were any number of women eager to satisfy him, it was always Ruby who fired Luke's imagination. He detested the way she had come up in the world and made a name for herself. He loathed ambition in a woman because it was unseemly. But he could forgive it in Ruby. Especially if, after all this time, she was to receive him with favour – a beautiful woman who was also clever. He smiled to himself. It would be a new experience for him.

As for the docile and irritating Cicely, he had never really been able to touch her in the way he liked to touch a woman. In her present state, large with child and cumbersome of movement, she was even more repulsive to him. *He wanted Ruby*. He had always wanted Ruby. The more he thought of her, the more he savoured her. She made him feel good inside. She fired him with longing. Just now, his cowardly spirit was glowing from the wine he had downed at his father's table and he could hardly wait. Oh, yes, he wanted Ruby like he had never wanted anything in his life. And tonight he would have her!

Johnny wasn't surprised when the bell rang on the wall above his head. With his stable work finished and the groom gone home some hours since, he had taken a moment to sup a warming brew of tea with old Thomas.

'There you go,' Thomas muttered from the depths of his chair. 'The buggers are ready to be tekken home.' He was snuggled into a blanket, with his feet tucked into a muffler on the floor and his gloved hands wrapped round the hot mug which Johnny had just given him.

'You'll be all right, won't you?' asked Johnny, thrusting his arms into his coat. It was a bitter night outside – but not in here, not when he had piled the stove high and the room was cosy.

Thomas was his old crusty self. 'Away with yer!' he grumbled. 'I may have been retired from my work, but I don't take kindly to you staying over whenever yer think I'm falling apart. Well, I ain't dead yet, so bugger off. Go on. BUGGER OFF!'

'Now then, old fella,' Johnny gently chided, 'it's not because I think you're falling apart that I stay over, and well you know it,' he lied. In fact, he was staying over more and more these days. And now that Maureen was more able to negotiate the stairs with the help of her mam, he wasn't needed quite so much at home. He smiled to himself. Women were an independent lot, he thought. And his mind flew straight to Ruby.

'Aye, well, just remember, young man, there's many a trick left in the old dog yet!' Thomas raised his head proudly, but the plain truth was that he didn't have so many 'tricks' left. Until recently, he was able to do any number of tasks around the stables, but now he was riddled with gout and even walking was becoming painful.

Not wanting to hurt the old fella's feelings, Johnny went along with him. 'I know that,' he answered. 'All the same, you can't deny there are times when two pairs of hands are better than one. Especially when a mare might be foaling. And then, like tonight, when we know there'll be need of the carriage. So stop feeling sorry for yourself.'

'And don't you be so bloody lippy.' Thomas sank his chin into his neck and began muttering, 'Anybody'd think I were on me last legs, so they would. What with you and that snotty-nosed lad they've put at my beck and call, I'm watched like a sodding 'awk!'

Kindly ignoring him, Johnny checked the fire and drew the curtains against the night. 'I'll not be long,' he promised, 'I expect it's Miss Cicely wanting to be run back to Preston New Road.'

Thomas laughed out loud. 'Yer stubborn bugger! You know very well it ain't "Miss Cicely" no more.' He jerked his head up, saying in a snooty voice, 'It's Mr Luke and his wife . . . that's who they are. Why can't yer bring yerself to say his name, eh?'

Johnny gave no answer. Instead, he strode across the room and halfway out the door when Thomas guffawed, ''Cause he's a bastard, is that it?'

Johnny looked at him for a moment. Suddenly he was angry, but didn't know who he was angry at. 'Well, it was *you* who said it this time,' he chuckled. 'But you're right. Luke *is* a bastard and I'll not deny it. See you later.' Before Thomas could retaliate, Johnny was gone running down the stairs two at a time and smiling to himself as his anger faded to amusement. Thomas was always a law unto himself. But what he'd said was true. Johnny couldn't bear the name of that man on his lips. Thomas had hit the nail on the head and no mistake. Luke Arnold was a bastard, and as far as Johnny was concerned, he would never be anything else. Cicely might not know it, and then again it might be a mercy that she didn't, but her husband was cheating on her at every turn. The man was worse than a street cur, chasing after bitches on heat.

Luke Arnold was making other enemies too – men on the foundry floor. Since Ted Miller was killed, no man had dared to set themselves against their employers, but there was a growing unrest. Things were being muttered about. When questions were asked, fear stilled the men's tongues and as yet nothing damning had carried beyond the foundry walls. But everyone knew it was only a matter of time before the voices grew louder and the truth spilled out. Johnny hoped it would be sooner rather than later.

'Yes, of course I'll take care of her. I always do.' Luke appeared suitably offended at his father's concern. He smiled at Cicely and draped his arm round her, drawing her close to him. 'She's very precious to me,' he said. Then he shook his father's hand and hurried Cicely into the waiting carriage.

Oliver Arnold stood by the door as Johnny manoeuvred the carriage out of the drive and on to the main road. 'I wonder, Luke, have you really changed?' he asked the emptiness. 'Or is it just an old man seeing only what he wants to see?'

Sadly he turned and went inside that great quiet house. Lately, he too had sensed the simmering atmosphere at the main foundry. He had long toyed with the idea of reviewing the situation of

Luke's free hand there. He was suddenly glad that he had not yet succumbed to Luke's wishes and given over even more responsibility.

'But then, he has done nothing to rouse my suspicions,' he reminded himself. Still, he mused, there was something, and perhaps it wouldn't hurt to keep a closer eye on things in the future? He may be old, but Oliver did not see himself as a fool. In his heart, he had always known that the only real worthwhile person in his life was the young girl who slept soundly upstairs. Ida was his everything, and unbeknown to anyone but the solicitor concerned, he was already taking steps to protect her inheritance from his greedy grasping son.

Easing the carriage into the kerb outside the big house on Preston New Road, Johnny jumped down to help Cicely out. He was surprised when Luke remained inside. 'See the lady into the house,' he told Johnny. 'Then you can run me into town. I have urgent business there.' He smiled sweetly into the dimly-lit street. 'Goodnight, my dear,' he called to Cicely. 'Don't wait up. I could be some considerable time.'

Cicely's answer was to pause in her steps and turn to look at him. She said nothing for a moment then she softly pleaded, 'Don't leave me, Luke. Not tonight.' She had not felt well all day. In spite of his callous treatment of her, there were times when she desperately needed him, but he was never there. When he merely smiled and waved his hand in a gesture of dismissal, she stared at him in a strange manner. In that moment Cicely recalled Ruby's words. 'He'll make your life a misery,' she had warned. And Ruby had been right.

'Please, let me get you inside, out of the cold,' Johnny urged. Earlier, he had wondered whether Cicely knew of her husband's womanising, and now he saw his answer. It was there in her sad face. And he loathed the fellow even more.

Once Cicely was safe inside and her maid attending to her, Johnny returned to the carriage. 'Hurry, you fool!' came the other man's voice. 'Take me to Derwent Street.'

Johnny was shocked when the destination was given. 'That's where Ruby lives,' he muttered to himself as he took his place up front. Maureen had told him that Ruby was renting number four Derwent Street. Oh, the times he had been tempted to go and see her. The times he had walked along Montague Street and stared into the long broad street where Ruby had set up home. But always he came away. Later, when Maureen asked if he had managed to see her, he replied angrily, 'If Ruby wants to see me, she knows where I am. I've never been a man to go begging.'

As he drove into Derwent Street, visions of a certain night came into Johnny's tortured mind. Visions of Ruby, all dressed up as a lady and dancing in this bastard's arms? The more he thought about it the more furious he became, until he was ready to drag his seedy passenger onto the street and leather the hell out of him.

'Here. Stop here,' came the instructions from behind. Johnny visibly relaxed. The carriage was coming to a halt halfway down the street, some way from the house where Ruby lived. So, whoever Luke Arnold was visiting at this late hour, it certainly wasn't Ruby. But then Johnny knew all along that she would never really entertain such a low creature.

Climbing down to the pavement and coming to the front of the carriage, Luke stared up. In the light from the street lamp, his face was a study in cunning. 'Wait here,' he instructed. He laughed then. 'Don't grow impatient. I might not be in such a hurry to go home tonight.'

Johnny's answer was deliberately to turn away and busy himself with the tangled leather reins. He thought of how Luke had left his wife without a second thought, and it was all he could do not to jump down and put his fist in that grinning mouth. He heard low laughter and unstable footsteps moving away, and shifted his dark brooding eyes towards that detestable figure going down the street. He watched how it lumbered along, squinting in the dim light, noting the door numbers, then cursing before moving on; moving ever on, towards the top of Derwent Street.

When suddenly he stopped, Johnny's heart missed a beat. Slowly, he edged the carriage on, placing it where he could see more easily. 'Whoah, there,' he hissed in a harsh whisper, gently tugging at the reins as the horses strained their great bulging muscles to go on. When the carriage was halted almost opposite the house where Luke was waiting, Johnny leaned forward in his seat and focussed his anxious eyes on the top panel of the door. The number four was clear enough. 'No!' he muttered, his suspicious eyes fixed on that door in disbelief. 'It can't be Ruby's house.' And yet Maureen had definitely said number four. Craning his neck, he watched Luke knock on the door and he waited with bated breath, to see who might answer. He prayed it would not be his Ruby.

When the knock came on the door, Ruby was deep in thought, toying with the idea of going to see her mam tomorrow, when she would thrash this thing out once and for all. But then she recalled Dolly's innocent words on her last visit here. 'Our mam says we ain't to talk to you. She says you've chosen what you want and you ain't welcome in her house 'til you come to your senses.' The child had been close to tears, asking, 'Why don't our mam love you no more, Ruby?' These were harsh words that stuck in her heart like a clenched fist.

The knock came on the door again. 'All right,' she called impatiently. 'I'm on my way.' Hurrying down the passage, Ruby gasped at the cold that lingered there. Drawing her robe tighter about her, she leaned her ear to the door and asked, 'Yes? Who is it?' She still hadn't got used to living on her own, and was always wary.

The voice came back in a hoarse mutter. 'It's Lenny.'

'Lenny!' She was thrilled. At last, he had found his way to Derwent Street. It was a start. Happen her mam wouldn't be far behind. Taking the big iron key from its nail above, Ruby slid it into the lock and flung open the door. The night was pitch black and the man's shadow was vaguely familiar. Her ready smile lit up the darkness as she quickly ushered him in. 'I'm glad you decided to visit me,' she said. Even as she spoke, a terrible suspicion flickered through her mind. But there was no time to satisfy herself that it was Lenny because the shadow was suddenly in the passage and the forceful weight of his body was sending her backwards.

In the half-light, Ruby recognised the intruder, 'Luke!' She struggled but his arms were like steel bands locked round her.

'Oh, so you haven't forgotten my name then?' he leered, his smile dark. His warm breath fanned over her face and she realised with horror that she was in terrible danger. 'Been dreaming of me, have you?' he chuckled, bending his head to hers and pressing his mouth to her neck. He laughed out loud when she fought like a wild thing. 'Now, now. Let's not spoil it,' he murmured, pressing his hand over her lower face and propelling her backwards into the parlour. 'It's been a long time, Ruby my love, and we've a great deal to catch up on, wouldn't you say?' Against his brute strength she was helpless.

'Take your filthy hands off me and get out of my house!' Mustering all her strength she pushed him towards the door.

He laughed at her futile efforts. '*Your* house, is it?' he mocked. 'My, my! We're quite the little property owner, aren't we?' Gripping her wrists harder he said cuttingly, 'What would you do, I wonder, if it was all taken away from you? How would you survive without your precious business?' Jerking her backwards, he insisted, 'Somehow I don't think you'd like it . . . back in the gutter. Too high and mighty for all of that now, aren't you, eh?' He saw the shock on her face, and misunderstood. 'That frightens you, doesn't it?' He grinned, bending his head to kiss her. 'Oh, but there's no reason for you to be paupered, my sweet . . . not if you're nice to me, there isn't.'

A terrible fight ensued when he locked her arms behind her back and began tearing at her nightclothes with his free hand. In a minute both robe and gown were flung on the floor and he was softly laughing. Terrified, yet determined that he wouldn't violate her, Ruby kicked and squirmed; but her fierce resistance only served to excite him. 'I've waited a long time for this, my beauty,' he told her. Keeping one arm secured round her slim body and bunching her small fists tight behind her back, he had her at his mercy. His glittering eyes ravaged her nakedness. He had dreamed so often of seeing her like this, and now here she was, flesh and blood in his arms, stripped before his eyes and ripe for him to take her.

He was in a frenzy, clumsily undoing the buttons on his trousers. His released member was thrust out large and erect as he feverishly probed between her thighs. He crushed her over the table, roughly opening her legs with the force of his body and crying out with delicious pleasure when he felt the heat of her skin against his belly. When Ruby frantically twisted away in an attempt to grab the centrepiece from the table, he snatched her towards him, ignoring her cries of pain.

'You little witch!' he snarled, gripping the tablecloth and sending the whole lot crashing to the floor. 'I've waited long enough for this. *Too long for you to stop me now!*'

He whipped the back of his hand against her face. The blood spurted from her lip, but she wouldn't be still. She twisted and turned, and when he leaned close she pinched the skin of his face between her teeth and bit hard, until she could taste his blood in her mouth. Jerking back in agony, he was like a thing demented. Still he held on to her. He meant to have her. He was too far gone to stop now.

Out in the street, Johnny waited. He couldn't believe it, but he couldn't deny it. Ruby had opened the door to Luke Arnold, and with a smile had taken him inside. Unable to sit still, he had climbed down to the pavement and was pacing up and down. In the light from the street lamp, he could see that the door was slightly open. 'Couldn't even wait to close the door,' he muttered angrily. In his mind's eyes he could imagine them inside. But then he *couldn't* imagine them. He couldn't bring himself to believe it even now; even though he had seen the way Ruby had welcomed him. He paused beneath the street lamp and stared at the door. He lowered his gaze, and then he brought it back to the door again. His whole body ached with fury. It was all he could do not to tear in there and turn the whole house upside down. He began pacing the pavement again. Pacing and stopping, staring at the house, then pacing again. 'She wouldn't,' he murmured. 'I was mistaken. It can't have been Ruby.'

Almost without realising it, he was walking across the cobbled road towards the house. Suddenly he was outside the door, staring up, wondering whose house it could be, for he had made himself believe that it was not Ruby's. But I saw her with my own eyes, he recalled. He was in a turmoil. He was bitterly jealous and deeply ashamed. Ashamed for her, ashamed that she could stoop to entertain such a low creature. But then he was ashamed of himself. How could he believe that it was Ruby he had seen? It was someone who looked like her, that's all, he told himself. But then he knew there was no other woman who looked like her. Ruby's image was etched on his heart, seared into his mind, so how could he ever mistake her?

Confused, he turned away, retracing his steps. It was then that he heard the muffled cries from inside. Before he drew a second breath he was leaping up the steps and flinging open the door. Going down the passage at a run, he could hear the cries more clearly now. There was no mistaking Ruby's voice. Enraged, he kicked open the parlour door. The scene before him was one of mayhem; chairs turned over and ornaments smashed on the carpet. The tablecloth and centrepiece strewn on the floor, and beside it Ruby's nightclothes. She was naked, pressed backwards over the table with the half-clothed Luke on top; his face was scarred and bleeding, and the blood was dripping on to her bare shoulder, making a weird meandering pattern across the pale, creamy skin. As Johnny rushed forward, Ruby's wide frightened eyes swivelled towards him. The fear was superimposed with shame. In her helplessness, she turned away.

What happened next took place with such speed that Ruby could never recall it completely. All she felt was the weight snatched from her, followed by the confusing sense of a struggle, the nauseating crack of knuckle against bone as one man fell sideways and the other stood over him. Then Johnny's face staring at her, wilder and angrier than she had ever imagined. 'How could you let him into your house?' he asked. His voice was low and condemning as he collected the tablecloth from the floor and threw it over her nakedness.

'I didn't know,' she said lamely, sinking into the chair. Every bone in her body was hurting. Out of the corner of her eye she saw Luke's misshapen form. Johnny's vicious punch had struck home, sending him across the room. Like a rag doll, he lay sprawled unconscious in the armchair. 'He said he was Lenny,' she explained in a whisper. When Johnny gave no answer to that, she assumed that he thought her a liar. 'I'M NO LIAR!' she snapped, flinging the cover tighter round her body. Struggling out of the chair, she stood defiantly before him.

He wanted so much to take her in his arms, for he believed

her, and knew he had been wrong. Yet he sensed that if he was to put out one hand to her, she would shrink from him. His instincts warned him it wasn't right for them yet. She wasn't ready for him. So instead he asked simply, 'Why don't you go home, Ruby?'

She realised his good intention, but she resented it. 'I *am* home,' she answered. Her dark eyes blazed into his. Beneath all that defiance was a mountain of shame. 'And anyway, I'm not answerable to you.' She glanced scornfully at Luke's prostrate figure. 'Thank you for what you did just now, but I'd be grateful if you would just get him out,' she said. 'I don't expect you to believe it, but he did trick his way into this house.'

He continued to look down on her with questioning eyes. In spite of himself there still lingered the smallest of doubts. After all, he had seen her smile at Luke at the door. 'You don't believe me, do you?' she demanded.

'Does it matter what I believe?'

Unable to contain her anger she hit out at him with her fist. It made no impact. He stood his ground while she screamed at him. 'I don't give a damn whether you believe me or not, so *get out* and take him with you!' The awful incident had left more than its physical mark on her. She had been terrified for her very life, and now the relief was too much. That Johnny had seen it all was both shocking and infuriating to her. The bitter tears fell down her face. 'I said, get out!' she cried, going to the door and willing him away from this awful scene.

It was a moment before he moved, and when he did it was to stride across the room and tower over her. 'You don't belong here,' he told her in a soft firm voice. 'Go home to Lizzie . . . to your family.' When he saw that he had touched a nerve, he dared to go on, 'Better still, let me take care of you.'

Ruby felt herself weakening. What she wanted was to fall into his arms and admit she had been wrong. Yet what she actually did was to order him in a stiff voice to: 'Leave me alone.'

For what seemed an age he continued to look down on her. She seemed so vulnerable. The tears were still wet on her face, and even though she wanted him to think how independent and able she was, he saw the helpless little girl in her. His heart turned over at her beauty. One minute he was looking into her upturned face, and the next she was in his arms and they were kissing; a tender warm kiss filled with passion and a love that could not easily be denied. 'Come home,' he said, gently holding her, his dark eyes softly smiling.

She drew away, shaking her head. 'I am home,' she said again. 'My mam turned me out, and now I'm turning you out. Please go.' She knew if he stayed, she would be lost.

He made a deep groaning noise in the back of his throat. 'You little fool!' he said in a controlled voice. 'What is it that drives you? Is it money? Is it power? Is it the fear of leaning on someone else?' He shook his head slowly from side to side, 'Oh, Ruby. RUBY!' Placing his two hands on her shoulders, he held her there. 'Whatever it is, don't you think the price is too high?'

'What do you mean?' The touch of his strong hands on her shoulders was wonderful.

'I mean that nothing in the world is worth the loneliness you must be feeling right now.' He jerked his head sideways and moved his dark eyes round the room. It was a pleasant enough place, but it had no heart. 'Look around you, Ruby. Where's your mam? Where are your brothers and sisters? Your family? Where are the things you've always cherished? I thought the very reason you wanted to move out of Fisher Street and go up in the world was so you could give your family a better life?' He looked on her with the love of a man who believed that love may be lost. 'Lizzie adores you, but she can't give up what she's had all these years, and you're wrong to expect it. Her home is where she brought up her children. It's that damp and draughty house where she lived content with her husband for all those years. *You* were born in that house . . . all the children were. Your father was buried from that house.' He shook her gently. 'Oh, Ruby, can't you see what I'm saying? Your mam is afraid of you.'

'Afraid of me?' She was shocked. Until she recalled how violently her mam had reacted when she asked her: 'What is it you're afraid of?'

'You're asking her to do something that she just can't do. You are asking her to be a stranger in a strange place. Think hard, Ruby. Think of her, and you'll see that it would break her heart. She has her memories, and they're all back in that house on Fisher Street. Lizzie will never set foot in this house. It's *you* who will have to go to her.' He stroked her hair. 'And then there's *me*. No man will ever love you more.' His voice hardened when he felt her stiffen beneath his hands. 'I want you to be my wife, but I have little to offer.'

Without another word he went to the chair and lifted Luke's limp body on to his shoulder. As he passed her, he kept his eyes straight ahead, a tall proud man who had been rejected yet again. Will I never learn? he asked himself bitterly as he went out of the house and into the street. God knows, no man could ever love her more than me. But it wasn't enough. She was a woman who had made herself a good business, and he admired her for it. Sadly for him, though, it had carried her further away, and now he could never see her making a life with him.

From the doorway, Ruby watched as he threw his passenger into the carriage. When he glanced back at her, she stepped quickly into the passage and closed the door. For a long time she leaned against the door. The sound of the carriage wheels made a distant and musical sound against the raised cobbles. Another moment, and then the silence was thick and unnerving. Coming into the parlour, she looked with sorry eyes at the wreck there. She heard Johnny's words: 'Where's your mam? And your family? *Nothing in the world is worth this loneliness.*' The tears fell freely down her face. 'Oh, Mam, what have I done to us?' she murmured. Something else he'd said came into her mind. 'I want you to be my wife.' How many times was he prepared to say those wonderful words to her? Perhaps never again.

It was some time later, after the parlour was tidied and she had bathed, that Ruby went to bed. She couldn't sleep. Her thoughts were too alive with memories of Johnny. I can't give it all up, she reminded herself. It was too hard, and now I have it all. But what *did* she have? More and more, his words had made her think. On the one side, she felt that it ought not to be just her who made sacrifices. On the other, she began to realise the 'sacrifices' she was already making, and it opened her eyes.

Weary and undecided, she closed her eyes and drifted into a restless sleep. Her mind was alive with images; Johnny, Luke; her mam. And all she could hear was Luke's veiled threat: 'What would you do if it was all taken away?' What did he mean by it? Nothing of course, she told herself. He was a loud-mouthed thug who thought with his tongue. Her business was safe from him. She was safe from him.

Ruby gave herself up to sleep. But, even as she slept, disturbing events were taking place that would determine her future.

A week later, an official-looking gentleman paid a visit to Scarborough and Widow Reece. When she opened the door, he was secretly delighted to see that she looked harassed and somewhat unhappy. 'Mr Lawton, ma'am,' he said, in a warm polite voice. 'From the firm of Lawton, Armitage and Castle.'

At once her expression lifted. 'Oh. Please, come in.'

Removing his trilby, he followed her into the parlour. It smelt of medicines and liniment. He didn't want to stay long so he promptly declined her offer of tea and biscuits. At that same moment, there came a sharp knock on the ceiling. They both glanced up, 'I'm sorry,' Mrs Reece muttered, going at a painful rush across the room. 'It's my sister. She's very poorly, you know.'

He waited patiently while she went up the stairs, then down again, then up and down once more; the first time to collect a bowl of hot water, and the second to carry out a tray of refreshments. When she came into the parlour again, she brought the pungent smell of disinfectant with her. 'Forgive me,' she said, settling into the chair and regarding him carefully. 'My sister needs constant attention, otherwise I would never have entertained your business proposal.'

He smiled knowingly. 'Of course. I can see that you have been placed in a difficult situation. It's very sad when loved ones fall prey to illness.'

She was impatient now, and desperately tired. 'Please, I have little time to spare for you.'

'Indeed,' he agreed. Without delay he opened his briefcase and withdrew a sheaf of papers. 'It's all there,' he explained, putting them into her gnarled fingers. 'My client has been extremely generous and, if I may say, you will not better his offer.'

After she had glanced through the documents, Widow Reece looked up with regret. Most of her money was gone, used up by endless medical bills for herself and her sister. Now it was necessary to employ constant care round the clock for her, and this was why he was here. This man had offered her a lifeline, and though she would rather not have deceived Ruby in this way, she felt there was no alternative.

His client was willing to buy Ruby's debt. On top of that, he was prepared to pay a hundred guineas for the privilege. How could she refuse?

'Are we agreed then?'

'On two conditions.'

'Name them.'

'First, the transactions must be approved by my solicitor. Second . . .' Widow Reece lowered her gaze. She felt guilty. But the guilt was fleeting. Ruby was young and strong, and what did it matter who owned the debt? Ruby would pay it off, just as she had promised, and be none the wiser. 'The second condition is that Ruby's monthly payments should still come to my solicitor. That way she will not know that I've sold her debt.' Her face flushed with shame.

'Agreed.' In fact, his own client had issued the very same instructions. Ruby Miller must not yet know of this transaction.

With the proposal generally agreed, he took his leave. It needed only a consultation with Mrs Reece's solicitor, and the deed would be done. He felt he had done a good day's work here. And no doubt Luke Arnold would wholeheartedly agree with him!

Chapter Seventeen

Ruby was desperately worried. Christmas and the coming New Year should have been her busiest time. Instead, she had already been forced to dismiss one of the assistants, and most of the time she herself was standing idle.

'It's very quiet in here, my dear.' Lady Lloyd-Briggs was still a loyal customer. Looking into the mirror, she roved her concerned gaze around the shop. 'I recall the time when this place was bursting at the seams,' she said curiously.

'Oh, we've had a rush this morning,' Ruby lied shamefully.

'I'm not complaining. It's nice to have the shop all to myself,' she replied with a warm smile. All the same, she was most surprised at the lack of customers. It was very odd. Very odd indeed.

Later, when the shop was closed and she was alone with her thoughts, Ruby pored over the accounts ledger. It told a shocking tale. Already she was a month behind with the payment to Widow Reece's solicitor, and it looked increasingly as though she might have to ask for some more time.

With a heavy heart, she put pen to paper, explaining the situation which she promised was 'of a temporary nature', and then she posted the letter on her way home. More and more, Ruby was learning what a cold unfriendly world it was when you aspired to heights that left your loved ones behind.

In the days that followed, Ruby arrived daily at the shop, dressed smartly with her hair brushed to a deep shine and a heart filled with determination. The customers will return, she told herself. But they never did. And she was at a loss to understand why.

One Monday morning she arrived at the shop, looking every inch the businesswoman, in her expensive brown jacket and long straight skirt. She wondered whether today would be any better. Unfortunately it was not. In spite of her splendid window display and a sign telling the world she had reduced the price of her best hats, only two customers took advantage; one was a passer-by, and the other was Lady Lloyd-Briggs. This time she made no comment about the lack of customers. Instead, she told Ruby, 'Foolish women, my dear. Some of them wear a hat, not to cover their hair but to smother their pitiful brains,' leaving Ruby to wonder at such an odd statement.

Before the day was over, there was a great deal more for Ruby to wonder about. She received an official letter that shocked her to the core, and a certain visitor who brought news of a deeply disturbing nature. The letter was from Widow Reece's solicitor and read:

Dear Miss Miller,

While we are sympathetic to the fact that the business appears to be in decline, we must nevertheless act in the interest of our client. We are advised not to accept your offer of late payment.

In accordance with the agreement, we issue notice that, unless the outstanding amount of the entire monies owed is paid forthwith, you will forfeit all claim to the lease, contents, and goodwill of the milliner's establishment.

To this effect, our representative will call on you shortly with formal papers and requisition order.

Ruby was still reeling from that letter when her unexpected visitor arrived.

'Are you all right, miss?' As Katie handed Ruby a freshly brewed cup of tea, she couldn't help but notice her employer's tired features and preoccupied manner.

'I'm fine,' Ruby assured her. Right now, the last thing she wanted was company.

'It doesn't look as though we're going to be busy, does it?' Katie observed dolefully.

Ruby agreed, 'Give it a while longer, then take yourself off home, Katie,' she said. 'There's no point in both of us wasting our time.'

'Well, if you're sure?'

Ruby nodded impatiently. 'It's all right,' she assured the young woman. And Katie didn't argue.

Alone with her uneasy thoughts, Ruby mulled over these past weeks. Somehow, everything she had ever dreamed of had gone horribly wrong. She felt bone-tired and desperately unhappy. Had all of her ambitions been for nothing? Where did she go from here? So much had happened. Not just to the business either. There was her darling mam and Johnny.

She didn't know herself any more. And what of Luke? A bad enemy if ever there was one. And yet, hadn't she brought it all on herself? Stop tormenting yourself, Ruby Miller! she chided. It's time you stopped blaming yourself for everything that's happened.

Her mam was still on her mind. Oh, how she adored that little woman. But through all these years Ruby had never really understood her. Why was she so set against Ruby making good in the world? Why was it that every step forward she took, her mam fought to drag her back? Even her friendship with Cicely had been frowned on. Ruby could not forget the delight on her mam's face when she knew that friendship was at an end. It was

Josephine Cox

all a mystery to her. Every question she had ever asked was dismissed with the angry statement: 'Folks like us don't mix with gentry, and we don't yearn for more than the good Lord sees fit to give us, my girl!'

It was a view which Ruby found increasingly difficult to share. She was puzzled and hurt because Lizzie found no pride in her daughter's considerable achievements. Instead, she chose to turn her back on her. She was a hard little woman when she set her mind to it, and yet there was such a deep and special love between these two women that it broke both their hearts to be parted in that way. Ruby knew that. But, just as her mam felt that she was right, Ruby felt that she also was doing what she believed in. They were both proud and stubborn, and each was determined that the other would give in first. Lizzie had her reasons for being stubborn and afraid, and Ruby had her reasons for clinging to what she had worked so hard to achieve. Lately, though, just as Johnny had said, all she seemed to have achieved was unbearable loneliness. 'Oh, Mam, whatever have we come to?' she groaned, closing her eyes and picturing that dear familiar face.

When the door opened and the little bell above tinkled through her thoughts, Ruby gave a little cry and sat bolt upright in the chair. She was shocked to see Cicely coming hesitantly into the shop. 'Cicely!' At once she was on her feet and hurrying towards the door. 'Oh, Cicely, it's so good to see you.' It was then that she realised the woman was unwell. More than that, she had a dark red bruise just below her cheekbone. Ruby didn't need to ask who had done that to her, because she instinctively knew. Luke was not averse to hitting any woman; it wouldn't matter that this one was his wife and bearing his child.

'Here, come and sit down,' Ruby said. Taking her by the arm she guided her to the chair she had just vacated. Cicely was extremely large with child and obviously uncomfortable. She wedged herself into the chair and looked up at Ruby with large

458

sad eyes. 'I had to come and see you,' she said in a low voice.

Ruby was thrilled. She wanted so much to throw her arms round that poor soul and hug her tight. But there was something in the other woman's manner that stopped her. 'You shouldn't be out,' she chided gently. 'How long is it to the birthing?' she glanced at the great mound on Cicely's lap. 'Not long by the looks of things,' she chuckled.

'Three weeks . . . maybe four.' Cicely's eyes grew moist. 'I don't really care.'

'No, no. You mustn't say that, Cicely.' Ruby was astonished. 'I'll tell you what, why don't I make you a strong brew? We can go into the back room, you can have a rest and we'll chat for as long as you like. Afterwards I'll take you home. What about that, eh?'

Cicely shook her head. 'I haven't come to socialise,' she said in a sharper voice. 'And I can find my own way home. I have a carriage waiting for me outside.' Her blue eyes hardened. 'I've come to ask you something, and I would appreciate the truth.'

Ruby was puzzled. 'Of course,' she said, 'I have no reason to lie to you, Cicely.' In two strides she had gone to the door and turned the CLOSED sign over. Normally she stayed open at lunch-times, but judging by Cicely's face, she realised it might be better if they were not interrupted. Coming back to her, she sat in the opposite chair. 'What is it you want from me?' she asked curiously.

Cicely fidgeted. Instead of answering Ruby's question straightaway, she observed, 'You've come up in the world.' She glanced around, admiring what she saw. 'I always knew you would.'

'Cicely, please. You said you came here to ask me something,' Ruby entreated. Now, when those pale blue eyes looked at her, she saw such pain there she was visibly moved. 'What is it you want to know?'

In her wildest dreams Ruby could not have prepared herself for the question which Cicely put. '*Are you having an affair with my husband?*'

At first, Ruby felt like laughing out loud. God above! What self-respecting woman would ever have an affair with Luke Arnold? But then she realised that here was the woman who had actually married him. Cicely was gentle and caring, she was vulnerable and kind, yet he had taken her for his own sinister purposes and used her as though she was a thing without feeling. 'Oh, Cicely, do you really have to ask that question?' Ruby whispered. 'You must know it isn't true.' Her heart went out to this woman whose past friendship she still greatly valued. 'You said I was to answer you truthfully,' she reminded her, 'and the truth is this . . . I detest your husband, and I always have. And even if, by some remote possibility, I wanted an affair with him, my affection for you and the friendship we once enjoyed would not allow it.' She shook her head as though ridding herself of the idea. 'Believe me, Cicely, I could no more have an affair with Luke Arnold than I could become Queen of England.'

Cicely stared at her for a moment before fishing in her bag and holding aloft a folded note. 'Then how do you explain this?' she asked in a hostile voice, thrusting the note into Ruby's hand.

With trepidation, she unfolded the note. It was a small grubby piece of paper. At the top was her name, and beneath her full address: number four Derwent Street. She was instantly curious. 'What does it mean?' she wanted to know. 'Where did you get it?'

'I found it.' Cicely's burning gaze never left Ruby's face. 'I found it in Luke's bedroom after he was put to bed on Saturday night. He arrived home in a terrible state. From the look of him, he'd either been drinking or fighting . . . or both.' She pointed to the paper in Ruby's hand. 'I can only assume this fell out of his pocket. Even if your name hadn't been there,

I would have known your address.' She didn't admit to the many times she had considered visiting, and then dismissed the idea. 'There aren't many people who don't know the success story of Ruby Miller.' She gave a small sound that could have been a laugh. 'You're the talk of Blackburn town. There isn't one member of my own household who hasn't followed your upward career with interest.' She lowered her eyes, reluctantly admitting, 'Myself included.'

Ruby returned the paper. 'I honestly can't explain this.' In fact, she had been wondering how Luke found out where she was living.

'Are you telling me he would carry your address in his pocket for no reason?' Before Ruby could answer, she insisted, 'He's been to your house, hasn't he? Don't lie to me, Ruby. I need to know. And I have no intention of leaving until you tell me the truth. If you are not having relations with Luke, why would he come to your house?'

Ruby had wanted to spare Cicely the shocking truth, but she knew now that nothing else would satisfy her. 'I wish you hadn't found that note,' she murmured, 'I don't want to hurt you.'

Cicely laughed then, and it was a hollow painful sound. 'I've been hurt many times since Luke and I were married,' she replied. 'Only I never thought you and I would be sitting here, having this kind of conversation. I am hurt by that.'

'First of all, Cicely, I was telling you the truth just now when I denied that your husband and I were having an affair. And I meant what I said when I told you that I have always detested him. Right from the start, I took against him. Unlike you, I saw through his charming ways. You remember I didn't want you to wed him. That was why we went our different ways. I've always been sorry about that. I miss you, Cicely. I miss our friendship.' She saw the other woman's face soften and was encouraged. She took a deep breath before going on, 'Yes. You're right. He did come to my house on Saturday night.' She looked into Cicely's eyes with compassion. 'What I'm going to tell you now will be painful for you.'

Cicely squared her slim shoulders. 'I want to know everything,' she said.

Ruby did as she was asked. She told Cicely exactly what had taken place that night . . . how Luke made her believe he was Lenny; how he forced himself on her. She left nothing out, including her own stupidity at being taken in so easily. And as she went on, Cicely didn't even bat an eyelid. Instead, her face grew hard and stiff, and her fists were clenched so tightly that her bony white knuckles poked through her skin. 'It was Johnny who dragged him off.' As she finished, Ruby felt the shame burn through her. Lowering her gaze to the floor, she murmured, 'I'm sorry you had to know.'

Cicely reached out her hand and took Ruby's slim fingers into her own. 'I'm not sorry,' she said softly, 'I'm glad you told me. And I'm glad my suspicions were wrong, Ruby, for I've never stopped loving you. You were always my one and only friend.' Her smile was sweet always, only this time pleasure was tainted by pain. 'You were right about him, Ruby. He's everything you warned he would be. At first it was good, but that didn't last long.' Her voice broke. 'Oh, Ruby, I've been so unhappy. Why didn't I listen to you?'

'Because you were lonely,' Ruby told her kindly. It was good to feel Cicely's hand in hers. The friendship was still there. Perhaps even stronger than ever. 'We're all lonely at times,' she admitted. 'We've both made mistakes, Cicely, and now we're paying for them in different ways.' Suddenly the thought of Luke loomed up between them. 'What will you do?' she asked. 'Will you stay with him?'

'No. My father is home. I shall have the child in his house.' She shook her head as though imagining him there. 'All of this will come as a shock to him. You see, I wasn't the only one who failed to see the badness in Luke.'

At the door, the two women embraced. 'You will come and see me, won't you, Ruby?' Cicely asked.

'Just try and keep me away!' she told her. Suddenly, she sensed there was something else on Cicely's mind. 'What is it?' she asked, when Cicely seemed reluctant to leave.

Cicely was unsure as to whether she should speak her mind. It was a dangerous thing that she had found out. At length, she answered, 'You were truthful with me, Ruby, and I must be the same with you. Some time ago, the manager of Arnold's main foundry came to see Luke. He seemed very agitated and afraid. I know I shouldn't have done it, but I listened, and what I heard has to do with trickery and fraud. It seems that Luke and this man have been cheating Luke's father; embezzling funds and using inferior materials for the new construction inside the foundry. According to what the manager came to tell Luke, some of the men have been calling meetings, and it appears they're about to organise a strike. He was terrified they'd be found out and imprisoned.'

'Have you told Oliver Arnold?' Somehow Ruby wasn't surprised to hear that Luke was a thief.

'Not yet. Luke found me outside the door and threatened all kinds of retribution if I didn't keep my mouth shut.' She shivered. 'If he knew I'd told you, he would beat me within an inch of my life.'

Ruby was furious. 'He'll never beat you again. Go to your father's and stay there. Tell him what you've told me. Let *him* go to Oliver Arnold with the news. He'll deal with it.' She gently shook her. 'Promise me, Cicely. You won't go back to him?' When Cicely agreed, Ruby hugged her warmly. 'God bless,' she whispered. She felt Cicely tremble in her arms. 'You mustn't be afraid. You're doing the right thing, I know.'

'Ruby?'

'Yes?'

'Luke is saying that he'll break you . . . take your business from you.'

Ruby smiled sadly. 'My business may well be taken from me, but it won't be because of anything *Luke* can do.'

'You're wrong.' Before Ruby could reassure her, she went quickly on, 'I've heard things, Ruby . . . listened when I shouldn't. I know that Luke has bought your debt from Widow Reece. Since then, he's started a whispering campaign against you . . . belittling your high standards and persuading your customers away. You know he can do that. He mixes with very influential people.'

Ruby was horrified. 'Why in God's name would he do such a thing? Why would he use a substantial amount of money to buy my debt, then set out to ruin me? Surely he would suffer too?'

'Not Luke. He's cunning. You see, he plans to kill two birds with one stone. No doubt ruining you would give him a great deal of satisfaction. But he's also playing another game. He's already talking to Gabriel's outfitters. Once he forecloses on you, he stands to make a healthy profit by selling the business to them.'

Ruby was stunned. It was one blow after another. Before she could respond, Cicely added softly, 'There's something else. Something terrible. And you of all people have a right to know.'

There was fear in Cicely's face, and it transmitted itself to Ruby. Suddenly, she didn't want to know what was in her friend's mind. For a long awkward moment the silence between them was crucifying, then, in soft hushed tones, Cicely told her the shocking truth. 'Luke ordered your father to be murdered.'

The colour drained from Ruby's face. She couldn't speak. The words wouldn't register; they went round and round, bouncing off the walls of her mind. LUKE ORDERED YOUR FATHER TO BE MURDERED . . . MURDERED . . . MURDERED . . .

YOUR FATHER. Of all the dreadful things she knew him to be guilty of, she had never suspected this. And yet it all came flooding back: the way her father had grown morose and troubled; the deep conversations he had with her mam when he would speak of his fears. Lizzie always said he would get himself into trouble if he didn't watch whose path he crossed. 'Be careful what you say, Ted. The gentry are a powerful lot!' That's what she had warned, and Ruby had heard it with her own ears. *But neither she nor her mam had dreamed in their worst nightmare that his life was truly in danger.* A great tide of rage washed through her now, red searing rage that lifted her very soul. 'Where's Luke now?' she murmured, and her eyes were bright with burning tears. Now, there was murder in her own heart.

Cicely was mortified. 'No, Ruby! It's a matter for the authorities,' she cried. 'I shouldn't have told you. Oh, I wish I hadn't told you.' She was becoming distressed.

Forcing herself to stay calm, Ruby assured her, 'There's nothing for you to worry about.' She gently propelled her out of the shop and into the carriage. 'Go to your father's house,' she said. 'I'll come and see you soon, I promise.'

As the carriage pulled away, Cicely leaned out of the window. 'You won't do anything foolish, will you?'

Ruby shook her head. A moment later she had gone back into the shop. Katie was accompanying her client down the stairs. 'I'm going out,' Ruby told her, collecting her coat from the cupboard, 'and I don't know how long I'll be.'

Her emotions must have been written on her face, because Katie stared at her, 'Is anything the matter?' she asked with concern.

Ruby cursed herself. 'I'd better go,' she answered. 'There's something urgent I have to attend to.' Throwing her coat round her shoulders, she grabbed her bag and rushed out, leaving both women gaping after her. In the street, she hailed a cab. 'Arnold's

Foundry,' she told him breathlessly. 'The big one the other side of Eanam.'

Clambering into the cab, she leaned back into the seat where, with incredible calm, she began to plan how she would see Luke Arnold behind bars before the day was out. But first she wanted to meet him face to face. As the cab sped out of Blackburn centre, Ruby's heart was black with loathing. Never before in her life had she felt like committing murder. But she felt like it now.

'He killed my father,' she muttered through her tears, 'I should have known.'

'God in Heaven, what's wrong, child?'

Oliver Arnold jumped out of his comfortable chair when Cicely burst into the room. She was distraught and dishevelled. With a cry she fell into his arms.

'You have to stop her,' she begged. 'He'll hurt her, I know he will.' In a torrent of words she told how she had watched Ruby come out of the shop and get into a cab. 'She was wild because of what I told her.'

She confessed to him then, about the awful things she had overheard between Luke and the manager, about how his son regularly beat her and then forbade her to leave the house. 'Oh, and I told Ruby that he had her father killed.' She was sobbing now. She had not seen the shock on Oliver's face. 'If anything happens to her, it will be my fault. You've got to stop her. Please, stop her!'

When she gave a groan, he saw her face crumple in pain and feared she was going into early labour. Yelling for the housekeeper, he carried Cicely upstairs and laid her on his own bed. It was only a moment before the older woman came in at a rush. 'Get the doctor quickly!' he ordered. She saw how it was and, without acknowledgement, ran from the room to summon help. It was some ten minutes before the doctor arrived. By that time, Cicely was in the full throes of labour, and all but doctor and housekeeper were banned from the room.

'She's in good hands, sir,' the housekeeper assured Oliver as he left.

Satisfied that everything was in hand, he took his leave. Downstairs in the kitchen, he told the astonished scullery lad, 'Go as fast as you can and send the authorities to the Eanam foundry.' Excited, the boy went off at a run while Oliver hurried to the stables. Johnny was seated on a stool, repairing one of the hunter's best saddles. It was only a matter of minutes before he had readied the carriage and was driving his master away at a furious speed.

Seated up front, his dark eyes intent on the road, he wondered why the master would want to get to the foundry in such a rush. In all the time he had worked for him, he had never seen him so agitated. Something was very wrong, and that was a fact.

'Get out of here, you blasted fool!' Ruby had forced her way into the office and now, frightened by her accusations, Luke was desperate to shut her up. The cowardly manager stood back while Luke grabbed Ruby and, twisting one arm behind her back, thrust her out on to the platform. 'One more word,' he warned, 'and there might be the most awful accident.' Gripping his fingers round her neck, he bent her head down. 'See there,' he laughed, pressing her hard against the railings and staring at the bubbling cauldron beneath. 'You wouldn't want to end up in that, would you now?'

He cursed when the manager came up behind him. 'Don't be a bloody fool, man,' he hissed, prodding Luke in the side. 'The game's up. I won't be party to *another* murder. If your wife's blabbed to this one, who *else* has she told, eh? Answer me that!'

'Murderers, the pair of you!' Ruby shouted defiantly. 'You killed my father, and I swear I'll see you hang for it.' Enraged, Luke smacked a hard flat hand across her mouth. But she wouldn't be silenced. From the corner of her eye, she saw one of the steel-workers staring up, wondering what was going on. 'GET THE POLICE!' she yelled. From the way she was struggling, the fellow could see that she was in some sort of difficulty, but her voice was lost in that great place.

Outside, Oliver impatiently waited for the carriage to come to a halt. Quickly clambering out, he ordered Johnny to: 'Come with me. There might be trouble here.' The two of them strode across the yard and into the choking heat of the foundry. There, beneath the gantry, a group of men had gathered anxiously. Almost immediately Oliver and Johnny were approached. 'There's summat going on up top,' one of the workers said. 'Two of the chaps are making their way up now. Your son's up there, and if I'm not mistaken I reckon that's Ted Miller's lass he's got hold of.' He cast his eyes upwards to indicate the spot where the struggle was taking place. When he looked down again, Johnny was gone.

'LET GO OF HER!' Johnny's voice sailed above the rafters. He had climbed the outer platform and swung right above to where Ruby was fighting to free herself. She wasn't afraid. She was too distressed at her father's untimely fate to be frightened. But, oh, she was grateful to hear Johnny's familiar voice.

'Be careful, Johnny,' she warned. She couldn't see him, but knew he was somewhere above. And there was no doubt in her mind that Luke Arnold was insane and desperate. The men below had long suspected his underhand dealings and now some were already on their way up, their faces like stone, and every one of them out for his blood.

'KEEP BACK OR I SWEAR I'LL SEND HER TO A FIERY DEATH!'

To make his point, he edged her closer to the railings. Ruby hadn't been afraid until now but when she saw that great open-mouthed cauldron bubbling with white-hot metal directly below, her heart came into her mouth. 'I MEAN IT!' Luke yelled again, twisting his neck to see where Johnny was coming from. Like a trapped rat, he glared at the workers who had climbed to the far end of the platform. And, sensing a real danger that he would topple Ruby over the railings, they stopped where they were.

Emerging through the cluster of men who had found their way up, Oliver Arnold stood before them, his eyes seeking out his only son. 'Give yourself up,' he coaxed. There was no love in his heart for this man who now seemed like a stranger, had *always* seemed like a stranger to him. But he knew he must not let his loathing show through. 'You don't want to hurt her, do you?'

He glanced down. Uniformed officers were infiltrating the area, fanning out like ants below. 'It's too late, don't you see?' he said in a controlled voice. 'There mustn't be any more bloodshed.' He began walking towards Luke. 'I know what's been going on. But we can talk. You and I can talk it through. What do you say?' All the while he advanced he was aware of Johnny, slowly descending behind the trapped man. He knew he had to hold Luke's attention. 'Look below, son. The authorities are here. If you give yourself up, it'll go easier for you.'

'Liar!' He twisted Ruby's arm and laughed aloud when she winced. 'Don't take me for a fool. If I'm going, she's going with me.' Suddenly he was crying, blubbering like a baby, 'You're two of a kind, you and her. *You* never wanted me either. All my life you've treated me like an inferior. You never gave me a proper chance to prove myself. Everything I've ever done has been for you. DON'T YOU KNOW THAT?' Swamped by his own memories, he was unaware that one of the officers was climbing the platform immediately behind him.

'You're wrong, son.' Oliver kept advancing. 'I've done everything a father could do for you. But it's not too late. Maybe we can put it right?'

In that moment, Luke suspected they were quietly closing in.

'I did warn you!' he yelled, pushing Ruby further over the railings. The intense heat came up to her in relentless waves. She felt her senses going and feared she would never leave this place alive.

Suddenly, all hell was let loose. Johnny had seen the officer's intention of leaping on to his unsuspecting prey and the fear of God shot through him. 'NO!' he yelled. But it was too late. The officer sprang. Luke spun round and, as he went to throw both himself and Ruby over the top, the whole platform lurched sickeningly to one side. There were shouts as the men ran for their lives. Ruby felt Luke's grip loosen, then as he tumbled past, he took her with him.

The last thing she saw was the mouth of that horrifying crater looming up towards her. She heard Johnny's frantic cry, and Luke's mind-splitting scream as he slid beneath the sizzling surface. All around her was mayhem. And then nothing at all. Only the searing heat and the white bubbling liquid. In that last moment the faces of her loved ones flashed through her mind. There was no terror, only bitter regret.

Part Four

December 1895

GOING HOME

Chapter Eighteen

'There's a fella at the door, Mam.' The twins came bounding in from school, red-faced and excited. 'He's got out of a posh carriage an' all,' Frank went on. He slapped Ralph hard when the lad pushed himself in front to tell Lizzie, 'And the dirty old horse plopped in the street right outside our door.'

Lizzie had been playing with Lottie on the rug in front of the fire. Snatching the infant into her chubby arms, she said impatiently, 'There's no "posh" fella coming here, I can promise yer that.' Putting the young 'un to the floor, she told it to: 'Behave yerself while yer mammy gets the tea, eh?' When it giggled and hugged her skirt, she laid a gentle hand on its head. 'Aw, yer a little darlin', that yer are,' she declared. Swinging round, she demanded of the twins, 'Where's our Dolly?'

'She's talking to that posh fella,' Frank said proudly. And Ralph added indignantly, 'She'd talk to anybody, that one!' There was a sudden sharp knock on the door and the two of them soon scooted out of the scullery and down into the yard. 'We ain't done nothing wrong, honest our mam,' wailed Frank as Ralph dragged him out.

'We're going to play in the cellar,' he informed Lizzie, 'and we ain't coming out for nobody!' She had threatened them both with hell and high water after she discovered that they'd played

473

truant last Friday week. They hadn't played truant since, and they hadn't forgotten her warning either. Every time there was a knock on the door they feared it was the 'man from the Church school, come to take 'em away'.

Lizzie laughed when she heard the cellar door bang behind them. The smile didn't live long on her face though, because here was Dolly telling her, 'There's a gentleman come to see you, Mam.' Dolly was growing fast, making a lovely girl. She spoke with a soft refined voice that put Lizzie in mind of Ruby.

'Come to see *me*?' she asked. 'Are yer sure, lass?' She was saddened by the way her family was growing up so frighteningly fast.

It was a man's voice that answered. 'Yes, Lizzie,' it said. 'I've come to see you.' Jeffrey Banks's figure seemed to fill that humble little parlour.

'God bless and love us!' Lizzie exclaimed, unconsciously patting her dishevelled hair. She still had her old pinnie on which was slightly stained where the flour had showered it when she was baking the bread. Momentarily flustered, she told Dolly, 'Take Lottie into the scullery, sweetheart. She can help you butter the scones for tea.' Dolly gave her a little smile then took Lottie by the hand and walked her into the scullery, closing the door behind them.

Taking his trilby off, Jeffrey laid it on the chair. 'You have a delightful family, Lizzie,' he said. 'They're a credit to you.'

Lizzie's heart was going nineteen to the dozen. Jeffrey Banks! Here, in her own little house. What did he want? Suddenly she was fearful, not knowing if she should ask him to sit down or to leave. She chose to ask him, 'Come in, sir. Sit yerself aside o' the fire. There's no need to stand on ceremony in this house.' When he was seated, she offered, 'Would yer like a brew?' It was a strange thing, but whenever she was in this good man's company, her shyness was short-lived. He'd always had that effect on her.

She watched his expression change. At first he too had been self-conscious, but now he was smiling with a warmth that soothed her heart. His hair was greyer than when she had last seen him, and he stooped more at the shoulders. But then, like the rest of them, he had suffered a blow. Cicely was widowed, and her new son was without a father – but then, happen no father at all was better than the one who spawned him, thought Lizzie bitterly. In one way or another, Luke Arnold's badness had touched all of them.

'No, thank you, Lizzie,' he said softly. 'It's only a short visit before I take my daughter and grandson away for a while.'

'How is the lass?' Lizzie came to seat herself opposite.

'She's bearing up very well.' He shook his head in disbelief. 'When I think what she went through with him . . . well, it doesn't bear thinking about. What hurts is that she couldn't bring herself to confide in me, her own father who loves her.'

Lizzie smiled knowingly. 'That's what yer call pride,' she explained sadly. 'It's a shocking thing, but we all let it rule us at some time or another.' She was remembering how it was with Ruby, and how she had let her down badly. All these years Lizzie had believed it was shame that set her against the gentry and made her loathe Ruby's driving ambition to raise herself up in the world; an ambition that had come from this man. It was only lately that she had been made to wonder whether her bitterness wasn't born out of foolish pride and not shame – a pride that had been deeply wounded when this man persuaded her into his bed. He didn't force her. She went willingly. And ever since Ruby was born, that poor lass had been made to pay for her mother's disgrace. Even now, Lizzie couldn't fathom her own feelings. All she knew was that they had caused her darling Ruby so much pain and Lizzie would regret that for the rest of her days. 'What is it yer want with me?' she had to know.

He gazed at her, searching for the right words for he knew

how proud Lizzie was. 'I want to help,' he said in a whisper. 'For Ruby's sake, and because it was my son-in-law who left you widowed. I have more money than I know what to do with.' Seeing the indignant look on her face he bowed his head. 'I'm sorry.'

''Tain't your fault,' she declared wisely. 'Though I still blame you for paying Ruby all that money when she left your household. If it hadn't been for that, she would never have bought into the milliner's and never have left home. That money opened a door for her which I had always prayed would stay shut, 'cause I've lived long enough to know that there ain't no happiness to be got from trying to be summat you ain't.' Seeing how sad he was, she brightened her tone. 'All the same, it's good of yer to come here and offer yer help, but like I say, this family don't need it, thank you.' Lizzie had already received a visit from the ailing Oliver Arnold, offering the very same. In the five weeks since the tragedy, that sorry man had aged a hundred years. Johnny even had to help the poor fellow up the steps to her front door.

Now, Lizzie told Jeffrey Banks what she had told Oliver Arnold. 'Folks like us don't need no help from the gentry,' she declared, and never was she more proud than at that moment. 'I've managed all this time, and God willing I'll manage again.' She stood up, head high and her eyes bright. 'Is that all yer came to say?'

He knew he was being dismissed. 'Ruby was always a good friend to Cicely,' he said, then glancing towards the scullery door, lowered his voice. 'Whether you like it or not, Lizzie . . . Ruby is *my* daughter as well. And I feel responsible.' Almost as soon as the words were out of his mouth he knew he had said the wrong thing because Lizzie stiffened and her brown eyes darkened.

'I thank you for your trouble, sir,' she said, in a servile manner which made her the stronger of the two, 'but this family looks after its own. Whatever needs to be done will be taken care of by us.' Before he went, she had to make certain. 'You once made me a promise,' she whispered anxiously. 'You told me that our secret would never be told.' While she waited, her heart was in her mouth.

'And it never will, Lizzie. Not by me, anyway.'

'And not by me,' she declared with relief. No one must ever know that Ruby was not her beloved Ted's daughter.

Like the gentleman he was, he took her hand into his and placed the softest kiss there. 'You're a good woman, Lizzie Miller,' he murmured. 'And, God forgive me, but I think I'll always love you a little.'

His action had moved her deeply, and she was too full for words. Instead she squeezed his fingers in her own. As he went out of the parlour, she said in a murmur, 'God keep yer safe. Look after the lass and the bairn.'

He looked at her for a moment before replying, 'We'll be gone for three months . . . coming back with the spring. That's time enough for the wounds to heal, don't you think, Lizzie?' he asked hopefully.

'Yer right,' she told him with a warm smile. 'A good friendship will travel through all weathers, I reckon.'

His fond gaze lingered on her, then he placed his trilby on his grey hair and departed. Before closing the front door he paused to look back down the passage, and there she was, lively and bright, her pretty brown eyes following his every move. He didn't speak. Neither did she. But it was there, like a beacon burning between them, that special emotion that had drawn them to each other over twenty years ago. He knew now that they would always be there for each other, Lizzie and he. Once it was a burning passion. Now it was a gentler thing. But it would endure for ever. It was enough.

Chapter Nineteen

Johnny's eyes lit up at the doctor's words. 'Well, we've done our tests and the results are as we expected. The injuries to her left side are healing well, and she has almost full use of her arm.' He added with a shake of his head, 'I don't need to tell you how lucky she is to be here at all. If she hadn't been caught by the steel band that holds the cauldrons, well . . .' He rolled his eyes upwards.

Johnny knew only too well. When he saw Ruby falling through the air, he suffered emotions he would never want to feel again as long as he lived. And, oh, the enormous tide of relief and shock when her fall was broken by the steel cradle. Even so, it was a while before they knew whether she was alive. Like the others who watched it happen before their eyes, he was utterly helpless. The platform crumbled, and it was a miracle that more people hadn't been killed. As it was, a young police officer was lost together with the man who had brought the whole tragedy upon them. There were those who said that Luke Arnold met the end he deserved. But Johnny had seen it, and he believed that no man, however evil, should have to die like that.

Interrupting his thoughts, the doctor went on, 'Of course, she will need to attend the infirmary for some time after she's discharged. The nerves in her left side were severely damaged.

An injury like that takes time to heal. But, thankfully she's a woman of remarkable determination.' He smiled, and in answer to Johnny's earlier question, answered, 'I see no reason why she shouldn't go home by the end of the week.' He knew his next words would lighten Johnny's heart even more. 'Perhaps you would like to give her the good news?'

'Whatever it costs, she must continue to have the very best attention,' he asserted.

The doctor nodded in his official manner. 'Apparently, there's no problem in that direction. I understand it's all taken care of. The young lady herself has given instructions with regard to funds.' He patted Johnny on the shoulder as he saw him out of the office. 'You're a very lucky man. Ruby will make a glorious Easter bride.'

Johnny made a wry expression. 'That's if she'll have me.'

'What? You mean you haven't asked yet? Well, from what I've seen of the way her eyes light up when she sees you coming down the ward, you've no need to worry.' He had only been married himself these past few weeks, and he fully understood what Johnny was going through.

Johnny wasn't so certain. 'You don't know her,' he said. 'Besides being beautiful and courageous, Ruby is also headstrong and fiercely independent. I've lost count of the times before when I've asked her to wed me,' he confessed. But with a heart as big and strong as an ox's, and the determination not to take no for an answer this time, Johnny left the doctor's office and made his way towards the ward.

Ruby saw him coming. She had been watching the clock for over an hour. Now at last he was here, and oh, he looked so handsome in his new white shirt and dark blue tie, with his long legs clad in brown cords and his dark jacket slung casually over his shoulder. 'There you are, miss,' chirped the little Irish nurse, 'I said he'd be on his way, didn't I now? And there was yourself thinking he'd forgotten all about visiting.'

She tutted, playfully digging Ruby in the shoulder. 'Oh, it'll be all kissing and cooing, that it will,' she teased, hurrying away when Johnny drew closer. As she went by, she had a naughty thought. 'Sure I wouldn't mind a fella like that meself,' she muttered. 'By! He's a long-legged, strong-looking bloke.' In fact, as she looked back and Johnny glanced up, she gave him a cheeky wink. But he had eyes only for Ruby. 'Behave yerself, Bridie girl,' she chided. 'Like all the best ones, he's already spoken for.'

'How are you feeling?' Johnny thought Ruby had never looked more beautiful. Her short-cropped dark hair was a perfect frame for that delightful face. Tonight, her eyes shone as though a light was switched on inside. Like a raven's wing, they were neither blue nor black, but speckled with a midnight sheen that took his breath away.

'Don't I get a kiss then?' she asked teasingly.

Her unexpected words took him aback and he blushed to the roots of his hair. 'Why! You brazen hussy!' he laughed, placing the bunch of chrysanthemums on the bedside locker. Leaning over he slid his hand behind her neck and brought his mouth down on hers. Her lips were soft, deliciously warm and inviting. One minute he sensed her need of him, and the next she was sitting back, leaning against the pillow and smiling coyly at him. He was wonderfully astonished. She never failed to take him by surprise.

'Have you been to see the doctor?' She knew he had, because she knew him.

'Yes.'

'What did he say?'

'First, I want you to tell me how you are.'

'Hmh! You always were a bully, Johnny Ackroyd.' She wanted to tell him so much. She wanted him to know how badly she had missed him since his last visit. Days and nights she had thought and thought about him, about her family and her life. For the first time in a very long while she felt at peace with herself. At long last she had given in to her love for Johnny; a deep abiding love which had crept up and overwhelmed her.

Ruby wanted to tell him all of these things, and oh so very much more. But she didn't know whether he would ever forgive her for the way she had so foolishly rejected him; not once but time and again. She still wasn't certain that he wanted her as much as he did before. And even if he did, and though she had all the words off pat, she still didn't have the courage actually to speak them. In all her life Ruby Miller had never been afraid of failure. And, the one time when it meant so much to her to succeed, her courage deserted her. 'I'm fine,' she answered, cursing herself for her cowardice. 'See for yourself.' She sat up straight and swung her legs out of the bed. She stretched out her left leg and made an effort to reach high with her left arm, but it wouldn't go all the way and she groaned with frustration. 'Still, I can move my limbs with greater ease now,' she told him, 'and there's very little pain.'

In that moment she had mustered enough bravado to tell him what was in her heart. But just then the little Irish nurse came hurrying down the ward. 'Shame on yer!' she called, gently taking Ruby's ankles one in each hand and tucking her legs back under the bedcovers. 'What will folk think of yer . . . showing yer legs to all and sundry?'

Johnny smiled. 'Nice legs though, don't you think?' he said with a cheeky grin.

She couldn't help but agree as she went about her duties. 'Yer as bad as each other, sure yer are,' she chuckled.

'You can see for yourself that I'm doing very well. I have these exercises every day and they're doing what they're supposed to do,' Ruby explained. 'Now it's your turn. What did the doctor tell you just now?'

'More or less what you're telling me, except that you'll need to come in for exercises after you're discharged from here.' It was obvious that Ruby was working hard towards a complete recovery. But then she was not the sort to feel sorry for herself. 'Are you in much pain, Ruby?' He guessed she wouldn't tell him the whole truth.

'Some,' she admitted. 'But it's getting less and less.'

'Ruby?' His heart was beating so hard he feared it would leap straight out of his chest. 'There's something I want to ask you.' He had the wonderful news the doctor had just given him about her coming home soon. But there was another excitement in him, and that wouldn't wait any longer.

'Oh?' For one fleeting wonderful moment she wondered but she dared not believe. 'What is it?' She made her voice sound casual, even though her every nerve end was tingling with anticipation.

His mind was running ahead. 'Marry me,' it cried. 'Marry me.' But only he could hear it. His mouth formed the words. They played on his lips and took his breath away. Unable to contain them any longer he then blurted out, 'I know I said I may never ask you again, but I must. I want you to walk down the aisle with me. Be my wife. Oh, Ruby . . . say you will?' If she refused him now, he would walk away and never ask again.

Slowly, she brought her two hands up to his face, and with the gentlest of touches bent his head towards her. He was astonished to see the tears tumble down her long lashes. 'Don't you know how much I love you?' she whispered. 'Marry you?' She shook her head. 'Oh, sweetheart. Nothing in the world would make me happier.'

Ruby had thought she would never say those words. But she had been to a place where everything was crystal clear. After her terrifying experience, she had suffered more than physical pain. Lying here in this lonely infirmary, she had plenty of time to put things into perspective. When she feared she was about to die, there was only one regret that burned through her soul: the knowledge that she had lost everyone she had ever loved. Thanks to the good Lord, she had been given another chance. And this time, she would not waste it on empty values. 'I love you, Johnny,' she murmured, and the love inside lit up her face.

At first he couldn't believe what he was hearing. When he realised that at long last she would be his wife, he let out a great whoop of joy. Spinning round, he yelled to the watching patients and their amused visitors, 'DID YOU HEAR THAT? WE'RE GETTING WED!' A great cheer went up, and through it all Ruby was laughing and crying. There was bedlam from one end of the ward to the other until Sister Macarthy marched through the door and put an end to it.

Ruby had made Johnny promise to keep the wonderful news to himself until today. It was Friday, and he had brought her home from the infirmary in the carriage. 'It's so good to be back,' she said, coming into the parlour with her arm linked in Johnny's. Seated round the cheery fire were all those she knew and loved; the childer, old Thomas puffing at his pipe, Maureen and her mam, Cicely and Lizzie. It was good to see them all here.

Lizzie ran to greet her. 'Oh, lass, welcome home, bless yer heart. Welcome home.' Suddenly everyone was crowding round and she was hugged from all sides. Through it all, Johnny kept a firm hold on her.

Ruby hugged them back and then was seated in a chair. With her lovely eyes shining, she broke the news. 'Johnny and I are getting wed.' There was instant uproar. Cicely ran and embraced her again, Maureen cried into her hankie, and the childer started fighting amongst themselves.

Lizzie cried buckets. 'Come here, me darling lass,' she

laughed, covering her daughter in kisses. 'And to think I were afraid you'd never be nobody's darling.'

Ruby had an answer to that. Leaning into Johnny's strong arms, she gazed round the room at all those lovely people. 'How could you think that, Mam?' she asked softly. 'While I have all of you, and my man,' she looked up into his face with adoring eyes, 'I'll always be somebody's darling.'

Lizzie started crying all over again. Dipping her hand into her pinnie pocket, she took out her big brown purse. 'Lenny, go to the pub on the corner and fetch a jug o' summat good,' she told him, crushing a handful of coins into his hand. 'Tell the landlord we've got a double celebration here tonight.'

She sniffed and sobbed and wiped her nose on the end of her pinnie, and with the love of a mother she gazed at all her childer, then at Johnny and Ruby, so close and so much in love. 'Our Ruby's home,' she said in a broken voice, 'and there's to be a wedding.' She raised both her arms in the air and did a little jig on the spot. 'You tell the landlord,' she ordered through everyone's laughter. 'Tell him there's to be a wedding atween Ted Miller's gal and our Johnny here!' It was her dream come true, and she wanted everyone to share in it.

Chapter Twenty

Easter Saturday was a glorious day. Ruby looked delightful in a straight dress with scalloped hem and sweetheart neckline. Her unruly brown hair was held secure by a pretty band of rosebuds and blue silk ribbon. Johnny walked tall beside her, a proud good-looking fellow who had all he wanted out of life.

Maureen and Cicely were maids of honour; Maureen wore a cornflower blue gown that draped over her wheelchair and made it look like a splendid carriage, and Cicely paired up with a matching gown that swept the ground as she walked.

The reception was upstairs at the Rose and Crown where Ted used to drink with his pals. All in all, it was a wonderful affair, and everyone said so.

When they had a moment alone, Ruby and Maureen talked about all the things that were closest to their hearts. 'I never really thought you would sell the milliner's, Ruby,' Maureen told her. 'I'm very glad you did, but you worked so hard for it, I never thought you would let go.'

Ruby told her something then. A secret she had not told anyone else. 'I fell out of love with it.'

'But I thought it was all you ever wanted . . . a business of your own?'

'So did I,' Ruby admitted. 'But sometimes we can be wrong.

Sometimes the stars in our eyes blind us to the love in our hearts.'

'You don't regret it then?'

'No. I don't regret it. Luke's estate will sell the business to Gabriel's just as he planned. But, thanks to his father, I've been fairly compensated and now I don't owe anyone a penny. In fact, there's even a little money left over in the bank.'

She lapsed deep into thought before saying softly, 'I'll never know whether, if things had turned out differently, I might have fought tooth and nail to keep the business going. To be honest, Maureen, Johnny said something very wise to me when he came to Derwent Street. He asked me where my family and loved ones were. He made me realise just how empty my life had become.'

Maureen squeezed her hand. 'I'm glad you've come back to us, Ruby.' She saw a certain glint in her eye then, and it made her ask, 'Have you really done with ambition and all that?'

Ruby thought for a moment before saying wickedly, 'Who knows? When Johnny and I have raised our family and the world begins to open up to us, who knows?' She bent forward and whispered into her friend's ear, 'But I'll tell you this. Whatever I do in the future, it won't be on borrowed money. More importantly, it will be with Johnny by my side and my family around me. Or it won't be worth doing. I've learned that much.'

Johnny came to her then. 'All right, sweetheart?' he asked, bending to kiss her.

Ruby pressed her face to his. 'We're so lucky,' she said. 'We have each other, and we have our families.' The two of them gazed across the room to where Lizzie and Johnny's mam were looking so proud and pleased with themselves. 'Oh, Ruby Miller, I do love you,' he murmured.

'And I love you,' she whispered, reaching up to put her arms round his neck. She thought about all those wasted years when she had fought against that love. And she knew that in the years to come she would treasure their every moment together.

Suddenly, Lizzie's voice sailed through the room. 'Would yer look at that!' she called, pointing to where Lottie was stuffing a cake into her mouth. 'Anybody'd think the little bugger were half starved!' The room echoed with laughter. Ruby felt her hand in Johnny's, and her heart soared with joy. For a while she had been lost, but now she was home again. It was a wonderful feeling.

Now you can buy any of these bestselling books
by **Josephine Cox** from your bookshop
or *direct from the publisher*.

TO ORDER SIMPLY CALL THIS NUMBER

01235 400 414

or visit our website: www.headline.co.uk

Prices and availability subject to change without notice